BETHAN ROBERTS

Bethan Roberts has published five novels and writes stories and drama for BBC Radio 4. Her books include *The Good Plain Cook* (Serpent's Tail, 2008), which was a Radio 4 Book at Bedtime and *Mother Island* (Chatto, 2014), which received a Jerwood Fiction Uncovered prize. Her latest novel, *Graceland*, tells the story of Elvis Presley and his mother, Gladys. Bethan has taught Creative Writing at Chichester University and Goldsmiths College, London. She lives in Brighton with her family.

ALSO BY BETHAN ROBERTS

The Pools
The Good Plain Cook
Mother Island
Graceland

BETHAN ROBERTS

My Policeman

VINTAGE

1 3 5 7 9 10 8 6 4 2

Vintage is part of the Penguin Random House group of companies
whose addresses can be found at global.penguinrandomhouse.com

Penguin
Random House
UK

First published in Great Britain in 2012 by Chatto & Windus

First published by Vintage in 2012
This edition published by Vintage in 2022

penguin.co.uk/vintage

A CIP catalogue record for this book is available from the British Library

ISBN 9781529115765

Printed and bound in Great Britain by Clays Ltd, Elcograf S.p.A.

The authorised representative in the EEA is Penguin Random House Ireland,
Morrison Chambers, 32 Nassau Street, Dublin D02 YH68

Penguin Random House is committed to a sustainable future
for our business, our readers and our planet. This book is made
from Forest Stewardship Council® certified paper.

For all my Brighton friends, but most especially for Stuart

I

Peacehaven, October 1999

I considered starting with these words: *I no longer want to kill you* – because I really don't – but then decided you would think this far too melodramatic. You've always hated melodrama, and I don't want to upset you now, not in the state you're in, not at what may be the end of your life.

What I mean to do is this: write it all down, so I can get it right. This is a confession of sorts, and it's worth getting the details correct. When I am finished, I plan to read this account to you, Patrick, because you can't answer back any more. And I have been instructed to keep talking to you. Talking, the doctors say, is vital if you are to recover.

Your speech is almost destroyed, and even though you are here in my house, we communicate on paper. When I say on paper, I mean pointing at flashcards. You can't articulate the words but you can gesture towards your desires: *drink, lavatory, sandwich*. I know you want these things before your finger reaches the picture, but I let you point anyway, because it is better for you to be independent.

It's odd, isn't it, that I'm the one with pen and paper now, writing this – what shall we call it? It's hardly a journal, not of the type you once kept. Whatever it is, I'm the one writing, while you lie in your bed, watching my every move.

*

You've never liked this stretch of coast, calling it suburbia-on-sea, the place the old go to gaze at sunsets and wait for death. Wasn't this area – exposed, lonely, windswept, like all the best British seaside settlements – known as Siberia in that terrible winter of '63? It's not quite that bleak here now, although it's still as uniform; there's even some comfort, I find, in its predictability. Here in Peacehaven, the streets are the same, over and over: modest bungalow, functional garden, oblique sea view.

I was very resistant to Tom's plans to move here. Why would I, a lifelong Brighton resident, want to live on one floor, even if our bungalow was called a Swiss chalet by the estate agent? Why would I settle for the narrow aisles of the local Co-op, the old-fat stench of Joe's Pizza and Kebab House, the four funeral parlours, a pet shop called Animal Magic and a dry-cleaner's where the staff are, apparently, 'London trained'? Why would I settle for such things after Brighton, where the cafés are always full, the shops sell more than you could possibly imagine, let alone need, and the pier is always bright, always open and often slightly menacing?

No. I thought it an awful idea, just as you would have done. But Tom was determined to retire to a quieter, smaller, supposedly safer place. I think, in part, he'd had more than enough of being reminded of his old beats, his old busyness. One thing a bungalow in Peacehaven does not do is remind you of the world's busyness. So here we are, where no one is out on the street before nine thirty in the morning or after nine thirty at night, save a handful of teenagers who smoke outside the pizza place. Here we are in a two-bedroom bungalow (it is not a Swiss chalet, it is *not*), within easy reach of the bus stop and the Co-op, with a long lawn to look out on and a whirligig washing line and three outdoor buildings (shed, garage, greenhouse). The saving grace is the sea view, which is indeed oblique – it's visible from the side bedroom window. I've given this bedroom to you, and have arranged your bed so you may see the glimpse of the sea as much as you like. I've given all this to you, Patrick, despite the fact that Tom and I never before had our own view. From your Chichester Terrace flat, complete with Regency finishings, you enjoyed the sea every day. I remember the view from your flat very well, even though I rarely visited you: the Volk's railway, the Duke's Mound gardens, the breakwater with its crest of white on windy days, and of course the sea, always different, always the same. Up in our terraced house on Islingword Street, all Tom and I saw were our own reflections in the neighbours' windows. But still. I wasn't keen to leave that place.

So I suspect that when you arrived here from the hospital a week ago, when Tom lifted you from the car and into your chair, you saw exactly what I did: the brown regularity of the pebble-dash, the impossibly smooth plastic of the double-glazed door, the neat conifer hedge around the place, and all of it would have struck terror into your heart, just as it had in mine. And the name of the place: *The Pines*. So inappropriate, so unimaginative. A cool sweat probably oozed from your neck and your shirt suddenly felt uncomfortable. Tom wheeled you along the front path. You would have noticed that each slab was a perfectly even piece of pinkish-grey concrete. As I put the key in the lock and said, 'Welcome,' you wrung your wilted hands together and pulled your face into something like a smile.

Entering the beige-papered hallway, you would have smelled the bleach I'd used in preparation for your stay with us, and registered the scent of Walter, our collie-cross, lurking beneath it. You nodded slightly at the framed photograph of our wedding, Tom in that wonderful suit from Cobley's – paid for by you – and me in that stiff veil. We sat in the living room, Tom and I on the new brown velvet suite, bought with money from Tom's retirement package, and listened to the ticking music of the central heating. Walter panted at Tom's feet. Then Tom said, 'Marion will see you settled.' And I noticed the wince you gave at Tom's determination to leave, the way you continued to stare at the net curtains as he strode towards the door saying, 'Something I've got to see to.'

The dog followed him. You and I sat listening to Tom's footsteps along the hallway, the rustle as he reached for his coat from the peg, the jangle as he checked in his pocket for his keys; we heard him gently command Walter to wait, and then there was only the sound of the suction of air as he pulled the double-glazed front door open and left the bungalow. When I finally looked at you, your hands, limp on your bony knees, were shaking. Did you think, then, that being in Tom's home at last might not be all you'd hoped?

Forty-eight years. That's how far I have to go back, to when I first met Tom. And even that may not be far enough.

He was so contained back then. *Tom.* Even the name is solid, unpretentious, but not without the possibility of sensitivity. He wasn't a Bill, a Reg, a Les or a Tony. Did you ever call him Thomas? I know I wanted to. Sometimes there were moments when I wanted to rename him. *Tommy.* Perhaps that's what you called him, the beautiful young man with the big arms and the dark blond curls.

I knew his sister from grammar school. During our second year there, she approached me in the corridor and said, 'I was thinking – you look all right – will you be my friend?' Up until that point, we'd each spent our time alone, baffled by the strange rituals of the school, the echoing spaces of the classrooms and the clipped voices of the other girls. I let Sylvie copy my homework, and she played me her records: Nat King Cole, Patti Page, Perry Como. Together, under our breath, we sang *Some enchanted evening, you may see a stranger* as we stood at the back of the queue for the vaulting horse, letting all the other girls go before us. Neither of us liked games. I enjoyed going to Sylvie's because Sylvie had *things*, and her mother let her wear her brittle blonde hair in a style too old for her years; I think she even helped her set the fringe in a kiss-curl. At the time, my hair, which was as red as it ever was, still hung in a thick plait down my back. If I lost my temper at home – I remember once shutting my brother Fred's head in the door with some force – my father would look at my mother and say, 'It's the red in her,' because the ginger strain was on my mother's side. I think you once called me *the Red Peril*, didn't you, Patrick? By that time, I'd come to like the colour, but I always felt it was a self-fulfilling prophecy, having red hair: people expected me to have a temper, and so, if I felt anger flaring up, I let it go. Not often, of course. But occasionally I slammed doors, threw crockery. Once I rammed the Hoover so hard into the skirting board that it cracked.

When I was first invited to Sylvie's house in Patcham, she had a peach silk neckerchief and as soon as I saw it I wanted one too. Sylvie's parents had a tall drinks cabinet in their living room, with glass doors painted with black stars. 'It's all on the never-never,' Sylvie said, pushing her tongue into her cheek and showing me upstairs. She let me wear the necker-chief and she showed me her bottles of nail varnish. When she opened one, I smelled pear-drops. Sitting on her neat bed, I chose the dark purple polish to brush over Sylvie's wide, bitten-down nails, and when I'd finished, I brought her hand up to my face and blew, gently. Then I brought her thumbnail to my mouth and ran my top lip over the smooth finish, to check it was dry.

'What are you doing?' She gave a spiky laugh.

I let her hand fall back into her lap. Her cat, Midnight, came in and brushed up against my legs.

'Sorry,' I said.

Midnight stretched and pressed herself along my ankles with greater urgency. I reached down to scratch her behind the ears, and whilst I was doubled over the cat, Sylvie's bedroom door opened.

'Get out,' Sylvie said in a bored voice. I quickly straightened up, worried that she was speaking to me, but she was glaring over my shoulder towards the doorway. I twisted round and saw him standing there, and my hand came up to the silk at my neck.

'Get out, Tom,' Sylvie repeated, in a tone that suggested she was resigned to the roles they had to play out in this little drama.

He was leaning in the doorway with the sleeves of his shirt rolled up to the elbows, and I noticed the fine lines of muscle in his forearms. He couldn't have been more than fifteen – barely a year older than me; but his shoulders were already wide and there was a dark hollow at the base of his neck. His chin had a scar on one side – just a small dent, like a fingerprint in plasticine – and he was wearing a sneer, which even then I knew he was doing deliberately, because he thought he should, because it made him look like a Ted; but the whole effect of this boy leaning on the door frame and looking at me with his blue eyes – small eyes, set deep – made me blush so hard that I reached down and plunged my fingers back into the dusty fur around Midnight's ears and focused my eyes on the floor.

'Tom! Get out!' Sylvie's voice was louder now, and the door slammed shut.

You can imagine, Patrick, that it was a few minutes before I could trust myself to remove my hand from the cat's ears and look at Sylvie again.

After that, I did my best to remain firm friends with Sylvie. Sometimes I would take the bus out to Patcham and walk past her semi-detached house, looking up at her bright windows, telling myself I was hoping she would come out, when in fact my whole body was strung tight in anticipation of Tom's appearance. Once, I sat on the wall around the corner from her house until it got dark and I could no longer feel my fingers or toes. I listened to the blackbirds singing for all they were worth, and smelled the dampness growing in the hedges around me, and then I caught the bus home.

My mother looked out of windows a lot. Whenever she was cooking, she'd lean on the stove and gaze out of the tiny line of glass in our back door. She was always, it seemed to me, making gravy and staring out of the window. She'd stir the gravy for the longest time, scraping the bits of meat and gristly residue around the pan. It tasted of iron and was slightly lumpy, but Dad and my brothers covered their plates with it. There was so much gravy that they got it on their fingers and in their nails, and they would lick it off while Mum smoked, waiting for the washing-up.

They were always kissing, Mum and Dad. In the scullery, him with his hand gripped tight on the back of her neck, her with her arm around his middle, pulling him closer. It was difficult, at the time, to work out how they fitted together, they were so tightly locked. It was ordinary to me, though, seeing them like that and I'd just sit at the kitchen table, put my *Picturegoer* annual on the ribbed tablecloth, prop my chin in my hand and wait for them to finish. The strange thing is, although there was all that kissing, there never seemed to be much conversation. They'd talk through us: *You'll have to ask your father about that.* Or: *What does your mother say?* At the table it would be Fred, Harry and me, and Dad reading the *Gazette* and Mum standing by the window, smoking. I don't think she ever sat at the table to eat with us, except on Sundays when Dad's father, Grandpa Taylor, would come too. He called Dad 'boy' and would feed his yellowing Westie, crouched beneath his chair, most of his dinner. So it was never long before Mum was standing and smoking again, clearing away the plates and crashing the crocks in the scullery. She'd station me at the drainer to dry, fastening a pinny round my waist, one of hers that was too long for me and had to be rolled over at the top, and I'd try to lean on the sink like her. Sometimes when she wasn't there I'd gaze through the window and try to imagine what my mother thought about as she looked out on our shed with the slanting roof, Dad's patch of straggly Brussels sprouts, and the small square of sky above the neighbours' houses.

In the summer holidays Sylvie and I often went to Black Rock Lido. I always wanted to save my money and sit on the beach, but Sylvie insisted that the Lido was where we should be. This was partly because the Lido was where Sylvie could flirt with boys. All through school, she was seldom without some admirer, whereas I didn't seem to attract anyone's interest. I never relished the thought of spending another afternoon watching my friend being ogled, but with its sparkling windows, glaring white concrete and striped deckchairs, the lido was too pretty to resist, and so more often than not we paid our ninepences and pushed through the turnstiles to the poolside.

I remember one afternoon with particular clarity. We were both about seventeen. Sylvie had a lime-green two-piece, and I had a red swimsuit that was too small for me. I kept having to yank up the straps and pull down the legs. By this time, Sylvie had rather impressive breasts and a neat waistline; I still seemed to be a long rectangular shape with a bit of extra padding around the sides. I'd had my hair cut into a bob by then, which I was pleased with, but I was too tall. My father told me not to stoop, but he also made a point of telling me to always choose flat shoes. 'No man wants to look up a woman's nose,' he'd say. 'Isn't that right, Phyllis?' And Mum would smile and say nothing. At school they kept insisting that with my height I should be good at netball, but I was dreadful. I'd just stand at the side, pretending to be waiting for a pass. The pass never came, and I'd gaze over the fence at the boys playing rugby. Their voices were so different to ours – deep and woody, and with that confidence of boys who know what the next step in life will be. Oxford. Cambridge. The bar. The school next door was private, you see, like yours was, and the boys there seemed so much more handsome than the ones I knew. They wore well-cut jackets and walked with their hands in their pockets and their long fringes falling over their faces, whereas the boys I knew (and these were few) sort of charged towards you, looking straight ahead. No mystery to them. All up-front. Not that I ever talked to any of those boys with the fringes. You went to one of those schools, but you were never like that, were you, Patrick? Like me, you never fitted in. I understood that from the start.

It was not quite hot enough for bathing outside – a freshening wind was coming from the sea – but the sun was bright. Sylvie and I lay flat on our towels. I kept my skirt on over my costume, whilst Sylvie arranged her things in a neat row next to me: comb, compact, cardigan. She sat up and squinted, taking in the crowds on the sun-drenched terrace. Sylvie's mouth always seemed to be pulled in an upside-down smile, and her front teeth followed the downward line of her top lip, as if they'd been chiselled especially into shape. I closed my eyes. Pinkish shapes moved around on the insides of my eyelids as Sylvie sighed and cleared her throat. I knew she wanted to talk to me, to point out who else was at the pool, who was doing what with whom and which boys she knew, but all I wanted was some warmth on my face and to get that far-away feeling that comes when you lie in the afternoon sun.

Eventually I was almost there. The blood seemed to have thickened behind my eyes and all my limbs had gone to rubber. The slap of feet and the crack of boys hitting the water from the diving board did nothing to rouse me, and although I could feel the sun burning my shoulders I remained flat on the concrete, breathing in the chalky smell of the wet floor and the occasional waft of cold chlorine from a passer-by.

Then something cool and wet fell on my cheek and I opened my eyes. At first all I could see was the white glare of the sky. I blinked, and a shape revealed itself, outlined in vivid pink. I blinked again and heard Sylvie's voice, petulant but pleased – 'What are *you* doing here?' – and I knew who it was.

Sitting up, I tried to gather myself together, shading my eyes and hastily wiping sweat from my top lip.

There he was, with the sun behind him, smirking at Sylvie.

'You're dripping on us!' she said, brushing at imaginary droplets on her shoulders.

Of course, I'd seen and admired Tom at Sylvie's house many times, but this was the first time I'd seen quite so much of his body. I tried to look away, Patrick. I tried not to stare at the bead of water crawling its way from his throat to his navel, at the wet strands of hair at the nape of his neck. But you know how hard it is to look away when you see something you want. So I focused on his shins: on the glistening blond hairs that covered his skin; I adjusted the straps of my one-piece, and Sylvie asked again, with an overly dramatic sigh: 'What do you want, Tom?'

He looked at the two of us – both bone-dry and sun-blotched. 'Haven't you been in?'

'Marion doesn't swim,' announced Sylvie.

'Why not?' he asked, looking at me.

I could have lied, I suppose. But even then I had a terrible dread of being found out. In the end, people always found you out. And when they did, it would be worse than if you'd simply told the truth in the first place.

My mouth had dried, but I managed to say, 'Never learned.'

'Tom's in the sea-swimming club,' said Sylvie, with what sounded almost like pride.

I'd never had the urge to get wet. The sea was always there, a constant noise and movement on the edge of town. But that didn't mean I had to join it, did it? Until that moment, not being able to swim hadn't seemed the least bit important. But now I knew that I would have to do it.

'I'd love to learn,' I said, trying to smile.

'Tom'll teach you, won't you, Tom?' said Sylvie, looking him in the eye, challenging him to refuse.

Tom gave a shiver, then snatched Sylvie's towel and wrapped it about his waist.

'I could,' he said. Rubbing roughly at his hair, trying to dry it with one hand, he turned to Sylvie. 'Lend us a bob.'

'Where's Roy?' asked Sylvie.

This was the first I'd heard of Roy, but Sylvie was obviously interested, judging by the way she dropped the question of swimming lessons and instead craned her neck to see past her brother.

'Diving,' said Tom. 'Lend us a bob.'

'What are you doing after?'

'None of your business.'

Sylvie opened her compact and studied herself for a moment

before saying, in a low voice, 'I bet you're going to the Spotted Dog.'

At this, Tom stepped forward and made a playful swipe for his sister, but she ducked to avoid his hand. His towel fell to the floor and again I averted my eyes.

I wondered what was so bad about going to the Spotted Dog, but, not wanting to appear ignorant, I kept my mouth shut.

Sylvie let a small silence pass before she murmured, 'You're going there. I know it.' Then she grabbed the corner of the towel, jumped up, and began to twist it into a rope. Tom lunged for her, but she was too quick. The end of the towel landed across his chest with a crack, leaving a red line. At the time, I fancied I saw the line pulsing, but I'm not sure of that now. Still, you can picture it: our beautiful boy beaten by his little sister, marked by her soft cotton towel.

A flash of anger passed across his face, and I bristled; it was getting cooler now; a shadow was creeping over the sunbathers. Tom looked to the ground and swallowed. Sylvie hovered, unsure of her brother's next move. With a sudden grab, he had the towel back; she was ducking and laughing as he flicked the thing madly about, occasionally slapping her with its end – at which she'd let out a high-pitched squeal – but mostly missing. He was gentle now, you see, I knew it even then; he was padding about and being deliberately clumsy, teasing his sister with the idea of his greater strength and accuracy, with the idea that he *might* strike her hard.

'I've got a bob,' I said, feeling for change in my cardigan pocket. It was all I had left, but I held it out to him.

Tom stopped flicking the towel. He was breathing hard. Sylvie rubbed at her neck where the towel had hit. 'Bully,' she muttered.

He held out his palm, and I placed my coin in it, letting my fingertips brush his warm skin.

'Thanks,' he said, and he smiled. Then he looked at Sylvie. 'You all right?'

Sylvie shrugged.

When he'd turned his back, she stuck out her tongue.

On the way home, I smelled my hand, breathing in the metallic scent. The tang of my money would be on Tom's fingers now, too.

Just before Tom left for his National Service, he gave me a glimmer of hope that I clung to until his return, and, if I'm honest, even beyond that.

It was December and I'd gone to Sylvie's for tea. You'll understand that Sylvie rarely came to my house, because she had her own bedroom, a portable record-player and bottles of Vimto, whereas I shared a room with Harry and the only thing to drink was tea. But at Sylvie's we had sliced ham, soft white bread, tomatoes and salad cream, followed by tinned mandarins and evaporated milk. Sylvie's father owned a shop on the front that sold saucy postcards, rock dummies, out-of-date packets of jellied fruits, and dolls made from shells with dried seaweed for collars. It was called Happy News because it also sold newspapers, magazines and copies of the racier titles wrapped in cellophane. Sylvie told me that her father sold five copies of the *Kama Sutra* every week, and that figure trebled over the summer. At the time, I'd only a dim idea that the *Kama Sutra* was, for reasons unknown to me, a forbidden book; but I'd pretended to be impressed, opening my eyes wide and mouthing 'Really?' as Sylvie nodded, triumphant.

We ate in the front room, and Sylvie's mother's budgerigar provided a constant background tweep. There were plastic chairs with steel legs and a wipe-clean dining table with no cloth. Sylvie's mother was wearing an orangey shade of lipstick, and from where I was sitting I could smell the lavender cleaning fluid on her hands. She was extremely overweight, which was strange, because all I ever saw her eat were salad leaves and cucumber slices, and all I ever saw her drink was black coffee. Despite this apparent self-denial, her features seemed lost somewhere in the swollen flesh of her face, and her bosom was enormous and always propped up on display, like an oversized, well-whipped meringue in a baker's window. When I knew I shouldn't spend any more time looking at Tom, who was sitting next to his mother, I would fix my eyes on Mrs Burgess's cushiony cleavage. I knew I shouldn't really look there, either, but it was better than being caught with my eyes wandering all over her son. I was convinced I could feel the heat rising from him; his naked forearm rested on the table, and it seemed to me that his flesh was warming the entire room. And I could smell him (I wasn't just imagining this, Patrick): he smelled – do you remember? – he smelled of hair oil, of course – Vitalis, it would have been then – and of pine-scented talc, which I later learned he dashed liberally beneath his arms every morning before pulling on his shirt. At that time, as you'll recall, men like Tom's father did not approve of talc. It's different now, of course. When I go to the Co-op in Peacehaven and pass all the young boys, their hair so closely resembling Tom's as it once was – slicked with oil and teased into impossible shapes – I'm overwhelmed by the fabricated scent of their perfume. They smell like new furniture, those boys. But Tom didn't smell like that. He smelled exciting, because, back then, men who covered their own sweat with talc were rather suspect, which was very interesting to me.

And you got the best of both worlds, you see: the fresh odour of the talc, but if you were close enough, the warm, muddy smell of skin beneath.

When we'd finished our sandwiches, Mrs Burgess brought through the tinned peaches on pink dishes. We ate in silence. Then Tom wiped the sweet juice from his lips and announced, 'I went down the conscription office today. To volunteer. That way I get to choose what I do.' He pushed his dish away and looked his father in the face. 'I start next week.'

After giving a brief nod, Mr Burgess stood up and held out his hand. Tom also stood, and clasped his father's fingers. I wondered if they'd ever shaken hands before. It didn't look like something they did often. There was a firm shake and then they both glanced around the room as if wondering what to do next.

'He always has to outdo me,' Sylvie hissed in my ear.

'What'll you be doing?' asked Mr Burgess, still standing, blinking at his son.

Tom cleared his throat. 'Catering Corps.'

The two men stared at one another and Sylvie let out a giggle.

Mr Burgess suddenly sat down.

'This is news, isn't it? Shall we have a drink, Jack?' Mrs Burgess's voice was high, and I thought I heard a little crack in it as she pushed back her chair. 'We need a drink, don't we? For news like this.' As she stood, she knocked the remains of her black coffee over the table. It spread across the white plastic and dripped on to the rug below.

'Clumsy cow,' muttered Mr Burgess.

Sylvie let out another giggle.

Tom, who seemed to have been standing in a trance, his arm still slightly outstretched where he'd shaken his father's hand, moved towards his mother. 'I'll get a cloth,' he said, touching her shoulder.

After Tom had left the room, Mrs Burgess looked around the table, taking in each of our faces. 'Whatever will we do now?' she said. Her voice was so quiet that I wondered if anyone else had heard her speak. Certainly no one responded for a few moments. But then Mr Burgess sighed and said, 'Catering Corps isn't exactly the Somme, Beryl.'

Mrs Burgess gave a sob and followed her son out of the room.

Tom's father said nothing. The budgie tweeped and tweeped as we waited for Tom's return. I could hear him talking in a hushed voice in the kitchen, and I imagined his mother weeping in his arms, devastated, as I was, that he was leaving.

Sylvie kicked my chair, but instead of looking at her, I fixed Mr Burgess with a stare and said, 'Even soldiers have to eat, though, don't they?' I kept my voice steady and neutral. Later on, this was what I did when a child answered me back in class, or when Tom told me it was your turn, Patrick, at the weekend. 'I'm sure Tom will make a good chef.'

Mr Burgess gave a tight laugh before pushing back his chair and hollering towards the kitchen door: 'For God's sake, where's that drink?'

Tom came back in, holding two beer bottles. His father snatched one, held it up to Tom's face and said, 'Well done for upsetting your mother.' Then he left the room, but instead of going into the kitchen and comforting Mrs Burgess, as I thought he might, I heard the front door slam.

'Did you hear what Marion said?' squawked Sylvie, snatching the other bottle from Tom and rolling it between her hands.

'That's mine,' said Tom, grabbing it back from her.

'Marion said you'll make a good chef.'

With a deft flick of his wrist, Tom released the air from the bottle and tossed the metal cap and the opener aside. He took a glass from the top of the sideboard and carefully poured himself half a pint of thick brown ale. 'Well,' he said, holding the drink before his face and inspecting it before taking a couple of gulps, 'she's right.' He wiped his mouth with the back of his hand and looked directly at me. 'I'm glad there's someone with some sense in this house,' he said, with a broad smile. 'Wasn't I going to teach you to swim?'

That night, I wrote in my hard-backed black notebook: *His smile is like a harvest moon. Mysterious. Full of promises.* I was very pleased with those words, I remember. And every evening after that, I would fill my notebook with my longing for Tom. *Dear Tom*, I wrote. Or sometimes *Dearest Tom*, or even *Darling Tom*; but I didn't allow myself that indulgence too often; mostly, the pleasure of seeing his name appear in characters wrought by my hand was enough. Back then I was easy to please. Because when you're in love with someone for the first time, their name is enough. Just seeing my hand form Tom's name was enough. Almost.

I would describe the day's events in ludicrous detail, complete with azure eyes and crimson skies. I don't think I ever wrote about his body, although it was obviously this that impressed me the most; I expect I wrote about the nobility of his nose (which is actually rather flat and squashed-looking) and the deep bass of his voice. So you see, Patrick, I was typical. So typical.

For almost three years, I wrote out all my longing for Tom, and I looked forward to the day when he would come home and teach me to swim.

Does this infatuation seem faintly ludicrous to you, Patrick?

Perhaps not. I suspect that you know about desire, about the way it grows when it's denied, better than anyone. Every time Tom was home on leave I seemed to miss him, and I wonder now if I did this deliberately. Was waiting for his return, forgoing the sight of the real Tom, and instead writing about him in my notebook, a way of loving him more?

During Tom's absence I did have some thoughts about getting myself a career. I remember I had an interview with Miss Monkton, the Deputy Head, towards the end of my time at the grammar, when I was about to sit my exams, and she asked me what my plans for the future were. They were quite keen on girls having plans for the future, although I knew, even then, this was all a pipe-dream that only stood up inside the walls of the school. Outside, plans fell apart, especially for girls. Miss Monkton had rather wild hair, for those days: a mass of tight curls, specked with silver. I felt sure she smoked, because her skin was the colour of well-brewed tea and her lips, which frequently curled into an ironic smile, had that dry tightness about them. In Miss Monkton's office, I announced that I would like to become a teacher. It was the only thing I could think of at the time; it sounded better than saying I'd like to become a secretary, but it didn't seem completely absurd, unlike, say, becoming a novelist or an actress, both of which I'd privately imagined myself being.

I don't think I've admitted that to anyone before.

Anyway, Miss Monkton twisted her pen so the cap clicked and said, 'And what's made you reach this conclusion?'

I thought about it. I couldn't very well say, *I don't know what else I could do.* Or, *It doesn't look like I'll be getting hitched, does it?*

'I like school, miss.' As I spoke the words, I realised they were true. I liked the regular bells, the cleaned blackboards, the dusty desks full of secrets, the long corridors crammed with girls, the turpentine reek of the art class, the sound of the library catalogue spinning through my fingers. And I suddenly imagined myself at the front of a classroom, in a smart tweed skirt and a neat chignon, winning the respect and affection of my pupils with my firm but fair methods. I had no conception, then, of how bossy I would become, or how teaching would change my life. You often called me bossy, and you were right; teaching drills it into you. It's you or them, you see. You have to make a stand. I learned that early on.

Miss Monkton gave one of her curled smiles. 'It's rather different,' she said, 'from the other side of the desk.' She paused, put her pen down and turned to the window so she was no longer facing me. 'I don't want to dampen your ambitions, Taylor. But teaching requires enormous dedication and considerable backbone. It's not that you're not a decent student. But I would have thought something office-based would be more your line. Something a little quieter, perhaps?'

I stared at the trail of milk on top of her cooling cup of tea. Apart from that cup, her desk was completely empty.

'What, for example,' she continued, turning back towards me with a quick look at the clock above the door, 'do your parents think of the idea? Are they prepared to support you through this venture?'

I hadn't mentioned any of this to Mum and Dad. They could hardly believe I'd got in to the grammar in the first place; at the news, my father had complained about the cost of the uniform, and my mother had sat on the sofa, put her head in her hands and cried. I'd been pleased at first, assuming she was moved to tears by her pride in my achievement, but when she wouldn't stop I'd asked her what was wrong and she'd said, 'It'll all be different now. This will take you away from us.' And then, most nights, they complained that I spent too long studying in my bedroom, rather than talking to them.

I looked at Miss Monkton. 'They're right behind me,' I announced.

When I look over the fields to the sea, on these autumn days when the grass moves in the wind and the waves sound like excited breath, I remember that I once felt intense and secret things, just like you, Patrick. I hope you will understand that, and I hope you can forgive it.

Spring 1957. Having finished his National Service, Tom was still away, training to become a policeman. I often thought with excitement of him joining the force. It seemed such a brave, *grown-up* thing to do. I didn't know anyone else who'd do such a thing. At home, the police were rather suspect – not the enemy, exactly, but an unknown quantity. I knew that as a policeman Tom would have a different life to our parents, one that was more daring, more powerful.

I was attending teacher training college in Chichester but still saw Sylvie quite a bit, even though she was becoming more involved with Roy. Once she asked me to go with her to the roller rink, but when I got there she turned up with Roy and another boy called Tony, who worked with Roy at the garage. Tony didn't seem to be able to speak much. Not to me, anyway. Occasionally he'd shout a comment to Roy as we skated round, but Roy didn't always look back. That was because his eyes were caught up with Sylvie's. It was like they couldn't look anywhere else, not even where they were going.

Tony didn't hold my arm as we skated round, and I managed to get ahead of him several times. As I skated I thought of the smile Tom had given me the day he'd announced he was joining the Catering Corps, how his top lip had disappeared above his teeth and his eyes had slanted. When we stopped for a Coke, Tony didn't smile at me. He asked me when I was leaving school, and I said, 'Never – I'm going to be a teacher,' and he looked at the door like he wanted to skate right through it.

One sunny afternoon not long after that, Sylvie and I went to Preston Park and sat on the bench beneath the elms, which were lovely and rustly, and she announced her engagement to Roy. 'We're very happy,' she declared, with a secretive little smile. I asked her if Roy had taken advantage of her, but she shook her head and there was that smile again.

For a long time we just watched the people going by with their dogs and their children in the sunshine. Some of them had cones from the Rotunda. Neither Sylvie nor I had money for ice cream and Sylvie was still silent, so I asked her: 'How far have you gone, then?'

Sylvie looked over the park, swinging her right leg back and forth impatiently. 'I told you,' she said.

'No. You didn't.'

'I'm in love with him,' she stated, stretching out her arms and closing her eyes. 'Really in love.'

This I found hard to believe. Roy wasn't bad looking, but he talked too much about absolutely nothing. He was also slight. His shoulders didn't look as though they could bear any weight at all.

'You don't know what it's like,' Sylvie said, blinking at me. 'I love Roy and we're going to be married.'

I gazed at the grass beneath my feet. Of course I couldn't say to Sylvie, 'I know exactly what it's like. I'm in love with your brother.' I know that I would've ridiculed anyone who was in love with one of *my* brothers, and why should Sylvie have been any different?

'I mean,' she said, looking straight at me, 'I know you've got a crush on Tom. But it's not the same.'

Blood crawled up my neck and around my ears.

'Tom's not like that, Marion,' said Sylvie.

For a moment I thought of standing up and walking away. But my legs were shaking, and my mouth had frozen in a smile.

Sylvie nodded towards a lad passing by with a large cornet in his hand. 'Wish I had one of those,' she said, loudly. The boy twisted his head and gave her a quick glance, but she turned to me and gently pinched my lower arm. 'You don't mind that I said that, do you?' she asked.

I couldn't reply. I think I managed to nod. Humiliated and confused, all I wanted was to get home and think properly about what Sylvie had said. My emotions must have shown on my face, though, because after a while Sylvie whispered in my ear, 'I'll tell you about Roy.'

Still I couldn't respond, but she continued, 'I did let him touch me.'

My eyes shifted towards her. She licked her lips and looked to the sky. 'It was strange,' she said. 'I didn't feel much, except scared.'

I fixed her with a stare. 'Where?' I asked.

'Round the back of the Regent . . .'

'No,' I said. 'Where did he touch you?'

She studied my face for a moment and, seeing that I wasn't joking, said: 'You know. He put his hand there.' She gave a quick glance down to my lap. 'But I've told him the rest will have to wait until we're married.' She stretched back on the seat. 'I wouldn't mind going the whole way, but then he won't marry me, will he?'

That night, before sleep, I thought for a long time about what Sylvie said. I re-imagined the scene again and again, the two of us sitting on the bench, Sylvie kicking her skinny legs out and sighing as she said, 'I did let him touch me.' I tried to hear her words again. To hear them clearly, distinctly. I tried to find the right meaning in what she'd said about Tom. But whichever way I formed the words, they made little sense to me. As I lay on my bed in the dark, listening to my mother's coughing and my father's silence, I breathed into the sheet I'd pulled up to my nose and thought, she doesn't know him like I do. I *know* what he's like.

My life as a teacher at St Luke's began. I'd done my best to put Sylvie's comment out of my mind and had got myself through training college by imagining Tom's pride in me on hearing I'd successfully become a teacher. I had no grounds for thinking he would be proud of me, but that didn't stop me picturing him arriving home from his police training, walking up the Burgess family's front path, his jacket slung carelessly over one shoulder, whistling. He'd pick Sylvie up and swing her round (in my fantasy, brother and sister were best of friends), then he'd go in the house and peck Mrs Burgess on the cheek and hand her the gift he'd carefully selected (Coty's Attar of Roses, perhaps, or – more racily – Shalimar), and Mr Burgess would stand in the living room and shake his son's hand, making Tom blush with pleasure. Only then would he sit at the table, a pot of tea and a Madeira cake set in front of him, and ask if anyone knew how I was getting on. Sylvie would reply, 'She's a schoolteacher now – honestly, Tom, you'd hardly recognise her.' And Tom would smile a secret smile and nod, and he'd swallow his tea with a shake of his head and say, 'I always knew she was capable of something good.'

I had this fantasy in my mind as I walked up Queen's Park Road on the first morning of my new job. Although my blood fluttered around my limbs, and my legs felt as though they might buckle at any moment, I walked as slowly as I could in an effort to keep from sweating too much. I'd convinced myself that as soon as term began it would turn cold and possibly wet, so I'd worn a woollen vest and carried a thick Fair Isle cardigan in my hand. In fact, the morning was unnervingly bright. The sun shone on the school's high bell tower and lit up the red bricks with a fierce glow, and every windowpane glared at me as I walked through the gate.

I'd arrived very early, so there were no children in the yard. The school had been shut for weeks over the summer, but, even so, as I went into the long empty corridor I was immediately assailed by the smell of sweet milk and chalk dust, mixed with children's sweat, which has a special, soiled aroma all of its own. Every day from then on, I'd come home with this smell in my hair and on my clothes. When I moved my head on the pillow at night, the taint of the classroom shifted around me. I never fully accepted that smell. I learned to tolerate it, but I never ceased to notice it. It was the same with the smell of the station on Tom. As soon as he got back to the house, he'd take off his shirt and have a good wash. I always liked that about him. Though it occurs to me now that he may have left his shirt on for you, Patrick. That you might have liked the bleach and blood stench of the station.

That morning, trembling in the corridor, I looked up at the large tapestry of St Luke on the wall; he stood with an ox behind him and a donkey in front. With his mild face and neatly clipped beard, he meant nothing to me. I thought of Tom, of course, of how he would have stood with his chin set in a determined pose, the way he would have rolled up his sleeves to show his muscled forearms, and I also thought about running home. As I walked along the corridor, my pace gradually increasing, I saw that every door was marked with a teacher's name, and none of them sounded like a name I knew, or a name I could imagine ever inhabiting. Mr R.A. Coppard MA (Oxon) on one. Mrs T.R. Peacocke on another.

Then: footsteps behind me, and a voice: 'Hi there – can I help? Are you the new blood?'

I didn't turn around. I was still staring at R.A. Coppard and wondering how long it would take me to run the length of the corridor back to the main entrance and out on to the street.

But the voice was persistent. 'I say – are you Miss Taylor?'

A woman whom I judged to be in her late twenties was standing before me, smiling. She was tall, like me, and her hair was strikingly black and absolutely straight. It seemed to have been cut by someone who'd traced the outline of an upturned bowl around her head, just as my father used to do to my brothers. She was wearing very bright red lipstick. Placing a hand on my shoulder, she announced: 'I'm Julia Harcourt. Class Five.' When I didn't respond, she smiled and added: 'You *are* Miss Taylor, aren't you?'

I nodded. She smiled again, her short nose wrinkling. Her skin was tanned, and despite being dressed in a rather outmoded green frock with no waist to speak of and sporting a pair of brown leather lace-ups, there was something rather jaunty about her. Perhaps it was her bright face and even brighter lips; unlike most of the other teachers at St Luke's, Julia never wore spectacles. I sometimes wondered if the ones who did so wore them mostly for effect, enabling themselves to look over the rims in a fierce way, for example, or take them off and jab them in a wrongdoer's direction. I'll admit to you now, Patrick, that during my first year in the school I thought briefly of investing in a pair of glasses myself.

'The infant school is in another part of the building,' she said. 'That's why you can't find your name on any of these doors.' Still holding my shoulder, she added, 'First day's always frightful. I was a mess when I started. But you do survive.' When I didn't respond, she let her hand drop from my shoulder and said, 'It's this way. I'll show you.' After a moment spent standing there, watching Julia walk away, swinging her arms by her sides as though she were hiking over the South Downs, I followed her.

Patrick, did you feel like this on your first day at the museum? Like they had meant to employ someone else but due to some administrative error the letter of appointment had been sent to your address? I somehow doubt it. But that's how I felt. And I was also sure I was about to vomit. I wondered how Miss Julia Harcourt would deal with that, with a grown woman suddenly turning pale and sweaty and throwing up her breakfast all over the polished corridor tiles, splashing the toes of her neat lace-ups.

I didn't vomit, however. Instead I followed Miss Harcourt out of the junior school and into the infants', which had its own separate entrance at the back of the building.

The classroom she led me to was bright, and even on that first day I could see this quality was underused. The long windows were half disguised by flowered curtains. I couldn't see the dust on those curtains at once, but I could smell it. The floor was wooden and not as gleaming as the corridor had been. At the head of the room was the black-board, on which I could still see the ghost of another teacher's handwriting – 'July 1957' was just visible on the top left-hand side, written in curling capitals. Before the board were a large desk and a chair, next to which was a boiler, encased by wire. At all the rows of low children's desks there were chipped wooden seats. It seemed depressingly usual, in other words, except for the light trying to get through those curtains.

It wasn't until I stepped inside (waved on by Miss Harcourt) that I saw the special area of my new classroom. In the corner, behind the door, tucked between the back of the stationery cupboard and the window, were a rug and some cushions. None of the classrooms I'd entered on my training sessions had had this feature, and I daresay I took a step back at the sight of soft furnishings in a school context.

'Ah yes,' murmured Miss Harcourt. 'I believe the woman who was here before you – Miss Lynch – used this area for story time.'

I stared at the red and yellow rug and its matching cushions, which were plump and tassled, and I imagined Miss Lynch surrounded by her adoring brood as she recited *Alice's Adventures in Wonderland* from memory.

'Miss Lynch was unorthodox. Rather wonderfully so, I thought. Although there were those that didn't agree. Perhaps you'd rather it was removed?' She smiled. 'We can have the caretaker get rid of it. There's a lot to be said for sitting at desks, after all.'

I swallowed and finally found enough breath to speak. 'I'll keep it,' I said. My voice sounded very small in the empty classroom. I suddenly realised that all I had to fill this entire space were my words, my voice; and it was a voice over which – I was convinced at that moment – I had very little control.

'Up to you,' chirped Julia, turning on her heel. 'Good luck. See you at break.' She gave a salute as she closed the door, the tips of her fingers brushing the blunt line of her fringe.

Children's voices were beginning to sound outside. I considered closing all the windows to keep the sound out, but the sweat I could taste on my top lip prevented me from doing so on such a warm day. I put my bag on top of the desk. Then I changed my mind and put it on the floor. I cracked my knuckles, looked at my watch. A quarter to nine. I paced the length of the room, looking at the distempered bricks, my mind trying to focus on some piece of advice from the training college. *Learn their names early on and use them frequently*, was all that would come to me. I stopped at the door and peered at the framed reproduction of Leonardo's *The Annunciation* hanging above it. What, I wondered, would six-year-old children make of that? Most likely they would admire the muscular wings of the Angel Gabriel, and puzzle over the wispiness of the lily, as I did. And, like me, they probably had very little comprehension of what the Virgin was about to go through.

Beneath the Virgin, the door opened and a little boy with a black fringe that looked like a boot mark stamped on his forehead appeared. 'Can I come in?' he asked.

My first instinct was to win his love by saying *Yes, oh yes, please do*, but I checked myself. Would Miss Harcourt let the boy straight in before the bell went? Wasn't it insolent for him to address me in this manner? I looked him up and down, trying to guess his intentions. The black boot-mark hair didn't bode well, but his eyes were light and he kept his feet on the other side of the door jamb.

'You'll have to wait,' I answered, 'until the bell goes.'

He looked at the floor, and for an awful moment I thought he might give a sob, but then he slammed the door shut and

I heard his boots clattering in the corridor. I knew I should haul him back for that; I should shout for him to stop running at once and come back here to receive a punishment. But instead I walked to my desk and tried to calm myself. I had to be ready. I took up the blackboard rubber and cleaned the remains of 'July 1957' from the corner of the board. I pulled open the desk drawer and took some paper from it. I might need that, later. Then I decided I should check my fountain pen. Shaking it over the paper, I managed to scatter the desk with black shiny dots. When I rubbed at these, my fingers became black. Then my palms went black as I tried to wipe the ink from my fingers. I walked to the window, hoping to dry the ink in the sunlight.

As I'd been arranging and decorating my desk, the noise of children playing in the yard had been steadily increasing. It was now loud enough, it seemed to me, to threaten to swamp the whole school. A girl standing by herself in the corner of the yard, one plait hanging lower than the other, caught my eye, and immediately I stepped back from the window. I cursed myself for my timidity. I was the teacher. It was she who should move away from my gaze.

Then a man in a grey overcoat and horn-rimmed spectacles stepped into the yard and a miracle occurred. The noise ceased completely even before the man blew his whistle. After that, children who'd been screaming with excitement in some game, or sulking under the tree by the school gate, ran and took part in the formation of orderly lines. There was a moment's pause, and in that moment I heard the footsteps of other teachers along the corridor, the confident clack of other class-room doors opening and closing, and even a woman laughing and saying, 'Only an hour and a half until coffee time!' before a door slammed shut.

I stood and faced my own classroom door. It seemed a long way from me, and as the marching children came closer, I took in the scene carefully, hoping to keep this sense of distance uppermost in my mind during the forthcoming minutes. The wave of voices began, gradually, to rise again, but was soon stemmed by a man bellowing 'Silence!' There followed the opening of doors and the swish and scrape of boots on wood as children were allowed to enter their classrooms.

It would be wrong, I think, to call what I felt *panic*. I was not sweating or feeling nauseous, as I had been in the corridor with Julia. Instead, an utter blankness came over me. I could not propel myself forward to open the door for the children, nor could I move behind the desk. Again I thought about my voice, and wondered where exactly it was situated in my body, where I might find it if I were to go looking. I might as well have been dreaming, and I think I did close my eyes for a minute, hoping that when I opened them again it would all become clear to me; my voice would come back and my body would be able to move in the right direction.

The first thing I saw when I opened my eyes was a boy's cheek pressed against the glass panel in the door. But still my limbs would not move, so it was a relief when the door opened and the boot-mark boy asked again, with the hint of a smirk, 'Can we come in now?'

'You may,' I said, turning to the blackboard so I wouldn't have to watch them appear. All those tiny bodies looking to me for sense, and justice, and instruction! Can you imagine it, Patrick? In a museum, you never face your audience, do you? In a classroom, you face them every day.

As they were filing in, whispering, giggling, scraping chairs, I took up the chalk and wrote, as I'd been taught at college, the day's date in the left-hand corner of the board. And then, for some strange reason, it struck me that I could write Tom's name instead of mine. I was so used to writing his name every night in my black book – sometimes a column of Toms would form, and become a wall of Toms, or a spire of Toms – that to do the same so boldly in this public place suddenly seemed entirely possible, and perhaps even sensible. That would shock the little bleeders. My hand hovered over the board and – I couldn't help it, Patrick – a laugh escaped me. Silence fell on the class as I stifled my guffaw.

A moment passed as I gathered myself, then the chalk touched the slate and began to form letters; there was that lovely, echoey sound – so delicate and yet so definite – as I wrote, in capitals:

MISS TAYLOR.

I stood back and looked at what my hand had written. The letters climbed towards the right-hand side of the board as if they, too, wanted to escape the room.

MISS TAYLOR

—my name from now on, then.

I hadn't meant to look directly at the rows of faces. I'd meant to fix my eyes on the Virgin above the door. But there they all were, impossible to avoid, twenty-six pairs of eyes turned towards me, each pair utterly different but equally intense. A couple stood out: the boy with the boot-mark hair was sitting on the end of the second row, grinning; in the centre of the front row was a girl with an enormous number of black curls and a face so pale and thin that it took me a second to look away from her; and in the back row was a girl with a dirty-looking bow in the side of her hair, whose arms were crossed tightly and whose mouth was bracketed by deep lines. When I caught her eye she did not – unlike the others – look away from me. I considered ordering her to uncross her arms straight away, but thought the better of it. There'd be plenty of time to tackle such girls, I thought. How wrong I was. Even now I wish I hadn't let Alice Rumbold get away with it on that first day.

Something strange is happening as I write. I keep telling myself that what I am writing is an account explaining my relationship with Tom, and everything else that goes with it. Of course, the *everything else* – which is actually the point of writing at all – is going to become much more difficult to write about very soon. But I find, unexpectedly, that I'm enjoying myself immensely. My days have the kind of purpose they haven't had since I retired from the school. I'm including all sorts of things, too, which may not be of interest to you, Patrick. But I don't care. I want to remember it all, for myself, as well as for you.

And as I write, I wonder if I will ever have the courage to actually read this to you. That has always been my plan, but the closer I get to the *everything else*, the more unlikely this seems.

You were particularly trying this morning, refusing to look at the television, even though I'd switched it from *This Morning,* which we both hate, to a rerun of *As Time Goes By* on BBC2. Don't you like Dame Judi Dench? I thought everyone liked Dame Judi. I thought her combination of classical actressiness and cuddly accessibility (that 'i' in her name says so much, doesn't it?) made her irresistible. And then there was that incident with the liquidised cornflakes, the tipping-over of the bowl, which made Tom exhale a hefty *tut*. I knew you weren't quite up to sitting at the table for breakfast, even with your special cutlery and all the cushions I'd provided to stabilise you, as Nurse Pamela suggested. I must say I find it difficult to concentrate on what Pamela says, so intrigued am I by the long spikes protruding from her eyelids. I know it's not particularly unusual for plump blondes in their late twenties to wear false eyelashes, but it's a very strange combination – Pamela's brisk white uniform, her matter-of-fact manner, and her partygoing eyes. She repeatedly informs me that she comes every morning and evening for an hour so I can have what she calls 'time out'. I don't take time out, though, Patrick: I use the time to write this. Anyway, it was Pamela who told me to get you out of bed as often as possible, suggesting that you could join the 'family table' for meals. But I could see your hand was utterly wild as you brought the spoon up to your face this morning, and I wanted to stop you, to reach out and steady your wrist, but you looked at me just before it reached your lips, and your eyes were so alight with something unreadable – at the time I thought it was anger, but now I wonder if it wasn't a plea of some kind – that I was distracted. And so: wham! Over it went, milky slop dribbling into your lap and dripping on Tom's shoes.

Pamela says that hearing is the last of the senses to go in a stroke patient. Even though you have no speech, you have excellent hearing, she says. It must be like being a toddler again, able to comprehend others' words but unable to make your mouth form the shapes necessary to communicate fully. I wonder how long you'll be able to stand it. No one has said anything about this. The phrase 'no one can say' has become detestable to me. How long until he's on his feet, Doctor?

No one can say. How long until he'll be able to speak again? *No one can say.* Will he have another stroke? *No one can say.* Will he ever recover fully? *No one can say.* The doctors and nurses all talk of the next steps – physiotherapy, speech therapy, counselling, even, for the depression we've been warned can set in – but no one is prepared to forecast the likelihood of any of it actually working.

My own feeling is that your greatest hope of recovery lies in just being here, under this roof.

Late September 1957. Early morning at the school gates, and the sky still more yellow than blue. Clouds were splitting above the bell tower, wood pigeons were purring their terrible song of longing. *Oh-oooh-ooh-oh-oh.* And there Tom was, standing by the wall, returned to me.

By then I'd been teaching for a few weeks and had grown more accustomed to facing the school day, so my legs were a little sturdier, my breath more controlled. But the sight of Tom made my voice disappear completely.

'Marion?'

I'd imagined his sturdy face, his moon-white smile, the solidity of his naked forearm, so many times, and now here he was, on Queen's Park Terrace, standing before me, looking smaller than I'd remembered, but more refined; after almost three years' absence his face had thinned and he stood straighter.

'I wondered if I'd bump into you. Sylvie told me you'd started teaching here.'

Alice Rumbold pushed past us singing, 'Good morning, Miss Taylor,' and I tried to pull myself together.

'Don't run, Alice.' I kept my gaze on her shoulders as I asked Tom, 'What are you doing up here?'

He gave me a flicker of a smile. 'I was just . . . taking a walk around Queen's Park, and thought I'd look at the old school.'

Even at the time, I didn't quite believe this statement. Had he actually come up here just to see me? Had he sought me out? The thought made me catch my breath. We were both silent for a moment, then I managed to say, 'You're a bobby now, aren't you?'

'That's right,' he said. 'Police Constable Burgess at your service.' He laughed, but I could tell he was proud. ''Course, I'm still on probation,' he added.

He looked me up and down then, quite brazenly, taking his time over it. My hands tightened around my basket of books while I waited to read the verdict on his face. But when his eyes met mine again, his expression remained the same: steady, slightly closed.

'It's been a long time. Things have changed,' I said, hoping to draw a compliment, no matter how insincere.

'Have they?' After a pause he added, 'You certainly have.' Then, briskly, before I could blush too hard: 'Well. I'd better let you get on.' I'm remembering now that he looked at his watch, but that may not be true.

I had a choice, Patrick. I could say a quick goodbye and spend the rest of the day wishing we'd had more time together. Or. Or, I could take a risk. I could say something interesting to him. He'd returned, and was standing before me in the flesh, and I could take my chance. I was older now, I told myself; I was twenty years of age, a redhead whose hair was set in brushed curls. I was wearing lipstick (light pink, but lipstick nevertheless). It was a warm September day, a gift of a day when the light was soft and the sun still glowing as though it were summer. *Ooh-oooh-ooh-oh-oh* went the wood pigeons. I could well afford to take a risk.

So I said: 'When are you going to give me that swimming lesson?'

He gave a big Tom laugh. It drowned out everything around us – the children's shouts in the schoolyard, the pigeons' calls. And he slapped me on the back, twice. On the first slap, I almost fell forwards on to him – the air around me became very warm and I smelled Vitalis – but on the second I steadied myself and laughed back.

'I'd forgotten that,' he said. 'You still can't swim?'

'I've been waiting for you to teach me.'

He gave a last, rather uncertain, laugh. 'I bet *you're* a good teacher.'

'Yes. And I need to be able to swim. I have to supervise the children, in the pool.'

This was an out-and-out lie, and I was careful to look Tom fully in the face as I uttered it.

He slapped me on the back again, lightly this time. This was something he did often in the early days, and at the time I was thrilled by the warmth of his hand between my shoulder blades, but now I wonder if it wasn't Tom's way of keeping me at arm's length.

'You're serious.'

'Yes.'

He put a hand to his hair – shorter now, less full, more controlled after the army, but still with that wave that threatened to break free at any moment – and looked down the road, as if searching for a response.

'Do you mind starting in the sea? It's not really advised for beginners, but it's so warm at the moment, it would be a shame not to; the salt, it aids buoyancy . . .'

'The sea it is. When?'

This time I did not blush when he looked me up and down.

'Eight on Saturday morning all right? I'll meet you between the piers. Outside the milk bar.'

I nodded.

He gave another laugh. 'Bring your costume,' he said, starting off down the road.

On Saturday morning I rose early. I'd like to tell you that I'd dreamed all night of being in the waves with Tom, but that wouldn't be true. I don't remember what I dreamed, but it was probably located in the school, and it would have involved me forgetting what I was supposed to be teaching, or being locked in the stationery cupboard, unable to get out and witness what kind of havoc the children were creating. All my dreams seemed to be along these lines at that time, no matter how much I longed to dream of Tom and myself in the sea, of the two of us going out and coming in, coming in and going out with the waves.

So: I rose early, having dreamed of desks and chalk and cardboard milk bottle tops pierced with a straw, and from my window I saw that it was not a promising morning. It had been a mild September, but the month was drawing to a close now, and as I walked past Victoria Gardens the grass was soaked. I was very early, of course; probably it wasn't yet seven, and this added to the delicious feeling I had of doing something secret. I'd left my parents sleeping, and had told no one where I was going. I was out of the house, away from my family, away from the school, and the whole day lay ahead.

To pass the time (I still had at least forty minutes to kill before the enchanted hour of eight in the morning arrived) I strolled along the front. I walked from the Palace to the West Pier, and on that morning the Grand Hotel in all its wedding-cake whiteness, with its porter already standing to attention outside, complete with top hat and gloves, looked incredibly average to me. I didn't experience the pang I usually felt on passing the Grand – the pang of longing for hushed rooms with potted palms and ankle-deep carpets, for discreet bells rung by ladies in pearls (for that was how I imagined the place, fuelled, I suppose, by films starring Sylvia Syms) – no; the Grand could stand there, ablaze with money and pleasure. It meant nothing to me. I was happy to be going to the milk bar between the piers. Hadn't Tom looked me up and down, hadn't he taken in the whole of me with his eyes? Wasn't he about to appear, miraculously tall, taller than me, and looking a bit like Kirk Douglas? (Or was it Burt Lancaster? That set of the jaw, that steel in the eyes. I could never quite decide which of the two he most resembled.) I was very far, at this point, from what Sylvie had told me about Tom on the bench in Preston Park. I was a young woman wearing a tight pointed bra, carrying a yellow flowered bathing cap in her basket, ready to meet her recently returned sweetheart for a secret early-morning swim.

So I thought as I stood by the milk bar's creaking sign and looked out to sea. I set myself a little challenge: could I avoid looking towards the Palace Pier, the way I knew he would come? Fixing my eyes on the water, I imagined him rising from the sea like Neptune, half draped in bladderwrack, his neck studded with barnacles, a crab hanging from his hair; he'd remove the creature and fling it aside as he shrugged off the waves. He'd make his way noiselessly up the beach towards me, despite the pebbles, and would take me in his arms and carry me back to wherever it was he'd come from. I started to giggle at myself, and only the sight of Tom – the real, living, breathing, land-walking Tom – stopped me. He was wearing a black T-shirt and had a faded brown towel slung over his shoulders. On seeing me, he gave a brief wave and pointed back the way he'd come. 'The club's got a changing room,' he called. 'This way. Under the arches.' And before I could reply, he walked off in the direction he was pointing.

I remained standing by the milk bar, still imagining Neptune-Tom coming out of the sea, dripping salt and fish, spraying the shore with brine and sea creatures from some deep, dark world beneath.

Without turning around, he shouted, 'Haven't got all day,' and I followed him, hurrying behind and saying nothing until we reached a metal door in the arches.

Then he turned and looked at me. 'You did bring a hat, didn't you?'

'Of course.'

He unlocked the door and pushed it open. 'Come down when you're ready, then. I'm going in.'

I went inside. The place was like a cave, damp and chalky-smelling, with paint peeling from the ceiling and rusty pipes running along one wall. The floor was still wet, the air clinging, and I shuddered. I hung my cardigan on a peg at the back of the room and unbuttoned my dress. I'd graduated from the red bathing costume I'd worn that day at the lido years ago, and had bought a bright green costume covered in swirly patterns from Peter Robinson's. I'd been quite pleased with the effect when I'd tried it on in the shop: the cups of the bra were constructed from something that felt like rubber, and a short pleated skirt was attached to the waist. But here in the cavern of the changing room there was no mirror on the wall, just a list of swimming races with names and dates

(I noticed that Tom had won the last one), so after pulling the flowered cap on my head and folding my dress on the bench, I went outside, wearing my towel around me.

The sun was higher now and the sea had taken on a dull glitter. Squinting, I saw Tom's head bobbing in the waves. I watched as he emerged from the sea. Standing in the shallows, he flicked his hair back and rubbed his hands up and down his thighs, as if trying to get some warmth back into his flesh.

Almost toppling, and having to grab my towel to keep it from falling to the ground, I managed to walk halfway down the beach in my sandals. The crunch and crack of the pebbles convinced me that this scene was real, that this was actually happening to me: I was approaching the sea, and I was approaching Tom, who was wearing only a pair of blue striped trunks.

He came up to greet me, catching my elbow to steady me on the stones.

'Nice cap,' he said, with a half-smirk, and then, glancing down at my sandals, 'Those will have to come off.'

'I know that.' I tried to keep my voice light and humorous, like his. In those days it was rare, wasn't it, Patrick, for Tom's voice to become what you might call serious; there was always a lot of up-and-down in it, a delicacy, almost a musicality (no doubt that's how you heard it), as though you couldn't quite believe anything he said. Over the years, his voice lost some of its musicality, partly, I think, in reaction to what happened to you; but even now, occasionally, it's like there's a laugh behind his words, just waiting to sneak out.

'OK. We'll go in together. Don't think about it too much. Hold on to me. We'll just get you used to the water. It's not too cold today, quite warm in fact, it's always warmest this

46

time of year, and it's very calm, so it's all looking good. Nothing to worry about. It's also very shallow here, so we'll have to wade out a bit. Ready?'

It was the most I'd ever heard him say, and I was a bit taken aback by his brisk professionalism. He used the same smooth tone I did when trying to coax my pupils to read the next sentence of a book without stumbling. I realised that Tom would make a good policeman. He had the knack of sounding as though he were in control.

'Have you done this before?' I asked. 'Taught people to swim?'

'In the army, and at Sandgate. Some of the boys had never been in the water. I helped them get their heads wet.' He gave a short laugh.

Despite Tom's assurances to the contrary, the water was extremely cold. As I went in, my whole body clenched and the breath was sucked out of me. The stones drove into my feet and the water chilled my blood immediately, leaving my skin pimpled, my teeth chattering. I tried to concentrate my energy on the point where Tom's fingers met my elbow. I told myself that this contact was enough to make it all worth while.

Tom, of course, made no sign of noticing the iciness of the water or the sharpness of the stones. As he walked in, the sea rocking at his thighs, I thought how springy his body was. He was leading me and so was slightly ahead; this allowed me to look at him properly, and as I did so I managed to steady my juddering jaw and breathe through the cold that was smashing into my body with each step. So much Tom in the waves, springing through the water. So much flesh, Patrick, and all of it shining on that bright September morning. He let the water splash up his chest, still holding my elbow. Everything was moving, and Tom moved too: he moved with

the sea or against it, as he wished, whereas I felt the movement too late and only just managed to retain my balance.

He looked back. 'You all right?'

Because he smiled at me, I nodded.

'How does that feel?' he asked.

How, Patrick, could I begin to answer him?

'Fine,' I said. 'A bit cold.'

'Good. You're doing well. Now we're going to do the tiniest
bit of swimming. All I want you to do is follow me, and when
we're deep enough, let your feet lift off the bottom and I'll
hold you up, just so you can feel what it's like. Is that all right?'

Was that all right? His face was so serious when he asked
me this that it was hard to keep from laughing. How could
I object to the prospect of Tom holding me?

We waded further out, and the water took my thighs and
waist, touching every part of me with its freezing tongue.
Then, when the sea was up to my armpits and beginning to
splash at my mouth, leaving a salty trail on my lips, Tom put
a hand flat on my stomach and pressed. 'Feet off the bottom,'
he commanded.

I needn't tell you, Patrick, that I obeyed, utterly mesmerised
by the huge strength of that hand on my stomach, and by
Tom's eyes, blue and changing like the sea, on mine. I let my
feet lift and I was borne upward by the salt and the rocking
motion of the water. Tom's hand was there, a steady platform.
I tried to keep my head above the waves, and for a second
everything balanced perfectly on Tom's flat hand and I heard
him say, 'Good. You're almost swimming.'

I turned to nod at him – I wanted to see his face, to smile
at him and have him smile back (proud teacher! best pupil!)
– and then the sea came up over my face and I couldn't see.
In my panic I lost his hand; water rushed backwards through

my nose, my arms and legs whipped about wildly, trying to find something to grip, some solid substance to anchor me, and I felt something soft and giving beneath my foot – Tom's groin, I knew it even then – and I pushed off from that and managed to come up for a breath of air, heard Tom shouting something, then, as I went under again, his arms were around me, gripping my waist and pulling me free of the water so my breasts were nigh on in his face, and I was still struggling, gasping the air, and it wasn't until I heard him say, 'You're all right, I've got you,' in a slightly annoyed tone, that I stopped fighting and clung to his shoulders, my flowered bathing cap flapping loose at the side of my head like a piece of skin.

He carried me back to shore in silence, and when he deposited me on the beach I couldn't look at him. 'Take a moment,' he said.

'Sorry,' I gasped.

'Get your breath back, then we'll try again.'

'Again?' I looked up at him. 'You are joking?'

He ran a finger along the length of his nose. 'No,' he said. 'I'm not joking. You have to get back in.'

I gazed down the beach; the clouds were gathering now and the day hadn't warmed up at all.

He held out a hand to me. 'Come on,' he said. 'Just once.' He smiled. 'I'll even forgive you for kicking me where you did.'

How could I refuse?

Every Saturday after that, we met in the same place and Tom tried to teach me to swim. I'd wait all week for that hour with Tom in the sea, and even as it got much colder I felt this warmth in me, a heat in my chest that kept me moving in the water, kept me swimming those few strokes towards his waiting arms. You won't be surprised to hear that I was a deliberately slow learner, and as the weather worsened we were forced to continue our lessons in the pool, even though Tom still swam in the sea every day. And, gradually, we started talking. He told me that he'd joined the police force because it wasn't the army, and everyone said he should, what with his height and his fitness, and it was better than working at Allan West's factory. But I could feel that he was proud of his job, and that he enjoyed the responsibility and even the danger of it. He seemed interested in my job, too; he asked a lot about how I taught the children and I tried to give him answers that would sound intelligent without being off-putting. We talked about Laika, the dog the Russians had just sent into space, and how we both felt sorry for her. Tom said he'd like to go into space, I remember that, and I remember saying, 'Perhaps you will, one day,' and him laughing hysterically at my optimism. Occasionally we talked about books, but on this subject I was always more enthusiastic than Tom, so I was careful not to say too much. But you've no idea, Patrick, how liberating – how *daring*, even – it felt to talk about these things with Tom. I'd always thought, up to then, that I should keep quiet about what I would now call my *cultural interests*. Too much talk about such things was tantamount to showing off, to getting ideas above your station. With Tom it was different. He wanted to hear about these things, because he wanted a part of them too. We were both hungry for this other world, and back then it seemed as though Tom could be my partner in some new, as yet undefined, adventure.

Once, as we were walking along the poolside back to the changing rooms, both wrapped in our towels, Tom suddenly asked, 'What about art?'

I knew a little about art; I'd taken art A level at school,

liked the Impressionists, of course, particularly Degas, and some of the Italian painters, and so I said: 'I like it.'

'I've been going to the art gallery.'

This was the first time that Tom had told me about anything he did – apart from swimming – in his spare time.

'I could get really interested in it,' he said. 'I've never looked at it before, you know? I mean, why would I?'

I smiled.

'But now I am, and I think I'm *seeing* something there, something special.'

We reached the door of the changing rooms. Cold water was dripping down my back, and I began to shiver.

'Does that sound stupid?' he asked.

'No. It sounds good.'

He grinned. 'I knew you'd think so. It's a great place. All sorts of paintings in there. I think you'd like it.'

Was our first date going to be at the art gallery? It wasn't a perfect location, but it was a start, I thought. So, smiling brilliantly, I took off my swimming cap and shook my hair in what I hoped was a seductive way. 'I'd love to go.'

'Last week I saw this picture, massive it was, just of the sea. It looked like I could jump into it. Really just jump into it and swim in the waves.'

'Sounds wonderful.'

'And there's sculpture, too, and watercolours, although I didn't like those as much, and drawings that look unfinished but I think they're supposed to be like that . . . there's all sorts.'

Now my teeth were chattering but I kept smiling, sure an invitation would follow.

Tom gave a laugh and slapped my shoulder. 'Sorry, Marion. You're cold. I should let you get dressed.' He rubbed his fingers through his wet hair. 'Same time next Saturday?'

It was like that every week, Patrick. We'd talk – we were good at talking, back then – and then he'd disappear into town, leaving me damp and cold, with only the trudge up Albion Hill and the weekend with my family to look forward to. Some Saturday nights or Sunday afternoons I met Sylvie at the pictures, but her time was mostly taken up by Roy, and so most of my weekends were spent sitting on my eiderdown, reading, or preparing next week's lessons. I also spent a lot of time at the windowsill, looking out at our tiny yard, remembering how it felt to be held by Tom in the water, occasionally spying a shiver in one of the neighbours' curtains, and wondering when it would all begin.

A couple of months later, Sylvie and Roy announced their wedding date. Sylvie asked me to be bridesmaid, and, despite Fred teasing me about how I should really be maid-of-honour, I looked forward to the event. It would mean a whole afternoon with Tom.

No one used the phrase *shotgun wedding*, and Sylvie hadn't confided in me, but there was a general feeling that the speed of the preparations meant that Sylvie must be expecting, and I presumed this was why Roy had been coaxed up the aisle of All Saints'. Certainly Mr Burgess's face, rust-red and clenched in a grin, suggested as much. And instead of the fancy three-tier cake and Pomagne affair that Sylvie and I had often discussed, the reception was held at the Burgess's house, with sausage rolls and mild ale for all.

You would have laughed, Patrick, at the sight of me in my bridesmaid's dress. Sylvie had borrowed it from a cousin who was smaller than me and the thing barely skimmed my knees; it was so tight around the middle that I had to wear a Playtex girdle before I could get the zip done up at the back. It was pale green, the colour you see on sugared almonds, and I don't know what it was made of, but it gave a soft crunching noise as I followed Sylvie into the church. Sylvie looked fragile in her brocade frock and cropped veil; her hair was white-blonde and despite the rumours there was no sign of any thickening about the waist. She must have been freezing: it was early November and the cold had bitten down hard. We both carried small posies of brownish chrysanthemums.

As I walked up the aisle I saw Tom, who was sitting in the front pew, holding himself very straight, staring at the ceiling. Seeing him in his grey flannel suit, rather than his swimming trunks, made him look unfamiliar, and I smiled, knowing I had seen the flesh beneath that stiff collar and tie. I stared at him, telling myself: *It will be us. Next time, it will be us.* And I could suddenly see it all: Tom waiting for me at the altar, looking back over his shoulder with a little smile as I entered the church, my red hair blazing in the light from the doorway. *What took you so long?* he'd tease, and I'd reply, *The best things are worth the wait.*

Tom looked at me. I snapped my gaze away and tried to concentrate instead on the back of Mr Burgess's sweating neck.

At that wedding, everyone was drunk, but Roy was more drunk than most. Roy was not a subtle drunk. He leant on the sideboard in Sylvie's living room, eating great chunks of wedding cake, staring at his new father-in-law. A few moments earlier, he'd shouted, 'Lay off me, old man!' at Mr Burgess's unmoving back, and then he'd retired to the sideboard to stuff his face. Now the room was quiet, and no one moved as Mr Burgess collected his hat and coat, stood at the door and stated in a steady voice, 'I'm not coming back in this house until you've hopped it and taken my trollop of a daughter with you.'

Sylvie fled upstairs, and all eyes turned to Roy, who was by now crushing cake crumbs in his little fists. Tom put on a Tommy Steele record and shouted, 'Who's for another?' while I made my way to Sylvie's room.

Sylvie's sobs were loud and breathy, but when I pushed the door open I was surprised to find she was not sprawled on the bed, beating the mattress with her fists, but standing before her mirror, naked except for her underwear, with both hands curled around her stomach. Sylvie had inherited her mother's expressive bosom.

Catching my eye in the glass, she gave a loud sniff.

'Are you all right?' I began, putting a hand on her shoulder.

She looked away, her chin quivering with the effort of suppressing another sob.

'Don't take any notice of your dad. He's overemotional. He's losing a daughter today.'

Sylvie gave another sniff and her shoulders drooped. I stroked her arm while she cried. After a while she said, 'It must be nice for you.'

'What must be?'

'Being a teacher. Knowing what to say.'

This surprised me. Sylvie and I had never really discussed my job; most of our conversations had been about Roy, or about films we'd seen, or records she'd bought. We'd been seeing less of each other since I'd started at the school, and perhaps this wasn't just because I had less time and she was busy with Roy. It was like at home; I never felt quite comfortable talking about the school, about my *career*, as I was afraid to call it, because no one else knew the first thing about teaching. To my parents and brothers, teachers were the enemy. None of them had enjoyed school, and although they were quietly pleased, if a little puzzled, by my success at the grammar, my decision to become a teacher had been met with stunned silence. The last thing I wanted was to be what my parents despised: a toffee-nosed show-off. And so, as often as not, I said nothing about how I spent my days.

'I don't know what to say all the time, Sylvie.'

Sylvie shrugged. 'It won't be long before you can get a place of your own now, though, will it? You're earning proper money.'

It was true; I'd started saving money and it had crossed my mind that I could rent a room somewhere, perhaps on one of the wide streets in the north of Brighton, nearer the downs, or even on the seafront at Hove, but I didn't relish the thought of living alone. Women didn't live alone then. Not if they could help it.

'You and Roy will have a place of your own, too.'

'I'd like to be *on* my own,' sniffed Sylvie, 'so I could do what I bloody well like.'

I doubted this, and said in a soft voice, 'But you're with Roy now. You'll be a family. That's much better than being alone.'

Sylvie turned away from me and sat on the edge of the bed. 'Got a hanky?' she asked, and I passed her mine. She blew her nose loudly. Sitting next to her, I watched as she took off her wedding ring, then slid it back on again. It was a thick dark-gold band, and Roy had one to match, which surprised me. I hadn't thought he was a man who would wear jewellery.

'Marion,' she said, 'I've got to tell you something.' Leaning close to me, she whispered, 'I lied.'

'Lied?'

'I'm not expecting a baby. I lied to him. To everyone.'

I stared at her, uncomprehending.

'We have done it and everything. But I'm not pregnant.'

She put a hand over her mouth and let out a sudden shrill laugh. 'It's funny, isn't it?'

I thought of Roy's open mouth, full of cake, of his eagerness to push Sylvie along at the roller rink, of the way he couldn't tell what was interesting to talk about and what was not. What an absolute fool he was.

I looked at Sylvie's stomach. 'You mean – there's nothing . . .?'

'Nothing in there. Well, just my insides.'

Then I too began to giggle. Sylvie bit down on her hand to stop herself from laughing too loudly, but soon we were both rolling on the bed, clutching one another, shuddering with barely suppressed mirth.

Sylvie wiped her face with my hanky and took a deep breath. 'I didn't mean to lie, but I couldn't think of any other way,' she said. 'It's a terrible thing, isn't it?'

'Not so terrible.'

She tucked her blonde hair behind her ears and giggled again, rather listlessly this time. Then she fixed me with her eyes. 'Marion. How am I going to explain it to him?'

The intensity of Sylvie's stare, the hysteria of our laughter just moments before and the stout I'd drunk must have made me reckless, Patrick, for I replied: 'Say you lost it. He's not to know, is he? Wait a bit, and then say it's gone. That happens, all the time.'

Sylvie nodded. 'Maybe. It's an idea.'

'He'll never know,' I said, clasping her hands in mine. 'No one will know.'

'Just us,' she said.

Tom offered me a cigarette. 'Is Sylvie all right?' he asked.

It was late afternoon now, and getting dark. In the gloom at the back of the Burgesses' garden, beneath a wedge of ivy,

I leant on the coal bunker, and Tom sat on an upturned bucket.

'She's fine.' I inhaled and waited for the dizzy feeling to knock me slightly out of time. I'd started smoking only recently. To enter the staff room you had to push your way through a curtain of smoke anyway, and I'd always liked the smell of my father's Senior Service. Tom smoked Player's Weights, which weren't as strong, but when the first hit came my mind sharpened and I focused on his eyes. He smiled at me. 'You're a good friend to her.'

'I haven't seen her much lately. Not since the engagement.' I blushed as I said the word, and was glad of the darkening sky, of the shade from the ivy. When Tom didn't respond, I galloped on: 'Not since we've been seeing one another.'

Seeing one another was not what we were doing. Not at all. But Tom didn't contradict me. Instead, he nodded and exhaled.

There was a noise of slamming doors from the house, and someone stuck their head out the back and shouted, 'Bride and groom are leaving!'

'We'd better see them off,' I said.

As I straightened up, Tom put a hand on my hip.

He'd touched me before, of course, but this time there was no solid reason for him to do so. This wasn't a swimming lesson. He didn't need to touch me, so he must have wanted to, I reasoned. It was this touch, more than anything, that convinced me to act as I did over the following few months, Patrick. It went right through my sugared-almond frock and into my hip. People say that love is like a lightning bolt, but this wasn't like that; this was like warm water, spreading through me.

'I'd like you to meet someone,' he said. 'I'd be interested to know what you think.'

This was not the utterance for which I'd hoped. I'd hoped for no utterance at all. I'd hoped, in fact, for a kiss.

Tom let his hand fall from my hip and he stood up.

'Who is it?' I asked.

'A friend,' he said. 'I thought you might have things in common.'

My stomach turned to cold lead. Another girl.

'We should see them off . . .'

'He works at the art gallery.'

To cover the relief I felt on hearing that masculine pronoun, I took a long drag on my cigarette.

'You don't have to,' said Tom. 'It's up to you.'

'I'd love to,' I said, exhaling a plume of smoke, my eyes watering.

We looked each other in the face. 'Are you all right?' he asked.

'I'm fine. Perfectly fine. Let's go in.'

As I turned to walk back to the house, he put his hand on my hip again, bent towards me and let his lips brush my cheek. 'Good,' he said. 'Sweet Marion.' And he strode indoors, leaving me standing in the gloom, my fingers touching the dampness he'd left on my skin.

~•~

There was progress this morning, I'm sure of that. For the first time in weeks, you spoke a word I could understand.

I was washing your body, which I do every Saturday and Sunday morning, when Pamela doesn't make her visit. She offered to send someone else at weekends, but I refused, telling her I'd cope. As always, I was using my softest flannel and my best soap, not the cheap white stuff from the Co-op but a clear, amber-coloured bar that smells of vanilla and leaves a creamy scum around the old washing-up bowl that I use for your bed bath. Wearing the scratched plastic apron I used to don for painting sessions at St Luke's, I pulled back the sheets to your waist, removed your pyjama jacket (you must be one of the few men left in the world to wear a blue striped pyjama jacket, complete with collar, breast pocket and swirling piping on the cuffs) and apologised for what was coming next.

I will not avert my eyes at the necessary moment, or at any moment. I will not look away. Not any more. But you never look at me as I tug down your pyjama bottoms. Leaving you the modesty of the sheet over your lower half, once I've whipped the things from your feet (it's a bit like a conjuring trick, this: I rummage beneath the sheet and – hey presto! – produce a pair of pyjama bottoms, fully intact), my hand, clutching the flannel, searches out your unclean places.

I talk all the while – this morning I remarked on the constant greyness of the sea, the untidiness of the garden, on what Tom and I watched on television the night before – and the sheet becomes damp, your eyes squeeze shut, and your drooping face droops even more. But I am not distressed. I am not distressed by the sight of this, nor by the feel of your warm, sagging scrotum, nor by the salty smell coming from the crinkled flesh of your armpits. I am comforted by all this, Patrick. I am comforted by the fact that I am tending you, cheerfully, by the fact that you let me do this with the minimum of fuss, by the fact that I can wash every part of you, rub it all clean with my Marks and Spencer's Pure Indulgence range flannel, and then throw the cloudy water down the drain. I can do all this without my hands shaking, without my heart-rate increasing, without my jaw slamming shut with such fierceness that I fear it may never open again.

That, too, is progress.

And this morning I was rewarded. As I was squeezing out the flannel for the last time, I heard you utter something that sounded like 'Eh um,' but – forgive me, Patrick – at first I dismissed it as your usual inarticulacy. Since the stroke, your speech has been strangled. You can do little more than grunt, and I'd sensed that, rather than face the indignity of being misunderstood, you had chosen silence. As you are a man whose speech was once impressively articulate – charming, warm and yet erudite – I had rather admired your sacrifice.

But I was wrong. The right side of your face still droops badly, giving you a slightly canine appearance, but this morning you summoned up all your energy, and your mouth and voice worked together.

Still I ignored it, the sound you made, which now had changed to 'Whu om'; I lifted the window slightly to let the stale night smell out, and when I finally turned to you, you were staring up at me from your pillows, your sunken chest still naked and damp, your face screwed into a ball of agony, and you made the sounds again. But this time I almost understood what you said.

I sat on the bed and pulled you forward by the shoulders, and with your limp torso resting on mine, I felt behind you for the pillows, dragged them upright and rested you back on your nest.

'I'll get you a new jacket.'

But you could not wait. You blurted again, even clearer this time, with all the urgency you could muster, and I heard what you said: 'Where's Tom?'

I went to the chest of drawers so you wouldn't see my expression, and found you a clean pyjama jacket. Then I helped you push your arms into the sleeves, and I fastened your buttons. I performed all this without looking you in the face, Patrick. I had to look away, because you kept saying it: 'Where's Tom where's Tom where's Tom where's Tom where's Tom', each time a little quieter and a little slower, and I had no answer for you.

Eventually I said, 'It's wonderful that you're talking again, Patrick. Tom will be very proud,' and I made us both some tea, which we drank together in silence, you exhausted and drooping over your straw, with your bottom half still naked under the sheets, and me blinking at the grey square of the window.

I'm sure you knew it was my first time in the place. I'd never found cause to step into Brighton Art Gallery and Museum before. Looking back, I'm astonished at myself. I'd just become a teacher at St Luke's Infants' School, and I'd never been to an art gallery.

When Tom and I pushed through the heavy glass-panelled doors, I thought how the place looked like nothing so much as a butcher's shop. It was all the green tiles, not that Brighton swimming-pool green that's almost turquoise and makes you feel sunny and light just looking at it, but a mossy, dense green. And the fancy mosaic floor, too, and the polished mahogany staircase, and the glinting cabinets of stuffed things. It was a secret world, all right. A man's world, I thought, just like butchers' shops. Women can visit, but behind the curtain, in the back where they do the chopping and sorting, it's all men. Not that I minded that, at the time. But I wished I hadn't worn that dress with the full skirt and kitten-heeled shoes – it was mid-December and the pavements were frosty, for one thing, and for another, I noticed that people didn't dress for a museum. Most of the others were in brown serge or navy-blue wool, and the whole place was dark and serious and quiet. And there were my kitten heels, tapping inappropriately on the mosaic, echoing around the walls like scattered coins.

Those shoes made me almost level with Tom, too, which can't have pleased him. We walked up the stairs, Tom slightly ahead, his wide shoulders pushing at the seams of his sports jacket. For a big man, Tom walks lightly. At the top of the stairs an enormous guard was nodding off. His jacket had fallen open to reveal a pair of yellow polka-dot braces. As we passed, his head flicked up and he barked, 'Good afternoon!', swallowing hard and blinking. Tom must have said hello, he always answered people, but I doubt I managed anything but a smirk.

Tom had told me all about you. On our way to the museum I'd had to listen again to his descriptions of Patrick Hazlewood, Keeper of Western Art at Brighton Museum and Art Gallery, who was down to earth, just like us, friendly, normal, no airs and graces, yet educated, knowledgeable and cultured. I'd heard it so many times that I'd convinced myself you would be just the opposite. Trying to picture you, I saw the face of the music teacher at St Luke's – a small, pointed face flanked by meaty ear lobes. I was always amazed that that teacher, Mr Reed, looked so much like a musician. He wore a three-piece suit and a fob watch, and his thin hands were often pointing at something, as if he were about to start conducting an orchestra at any moment.

We leant on the banister at the top of the stairs and took a look round. Tom had been there many times before, and was eager to name things for me. 'Look,' he said. 'That's a famous one.' I squinted at it. 'Well, it's by a famous artist,' he added, not telling me the name. I didn't press him for it. I didn't press him for anything, back then. It was a dark picture – everything almost black, the paint dusty-looking – but after a few seconds I saw the white hand stretching up in the corner. '*The Raising of Lazarus*,' said Tom, and I nodded and smiled at him, proud that he knew this information, wanting him to know I was impressed. But when I looked at his usually solid face – that broad nose, those steady eyes – it seemed to have gone a little soft. His neck was pink, and his lips hung drily open.

'We're early,' he stated, looking at his fat wristwatch, a present from his father when he joined the force.

'Will he mind?'

'Oh no,' said Tom. 'He won't mind a bit.'

It was then I realised that Tom was the one who would mind. Whenever we met, he was always exactly on time.

I looked down into the foyer and noticed, tucked by the side of the stairs, a huge multicoloured cat that seemed to be made of papier mâché. I don't know how I'd missed it when I'd first come through the door, but, needless to say, it wasn't the sort of thing I'd expected to see in a place like this. It would look more at home on the Palace Pier, that cat. I still hate its Cheshire grin and drugged-looking eyes. A small girl put a ha'penny into the slot on its belly and spread her hands wide, waiting for something to happen. I nudged Tom, pointing downwards. 'What's that thing?'

Tom gave a laugh. 'Pretty, isn't it? Its stomach lights up and it purrs when you feed it money.'

The girl was still waiting, and so was I.

'Nothing's happening now,' I pointed out. 'What's it doing in a museum? Shouldn't it be in a fairground?'

Tom gave me a slightly puzzled look before breaking into a big Tom-laugh: three short trumpets, eyes squeezed shut. 'Patience, sweet Marion,' he said. I felt the blood in my chest warm.

'He *is* expecting us?' I asked, ready to become annoyed if he wasn't. It was early on in the school's Christmas holidays, and Tom had taken a day's leave, too. There were plenty of other things we could be doing with our time off.

''Course. He's invited us. I told you.'

'I never thought I'd get to meet him.'

'Why not?' Tom was frowning, looking at his watch again.

'You've said so much about him . . . I don't know.'

'It's time now,' said Tom. 'He's late.'

But I was determined to finish. 'I thought he might not really exist.' I laughed. 'You know. That he was too good to be true. Like the Wizard of Oz.'

Tom looked again at his watch.

'What time did he say?' I asked.

'Twelve.'

My own watch said two minutes to midday. I tried to catch Tom's gaze, give him a reassuring smile, but his eyes kept darting about the place. Everyone else was focused on a particular exhibit, head on one side or chin in hand. Only we were just standing there, staring at nothing.

'It's not twelve yet,' I ventured.

Tom made a strange noise in his throat, something that sounded like it was meant to be a carefree 'huh' but which came out more like a whimper.

Then, stepping from my side, he raised his hand.

I looked up, and there you were. Average height. Mid thirties. White shirt, crisply ironed. Navy-blue waistcoat, a good fit. Dark curls worn slightly too long but well under control. A neat face: thick moustache, pinkish cheeks, wide forehead. You were looking at Tom without smiling, with an expression of deep absorption. You considered him, in the same way that others in the room were considering the displays.

You walked briskly forward, and only when you'd reached your goal and clasped Tom's hand did your mouth jump into a smile. For someone with a well-cut waistcoat and thick moustache, someone in charge of Western Art 1500–1900, you had a surprisingly boyish grin. It was small, and went up at the side, as if you'd been studying how Elvis Presley performed the same movement. I remember thinking that at the time, and almost giggling at the preposterousness of it.

'Tom. You came.'

The two of you shook hands vigorously, and Tom ducked his head. I'd never seen him do that before; he always caught my own gaze squarely, kept his face steady.

'We're early,' said Tom.

'Not at all.'

Your shake had gone on a little too long, and Tom withdrew his hand and you both looked away. But you recovered first. Facing me for the first time, your boyish grin flattened out to a wider, more professional, smile and you said, 'You've brought your friend.'

Tom cleared his throat. 'Patrick, this is Marion Taylor. Marion's a teacher. St Luke's Primary. Marion, Patrick Hazlewood.'

I held your cool, soft fingers for a moment and you held my gaze.

'Delighted, my dear. Shall we lunch?'

'Our usual place,' announced Tom, holding open the door to the Clock Tower Café.

I was astonished on two counts. Firstly, that you and Tom had a 'usual' place, and secondly, that the Clock Tower Café was it. I knew it as somewhere my brother Harry occasionally went for mugs of tea before work; he said it was snug, and the tea was so strong it'd take not only the enamel off your teeth but the skin off your gullet, too. But I'd never been in there myself. As we'd walked up North Street, I'd imagined you would take us to some place with white tablecloths and thick napkins for a mixed grill and a bottle of claret. Maybe the restaurant in the Old Ship Hotel.

But here we were in the greasy fug of the Clock Tower Café, your smart suit an awful beacon amongst the ex-army trench coats and grey macs, my kitten heels almost as outlandish here as they'd been at the museum. Apart from the young girl in a pink apron behind the counter, and an old woman hunched over a mug of something in the corner, curlers and hairnet still in place, there were no other women in the café. At the counter, men queued and smoked, their faces shiny with steam from the tea urn. At the tables, few

66

people talked. Most ate or read a newspaper. This wasn't the kind of place for conversation; at least, not the kind of conversation I imagined you would have.

We gazed up at the plastic letters attached to the menu board:

PIE MASH GRAVY
PIE CHIPS BEAN'S
SAUSAGE BEANS EGG'S
SAUSAGE BEANS CHIPS
SPAM FRITTER BEANS
SPOTTED DICK CUSTARD
APPLE SURPRISE
TEA COFFEE BOVRIL SQUASH

Beneath was a handwritten sign: ONLY THE BEST MARGARINE SERVED IN THIS EST'BLMENT.

'You two sit, I'll order,' said Tom, pointing at a free table by the window, which was still covered in dirty plates and pools of spilled tea.

But you wouldn't hear of it, and so Tom and I sat and watched as you shifted about in the queue, keeping your flattened smile bright throughout, and said, 'Thank you so much, my dear,' to the girl behind the counter, who giggled in reply.

Tom's knee was bouncing up and down beneath the table, making the bench on which we sat vibrate. You took a chair opposite and arranged a shiny paper serviette on your lap.

We each had a steaming plate of pie and mash, and although it looked terrible – sunk in gravy, spilling over the sides of the plate – it smelled delicious.

'Just like school dinners,' you said. 'Except I hated them.'
Tom gave a big laugh.

'Tell me, Marion, how do you and Tom know each other?'

'Oh, we're old friends,' I stated.

You glanced at Tom as he attacked his pie with enthusiasm. 'Tom's been teaching you to swim, I hear.'

I brightened at this. He'd been talking about me, then. 'I'm not a very good student.'

You smiled and said nothing; wiped your mouth.

'Marion's very interested in art, too,' said Tom. 'Aren't you, Marion?'

'Do you teach art to your class?' you asked.

'Oh no. The oldest is only seven.'

'It's never too young to start,' you said softly, smiling. 'I'm trying to persuade the powers-that-be at the museum to hold special art appreciation afternoons for children of all ages. They're hesitant – a lot of old-fashioned types, as you can imagine – but I think it would go down well, don't you? Get them young and you've got them for life and all that.'

You smelled of something very expensive. It came towards me as you rested your elbows on the table: a beautiful scent, like freshly carved wood. 'Forgive me,' you said. 'I shouldn't talk shop at lunch. Tell me about the children, Marion. Who's your favourite?'

I thought immediately of Caroline Mears, gazing up at me during story time, and I said: 'There is one girl who might benefit from an art class . . .'

'I'm sure they all adore you. It must be splendid to have a beautiful young teacher. Don't you think so, Tom?'

Tom was watching the condensation crawl down the window. 'Splendid,' he echoed.

'And won't he make a wonderful policeman?' you said. 'I must say I have my reservations about our boys in blue, but with Tom on the force, I think I'll sleep more easily in my bed at night. What was the book you were studying again, Tom? It had a marvellous title. Something like *Vagrants and Burglars . . .*'

'*Suspects and Loiterers*,' said Tom. 'And you shouldn't make light of it. It's serious stuff.' He was smiling; his cheeks glowed. 'The really good one, though, is *A Guide to Facial Identification*. Fascinating, that is.'

'What would you remember of Marion's face, Tom? If you had to identify her?'

Tom looked at me for a moment. 'It's difficult with people you know . . .'

'What would it be, Tom?' I asked, knowing I shouldn't be so eager to find out. I couldn't help myself, Patrick, and I think you probably knew that.

Tom looked at me with mock scrutiny. 'I suppose it would be . . . her freckles.'

My hand went up to my nose.

You gave a light laugh. 'Very fine freckles they are, too.'

I was still holding my nose.

'And your lovely red hair,' added Tom, with an apologetic look in my direction. 'I'd remember that.'

As we left the place, you helped me with my coat and murmured, 'Your hair *is* very arresting, my dear.'

It's difficult, now, to remember exactly how I felt about you on that day, after all that's happened since. But I think I liked you then. You talked so enthusiastically about your ideas for the museum – you wanted it to be an open place, *democratic* was the word you used, where everyone would be welcome. You were planning a series of lunchtime concerts to bring in new people, and you were absolutely set on getting the school-children into the gallery, doing their own work. You even suggested I could help you with this, as though I had the power to change how the education system worked. You almost made me believe that I could do such a thing. I was sure, back then, that you didn't fully appreciate the noise and mess a group of children could make. Still, Tom and I listened, enthralled. If the other men in the café stared at you, or craned their necks at the fulsome note your voice often struck, you merely smiled and carried on, confident that no one could take offence at Patrick Hazlewood, whose manners were impeccable and who himself took no individual at face value. That's what Tom had told me, early on: *He doesn't make assumptions just because of how you look.* You were too gracious for that.

I liked you well enough. And Tom liked you, too. I could tell he liked you because he listened. I suspect that's how it always was between the two of you. Tom was full of concentration as you spoke. He was immensely focused, as if afraid to miss a key phrase or gesture. I could see him swallowing it all down in great gulps.

When we left you that lunchtime, we stood in the doorway of the museum and Tom slapped me on the shoulder. 'Isn't it funny?' he said. 'You started all this, Marion.'

'All what?'

He looked suddenly shy. 'You'll laugh.'

'I won't.'

He pushed his hands in his pockets. 'Well – this sort of self-improvement. You know. I've always enjoyed our chats – about art and books and all that – with you being a teacher, and now Patrick's helping me too.'

'Helping you?'

'To improve my mind.'

After that, for a few months we became quite the threesome. I'm not sure how often you saw Tom alone – I suspect once

70

or twice a week, depending on what his police duties allowed. And what Tom said about self-improvement was true. You never laughed at our ignorance, and you always encouraged our curiosity. With you we went to the Dome to hear Elgar's cello concerto, we saw French films at the Gaiety Cinema (which, generally, I hated: so many beautiful, miserable people with nothing to say to one another), *Chicken Soup with Barley* at the Theatre Royal, and you even introduced us to American poetry – you liked e. e. cummings, but neither Tom nor I went that far.

One evening in January you took the pair of us to London to see *Carmen*, because you were keen to introduce us to opera, and you thought this story of lust, betrayal and murder a good place to start. I remember Tom was in the suit he'd worn to his sister's wedding, and I wore a pair of white gloves I'd bought especially, thinking these were obligatory for the opera. They didn't quite fit and I kept trying to flex my constricted fingers. My palms were sweating, even though it was a frosty night. On the train, you had your usual conversation with Tom about money. You always insisted on paying the bill, wherever we went, and Tom always protested noisily, getting to his feet, rummaging in his pockets for change; occasionally you would let him pay his way, but it was with a droop of your mouth and an impatient wipe of your brow. 'It's common sense that I should get this, Tom, really . . .'

Now Tom insisted that he was in full-time employment, albeit still in his probationary period, and he should at least pay for himself and for me. I knew it was useless to get involved in this conversation, so I fiddled with my gloves and watched Haywards Heath slip past the window. At first you shrugged him off with a laugh, a teasing comment ('You can owe it to me, how's that? We'll put it on the tab'), but Tom wouldn't leave it alone; he pulled his wallet from his jacket pocket and began counting out the notes. 'How much, Patrick?'

You told him to put it away, not to be absurd, but still he waved the money in your face and said, 'Grant me this. Just once.'

Eventually you raised your voice. 'Look, they cost almost seven pounds each. Now will you put that ridiculous thing away and be quiet?'

Tom had already told me, proudly, that he earned about ten pounds a week, and so I knew, of course, that he would have no answer to this.

We sat in silence for the rest of the journey. Tom shifted in his seat, gripping his roll of notes in his lap. You looked out at the passing fields, your eyes at first sharp with anger, then strained with remorse. As we pulled in to Victoria, you glanced at Tom every time he twitched, but he refused to catch your eye.

We pushed through the crowd clicking busily along the station, you following Tom, twisting your umbrella in your hands, licking your bottom lip as if about to venture an apology, but then thinking the better of it. As we descended the steps into the tube station, you touched my shoulder and said in a low voice, 'I've gone and blown it, haven't I?'

I looked at you. Your mouth was pulled downwards and your eyes were sharp with fear, and I stiffened. 'Don't be an idiot,' I commanded. And I walked on, reaching for Tom's arm.

London was noise and smoke and grime to me, that first time. Only later did I appreciate the beauty of it: the plane trees peeling in the sunshine, the rush of air on the tube platform, the crash of cups and the smack of steel on steel in the coffee bars, the hidden-ness of the British Museum, with its fig-leaved David.

I remember looking at my own reflection in the shop windows as we walked, and feeling ashamed that I was taller than you, especially in my heels. Next to you I looked gangly, overstretched, altogether too much, whereas next to Tom I looked almost a normal height; I could pass as someone who was statuesque, rather than slightly mannish.

Watching the opera, my mind slid about, unable to concentrate fully on the stage, distracted as I was by Tom's body in the chair next to mine. You'd insisted that I sit between the two of you ('A rose between two thorns,' you'd said). Occasionally I sneaked a look in your direction, but you didn't once take your eyes off the stage. I'd thought I would dislike the opera – it seemed so hysterical, like a pantomime with strange music, but when Carmen sang *L'amour est un oiseau rebelle que nul ne peut apprivoiser*, my whole body seemed to lift upwards, and then, in that final, awful, wonderful scene, Tom reached for my hand. The orchestra raged and Carmen swooned and died, and Tom's fingers were on mine in the darkness. Then it was all over and you were up on your feet, Patrick, clapping and bravo-ing and hopping on the spot with excitement, and Tom and I joined you, ecstatic in our appreciation.

I've been thinking about the first time I heard the phrase *unnatural practices*. Believe it or not, it was in the staff room at St Luke's, on the lips of Mr R.A. Coppard MA (Oxon) – Richard to me, Dickie to his friends. He was sipping coffee from a brown flowered cup, and, taking off his spectacles and folding one hand over them, he leaned towards Mrs Brenda Whitelady, Class 12, and frowned. 'Was it?' I heard her say, and he nodded. 'Unnatural practices, the *Argus* said. Page seven. Poor old Henry.' Mrs Whitelady blinked and sucked in her breath excitedly. 'His poor wife. Poor Hilda.'

They went back to their exercise books, filling the margins with vigorous red ticks and crosses, and didn't say a word to me. This wasn't a surprise, as I was sitting in the corner of the room, and my position seemed to render me utterly invisible. By this time I'd been at the school several months, but still didn't have my own chair in the staff room. Tom said it was the same at the station: a selection of chairs appeared to have the names of their 'owners' stitched somewhere in invisible thread – that must have been why no one else ever sat on them. There were a few chairs over by the door, with threadbare cushions or uneven legs, which were anybody's; that is to say, the newest staff members sat there. I wondered if you had to wait until another member of staff retired or died before getting the chance to stake a claim to a 'usual' chair. Mrs Whitelady even had her own cushion, embroidered with purple orchids, on hers, so confident was she that no one else's backside would ever touch her seat.

I've been thinking about it because I had the dream again last night, as vivid as it was forty years ago. Tom and I were beneath a table; this time it was my desk in the classroom at St Luke's, but it was the same in all other respects: Tom's weight on me, holding me down; the huge ham of his thigh on mine; his shoulder bowed and stretched across me like the bottom of a boat; and I'm part of him at last. There's no room for air between us.

And I'm coming to realise, writing this, that perhaps what worried me all along was what was inside *me*. My own unnatural practices. What would Mr Coppard and Mrs Whitelady have said if they knew how I felt about Tom? What would they have said if they knew I wanted to take him in my mouth and taste as much of him as I possibly could? Such desires, it seemed to me back then, must be unnatural in a young woman. Hadn't Sylvie warned me that she didn't feel much beyond fear when Roy touched her between her legs? My own parents were often stuck together in a long kiss in the scullery, but even my mother would slap my father's hand away when it went somewhere it shouldn't. 'Don't bother me now, Bill,' she'd say, shifting away from him on the sofa. 'Not now, love.'

In contrast, I wanted everything, and I wanted it now.

February 1958. All day at school I kept as close to the boiler as possible. In the playground I barked at the children to keep moving. Most of them did not have proper coats and their knees were bright with cold.

At home, Mum and Dad had begun to talk about Tom. I'd told them, you see, about our visit to the museum, the trip to London, and all our other outings, but I hadn't mentioned that Tom and I were not alone. 'Don't you go dancing together?' asked Mum. 'Hasn't he taken you to the Regent yet?'

But Tom hated dancing, he'd told me that early on, and I'd convinced myself that what we did was special, because it was different. We weren't like other couples. We were getting to know one another. Having proper conversations. And, having just turned twenty-one, I felt a bit old for all that teenage stuff, jukeboxes and jive.

One Friday evening, not wanting to go home and face the silent query that hung over the house about Tom's intentions towards me, I stayed late in the classroom, drawing up sheets for the children to fill in. Our project at the time was Kings and Queens of England, which I was beginning to think quite a dull topic, and I wished I'd done sheets on Sputnik or the Atom Bomb or something the children could at least get a little excited about. But I was young then, worried about what the headmaster would think, so Kings and Queens it was. Many of the children were still struggling to read the simplest of words, whilst others, like Caroline Mears, were already grasping the rudiments of punctuation. The questions were straightforward, with plenty of space for them to write out or draw their answers however fulsomely they wished: *How many wives did Henry VIII have? Can you draw a picture of the Tower of London?* and so on.

The boiler had gone off and even my corner of the classroom was cold, so I wrapped my scarf about my neck and shoulders and put on my bobble hat in an effort to keep warm. I always liked the classroom at this time of day, when all the children and the other teachers had gone home, and I'd straightened the desks, cleaned the blackboard and plumped the cushions in the reading corner, ready for a new morning.

There was such stillness and silence, apart from the scratching of my pen, and the whole place seemed to soften as the light outside disappeared. I had that lovely feeling of being brisk and organised, a teacher in control of her lessons, fully prepared for the work that lay ahead. It was during these moments, sitting alone at my desk, surrounded by dust and quiet, that I would convince myself that the children liked me. Perhaps, I thought, some of them even loved me. After all, hadn't they been well-behaved that day? And didn't every day now end with a triumphant story time, when I read aloud from *The Water-Babies* and the children sat around me, cross-legged on the rug? Some, of course (Alice Rumbold was one), fidgeted, plaiting each other's hair or picking at the warts on their fingers (Gregory Sillcock comes to mind), but others were clearly gripped by my narrative, their mouths open, their eyes wide. Caroline Mears would position herself at my feet and look up at me as if I held the keys to a kingdom she longed to enter.

'Isn't it time you went home?'

I jumped. Julia Harcourt was standing in the doorway, looking at her watch. 'You'll get locked in if you're not careful. I don't know about you, but I wouldn't relish a night with a blackboard.'

'I'm going in a moment. Just finishing off a few things.'

I was ready for her response: *Isn't it Friday night? Shouldn't you be getting ready for the pictures with your boyfriend?*

But instead she nodded and said, 'Freezing, isn't it?'

I remembered the bobble hat and my hand flew to my head.

'You've got the right idea,' Julia continued. 'It's like a larder in this place during the winter. I sometimes sneak a hot-water bottle under the cushion of my chair.'

She grinned. I put my pen down. She obviously wasn't going to leave without a chat.

Julia was in the privileged position of having her own chair in the staff room; she was pleasant to everyone, but I'd noticed that, like me, she tended to eat her lunch alone, her eyes rarely leaving her book as she took careful bites from her apple. It wasn't that she was shy; she looked the male teachers – even Mr Coppard – in the eye when she spoke, and she was also responsible for organising school field trips to the downs. She was famous for walking the children for miles without stopping, and for convincing them that this was the most enormous fun, whatever the weather.

I started to collect my worksheets into a pile. 'I hadn't realised the time,' I said. 'I'd better be going.'

'Where is it you live?' she asked, as if I'd mentioned it before now.

'Not so far.'

She smiled and stepped into the room. She was wearing a woollen cape, bright green, and she carried an expensive-looking briefcase made of soft leather, and I thought how much better it was than a basket. 'Shall we face the weather together?'

'So how are you getting on?' Julia asked as we walked briskly down Queen's Park Road. 'I wasn't sure if you'd survive that first day. You looked absolutely petrified.'

'I was,' I said. 'I thought I might be sick on your shoes.'

She stopped walking and looked me in the face without smiling. I thought she might be about to bid me good night and head off in the other direction, but instead she moved closer and said, gravely, 'That would have been a disaster. Those are my best teaching shoes. I've attached metal taps to the heels to warn the children I'm coming. I call them my hooves.'

For a moment I wasn't sure how to respond. But then Julia threw her head back and gave a loud roar, showing her straight teeth, and I knew it was all right to laugh.

'Do they work?' I asked.

'What?'

'The hooves.'

'You can count on it. By the time I've reached the classroom, they're silent as the dead. I can ride roughshod over them and they don't make a squeak.'

'I could do with a pair of those.'

'Giving you gyp, are they?'

'Not really.' I paused. 'Alice Rumbold is a little . . .'

'Shit?'

Julia's eyes were bright and narrow. She was daring me to laugh again. So I did.

'You definitely need the hooves with Alice,' she concluded.

When we reached the corner of my street, Julia squeezed my arm and said, 'Let's do this again.'

As spring approached, I began to feel more impatient. Tom had kissed my cheek and held my hand, and every week we saw each other at least once, usually in your presence. But this was no longer enough. As my mother was given to reminding me, it was not yet too late for me. Not yet.

I'm not sure exactly when the terrible moment used to fall, the moment at which a woman was judged to have been left on the shelf. Every time I thought of it, I thought of an old clock, ticking away the days. Many of the girls I'd known at school were already married. I knew I had a few years still to go, but if I wasn't careful, the other teachers would look at me in the same way they looked at Julia, a woman alone; a woman who has to work for her own living, reads too many books, and is seen out shopping on a Saturday with a trolley instead of a pram or a child in tow, wearing trousers and obviously in no hurry to get home. In no hurry to get anywhere, in fact.

I know it seems incredible now, and I'm sure I must have heard rumours of the existence of that fantastic beast, the career woman, at the time (it was almost 1960, for God's sake), but I'm also sure that I dismissed them, and that the last thing I wanted was to be one of those women. So there was a panic rising in me as I stood in front of the class and told them the story of Persephone in the underworld. I got them to draw pictures of Demeter bringing the spring back with her daughter, and I looked out at the bare trees in the playground, their branches like veins, black against the grey sky, and I thought: enough of this waiting.

And then the change happened.

It was a Saturday night, and Tom was coming to the house to pick me up. This was the first change. Usually we met at the pictures or the theatre, but on this Saturday he'd said he would come to the house. I hadn't told Mum and Dad about this, because I knew what would happen if I did: Mum would spend the whole day cleaning the place, making sandwiches, deciding which of her best frocks to put on and asking me questions, and Dad would spend the whole day silently preparing his questions for Tom.

All afternoon I pretended to be reading in my room. I'd hung my faux-silk pale blue dress on the back of the door, ready to step into, and it looked full of promise. I had a little cardigan, too, with angora in it; it was the softest thing I'd ever touched. I didn't have much in the way of fancy underwear – no sateen bras or frilly knickers or lacy camisoles – so I couldn't select anything particularly alluring, although I wished I could. I told myself that if Tom kissed me again I would get straight down to Peter Robinson's and buy myself something in black, something that would speak for itself. Something that would allow me to become Tom's lover.

Several times I was on the brink of going downstairs to announce the fact that Tom was coming over. But I couldn't decide which would be most delightful: sharing the knowledge that he was picking me up, or keeping it a secret.

I managed to wait until five to seven before positioning myself at the window in Mum and Dad's bedroom so I could watch for him. I didn't have to wait long. He appeared at a few minutes to the hour, looking at his watch. Usually Tom took long springy strides, but today he almost dawdled, glancing into windows as he passed. Still, there was something liquid about him as he moved, and I clutched the curtain to my face and breathed in its mustiness to steady myself.

I peeked out of the window again, half hoping that Tom would look up and catch me spying on him, but instead he straightened his jacket and reached for our knocker. I had a sudden wish that he'd worn his uniform, so my parents could open the door to a policeman.

Looking at myself in my mother's glass, I saw that my cheeks were flushed. The blue dress caught the light and flashed it back to me, and I smiled at myself. I was ready. He was here.

From the upstairs landing, I heard Dad answer the door and listened to the following conversation:

DAD (coughing): Hello. What can I do for you, then?

TOM (voice light, polite, every syllable carefully sounded): Is Marion in?

DAD (pause, a bit too loud): And who might you be?

TOM: Sorry. I should've said. I'm Tom Burgess. Marion's friend. You must be Mr Taylor?

DAD (after a long pause, shouting): PHYLLIS! MARION! Tom's here! It's Tom! Come in then, boy, come in. (Shouting up the stairs again.) It's Tom!

I took the stairs slowly, aware that both Tom and Dad were standing at the bottom, watching me descend.

We all looked at one another without speaking, then Dad showed us into the front room, where we sat only at Christmas and when Dad's posh sister, Marjory, came down from Surrey. The place smelled of polish and coal, and it was very cold.

'Phyllis!' Dad shouted. Tom and I looked at one another for a moment, and I saw the anxiety in his eyes. Despite the coolness of the room, his forehead was gleaming with perspiration.

'You're Sylvie's brother,' Dad stated.

'That's right.'

'Marion tells us you've joined the police.'

''Fraid so,' said Tom.

'Nothing to apologise for, not in this house,' said Dad, turning on the standard lamp. He glanced at Tom. 'Sit down then, boy. You're making me nervous.'

Tom balanced himself on the edge of a sofa cushion.

'We kept saying to Marion, bring Tom home for his tea, but she never did. Still. Here you are now.'

'We should get going, Dad. We'll be late for the pictures.'

'PHYLLIS!' Dad positioned himself by the door, blocking our exit. 'Let your mother meet Tom first. We've been waiting for this, Tom. Marion's kept us waiting ages.'

Tom nodded and smiled, and then Mum came in, wearing lipstick and smelling of hairspray.

Tom stood and held out a hand, which Mum took and held, gazing at his face. 'Well,' she said. 'Here you are.'

'Here he is,' echoed Dad, and we all looked at Tom, who suddenly let out a big laugh. There was a moment when no one responded, and I saw a frown begin to appear on Dad's brow, but then my mother giggled. It was a high, tinkling sound, one we didn't hear often.

'Here I am,' said Tom, and Mum giggled some more.

'Isn't he lovely and tall, Bill?' she said. 'You must be a good copper.'

'I've hardly started yet, Mrs Taylor.'

'They won't get away from you, will they? And you're a swimmer, too.' She looked at me with wide eyes. 'Marion's kept you a secret for too long.'

I thought she might be about to bat him playfully on the chest, but instead she patted me on the arm and looked coyly at Tom, who laughed again.

'We should go,' I repeated.

As we walked down the street, I was aware of Mum and Dad looking after us as if they couldn't believe such a man as Tom Burgess was by their daughter's side.

Tom paused to light us both a cigarette. 'They were impressed, weren't they?' he said, shaking out the match.

I took a jubilant drag and exhaled dramatically. 'Do you think so?' I asked, innocently.

We laughed. The Grand Parade was beginning to sing with people heading for town. I reached for Tom's hand and held it all the way to the Astoria. I held it tight and I didn't let go even as we approached the usual spot where we met you. But when we got there, you were nowhere to be seen, and Tom simply carried on walking.

'Aren't we meeting Patrick?' I asked, hanging back.

'No.'

'Are we meeting him somewhere else?'

A man pushed past us, knocking Tom's shoulder. 'Watch it!' he shouted, and the man – a boy really, younger than Tom, with a greased forelock – turned and scowled. Tom stood firm, glaring back, until the boy flicked his cigarette end into the road and walked on with a shrug.

'Patrick's in London this weekend,' Tom said.

We'd almost reached the pavilion now. Its turrets glowed cream against the blue-black sky. I knew you had a place in town, Patrick, but I'd never known you to stay there on a weekend. You were always with us at the weekend.

I couldn't help smiling as I realised what Tom was telling me. We were alone. Without you.

'Let's go for a drink!' I said, steering Tom into the King and Queen. I was determined to do what normal young couples did on Saturday nights, and I pretended not to hear Tom say that he'd something else in mind. It was so loud in there anyway; the jukebox was cracking out a beat as we stood near the bar, looking into our drinks. The crowd crushed us up against one another, and I wanted to stay there all night, feeling Tom's warmth as he stood next to me, watching the muscles in his arm move as he brought his pint of pale and mild to his mouth.

I'd hardly started my gin and tonic when Tom leant towards me and said, 'Shall we go somewhere else? I thought perhaps—'

'I haven't finished my drink,' I protested. 'How's Sylvie?' I wanted to keep the conversation away from the topic of you, Patrick. I didn't want to know why you were in London, or what you were doing there.

Tom finished his pint and put his glass down on the bar. 'Let's go,' he said. 'We can't talk in here.'

I watched him walk out of the place. He didn't look back for me, or call me from the doorway. He simply made his wishes clear, then left. I gulped back the rest of my gin and tonic. A cool rush of alcohol sped through my limbs.

Until I stepped outside and saw Tom, I didn't know I was furious. But in a second everything tightened and my breath came fast. I felt my arm going rigid, my hand drawing back, and I knew that if I didn't open my mouth and shout I would slap him, hard. So I stood with both feet planted firmly on the pavement, and I yelled: 'What the bloody hell is wrong with you?'

Tom stared at me, eyes bright with surprise.

'Can't we have a drink, like a normal couple?'

He looked up and down the street. I knew passers-by were staring at me, thinking, *Redheads. They're all the same.* But it was too late to care.

'Marion—'

'All I want is to be alone with you! Is that so much to ask? Everyone else manages it!'

There was a long pause. My arms were still rigid, but my hand had relaxed. I knew I should apologise, but I was frightened that if I opened my mouth a sob would come out.

Then Tom took a step forward, grasped my head in his hands, and kissed me on the lips.

Now, looking back, I think: did he do it just to silence me? To prevent any further public humiliation? After all, he was a police constable, albeit one still on probation, and probably not taken at all seriously by the local criminal population. But at the time, this thought did not cross my mind. I was so surprised to feel Tom's lips on mine – so sudden, so urgent – that I thought nothing. And it was such a relief, Patrick, to merely *feel* for a change. To allow myself to melt, as they say, into a kiss. And it was like melting. That letting go. That sliding into the sensations of another's flesh.

We said little after that. Together we strolled along the seafront, arms about each other's waists, facing the wind from the sea. In the darkness I could see the white tops of the waves, rising, rolling, dispersing. Boys on motorbikes raced up Marine Drive, giving me an excuse to hold Tom tighter every time one whipped by. I had no idea where we were going – I didn't even consider our direction. It was enough to be walking in the evening with Tom, past the upturned fishermen's boats on the shore, away from the bright blare of the pier and towards Kemp Town. Tom did not kiss me again, but I occasionally let my head rest on his shoulder as we walked. I felt very generous towards you then, Patrick. I even wondered if perhaps you'd gone away deliberately, to give us some time alone. *Take Marion out somewhere nice*, you'd have said. *And for heaven's sake give her a kiss, won't you!*

I'd hardly noticed where we were going until we reached Chichester Terrace. The wide pavements were quiet and empty. The place hasn't changed since you left: it's still a hushed, solid street where the glossy doors are set back from the pavement, each one announced by a sturdy set of Doric columns and a flight of black and white tiled steps. On that street, the brass knockers are shining and uniform. Each facade is flatly white, iced in brilliant plaster, and each railing is straight and unchipped. The long windows cleanly reflect the street lamps and the occasional flash of traffic. Chichester Terrace is grand yet understated, without the arrogance of Sussex Square or Lewes Crescent.

Tom stopped walking and felt in his pocket.

'Isn't this . . .'

He nodded. 'Patrick's place.' He dangled a set of keys in front of my face, gave a quick laugh, and skipped up the steps to your front door.

I followed him, my shoes making a lovely light clipping sound on the tiles. Tom opened the huge door to reveal a hallway papered deep yellow, patterned with gold trefoils, and a red carpet running right up the stairs.

'Tom, what's going on?'

Tom put a finger to his lips and beckoned me upwards. On the landing of the second floor, he paused and fumbled with the keys. We were facing a white door, to the side of which was a small gold-framed name plate: *P. F. Hazlewood*. Your door. We were outside your door, and Tom had the keys.

By now my mouth was dry and my heart was kicking in my chest. 'Tom,' I began again, but he'd already opened the door and we were inside your flat.

He let the door close without putting on the light, and there was a moment when I believed you were in there after all, that Tom would yell out, 'Surprise!' and you'd come blinking into the hallway. You'd be shocked, of course, but you'd recover quickly and you'd soon be your usual gracious self, offering drinks, bidding us welcome, talking into the small hours of the morning whilst we sat in separate chairs and listened appreciatively. But the only sound was Tom's breathing. I stood in the darkness, my skin prickling as I felt Tom move closer to me.

'He's not here, is he?' I whispered.

'No,' said Tom. 'It's just us.'

The first time Tom had kissed me, he'd pressed his mouth so hard upon mine that I'd felt his teeth; this time, his lips were softer. I was just reaching out to put my arms around his neck when he pulled away and switched on the light.

His eyes were very blue and serious. He looked at me for the longest time, there in your hallway, and I basked in the intensity of that gaze. I wanted to lie down and sleep in it, Patrick.

Then he grinned. 'You have to take a look at this place,' he said. 'Come on. I'll show you round.'

I followed him in a kind of daze. My whole body still felt doped from that look, those kisses. I remember, though, that it was very warm in your flat. You had central heating, even then, and I had to take off my coat and my angora cardigan. The radiators hummed and ticked, hot enough to burn.

First stop was the enormous living room, of course. That room was bigger than my classroom, with windows stretching from floor to ceiling. Tom scampered about, flicking on huge table lamps, and it all came into soft focus: the piano in the corner; the chesterfield, crammed with cushions; the cream walls covered in pictures, some of them with their own spotlight; the grey marble fireplace; the chandelier, which had glass flower petals rather than crystal drops and was all colours. And (Tom introduced this with a flourish) the television set.

'Tom,' I said, trying to make my voice stern. 'You're going to have to explain this to me.'

'Isn't it incredible?' He peeled off his sports jacket and threw it on an armchair. 'He's got everything.'

He was childlike in his wonder and excitement. 'Everything!' he repeated, gesturing again towards the television set.

'I'm surprised he has that,' I said. 'I'd have thought he'd be against that sort of thing.'

'He thinks it's important to keep up with new things.'

'I bet he doesn't watch ITV.'

It was a nice set: walnut veneer, carved into scrolls at the top and bottom of the screen.

'How come you've got his keys?' I asked.

88

'Shall we have a drink?' And Tom clicked open your cocktail cabinet to display deep rows of glasses and bottles. 'Gin?' he offered. 'Whisky? Brandy? Cognac?'

'Tom, what are we doing here?'

'Or how about a martini?'

I frowned.

'Come on, Marion. Stop acting like a schoolteacher and at least have a brandy.' He held out a glass to me. 'It's great here, isn't it? You can't tell me you don't like it.'

He smiled so widely that I had to join him. We sat together on the sofa, laughing as we lost ourselves in your cushions. Once I'd struggled to the edge of my seat, I fixed Tom with a look. 'So?' I said. 'What's going on?'

He sighed. 'It's all right. Really. Patrick's in London, and he's always said I could use the place whilst he's away . . .'

'Do you come here a lot?'

'Of course,' he said, taking a long drink from his glass. 'Well. Sometimes.'

There was a pause. I put my brandy down on your coffee table, next to a pile of art magazines.

'Those keys – are they yours?'

Tom nodded.

'How often do you—'

'Marion,' he said, leaning across to kiss my hair. 'I'm so glad you're here. And it's fine, believe me. Patrick would want us to come.'

There was something odd, something un-Tom-like in his voice, a theatricality which, at the time, I put down to nerves. I glimpsed our reflections in the long window, and we looked almost like a cultured young couple, surrounded by tasteful artefacts and quality furniture, enjoying a drink together on a Saturday night. Trying to ignore the feeling that this was all happening in the wrong place, to the wrong people, I finished my drink quickly and said to Tom, 'Show me some more of the flat.'

He took me to the kitchen. You had a spice rack, I remember – it was the first time I'd seen one – and a double sink and drainer, and the walls were tiled light green. Tom couldn't stop pointing things out for me. He opened the top door of the large fridge. 'Freezer compartment,' he said. 'Wouldn't you love one of these?'

I said that I would.

'He's a great cook, you know.'

I expressed surprise, and Tom opened all your cupboards, and showed me their contents, as evidence. There were copper pans, earthenware casseroles, a set of steel chopping knives, one with a curved blade that Tom announced was called a mezzaluna, bottles of olive oil and wine vinegar, a book by Elizabeth David on the shelf.

'But you cook too,' I said. 'You were in the Catering Corps.'

'Not like Patrick. Pie and mash is about all I do.'

'I like pie and mash.'

'Simple tastes,' said Tom, grinning, 'for a schoolteacher.'

'That's right,' I said, opening the fridge. 'A bag of fish and chips does me fine. What's he got in here?'

'He said he'd leave something. You hungry?' Tom reached past me for a plate of cold breaded chicken. 'Want some?' He took a wing and sucked the meat from the bone. 'It's good,' he said, holding the plate out to me, his lips glistening.

'Should we?' I asked. But my hand was already on a drumstick.

Tom was right: it was good; the crumbs were light and crisp, the meat fabulously rich and greasy.

'That's it!' Tom's eyes were still wild. He took piece

after piece, exclaiming all the while over the elegance of your kitchen, the tastiness of your chicken, the delicacy of your brandy. 'Let's have the lot,' he said. And we stood there in your kitchen, devouring your food, drinking your alcohol, licking our oily fingers, giggling.

Afterwards, Tom took my hand and led me to another room. I'd had a few drinks by then and, as I moved, I experienced the strange sensation of my surroundings not quite catching up with me. We didn't go to your bedroom, Patrick (although I would love to tell you that we did). We went to the spare room. It was small and white, with a single bed, primroses on the coverlet, a plain mirror above the skinny fireplace, and a wardrobe whose hangers clanged together in the empty space as we walked across the floor. A plain, practical room.

Still holding hands, we stood near the bed, neither one of us daring to look directly at it. Tom's face had gone very pale and serious; his eyes were no longer wild. I thought of him on the beach, how big and healthy and joyful he was in the water. I remembered my vision of him as Neptune, and almost told him about it, but something in his eyes kept me silent.

'Well,' he said.

'Well.'

'Would you like another drink?'

'No. Thank you.'

I began to shiver.

'Cold?' asked Tom, putting an arm around me. 'It's late,' he said. 'If you want to go . . .'

'I don't want to go.'

He kissed my hair, and when his fingers brushed my cheek, they were trembling. I turned to face him, and the ends of our noses touched.

'Marion,' he whispered. 'I haven't done this before.'

I was shocked by that statement, and even thought that he might be playing the innocent for my sake, to make me feel better about my own inexperience. Surely there must have been someone, whilst he was in the army?

Writing this now, picturing him confessing his weakness to me, I'm filled with love for him all over again. Whatever else he didn't tell me, daring to admit such a thing was a great achievement.

Of course, I had no idea how to respond to this confession, and so I think we stood like that, nose to nose, for a very long time, as though we were frozen together.

Eventually I sat on the bed, crossed my legs and said, 'It's all right. We don't have to do anything, do we?' I was rather hoping, of course, that this would spur him into action.

Instead, Tom paced to the window, hands in his pockets, and stared out into the darkness.

'We could have another drink,' I ventured.

Silence.

'I've had a lovely time,' I said.

Silence.

'One more brandy?'

Silence.

I sighed. 'I suppose it is getting late. Perhaps I'd better get back.'

Then Tom turned to face me, biting his lip and looking as though he was about to burst into tears.

'Whatever is it?' I asked. In answer, he knelt beside me and, clasping me around the stomach, leant his head on my bosom. He pressed into me so hard that I thought I might fall back on the bed, but I managed to keep myself upright. 'Tom,' I said, 'what's the matter?'

But he said nothing. I held his head to my chest and stroked his hair, my fingers clinging to his beautiful curls, digging into his scalp.

I tell you, Patrick, there was a part of me that wanted to pull him up by his roots, fling him on the bed, wrench the shirt from his back and plunge my body on to his. But I remained still.

He sat back on his heels, face flushed pink and eyes shining. 'I wanted it to be nice for you,' he said.

'It is. It really is.'

There was another long pause.

'And I wanted to let you know . . . how I feel.'

'How's that, Tom?'

'I want you to be my wife,' he said.

II

29th September 1957

Why write again? When I know that I must exercise caution. When I know that to commit my desires to paper is madness. When I know that those screaming bitch types who insist on trolling all over town spoil it for the rest of us. (I saw Gilbert Harding last week in his ghastly Roller, screeching out of the window at some poor lad on a bicycle. I didn't know whether to laugh or cry.)

Why write again? Because today things are different. One might even say everything's changed. And so here I am, writing this journal. And that means indiscretions. But I can't keep quiet about this one. I'm not going to name names – I'm not completely reckless – but I am going to write this: I have met someone.

Why write again? Because Patrick Hazlewood, thirty-four, has not given up.

I do think he's perfect. Ideal, even. And it's more than his body (though that is ideal, too).

My *affaires* – such as they've been, and they've been few – tend to be complicated. Drawn out. Reluctant, perhaps. How others like Charlie get along so damned carefree is beyond me. Those boys at the meat rack have their charms, but it's all so – I won't say sordid, I don't mean that – *fleeting*. Beautifully, awfully fleeting.

Will burn this after writing. It's one thing to commit oneself to paper; quite another to leave that paper lying about for any pair of eyes to devour.

It took place over a middle-aged lady sitting on a pavement. I was walking along Marine Parade. A bright, warm late-summer morning. The day: Tuesday. The time: approximately 7.30. Early for me, but I was on my way to the museum to catch up on some paperwork. Strolling along, thinking how pleasant it was to enjoy the quiet and the solitude, vowing to get up an hour earlier every day, I saw a car – a cream Ford, I'm sure it was – nudge the wheel of a bicycle. Just gently. There was a slight delay before the bicycle wobbled enough to tip its rider, hands splayed, legs tangled with wheels, on to the pavement. The car drove on regardless, leaving me to hurry over to the woman in distress.

By the time I reached her, she was sitting up on the edge of the kerb, so I knew there was no serious damage. She looked to be in her forties, and her basket and handlebars were loaded with bags of all types – string, paper, some kind of canvas construction – so it wasn't surprising that she'd lost her balance. I touched her on the shoulder and asked if she was all right.

'What does it look like?' she barked. I took a step back. Her voice had venom in it.

'You're shocked, of course.'

'Livid is what I am. That bastard knocked me off.'

She was a sorry sight. Her spectacles lopsided, her hat askew.

'Do you think you can stand?'

Her mouth twisted. 'We need the police here. We need the police, now!'

Seeing I had no alternative but to go along with her wishes, I dashed to the nearest police box on the corner of Bloomsbury

Place, thinking I could call from there, leave her with some obliging bobby and get on with the rest of my day.

I've never had much patience with our boys in blue. Have always despised their brutish little ways, their stocky bodies squeezed into thick wool, those ridiculous helmets rammed on their heads like black jam jars. What was it that officer said about the incident at the Napoleon, where that boy was left with half his face carved away from the bone? *Damned pansy's lucky that's all they cut off.* I think those were his exact words.

So I wasn't relishing the thought of coming face to face with a policeman. I steeled myself for the evaluating glance up and down, the raised eyebrows in response to my voice. The clenched fists in response to my smile. The chilled relations in response to *the cut of my jib*.

But the young man who stepped from the box as I approached was quite, quite different. I could see it straight away. He was properly tall, for a start, with shoulders that looked like they could take the weight of the world and yet were exquisitely shaped. Not a hint of bulk. I thought immediately of that wonderful Greek boy with the broken arm in the British Museum. The way he glows with beauty and strength, the way the warmth of the Mediterranean exudes from him (and still he manages to blend perfectly with his British surroundings!). This boy was like that. He wore his awful uniform lightly, and I could see at once there was life pulsing beneath the rough black wool of his jacket.

We looked at each other for a beat, he with a serious mouth, me with all my words vanished.

'Good morning,' he said as I tried to remember what it was I wanted. Why it was I'd sought out a policeman in the first place.

Eventually I stammered, 'I need your help, Officer.'

My actual words. And God knows I meant them. My plea for help, my cry for protection. It reminds me, now, of when I first became friends with Charlie at school. I went to him in desperation, thinking he could help me stop the bullying. And he did teach me not to care so much. Charlie always had something so nonchalant in his manner, something that made them back off – something so *fuck you*, is how he'd put it – and I've always loved that. Loved it and wished I could have it myself.

'There's been an accident,' I continued. 'A lady's come off her bicycle. I'm sure it's nothing serious, but—'

'Show me the way.' Despite his youth, he managed to sound very capable. And he walked with great energy and determination, frowning slightly now, asking me all the necessary questions – was I the only witness? What did I see? What make of car was it? Did I get a glimpse of the driver?

I answered as best I could, wanting to give him all the information he needed as I followed his great strides.

When we reached the woman, she was still sitting on the pavement, but I noticed she'd gained enough strength to gather her bags around her. As soon as she saw my policeman, her demeanour changed completely. Suddenly she was all smiles. Looking up at him, eyes ablaze, lips newly licked, she declared herself quite all right, thank you very much.

'Oh no, Officer, there's been a misunderstanding,' she said, without glancing in my direction. 'The car did come close, but it didn't *hit* me, I just slipped on the pedals – it's these shoes,' she displayed her scuffed black courts as though they were Hollywood dancing heels, 'and I *was* a little stunned, you know how it is, Officer, early in the morning . . .'

On and on she went, chattering away like an excited sparrow.

My policeman nodded, his face impassive, as she gabbled her nonsense.

When she'd run out of steam, he asked, 'So you weren't knocked off?'

'Not a bit of it.'

'And you're all right?'

'Right as rain.'

She held out a hand for him to help her up. He obliged, face still expressionless.

'It was lovely to meet you, Officer.' She was mounting her bicycle now, beaming for England.

My policeman granted her a smile. 'Mind how you go,' he said, and we both stood and watched as she cycled away.

He turned to me, and before I could begin any explanation he said, 'Batty old bird, wasn't she?' and gave a small grin, the like of which I'm sure young police constables are meant to have knocked out of them during their probationary period.

He had total confidence in what I'd told him. He believed me, not her. And already he trusted me enough to insult a lady in my presence.

I laughed. 'Not exactly a major incident . . .'

'They rarely are, sir.'

I held out a hand. 'Patrick Hazlewood.'

A hesitation. He considered my outstretched fingers. Briefly I wondered if there were some police regulation forbidding all physical contact – except the forcible kind – with the general public.

Then he took my hand and told me his name.

'I have to say I thought you handled that very well,' I ventured.

To my great surprise his cheeks went a little pink. Hugely touching.

'Thank you, Mr Hazlewood.'

I winced, but knew better than to ask for first names at this early stage.

'I suppose you get a lot of that sort of thing? Difficult people?'

'Some.' A moment's pause, then he added: 'Not so many. I'm new. Only been at it a few weeks.'

Again I was touched by his immediate, unquestioning trust. He's not like the rest. Didn't once give me the evaluating stare. Allowed no shadow to pass over his face at the sound of my voice. Didn't close down. He was open. He remained open.

He thanked me for my help and turned to go.

That was two weeks ago.

The day after the so-called accident, I walked past his police box again. No sign of him. Still I floated. All the girls in the museum commented on it. *You're chirpy today, Mr H.* And I was. Whistling Bizet wherever I went. I knew. That's what it was. I just knew. It was only a matter of time. A matter of playing it right. Of not rushing things. Not scaring him off. I knew we could be friends. I knew I could give him something he wanted. It's the long game with me. I'm well aware there are quicker, safer pleasures to be found down the Argyle. Or (heaven forbid) the Spotted Dog. And it's not that I dislike those places. It's the competitiveness that gets me down. All the moneyed minorities eyeing one another, positioning themselves for the evening, staking their claim on whatever comes through the door. Oh, it can be fun (I remember particularly a sailor fresh from Pompey, with a lazy eye and massive thighs). But what I want . . . well, it's really very simple. I want more.

So. Day two. Caught a glimpse of him on Burlington Street, but he was so far away that the only way to reach him would have been to run. And I wasn't going to do that. Still I whistled – perhaps a little quieter; floated – perhaps a little lower.

Day three: there he was, setting off from the box. I did hurry a little in an effort to catch up with him, but there was no running. I walked behind him – at a distance of about a hundred yards – for a while, watching his trim waist, the paleness of his wrists winking at me as he strode down the street. To call out for him would have been crass. Unwelcome. But I really couldn't walk any faster. He is a policeman, after all; I don't suppose he'd take kindly to being shadowed by any man.

And so I let him go. A whole weekend of waiting lay ahead. I'd forgotten, of course, that policemen do not keep the hours of mere mortals, and was not at all prepared when, on my way to buy a newspaper, I bumped into him on St George's Road. The day: Saturday. The time: 11.30-ish. Another warm early-September day, full of glowing light. He was walking towards me, on the edge of the pavement. As soon as I saw the uniform, my blood rose. I'd been doing that all week – warming at the sight of police uniforms. A very dangerous way to carry on.

My thought was: I'll glance his way, and if he doesn't glance back, that will be the end of it. I'll leave it up to him. He can return the look, or he can walk on. Through many years of experience, I've found this the safest way to conduct oneself. Don't invite trouble and it won't come looking for you. And fishing for a policeman's gaze is an extremely risky business.

So I glanced. And he was looking straight at me.

'Morning, Mr Hazlewood,' he said.

I was beaming, no doubt, as we stood and exchanged a few pleasantries about the clemency of the weather. His voice is light. Not high-pitched, but not a serious police voice. It's low, and delicate. Like very good pipe smoke.

'Quiet morning so far?' I asked. He nodded.

'No more trouble from our bicycle lady?'

He gave a small smile, shook his head.

'This must be when the job's at its best, I suppose,' I said, trying to prolong our chat. 'Just strolling along, everything in order.'

He looked me in the eye, his face suddenly serious. 'Oh no. I need a case. No one takes you seriously till you've had a case.'

He's trying to be a rather grave young man, I think. He has an eagerness to impress, a longing to say the right thing. It's quite at odds with that grin of his, with the life I can sense pulsing beneath his uniform.

There was a pause before he asked, 'What's your – line of work?'

He has a lovely Brighton accent, very non-U, which he doesn't in the least modify for my benefit.

'I work in the museum. The art gallery there. And I paint, a little.'

A light sprang up behind his eyes. 'You're an artist?'

'Of sorts. But that's not nearly as exciting as your work. Keeping the peace. Making the streets safe. Assailing criminals . . .'

There was another pause before he laughed. 'You're joking.'

'No. I'm quite serious.' I looked him in the face and he averted his eyes, mumbled something about having to get on, and we parted.

A cloud descended. All day I worried that I'd overstepped the mark, said too much, been too flattering, too eager. On Sunday it rained, and I spent many hours looking out of my window at the flat greyness of the sea, moping at having lost my policeman.

I can be a proper sulker. Have been that way since school.

Monday. Day six. Nothing. Walking through Kemp Town, I kept my head down, and did not allow myself to be distracted by any kind of uniform.

Tuesday. The seventh day. I was walking along St George's Road when I heard footsteps, quick and deliberate, behind me. Instinctively, I made to cross the road, but stopped when I heard a voice.

'Morning, Mr Hazlewood.'

The pipe-smoke tones unmistakable. I was so surprised that I swivelled right round and said, 'Please. Call me Patrick.'

There was that grin again, the one that policemen shouldn't have. A light colour in his cheeks. His quality of eager attentiveness.

It was that grin that made me plough on: 'I've been hoping to bump into you.' I fell in step by his side. 'I'm doing a project. Images of ordinary people. Grocers, postmen, farmers, shop girls, policemen, that sort of thing.'

He said nothing. Our steps were roughly in time now, although I was having to walk quickly to keep up with his long strides.

'And you'd be a perfect subject.' I knew this was all too fast; but once I've started talking I can never seem to stop myself. 'I'm making some studies, from life, of suitable subjects, such as yourself, and comparing them with past portraits – ordinary Brighton people, that's what the museum needs – what we need – don't you think? Real people, instead of all these stuffed shirts.'

I could tell by his cocked head that he was listening very carefully.

'It's something I hope will be in the museum. On display. It's part of my plan to bring more people in . . . more ordinary people, that is. I think that if they see people, well, like themselves, they'll be more likely to want to step inside.'

He stopped and looked me in the face. 'What would I have to do?'

I exhaled. 'Nothing at all. You sit. I draw. At the museum, if you like. A few hours of your time.' I tried to keep my face quite blank. Quite straight. I even managed a nonchalant wave of my hand. 'Up to you, of course. I just thought, since I'd bumped into you . . .'

Then he took off his helmet and I saw his hair for the first time, his hair and the exquisite shape of his head. This nearly knocked me off balance. His hair is waves and curls, cut short but with plenty of life in it. I noticed a little dent running all around his scalp where that ugly hat had been. He rubbed at the back of his hair, as if trying to erase the line, and then replaced the helmet.

'Well,' he said. 'I've never been asked to model before!'

I was afraid then. Afraid that he'd see through me, and close himself off completely.

But instead he gave a quick laugh and said, 'Will my picture be in the museum?'

'Well, perhaps, yes . . .'

'I'll do it. Yes. Why not?'

We shook hands – his large and cool – arranged a date, and parted.

As I walked away, I started to whistle, and had to stop myself. Then I almost looked back over my shoulder (pathetic creature!), and had to stop myself from doing that, too.

I heard nothing, save my policeman's 'yes', for the rest of the day.

30th September 1957

Very late, and no sleep. Shadowy thoughts – bad thoughts – chasing me. Have thought about burning my last entry many times. Cannot. What else can make him real, except for my words on paper? When no one else can know, how can I convince myself of his actual presence, of my actual feelings?

It's a bad habit, this writing things down. Sometimes, I think, a poor substitute for real life. Every year I have a clear-out – burn the lot. Even Michael's letters I burnt. And now wish I hadn't.

Since meeting my policeman, I'm more determined than ever that nothing can take me back to that dark room. Five years since Michael was lost, and I will not allow myself the luxury of dwelling there.

My policeman is nothing like Michael. Which is one of the many things I love about him. The words that come to mind when I think of my policeman are *light* and *delight*.

I won't go back to that dark room. Work has helped. Steady, regular work. Painting is all very well if you can take the rejection, the weeks of waiting for the right idea to come along, the yards of awful shit you have to turn out before you reach anything decent. No. What's needed are regular hours. Small tasks. Small rewards.

Which is why, of course, my policeman is very dangerous, despite the *light* and the *delight*.

We used to dance, Michael and I. Every Wednesday night. I'd make everything right. Fire laid. Dinner made (he loved anything with cream and butter. All those French sauces – *sole au vin blanc, poulet au gratin à la crème landaise* – and, to finish, if I'd had time, *Saint Émilion au chocolat*). A bottle of claret. The sheets fresh and clean, a towel laid out. A newly pressed suit. And music. All the sentimental magic that he loved. Caruso to start (I've always hated him, but for Michael I endured it). Then Sarah Vaughan singing 'The Nearness of You'. We'd cling to each other for hours, shuffle round on the rug like a couple of marrieds, his cheek burning against mine. Wednesdays were an indulgence, I know that. For him and for me. I made him his favourite butter-rich foods (which played havoc with my stomach), hummed along to 'Danny Boy', and, in return, he danced in my arms. Only when the records were all played, the candles burned down to pools of wax, would I slowly undress him, here in my sitting room, and we'd dance again, naked, in absolute silence, save for our quickening breaths.

But that was a long time ago.

He's so young.

I know I'm not old. And God knows my policeman makes me feel like a boy again. Like a nine-year-old, peeking out of the railings in front of my parents' London house at the butcher's boy who delivered next door. It was his knees. Thick but exquisitely shaped, scabbed, thrillingly raw. Once he gave me a backie on his bicycle, all the way to the shops. I trembled as I held on to the seat, watching his little arse bounce up and down as he pedalled. I trembled, but felt stronger, more powerful than I had my whole life.

Listen to me. Butchers' boys.

I tell myself that my age is an advantage, in this case. I am experienced. Professional. What I must never be is avuncular. An old quean with a young tough hanging on his every pound note. Is that what's happening to me? Is that what I'm becoming?

Must sleep now.

1st October 1957

7 a.m.

Better this morning. Writing this over breakfast. Today he comes. My policeman is alive and well and he is coming to meet me at the museum.

I mustn't be too eager. It's essential to maintain professional distance. At least for a while.

At work, I'm known as a gentleman. When they say I'm *artistic*, I don't believe there's any hint of malice there. It helps that it's mostly youngish women, many of whom have better things than my private life to concern themselves with. Quiet, loyal, mysterious Miss Butters – Jackie to me – stands by my side. And the head keeper, Douglas Houghton – well. Married. Two children, the girl at Roedean. Member of Hove Rotary Club. But John Slater told me he remembers Houghton from Peterhouse, where he was a definite aesthete. Anyway. It's his business and he's never given me so much as a hint that he knows about my minority status. Not a glance passes between us that isn't entirely official and above board.

I'll tell my policeman, when he comes, about my campaign to install a series of lunchtime concerts – free for all – in the downstairs entrance hall. Music spilling on to Church Street during the lunchtime rush. I'll say I'm thinking of jazz, even though I know anything more challenging than Mozart will be an impossibility. People will stop and listen, venture in, and maybe look at our art collection whilst they're about it. I know plenty of musicians who'd be glad of the exposure, and what does it cost to place a few seats in the hallway? But there's resistance from the powers that be (I'll stress this). Houghton's feeling is that a museum should be 'a place of peace'.

'It's not a library, sir,' I pointed out, the last time we had our usual discussion on this topic. We were having tea after our monthly meeting.

He raised his eyebrows. Looked into his cup. 'Isn't it? A kind of library for art, and artefacts? A place where objects of beauty are ordered, made available to the public?' He stirred triumphantly. Tapped his spoon on the side of the china.

'Well put,' I conceded. 'I only meant that it needn't be silent. It isn't a place of worship . . .'

'Isn't it?' he began again. 'I don't mean to be profane, Hazlewood, but aren't objects of beauty there to be worshipped? This museum provides respite from the trials of everyday life, does it not? Peace and reflection are here, for those who seek it. A little like a church, wouldn't you say?'

But not nearly as suffocating, I thought. Whatever else this place does, it does not condemn.

'Absolutely right, sir, but my concern is to widen the museum's appeal. To make it available, attractive even, to those who wouldn't normally seek out such experiences.'

He made a low gurgling noise in his throat. 'Most admirable, Hazlewood. Yes. We all agree, I'm sure. But remember, you can take the horse to water, but you can't make the bugger drink. Hmm?'

I shall make my changes. Houghton or no Houghton. And I'll make sure my policeman knows about it.

7 p.m.

Rain means a busy day at the museum, and today water sluiced down Church Street, raging against car tyres and bicycle wheels, soaking shoes and splashing stockings. And so in they came, faces damp and shiny, collars darkened by rain, seeking shelter. They pushed through the stiff doors, shook themselves, stuffed their umbrellas in the steaming rack, made for a dry place. Then they stood and dripped on the tiles, glancing at the exhibits, always keeping one eye on the windows, hoping for a change in the weather.

Upstairs, I was waiting. I had a gas heater installed in my office last winter. Considered lighting it to cheer the place up a bit on such a gloomy day, but decided this was unnecessary. The office would suffice, would impress him enough. Mahogany desk, rotating chair, large window looking out over the street. I removed some papers from the armchair in the corner so he would have somewhere to sit, gave Jackie instructions for tea at four thirty. A pile of correspondence kept me busy for a while, but mostly I watched the rain course down the panes. Checked my watch quite a bit. But I had no plan of action. I didn't quite know what I would say to my policeman. I trusted we would get off on the right foot somehow, and the way forward would become clear. Once he was here in this room, before me, everything would be all right.

Precisely four o'clock, and a call from Vernon on the front desk informed me that my policeman had arrived. Should he send him up? Although I knew the most sensible thing would've been to have him come straight to my office, thus avoiding any attention from other members of staff, I said no. I would go down and collect him.

Well, I wanted to show off. To show him the place. To walk up the sweeping staircase with him.

As he wasn't wearing his uniform, it took me a few seconds to locate him. He was admiring the huge cat in the hallway. Arms folded, back straight. He looked much younger without his silver buttons and tall helmet. And I liked him even more. Soft sports jacket (soaked on the shoulders), light-coloured trousers, no tie. His neck exposed. His hair slick with rain. He looked such a boy that I was struck by the sensation that I'd made a ghastly mistake. I almost decided to send him home on some excuse. He was too young. Too vulnerable. And far too beautiful.

Thinking all this, I stood on the bottom step and watched him for a moment as he studied the enormous cat.

'Feed it money and it purrs,' I said, approaching him. I held out a professional hand, which he took without hesitation. Immediately I changed my mind. This was no mistake. Sending him home was the last thing I was going to do.

'So glad you could come,' I said. 'You've been before?'

'No. I mean – I don't *think* so . . .'

I waved a hand. 'Why would you? Musty old place. But I call it home – of sorts.'

I had to stop myself from bounding up the steps two at a time as he followed me upstairs.

'We do have some exquisite displays, but I don't suppose you've time . . .'

'Plenty of time,' he said. 'Early shifts weekdays. On at six, off at three.'

What to show him? It's hardly the British Museum. I wanted to impress him, but I didn't want to over-egg it. My policeman should see something lovely, I decided, rather than challenging or in any way strange.

'Is there anything you'd particularly like to look at?' I asked as we reached the first floor.

He rubbed the side of his nose. Shrugged. 'Dunno much about art.'

'You don't have to. That's the wonderful thing about it. It's about reacting to it. Feeling it, if you like. It's not really anything to do with knowledge.'

I steered him into the watercolours and engravings room. The light was dim, greyish, and we were alone in there save for an old gent whose nose was almost touching the glass case.

'That's not the idea I get,' he said, grinning. He'd lowered his voice now we were near the artworks, as almost everyone does. It's a great pleasure and mystery to me, the way people change when they come into the place. I never know whether it's down to actual awe, or just slavish respect for museum protocol. Either way, voices are hushed, walks slowed, laughter stifled. A certain absorption takes place. I've always thought that in a museum people draw into themselves, and yet become more aware of their surroundings. My policeman was no different.

'The idea you get from where?' I asked, rocking on my heels, smiling back, also lowering my voice. 'School? The newspapers?'

'Just the general idea. You know.'

I showed him my favourite Turner sketch in the collection. All waves crashing and foam pounding, of course. But delicate, in that way of Turner's.

He nodded. 'It's – full of life, isn't it?' He was almost whispering now. The old gent had left us alone. I saw the colour rise in my policeman's cheeks, and understood what a risk he'd taken in uttering such an opinion in my presence.

'That's it,' I whispered back, like a conspirator. 'You've got it. Absolutely.'

Once in my office, he paced the room, examining my photographs.

'Is this you?' He was pointing at one of me squinting in the sun outside Merton. It's on the wall opposite my desk because Michael took it; his shadow is just visible in the foreground. Whenever I look at that photo I see not my own image – a bit skinny, far too much hair, slightly receding chin, standing awkwardly in an ill-fitting hound's-tooth jacket – but Michael, holding his beloved camera, telling me to pose as if I mean it, every sinew of his nimble body concentrated in this moment of capturing me on film. We hadn't yet become lovers, and in that photo there is something of the promise – and the threat – of what was to come.

I stood behind my policeman, thinking all this, and said, 'That's me. In another life.'

He stepped away from me, gave a little cough.

'Please,' I said, 'have a seat.'

'I'm all right standing.' His hands were locked in front of him.

A small silence. Once more I pushed down the fear that I'd made an awful mistake. Sat behind my desk. Coughed a little. Pretended to tidy some papers. Then I buzzed Jackie to bring in the tea, and we waited, not quite meeting one another's eyes.

'I'm most grateful to you for coming,' I said, and he nodded. I tried again: 'Please won't you sit down?'

He looked at the chair behind him, gave a little sigh and finally lowered himself on to the seat. Jackie came in with the tea and we both watched in silence whilst she poured two cups. She glanced over at my policeman, then looked at me, her long face utterly impassive. She's been my secretary since I came to the museum and has never betrayed any interest in my affairs, which is just the way I like it. Today was like any other day. She asked me no questions, gave no hint of curiosity. Jackie is always well-presented, not a hair out of place, lipstick firmly applied, and she is quietly efficient. Rumour has it that she lost her sweetheart in the TB outbreak some years ago, and so has never married. Sometimes I hear her laughing with the other girls, and there's something in that laugh that unnerves me a little – it's a noise not unlike radio static – but Jackie and I rarely share a joke. She has recently purchased new spectacles with tiny diamanté decorations in the wings of the frames, which give her a strange look, somewhere between glamour queen and headmistress.

As she bent over the trolley I watched my policeman's face, and noted that he did not follow her movements with his eyes.

When she'd gone and we'd both taken up our teacups, I launched into a long speech. I gazed out of the window so I wouldn't have to look at my policeman as I outlined my fictitious project. 'You probably want to know a bit more about this whole portrait business,' I began. Then I chatted on for goodness knows how long, describing my plans, using words such as 'democratic', 'new perspective' and 'vision'. All the time not quite daring to look at him. More than anything I wanted his big body to relax into those worn cushions, and so I went on and on, hoping my words would put him at ease. Or perhaps even bore him into submission.

When I'd finished, there was a pause before he put his cup down and said, 'I've never been drawn before.'

I looked at him then, and saw his grin, the soft open collar of his shirt, his hair resting on my antimacassar. I said, 'Nothing to it. All you have to do is keep still.'

'When do we start?'

I hadn't anticipated this eagerness. I'd supposed it would take a few meetings before we'd actually begin work. A bit of warm-up time. I hadn't even brought any materials with me.

'We have started,' I said.

He looked puzzled.

'Getting acquainted is part of the process. I won't make any sketches for a while yet. It's important we strike up a rapport beforehand. Get to know one another a little. Only then will I be able to translate your personality into a drawing . . .' I paused, wondering if I could get away with this line of persuasion. 'I can't draw you if I don't know who you are. Do you see?'

His eyes flickered towards the window. 'So no drawing today?'

'No drawing.'

'Seems a bit . . . strange.'

He looked directly at me, and I did not look away.

'Standard procedure,' I said. Then I smiled and added, 'Well, my procedure, anyhow.' From the surprised look on his face I sensed the best thing to do was to press on regardless. 'Tell me,' I said, 'do you like being a police constable?'

'Is this part of the procedure?' He was smirking a little, shifting about in his seat.

'If you like.'

He gave a short laugh. 'Yeah. I think so. It's a good job. Better than most.'

I selected a sheet of paper. Took hold of a pencil so as to look professional.

'It's good to know I'm doing something,' he continued. 'For the public. Protecting people, you know.'

I wrote down *protection* on my sheet. Without looking up, I asked, 'What else do you do?'

'What else?'

'Besides your job.'

'Oh.' He thought for a moment. 'I swim. In the sea-swimming club.'

That explained the shoulders. 'Even at this time of year?'

'Every day of the year,' he announced with simple pride. I wrote down *pride*.

'What does it take to be a good sea-swimmer, do you suppose?'

There was no hesitation in his answer. 'Love of the water. You've got to love being in it.'

I imagined his arms cutting the waves, his legs twisted with seaweed. I wrote down *love*. Then I put a line through that word and wrote *water*.

'Look, Mr Hazlewood—'

'Patrick, please.'

'Can I ask you something?' He leant forward in his seat.

I put my pencil down. 'Anything.'

'Are you one of those . . . you know . . .' He twisted his hands together.

'What?'

'One of those *modern* artists?'

I almost laughed. 'I'm not sure I know what you mean . . .'

'Well, like I said, I don't know about art, but what I mean is, when you draw me, it will look like *me*, won't it? Not like – one of those new tower blocks or something.'

I did laugh then. I couldn't help myself. 'I can assure you,' I said, 'I could never make you look like a tower block.'

He seemed a bit put out. 'All right. Just had to check. You never know.'

'You're right. Quite right.'

He looked at his watch.

'Same time next week?' I asked.

He nodded. At the door, he turned to me and said, 'Thank you, Patrick.'

I can still hear him saying my name. It was like hearing it uttered for the first time.

Same time next week.

An age until then.

3rd October 1957

Two days since he came, and already I am losing my mind with impatience. Today, Jackie suddenly asked, 'Who was that young man?'

It was early afternoon and she was handing me the minutes from my latest meeting with Houghton. She let the question drop without so much as a flicker. But she was wearing a look I hadn't seen on her before – one of genuine curiosity. Even with those diamanté frames obscuring her eyes, I saw it.

Avoiding the issue fuels the fire. So I replied: 'He was a subject.'

She had a hand on her hip as she waited for more.

'We're planning a portrait. A new project. Ordinary people of the town.'

She nodded. Then, after letting a moment pass: 'Is he ordinary, then?'

I knew she was prying. The other girls have been talking about him. About me. Of course they have. Throw her a titbit, I thought. Get rid of her.

'He's a policeman,' I said.

There was a pause as she digested this information. I half turned from her and picked up the telephone receiver in order to encourage her to leave. But she did not take the hint.

'He doesn't look like a policeman,' she said.

Pretending not to have heard this, I started dialling a number.

When she'd finally gone, I replaced the receiver and sat very still, letting my rushing heart calm. Nothing to worry about, I told myself. Just natural curiosity. Of course the girls want to know who he is. A handsome young stranger. We don't get many of those in the museum. And anyway. Everything is above board. Professional. And Jackie is loyal. Jackie is discreet. Mysterious, but trustworthy.

But. Rush, thump went the blood in my chest. It does this often. I've been to the doctor's. Langland. He's known as being sympathetic. Sympathetic up to a point, that is. Very keen on psychoanalysis, I believe. I explained to him: it most often comes in the night, when I'm trying to sleep. Lying still in my bed, I swear I can see it, this lump of muscle jumping in my chest. Langland says it's perfectly normal. Or, if not normal, then usual. An ectopic heartbeat, he calls it. Surprisingly common, he says. Sometimes the beat is the wrong way round, and that makes you aware of your heart thumping. He demonstrated: 'Instead of going de-DUM,' (he slapped his hand on the desk) 'it goes DUM-de. Nothing to worry about.' 'Ah,' I said. 'You mean it's trochaic, rather than iambic.' He seemed to appreciate this. 'Exactly,' he beamed.

Now I have a name for it, it's a little easier to dismiss, but no less difficult to ignore. My trochaic heart.

I sat at my desk until it calmed. Then I walked out of the place. Out of my office, through the long gallery, down the stairs, past the money cat and on to the street.

Amazed that no one stopped me. Not one single person looked my way as I marched by. Outside, it was raining lightly, and the wind was up. Gusts of damp salty air came at me across the Steine. Clanging notes from the pier blew this way and that. Crossed into St James's Street. Although the sky held a brownish tinge, the air was fresh after the museum. Quickened my pace. I knew where I was going, but I did not know what I was going to do once there. No matter. I pressed onward, elated at having escaped my office with so little fuss. Relieved at the regular beating of my heart. De-dum. De-dum. De-dum. Nothing outlandish or hurried. No rush of movement from chest to head, no thump of blood in the ears. Just that steady beat, and my steady walk towards the police box.

The rain became heavier. I'd come out without coat or umbrella, and my knees were wet. My collar, too, was damp. But I welcomed the feel of the rain on my skin. With every step I was closer to him. I didn't have to explain myself or provide excuses. I just had to see him.

The last time I was like this was with Michael. So anxious to see him that anything seemed possible. Conventions, other people's opinions, the law, all appear laughable in the face of your desire, your drive to reach your love. It's a blissful state. It's fleeting, though, this feeling. Soon you realise that you're walking in the rain, getting soaked, when you should be at your desk. Women with children jostle you, casting their eyes suspiciously over a single man without coat or hat in a shopping street during the middle of the afternoon. Old couples scurrying to bus stops charge at you with umbrellas. And you think, even if he is there, what can I possibly say to him? Of course, in the moment itself, in the blissful moment when anything's possible, there's no need for words. You'll simply fall into one another's arms, him understanding everything – *everything* – at last. But when the feeling starts to wane, when another woman has just said *excuse me* but stepped on your foot anyway, when you've glimpsed your reflection in Sainsbury's shop window and seen a wild-eyed, rain-scattering man past his first flush of youth gaping back at you, then you realise there will have to be words.

And what would I have said to him? What possible excuse could I give for arriving at his police box at this hour, soaked to the skin? *I just couldn't wait to see you?* Or, *I needed to make some urgent preliminary sketches?* I suppose I could have played the temperamental artist card. But it's probably just as well to keep that one in reserve for more testing times.

So I turned back. Then changed direction again, and headed for home. Once there, I telephoned Jackie and told her I was unwell. Said I'd popped out for a newspaper (this is not unheard of during the museum's afternoon lull) and had been overcome by nausea. I'd spend the rest of the day in bed and would be back in the morning. Tell all callers I'd deal with them tomorrow. She didn't sound surprised. She asked no questions. Good, loyal Jackie, I thought. What was I worrying about before?

I drew the curtains. Put the heating on. It wasn't cold in the flat, but I felt in need of any warmth I could get. Stripped out of my wet clothes. Got into bed wearing the pyjamas I hate. Flannel, blue stripes. I put them on because it's better than being naked in bed. Being naked just reminds you you're alone. If you're naked, there's nothing to rub against but the sheets. At least flannel on your skin is a layer of protection.

Thought I might weep, but did not. Lay there with heavy limbs and a foggy brain. I didn't think of Michael. I didn't think of myself, scurrying along the street after nothing like a fool. I just shook until the shaking stopped, and then I slept. I slept through the rest of the afternoon and into the evening. Then I woke and wrote this.

Now I will sleep again.

4th October 1957

Writing this Friday evening. A most satisfying day.

After my little weakness, I resigned myself to the long wait for Tuesday. But then this. Half past four. Monstrously dull meeting with Houghton over, I walked through the main gallery, thinking vaguely about my tea and custard cream biscuit, more specifically about the fact that there were only three days until Tuesday.

And then: the unmistakable line of his shoulders. My policeman was standing, head on one side, looking at a rather mediocre Sisley we've currently got on temporary loan. No uniform (the same jacket as before). Magnificently alive, breathing, and actually here, in the museum. I'd pictured him so many times over the past days that I rubbed my eyes, as disbelieving girls do in films.

I approached. He turned and looked straight at me, then at the floor. A little coy. As if he'd been caught out. DUM-de, went my trochaic heart.

'Beat finished for the day?' I asked.

He nodded. 'Thought I'd have another look. See what my mug'll have to compete with.'

'Do you want to come up? I was just about to have tea.'

Again he looked at the floor. 'I don't want to put you to no trouble.'

'No trouble,' I said, already leading the way to my office.

I showed him in, nodding at Jackie's offer of tea as I did so, ignoring her look of interest. He sat in the armchair. I perched on the edge of the desk. 'So. See anything interesting?'

He didn't hesitate in his response. 'Yeah. There's one of a woman, no clothes, sitting on a rock, her legs like a goat's . . .'

'*Satyrs*. French School.'

'That was pretty interesting.'

'Why was that?'

He looked at the floor again. 'Well. Women don't have goat's legs, do they?'

I smiled. 'It's a mythological thing . . . from the ancient Greeks. She's a creature called a satyr, only half human . . .'

'Yeah. But isn't all that just an excuse?'

'An excuse?'

'Art. Is it just an excuse to look at – well, naked people? Naked women.'

He didn't look down this time. He was staring at me so intently, his small eyes so clearly blue, that I was the one who had to look away.

'Well.' I straightened my cuffs. 'Well, there's certainly an obsession with the human form – with bodies – and yes, sometimes a celebration of the beauties of the flesh, I suppose you could say – male and female . . .'

I flicked a look at him, but Jackie chose this moment to come in with the tea trolley. She was wearing a daffodil-yellow frock, very tight about the waist. Matching yellow shoes. A string of yellow beads. The effect was almost blinding. I saw my policeman take in this golden vision with what I thought was some interest. But then he looked back at me and there was that small, rather secret grin.

Jackie, not seeing our exchange of glances, said, 'Good to see you back again, Mr . . .'

He told her his name. She passed him his tea. 'Having your portrait done?'

His cheeks flushed pink. 'Yeah.'

A little pause as she kept hold of his saucer, looking as though she were preparing herself to fish further.

I stood and held the door open. 'Thank you, Jackie.'

She pushed out her trolley with a tight smile.

'Sorry about that.'

He nodded, sipped his tea. 'You were saying?'

'Was I?'

'About naked bodies?'

'Oh, yes.' I settled on the corner of the desk again. 'Yes. Look, if you're really interested, I'll show you some fascinating examples.'

'Now?'

'If you have time.'

'All right,' he said, helping himself to a second biscuit. He eats rapidly, even noisily. His mouth slightly open. Enjoying himself. I offered him the plate. 'Take as many as you like,' I said. 'Then I'll show you something.'

We had half an hour before closing time. I decided to cut to the chase: the bronze Icarus. We walked side by side in silence until I said, 'I don't mean to be rude, but it's unusual, isn't it, for a policeman to be interested in art? Do any of your colleagues feel the same way, do you think?'

He gave a sudden laugh. It was loud and uninhibited, and it echoed around the gallery. 'God, no,' he said.

'That's a shame.'

He shrugged. 'Down the station, if you like art, you're wet. Or worse.'

A look at each other. His eyes were smiling, I swear it.

'Well – that's the *general* perception, I suppose . . .'

'I only know one other person who likes it.'

'And who's that?'

'Girl I know. A friend. She's a teacher, actually. Books are more her line, though. But we do have, you know, *discussions* . . .'

'About art?'

'About all sorts. I'm teaching her to swim.' He gave another laugh, softer this time. 'She's no good, though. Never gets any better.'

I'll bet she doesn't, I thought.

I pressed on, guiding him into the sculpture gallery. *Friend*, he'd said. A small revelation. Nothing to get panicked by. As he'd talked about her, the colour in his face had remained constant. He hadn't once avoided my gaze. *Friend* I can deal with. *Friend. Girlfriend. Sweetheart. Fiancée.* I can deal with all of those. I've had some experience. Michael had a girlfriend, after all. Dim little thing she was. Always feeding him sandwiches. Rather sweet, in her way.

Wife, even. I think I can deal with wife. Wives are at home, that's the good thing about them. They're at home, they're silent, and they're glad to see the back of him. Usually.

Lover, I cannot deal with. Lover is different.

'This,' I said, 'is *Icarus*, by Alfred Gilbert. It's a cast. On loan to us at the moment.'

There he was, his wings about him like a bullfighter's cape, and no fig leaf. The most impressive thing about him, to me, is his belief in those wings. Useless, fragile, attached to his arms by a couple of cuffs, and yet he believes in them as a child might believe a cloak will make him invisible. He is youthfully muscular, standing with his hip to the side, his leg bent, his gleaming chest catching the spotlight above. The line from his throat to his groin delicately curved. He stands alone on his rock, looking coyly down. He is both serious and absurd, and he is beautiful.

My policeman and I stood before him, and I said, 'You know the story?'

He gave me a sideways glance.

'Greek mythology again, I'm afraid. Icarus and his father, Daedalus, escaped from prison using wings they'd made from feathers and wax. But despite his father's advice, Icarus flew too close to the sun, his wings melted, and – well, you can guess the rest. It's a story often told to schoolchildren to warn them against being overambitious. And to impress upon them the importance of listening to their fathers.'

He was bending over, breathing on the glass case. He moved around, taking in the boy from all angles, whilst I stood back and watched. We caught each other's reflection in the glass, our faces merging and warping with Gilbert's golden Icarus.

I wanted to say to him: *I can't swim. Teach me. Teach me to cut through the waves with you.*

But I did not. Instead, as brightly as I could, I told him: 'You should bring her here.'

'Who?'

Exactly the response for which I'd hoped.

'Your friend. The schoolteacher.'

'Oh. Marion.'

'Marion.' Even the name's schoolteacherly. It brings to mind thick stockings, even thicker spectacles. 'Bring her.'

'To see the museum?'

'And to meet me.'

He straightened up. Put a hand to his neck, frowned. 'Do you want her to be part of the project?'

I smiled. Already he was worried about being usurped.

'Perhaps,' I said. 'But you're our first subject. We'll see how that goes, shall we? You are still coming?'

'Tuesday.'

'Tuesday.' On impulse, I added: 'Would you mind changing the venue? There's not really space in my office. Or the necessary equipment.' I pulled my card from my pocket and handed it to him. 'We could meet here instead. It would have to be a bit later. Say seven thirty?'

He looked at the card. 'Is this your studio?'

'Yes. And it's where I live.'

He turned the card over before tucking it into his jacket. He was smiling as he said, 'All right,' but I couldn't tell if his smile was one of happiness at the thought of coming to my flat, amusement at my wiles to get him there, or mere embarrassment.

But. He has the card in his pocket. And Tuesday it is.

5th October 1957

Terrible hangover this morning. I rose very late and have been sitting about drinking coffee, eating toast and rereading Agatha Christie in the hope that it will lift. It hasn't yet.

Last night, after writing, decided to go to the Argyle. I didn't relish the idea of another long evening, waiting for Tuesday, that was part of it. But in truth I was feeling puffed up at my success. The boy is to come here, to my flat. He has agreed. He is coming alone, Tuesday evening. We have looked at Icarus together and he has given me his secret smile and he is coming.

So I felt the Argyle might be fun. It is no good going to these places when one feels depressed and lonely. They just compound the misery, especially when one ends up leaving alone. But when one is feeling optimistic . . . well, then the Argyle is the place to be. It's a place of *possibilities*.

I hadn't been there for a very long time; since landing the curator's job a few years ago, I've needed to be very discreet. Not that I've ever been anything else, really. Certainly Michael and I went out very rarely. Wednesday night was our one whole night together, and I wasn't going to waste it by taking him out and sharing him with anyone else. I often visited him in the daytime but he always wanted me out of his room by eight o'clock, in case the landlady grew suspicious.

But even walking past the Argyle is risky. What if Jackie were to see me looking at that door? Or Houghton? Or any of the girls from the museum? Of course, if one does go to bars, one learns to take precautions – go after dark, go alone, don't catch anyone's eye whilst walking down the street, don't go into any establishment too near your own house. Which is why I enjoy my nights in London with Charlie. Much easier to be anonymous on those streets. Brighton, for all its cosmopolitan airs, is a small town.

It was a dreary night, wet and mild, very few stars. I was glad of the rain – it gave me an excuse to shelter beneath my largest umbrella. Walked right along the seafront, past the Palace Pier, and crossed King's Road to avoid the town centre. My steps rapid, but not hurried. Turned into Middle Street, keeping my head down. Thankfully, it was almost half past nine and the streets were fairly calm. Everyone was busy drinking up.

I slipped through the black door (graced only by the small gold plaque: ARGYLE HOTEL), signed in under the name I always use for places like this, removed my coat, slotted my soaking umbrella into the stand and went into the bar.

Candlelight. Log fire punching out too much heat. Leather armchairs. 'Stormy Weather' coming from the Oriental boy on the piano. They say he played at the Raffles Hotel in Singapore. The smell of gin, Givenchy cologne, dust and roses. There are always fresh roses on the bar. Last night's were pale yellow, very delicate.

Immediately I recognised the old familiar feeling of being appraised by more than a dozen pairs of male eyes. A feeling exquisitely balanced between pleasure and pain. It's not that they all turned and stared – the Argyle would never be that blatant – but my presence was noted. I'd taken care over my appearance, shaping my moustache, running some oil through my hair and selecting my most well-cut jacket (the grey marl from Jermyn Street) before I ventured out, so I was prepared. I keep myself fit – callisthenics every morning. The army did that for me, at least. And I don't yet have a grey hair on my head. I've never been obsessed with these matters but I do keep them in check. I was ready. I was, I thought, looking quite elegant. I was – in my head this is already taking on a strange reality – an artist about to embark on a daring new portraiture project.

Approached the bar, deliberately not looking anyone in the eye. I must have a drink in my hand before I can do that. The Miss Browns were, as usual, on their high stools behind the bar. The younger one – who must be approaching sixty by now – counts the takings. The older one greets the gentlemen and pours the drinks. Wearing a high lace collar and smoking a long cigarillo, she said hello, remembering my name.

'And how are we?' she asked.

'Oh, tolerable.'

'Like myself, like myself.' She smiled warmly. 'Wonderful to see you here again. One of the boys will take your order.'

Older Miss Brown is famous for relaying messages between her clients. You slip her your note over the bar and she will pass it on to the addressed gentleman. If he does not come in that night, she will store the note behind a bottle of crème de cacao on the bottom shelf. There are always a few new slips of paper behind that bottle. Nothing is ever said; the note is merely handed over with your change.

The Duchess of Argyle, as he's known, took my order for a dry martini and showed me to a table by the heavily draped bay window. His face was powdered and his red jacket was, as always, tightly fitting and just the right side of military. After a few sips I began to relax and take a look around the place. A couple of faces I recognised. Bunny Waters, as dapper as ever, sitting at the bar, wearing bright white shirt sleeves, several gold bracelets and a maroon waistcoat. He made a slight nod of recognition in my direction, lifted his glass, and I returned the gesture. One New Year I watched him foxtrotting round the floor with the most handsome boy. No one else was dancing. I wonder, now, if it really happened, this vision of two neat, dark-haired men gliding around the room, everyone aware of them, everyone admiring them, but no one feeling it necessary to make the slightest acknowledgement of what was happening. It was a gracious moment. We all silently agreed that it was beautiful, and rare, and not to be spoken of. We acted as though it was the most ordinary thing in the world. I heard, later, that Bunny was at the Queen of Clubs the night it was raided for, apparently, not having a supper licence. He avoided, somehow, the whole hullabaloo with the press, his employers and so on, and didn't face any charges. Others were not so lucky.

At a table not far from mine was Anthony B. I'm sure Charlie had a brief *affaire* with him, the year before he moved to London. Anton, he used to call him. He's looking just as respectable as ever – was reading the *Times*, a little more grey in his hair, and kept glancing towards the door, but he'd be at home in any gentleman's club. Still has the same red cheeks. There's something rather attractive about red cheeks on a very respectable man. A suggestion, perhaps, that his cup spilleth over. That he cannot always contain his emotions. That underneath the controlled exterior there lies much blood; blood that will eventually out.

I don't think I've blushed since school. It was my affliction, back then. *Cool, wet grass*, Charlie used to say to me. *Think of it. Allow yourself to lie in it.* It never worked. One of the sports masters called me the Pink Sap. *Come along, Hazlewood. Give it some welly, why don't you. Can't be a pink sap all your life, eh?* God, I hated him. I used to have dreams of throwing acid in his huge, sweating face.

I ordered another dry martini.

At about ten, a young man entered. Brown hair so short and coarse it looked like a pelt. A thin face and a compact, neat little body. Everyone stirred as he paused at the doorway, lit a cigarette and strode to the bar. He kept his eyes down as he walked, just as I had done. Let them get a look at you before you look back.

He took his time, this young man. Stood very square at the bar, refusing Older Miss Brown's offer of a seat. Ordered a baby tolly, which I thought very sweet. Then he continued to smoke, watching his own reflection in the mirror behind the bar.

My policeman wouldn't act like that. He would smile and nod, greet strangers warmly, show an interest in his surroundings. I allowed myself to picture the scene: the two of us making our entrance, shaking our coats free of rain. Older Miss Brown would ask if we were both tolerably well, and we would tell her that we were more than that, thank you, and would exchange a knowing smile before retiring to our usual table. All eyes would be on us, the gorgeous young man and his handsome gentleman. We'd discuss the film or show we'd been to see. There would be, as we stood to leave, a touch on the shoulder – I would touch my policeman's shoulder in a slight but unmistakable gesture, a gesture that said, *Come along, darling, it's getting late, let's go home to bed.*

But he would never step into a place like this. If he's come across the snatchers in vice squad by now, he's sure to know about it. The signs suggest that he's a sensible young man, though. Capable of being different. Capable of resistance. (I am so buoyant at the moment that I am incredibly, naively optimistic, despite my hangover.)

I ordered another dry martini.

And then I thought: why not? The young man at the bar hadn't yet been bought a drink, and was looking into his empty glass. So I positioned myself next to him. Not too close. Body facing away from his, into the room.

'What are you having?' I asked. Well, you have to start somewhere.

Without hesitation, he replied, 'Scotch.' I ordered him a double from the Duchess and we both watched Older Miss Brown pour his drink.

He thanked me as he took the whisky, drank half of it back in one gulp, did not look in my direction.

'Still wet out there?' I tried.

He drained his glass. 'Bucketing. Shoes are bloody soaked.'

I ordered him another drink. 'Why don't you join me by the fire? Soon have you dried out.'

Then he looked at me. Eyes large. Something drawn and hungry in his pale face. Something young but brittle. Without another word, I walked back to my table and sat down, certain he would follow.

Whatever happens, I thought, my policeman is still coming on Tuesday. He is coming to my flat. In the meantime, I can enjoy this, whatever it may turn out to be.

It took only a few moments for him to join me. I insisted he move his chair closer to the fire – closer to me. When he'd done so, there was a long silence. I offered him a cigarette. As soon as he took it, the Duchess moved in with a light. I watched the young man smoking. He lifted the cigarette slowly to his mouth, as if learning how to do it from a film, copying an actor's every move. Narrowing his eyes. Sucking in his cheeks. Holding his breath for a few seconds and then blowing out. As he brought his hand up to his mouth again, I noticed a bruise about his wrist.

I wondered how he'd ended up here, who had told him this was the right place to come. His jacket was slightly worn-looking, but his boots were brand new and pointed at the toes. He should have been in the Greyhound, really. Someone had advised him badly. Or perhaps – like I once did, years ago – he'd simply screwed up all his courage and gone into the first place about which he'd heard a scurrilous rumour.

'So, what brings you to this old dump?' I asked. (I was a bit squiffy by now.)

He shrugged.

'Let me get you another.' I nodded to the Duchess, who was leaning on the bar, closely observing the two of us.

Once the new drinks came, together with a clean ashtray, all provided with a lingering look from the Duchess, I moved a little closer to the boy. 'I haven't seen you in here before,' I said.

'Ain't seen you, neither.'

Touché.

'Not that I've been in much,' he added.

'It's a good place to come. Better than most.'

'I know.'

Probably due to the amount of dry martini I'd consumed, I suddenly lost patience. The boy was obviously bored; he'd just wanted a drink he couldn't afford to buy himself; he was not in the least interested in me.

I stood up and felt myself sway a little.

'You off?'

'It's getting rather late . . .'

He looked up at me. 'P'raps we could talk . . . somewhere else?'

Utterly brazen, really.

'Black Lion,' I said, grinding out my cigarette. 'Ten minutes.'

I paid the bill, leaving a large tip for the gaping Duchess, and left the place. I was completely calm as I crossed the road and entered the narrow alleyway that leads to Black Lion Street. It had stopped raining. I swung my umbrella and had that lightness in my feet you get after alcohol. I walked fast but felt no sense of exertion, and may even have whistled 'Stormy Weather'.

I did not hesitate to take the first steps down to the cottage. I didn't even look about me to check if I were being watched. I've never been much of a one for this sort of encounter. I've had my moments, of course, especially before Michael and I became a regular thing. But since then I've made very little contact with any man's flesh. Last night I suddenly realised how much I needed it. How much I'd missed it.

Then a tall man in a smart tweed overcoat, collar turned up, started up the steps. As he pushed past me, he muttered, 'Fucking queer.'

Not, God knows, the first time. Certainly not the last. But it shocked me. Shocked me and turned my yearning flesh utterly cold. Because I'd had too many martinis. Because the rain had stopped. Because my policeman was coming on Tuesday. Because I'd been foolish enough to imagine I could enjoy this boy and just, for once, bloody well get on with it.

I stopped halfway down and leant against the cold tiled wall. The stench of urine, disinfectant and semen rose from the cottage below. I could still go down there. I could still hold this boy, and imagine he was my policeman. I could touch his coarse brown hair and imagine soft blond curls.

But my trochaic heart protested. So I hauled myself out of there and took a taxi home.

Strange. What remains with me now is the satisfaction of knowing that I actually went there. I took fright, but at least I got first to the Argyle, and then to the Black Lion. Two things I've very rarely achieved since Michael. And, despite this wretched hangover, my mood is surprisingly light.

Only two days, and then . . .

8th October 1957

The day: Tuesday. The time: seven-thirty in the evening.

I am standing at my window, waiting for him. Inside, the flat is tidied to within an inch of its life. Outside, the dark sea lies still.

DUM-de, goes my heart.

I have opened the drinks cabinet, displayed the latest copy of *Art and Artists* on the coffee table, made sure the bathroom is spotless. The daily, Mrs Gunn, is actually a weekly in my case, and I'm not sure she can see as well as she once did. I've dusted off my old easel and arranged it in the spare room, together with a palette, a few tubes of paint, some knives and brushes stuffed in a jam jar. The room still looks far too neat to be a studio – the vacuumed carpet, the crisply made bed – but I'm presuming this will be the first artist's space he's seen, and he won't have many expectations.

Haven't put my photographs of Michael away, despite considering doing so. Thought about playing some music, but decided that would be too much.

It's just this evening turned quite chilly, so the heating's on and I'm in my shirt sleeves. Keep touching my own neck, as if in preparation for where my policeman's hand might go. Or his lips.

But I mustn't think of that.

I go to the drinks cabinet and pour myself a large gin, then stand again at the window, listening to the ice release itself into the alcohol. Next door's cat slinks along my sill and stares hopefully at me. But I won't let her in. Not tonight.

As I wait, I'm reminded of Wednesdays. Of how my preparations for Michael's arrival – the cooking, the arranging of the flat, of myself – were, for a while at least, almost more magical than the meetings themselves. It was the promise of what was to come, I know that. Sometimes, after we'd gone to bed and he was sleeping, I'd get up in the night and look at the mess we'd made. The dirty plates. Empty wine glasses. Our clothes strewn on the floor. Cigarette ends in the ashtray. Records lying on the sideboard without their sleeves. And I'd itch to put it all back into place, ready for the evening to begin all over again. If I could put everything back, I reasoned, when Michael rose before dawn he would see that I was ready for him. Waiting for him. Expecting him. And he might choose to stay the next night, and the next, and the next, and the next.

The buzzer goes. I put my drink down, run a hand through my hair. Take a breath. Go downstairs to the front door.

He's not wearing his uniform, for which I'm grateful. It's risky enough, having a lone male call at my door after six o'clock in the evening. He's carrying a bag, though, which he waves at me. 'Uniform. Thought you'd want me to wear it. For the portrait.'

He colours a little and glances down at the footplate. I wave him in. He follows me up the stairs (thankfully empty) and into the flat, his boots creaking.

'Join me?' When I hold up my glass, my hand shakes.

He says he'll have a beer if there is one; he's off duty now until six tomorrow morning. As I'm opening the only bottle of pale ale in the cabinet, I steal a glance at him. My policeman is standing on my rug, gloriously upright, the light from the chandelier catching his blond curls, and he's looking around with his mouth slightly agape. His gaze pauses at the newly acquired oil I've proudly hung over the fireplace – a Philpot portrait of a boy with sturdily naked torso – before he walks to the window.

I hand him his glass. 'Splendid view, isn't it?' I say, idiotically. There's not much to see apart from our own reflections. But he agrees and we both squint out at the black sky in silence. I can smell him now: something faintly carbolic that reminds me of school – undoubtedly the smell of the station – but also a hint of pine talc.

I know I should keep talking so he won't get too nervous, but I can't think of a thing to say. He's finally here, standing at my side. I can hear his breathing. He's so close that my head feels dizzy with it, with his scent and his breath and the way he's swallowing his drink in great gulps.

'Mr Hazlewood—'

'Patrick, please.'

'Shall I change? Shouldn't we get on with it?'

When he comes into the spare room he's carrying his helmet, but everything else is in place. The black wool jacket. The tightly knotted tie. The belt with silver buckle. The whistle chain, slung between his breast pocket and his top button. The polished number on his shoulder. The shiny boots. It's an odd thrill to have a policeman in my flat. Dangerous, despite his shy look. But also faintly ridiculous.

I tell him he looks splendid, and have him sit on the chair I've placed by the window. I've put a strong light beside it, and draped an old green tablecloth from the curtain rail as a backdrop. I've instructed him to place his hat on his knees and look into the corner of the room, over my right shoulder.

I settle myself on a stool, sketchpad on my lap, pencils to hand. The room is very quiet and I busy myself for a moment, getting to a clean page in the pad (which in truth hasn't been used in years), selecting the correct pencil. Then, realising I am now free to look at him as blatantly as I like, for hours if I want to, I freeze.

I can't do it. I cannot raise my eyes to him. My heart becomes frantic with the weight of it, this unfettered pleasure that lies ahead. I drop my pencil and paper and end up crouching on the floor before him, desperately trying to gather my things together.

'Everything all right?' he asks. His voice is light and yet grave, and I take a breath. Sit on the stool once more. Settle myself.

'Everything's fine,' I say.

The work begins.

It's strange. At first I can only take quick peeks at him. I'm worried I might start laughing with joy. I might start laughing at his youth, at the way he shines, at the way his cheeks are flushed, at the way his eyes are bright with interest. The way his thighs rest together as he sits. The way he holds his exquisite shoulders so square. Or, in this state, I might even start to weep.

I try to pull myself together. I realise I will have to convince myself I'm very serious about the drawing. It's the only way I can allow myself to study him. I must try to see him from the inside, as my art teacher used to say. See the apple from the inside. Only then can you draw it.

Holding my pencil before my face, squinting, I examine

his proportions: eyes to nose to mouth. Chin to shoulder to waist. Mark the points on the page. Note the lightness of his eyebrows. There's a slight knobble on the bridge of his nose. His nostrils are elegantly angled. His mouth has a firm line. The upper lip is slightly fleshier than the lower (I almost lose concentration at this point). His chin has a subtle cleft.

Sketching it in, I actually manage to become quite absorbed in the work. The whispery sound of the pencil is very calming. So it's something of a shock when he says: 'Bet you never thought you'd have a policeman sitting in your bedroom.'

I don't falter. I continue to draw, keeping my lines light, trying to remain focused on the work.

'I'll bet you never thought you'd be in an artist's studio,' I flash back, pleased with myself for remaining so composed.

He laughs a little. 'Maybe I did. Maybe I didn't.'

I look at him. Of course, he can't *not* be aware of how he looks, I remind myself. He must know some of his power, despite his youth.

'Seriously, though. I've always been interested in art and that,' he states. His voice sounds proud, but there's something boyish in his boast. It's charming. He's proving himself to me.

Then a thought strikes me: if I remain silent, he will continue to talk. He will let all this out. In this quiet room, with a tablecloth over the window and a lamp shining on his body, with my eyes on him but my voice silenced, he can be who he wants to be: the cultured policeman.

'The other coppers aren't interested, of course. They think it's hoity-toity. But I think, well, it's there, isn't it? You can take it if you want to. It's all there. It's not like it used to be.'

He's becoming more flushed; the hair around his temples is darkening with perspiration.

'I mean, I didn't have much education, really – secondary modern, all woodwork and technical drawing – and in the army, well. If you so much as hum a bit of Mozart they rip you to shreds. But now I'm my own man, aren't I? It's up to me.'

'Yes,' I agree, 'it is.'

''Course, you've got an advantage, if you don't mind me saying. You were born into it. Literature, music, painting . . .'

I stop drawing. 'True to an extent. But not everyone I knew approved of those things.' My father, for a start. And Old Spicer, the housemaster at school. Once he said to me: *English Literature is no subject for a man, Hazlewood. Novels. Isn't that what they study at these women's colleges?* 'I imagine my school was just as stuffed with philistines as yours,' I say.

There's a small pause. I start drawing again.

'But as you say,' I continue, 'you can show them now. They were wrong and you can show them.'

'Like you have,' he says.

Our eyes meet.

Slowly, I put down my pencil. 'I think that's enough for today.'

'Is it finished?'

'It will take several weeks. More than that, perhaps. This is just a preliminary sketch.'

He nods, looks at his watch. 'Is that it, then?'

And suddenly I can't bear for him to be in the flat. I know I won't be able to pretend for much longer. I won't be able to make small talk about art and schooling and the trials and tribulations of being a young police officer. I will have to touch him, and the thought of him turning away is so terrifying that before I can steady myself, I say, 'That's it. Same time next week?' The words come out in a rush and I can't look him in the eye.

'Right,' he says, getting to his feet, obviously a bit puzzled. 'Right.'

As soon as I've said it I want to take it back, to grab him by the arm and pull him to me, but he's heading for the sitting room, stuffing his uniform jacket into a bag and shrugging on his coat. As I show him the door he smiles and says, 'Thanks.' And I nod, dumbly.

13th October 1957

Sunday, a day I've always hated for its quiet respectability, seems to be the fitting time for a family visit. And so today I took the train to Godstone to see Mother. Every time I go, she is quieter. She is not, I often remind myself, alone. She has Nina, who does everything for her. Always has and always will. She has Aunt Cicely and Uncle Bertram, who visit often.

But it is – must be – three years since she's left the house. The place is as clean, as bright, as ever, but there is a deadness, a staleness, inside those walls. Which is what, amongst other things, makes me stay away more than I ought.

It was lunchtime when I made my way up the long brick drive, past the perfectly shaped privet and along the gravel path where I once pissed up the side of the house because I knew Father had kissed our neighbour, Mrs Drewitt, at that very spot, under the high kitchen window. He'd kissed her right there and Mother knew about it but was silent, as she always was on the subject of his betrayals. Mrs Drewitt came to our house every Christmas for mince pies and Nina's rum punch, and every Christmas my mother passed her a napkin and enquired after the health of her two appalling sons whose only interests were rugger and the stock market. It was after witnessing one of those conversations that I chose to decorate the wall of our house with an intricate pattern of my own urine.

Mother's house is stuffed with furniture. Since the old man died, she's been ordering it from Heal's. It's all modern, too – pale ash sideboards with pull-down doors, steel-legged coffee tables with smoked-glass tops, standard lamps with enormous white globes for shades. None of it blends with the house, which is pure mock-Tudor, a ghastly thirties creation, complete with leaded window-panes. I've tried to persuade Mother to move into somewhere more manageable, even (God forbid this should actually happen) a flat near me. She could easily afford Lewes Crescent, although Brunswick Terrace might be a safer distance away.

I let myself into the kitchen, where Nina had some cheese on toast under the grill and the radio on loud. Stealing up behind her, I pinched her lower arm and she jumped in the air.

'It's you!'

'How are you, Nina?'

'You gave me such a fright . . .' She blinked at me a few times, catching her breath, then turned down the radio's blare. Nina must be in her fifties herself by now. Still wears her hair in the same short bob, dyed coal black, as she did when I was a boy. Still has the same startled grey eyes and wary smile.

'Your mother's a bit distant today.'

'Have you tried electro-shock therapy? I've heard it can do wonders.'

She laughed. 'You always were too clever by half. Shall I do you some toast?'

'Is that all we're having?'

'I didn't know you were coming – she never said.'

'I didn't tell her.'

There was a pause. Nina looked at the clock. 'Bacon and egg?'

'Topping.' I always revert to schoolboy phrases with Nina.

I helped myself to a banana from the fruit basket on the dresser and sat at the kitchen table to watch Nina perform her fry-up. Bacon and egg doesn't mean just bacon and egg with Nina. It means grilled tomatoes, fried bread, possibly a devilled kidney.

'Aren't you going in to see her?'

'In a bit. What did you mean, distant?'

'You know. Not herself.'

'Is she ill?'

Nina laid three slices of bacon ever so gently in a pan. 'You should come more often. She misses you.'

'I've been busy.'

She sliced two tomatoes in half and put them under the grill. A pause, and then she said: 'Dr Shires says it's nothing. Old age, that's all.'

'The doctor came?'

'He says it's nothing.'

'When did the doctor come?'

'Last week.' She cracked two eggs into the pan without spilling a drop. 'Fried bread?'

'No thanks. Why didn't she tell me? Why didn't you tell me?'

'She didn't want a fuss.'

'But I don't understand. What's wrong with her?'

She put the food on a plate and looked me in the eye. 'Something happened, Patrick. The other week. We were playing Scrabble and she says to me, "Nina," she says, "I can't see the words." And she's all of a panic.'

I stared at her, unable to respond.

'I thought maybe she'd just had a few too many glasses, the night before,' Nina continued. 'You know how she likes her wine. But it happened again, yesterday. The newspaper this time. "It's gone all bleary," she says. I told her the print was funny, but I don't think she believed me.'

'The doctor will have to come back. I'll call him, this afternoon.'

When Nina looked at me, there were tears in her eyes. 'That would be good. Now eat your lunch,' she said. 'Or it'll get cold.'

I took Mother her cheese on toast in the conservatory. The sun had warmed the furniture and I could smell the earth of the large potted fern by the door. She was asleep in her wicker chair – her head hadn't drooped, but it was resting at an angle I recognised. She didn't stir, so I stood for a moment and looked out at the garden. Some roses were still hanging on and there were a few dried-out purple chrysanthemums, but the overall impression was one of bareness. We moved here when I was sixteen, so I don't feel very attached to the place. It was Father's way of starting again after the incident with the girl who worked at his tailor's, whom he was careless enough to impregnate. Mother cried for a week, so by way of atonement he allowed her to move back to Surrey.

She stirred. My sigh may have disturbed her.

'Tricky.'

'Hello, Mother.'

I bent to kiss her hair. She caught my cheek in her hand. 'Have you eaten?'

'Nina says you've been distant.'

With a tut, she let go of my cheek. 'Let me look at you.'

I stood in front of her, my back to the garden.

She sat up in her chair. Her skin is not as wrinkled as a sixty-five-year-old's should be, and her green eyes are clear. Her hair, rolled up on top of her head, is still thick, although now it's prison grey. She was wearing her usual ruby necklace. Her Sunday jewels. They used to come out for church, and then drinks, followed by lunch with friends and neighbours. At the time I hated all that, but just then I felt a sudden stab of nostalgia for the clink of ice in gin, the smell of roast lamb, the murmur of conversation in the sitting room. Now it's cheese on toast with Nina.

'You look well,' she said. 'Better than for a long time. Am I right?'

'You always are.'

She ignored this. 'It's lovely to see you.'

I placed her lunch tray on the table before her.

'Mother, Nina says you've been distant . . .'

She waved a hand in front of her face. 'Tricky, dear. Do I look distant to you?'

'No, Mother. You look quite close enough.'

'Good. Now what's going on in filthy old Brighton? Are you behaving yourself?'

'Certainly not.'

She uncurled her best devilish smile. 'Marvellous. Let's have a drink and you can tell me all about it.'

'Lunch first. Then I'm calling Dr Shires out to see you.'

She blinked. 'Don't be ridiculous.'

'I know all about these episodes you've been having. And I want him to come and see you.'

'It would be a complete waste of time. He's been already.' Her voice was quiet. She looked away from me, out into the garden.

'And what was his diagnosis?'

'I'm suffering from a common disease known as old age. These things happen. And they will happen, more and more.'

'Don't say that.'

'Tricky, darling. It's true.'

'If it happens again, you're to telephone me. Immediately.' I caught her hand. Held it fast. 'All right?'

She gave my fingers a squeeze. 'If you insist.'

'Thank you.'

'Now let's have that drink. I can't bear cheese on toast without a glass of claret.'

We left it at that. I spent the next couple of hours entertaining Mother with tales of my clashes with Houghton, my handling of Jackie, and even with the story of the lady on the bike, although I minimised my policeman's role in the incident.

Mother has never mentioned my minority status to me, and I have never brought it up with her. I doubt the subject will ever be broached by either of us, but I do feel she understands my situation in some vague, subconscious way. Not once, for example, has she asked when I am going to bring a nice girl home to meet her. When I was twenty-one, I overheard her field Mrs Drewitt's annual enquiry into my marital status with the words, 'Tricky's not made that way.'

Amen to that.

14th October 1957

I always know there's going to be trouble when Houghton pops his gleaming pate around my door and trills, 'Luncheon, Hazlewood? The East Street?' The last time the two of us luncheoned he demanded I display more local watercolours. I agreed, but have managed to ignore the demand thus far.

The East Street Dining Room is very Houghton: large white plates, silver gravy boats, knocking-on-a-bit waiters with crumbling smiles and no hurry to get your food to you, everything boiled. But the wine is usually passable and they do a good pud. Gooseberry pie, treacle sponge, spotted dick, that sort of thing.

Following a long wait for any service at all, we finally finished our main courses (a rather chewy Sussex lamb chop with what I'm sure were potatoes out of a tin, dressed up with a few sprigs of parsley). Only after this did Houghton announce he'd decided to give my art-appreciation afternoons for schoolchildren the go-ahead. However, he could not, on any account, agree to the lunchtime concerts. 'We're in the business of the visual, not the aural,' he pointed out, polishing off his third glass of claret.

I'd had a couple of glasses, too, so I countered: 'Does that matter? It would be a way of encouraging the aurally inclined towards the visual.'

He nodded slowly and took a deep breath, as if this was just the sort of challenge he'd expected from the likes of me and he was, in fact, glad I'd responded in a way for which he was fully prepared. 'It seems to me, Hazlewood, that your job is to ensure the continuing excellence of our collection of European art. The excellence of the collection – not some musical gimmick – is what will bring the public into the museum.' After a pause, he added, 'Do you mind if we skip pudding? I'm in rather a rush.'

Pudding, I wanted to say, was the only thing that would have made this experience worthwhile. But, of course, his question required no answer. He asked for the bill. Then, fiddling with his wallet, he made the following little speech: 'You reformers always push things too far. Take a tip from me and let it rest. It's all very well steaming in with new ideas, but you need to let a place settle around you before asking too much of it, d'you see?'

I said that I did. And I mentioned that I'd now been at the museum for almost four years, which, I thought, gave me the right to feel fairly settled.

'That's nothing,' he said, waving his hand. 'Been there twenty myself and the board still think I'm a newcomer. It takes time to allow your colleagues to get the real *measure* of you.'

Very politely, I requested he clarify this statement.

He looked at his watch. 'I didn't mean to bring this up now, but' – and I understood this was actually where our lunch had been heading all along – 'I was talking to Miss Butters the other day and she mentioned a project of yours about which I knew absolutely nothing. Which was rather odd. She said it involved portraits of ordinary townsfolk.'

Jackie. What on earth was Jackie doing in Houghton's office?

'Now, of course I don't listen to the prittle-prattle of office girls – at least one tries to block it out . . .'

On cue, I gave a laugh.

'. . . but on this occasion my ears were, as they say, pricked.' He looked at me, his eyes steady and clear. 'And so I'm asking you, Hazlewood, to please observe museum protocol. Each new project must be approved by me, and, if I think fit, by the board. Proper channels must be utilised. Otherwise, chaos reigns. Do you see?'

Didn't you ever ignore protocol, I wanted to ask, when you were an aesthete at Cambridge? I tried to imagine Houghton in a punt on the Cam, some dark-haired mystery of a boy resting his head on his knee. Did he ever follow through? Or was it merely a flirtation with him, like leftist politics and foreign food? Something to be experimented with at the Varsity and swiftly discarded upon entrance to the real world of adult male employment.

'Now. We'll take a walk back, and you can tell me what this portrait thingummy is all about.'

Out in the street, I insisted that Jackie must have got the wrong end of the stick. 'It's just an idea at the moment. I haven't taken any action.'

'Well, if you have an idea, for Christ's sake tell me and not the office girl, will you? Damned embarrassing, being wrong-footed by your Miss Butters.'

And then something quite beautiful happened. As we were crossing North Street, the Duchess of Argyle swanned past. And he *did* look like a swan. Gauzy white neckerchief. Tight-fitting cream jacket and trousers. Shoes the colour of a setting sun, with lipstick to match. My heart gave a big DUM-de, but I needn't have feared. The Duchess didn't throw me so much as a glance. I should've known the Argyle would never employ the type to scream at you in the street.

Someone hissed, 'Bloody queer,' and a few women giggled from the pavement. North Street on a weekday lunchtime is perhaps not the best place to troll. The Duchess is getting older, though – in the stark daylight I could see his crow's feet – and perhaps doesn't much care any more. I had a sudden itch to run after him, kiss his hand and tell him he was braver than any soldier, to wear that much make-up in an English seaside town, even if that town did happen to be Brighton.

This appearance silenced Houghton for a few moments, and I expected him to pretend the whole incident hadn't occurred. He was certainly walking fast, as if to escape the taint of the very air through which the Duchess had just swanned. But then he said, 'I suppose the fellow can't help it. But he needn't be so blatant. What I don't understand is what one gains from such behaviour. I mean, women are such lovely creatures. It's degrading to the fairer sex, his sort of carry-on, don't you think?' He looked me in the eye, but his own face was clouded with what I can only think was confusion.

Something – perhaps my policeman's presence at the flat the other night, perhaps pique with Houghton's attempts to put me in my place, perhaps bravado brought on by the Duchess's fine example – compelled me to reply: 'I try not to let it bother me, sir. Not *all* women are lovely, after all. Some look very like men and no one bats an eyelid at them, do they?'

For the rest of the way back I could feel Houghton searching for a reply. He found none, and we walked into the museum in silence.

Outside my office, Jackie looked up expectantly. I requested a word, almost addressing her as *Miss Butters* in my annoyance.

She sat in the armchair opposite my desk. I paced about a bit, hating myself for being in this situation. A dressing-down was necessary, I knew. Houghton had done it to me, and now I had to do it to Jackie. Who would Jackie do it to, though? Her dog, perhaps. I once saw her in Queen's Park, throwing a stick for a cocker spaniel. There was an enormous smile on her face and something unfettered in the way she knelt down to congratulate the creature for bringing the stick to her feet, letting it put its paws on her shoulders and cover every inch of her face with its reaching tongue. She looked almost beautiful in that moment. Free.

I was just clearing my throat when she said, 'Mr Hazlewood, I'm ever so sorry if I've caused any trouble.'

She clutched at the hem of her skirt – she was wearing the lemon ensemble again – pulling it down over her knees and shifting her feet about. 'It was such a long lunch with Mr Houghton, and I said to myself, that usually means trouble.' Her eyes were wide. 'And then I remembered that I'd mentioned your portrait project to Mr Houghton the other day and he looked so strange when I said it . . . and I wondered if perhaps I'd spoken out of turn?'

I asked her what, exactly, she had told him.

'Nothing really.'

I sat on the edge of my desk, meaning to smile benevolently down at her and thus appear powerful but essentially unthreatening. But God knows what expression was on my face – utter terror, probably, as I said, 'You must have said something.'

'He asked me if you were *up to anything new*. I think that's how he put it. But it was just . . . talking. Sometimes he does ask me things.'

'He *asks* you things?'

'After you've gone home. He comes in here and he asks me things.'

'What kinds of things?'

'Silly things. You know.' She batted her eyelids coyly and looked to the floor, but still I failed to grasp her meaning.

'You know,' she said again, 'chit-chat.'

Chit-chat? I wanted to hoot. Houghton does chit-chat? Then it dawned on me. 'Do you mean to tell me that old Houghton comes in here and flirts with you?'

She gave what can only be described as a giggle. 'I suppose you could call it that.'

I could see it, all too clearly. Him leaning over her shoulder, fingering her still-damp sheaf of carbon copy. Her taking off those winged specs and breathing all over his hot hands. And it completely wrong-footed me. So much so that I could think of nothing else to say.

There followed a long silence. Then Jackie piped up: 'It's nothing serious, Mr Hazlewood. He's a married man. It's just a bit of fun.'

'It doesn't sound like much fun to me.'

'Please don't be cross, Mr Hazlewood. I'm ever so sorry if I've caused any trouble.'

'You haven't,' I stated. 'But I'd rather you didn't mention the portrait project during your little . . . chats with Houghton again. It's at an embryonic stage and there's no need for anyone else to hear about it yet.'

'I didn't tell him much.'

'Good.'

'Only that that nice-looking copper dropped by. Nothing else.'

I certainly tried not to flinch. Jackie smoothed down her skirt again. Despite her careful grooming, her nails are bitten to the quick. I stared at these ragged stumps and managed to say, 'That's fine. It's simply best for me to present the project to Mr Houghton when I'm ready.'

'I understand.'

I told her she could go. At the door she repeated, 'I understand, Mr Hazlewood. I won't say anything.' And she took her leave.

Now, at home, I'm thinking of Michael's landlady. Mrs Esme Owens, widow. She lived downstairs, asked no questions, knitted endless socks for the poor and, on Fridays, made Michael fish pie, which he swore was delicious. He always said she was the soul of discretion. She'd seen a thing or two in the war, old Esme, and nothing shocked her. In return for his company, she offered her silence. For she must have noticed the frequency of my visits, and speculated on what it was that kept Michael out of the house every Wednesday night.

But I've often wondered who wrote those letters to Michael. He said it was no one we'd know, a professional outfit that probably made a good living from blackmailing homosexuals. The first letter was nothing if not to the point: SEEN YOU IN P RODIS WITH RENT. FOR SILENCE SEND FIVE POUNDS BY FRI. The address was a house in West Hove. Our righteous indignation caused us to blunder over there together that Sunday afternoon with no plan, no clue of what we were doing. Once we'd walked past the door a few times we realised the place was utterly empty. It was this emptiness that made me suddenly aware of the seriousness of the situation. This threat was faceless. It was something we couldn't see, let alone fight. We came home in silence. Although I tried to tell him not to, Michael sent the money. I knew he'd no choice, but felt I should be the voice of dissent. He refused to discuss it any further.

Some weeks later I found another note in his flat, and this

time the price of silence had doubled. Within two months of that first letter, Michael had killed himself.

So I do wonder, sometimes, about Mrs Esme Owens and her discretion. At Michael's funeral she was wearing a very expensive-looking fur stole. And acting rather more distraught than was necessary for a landlady.

15th October 1957

This business with Mother has been most distracting. On Sunday night, lying in bed wide awake, I was convinced she had only a few days left and I should prepare myself for her death. But on Monday I thought perhaps, at the very worst, she was in for a long illness and I should bring her to Brighton so I could nurse her. I even had a look in Cubitt and West's window on the way home from the museum, to see if any flats were available near mine. By this morning, though, I reckoned Mother to be the surviving type who'd probably see a good few years before my intervention was required. Nevertheless, I'd decided I should at least *ask* her to come here, if only to show willing. And I was sitting down this evening, gin and tonic to hand, to write a letter to that effect when the buzzer went.

Same time next week. I smiled. Despite the distraction of Mother's illness, I'd been waiting for him, of course, and had prepared the spare room. But only at the sound of the buzzer did I admit to myself that, despite sending him away last time, I had been expecting my policeman to return.

I sat for a few moments and relished the anticipation of his appearance. I took my time, and even read through what I'd written. *Dear Mother*, I'd begun, *I hope you won't think I'm interfering, or that I'm panicking about your condition.* I was, of course, doing both.

Then it went again. A long, impatient trill this time. He'd

come back. I'd sent him away, but he'd come back. And this meant everything was different. It was his decision. He was the insistent one, not me. There he was, outside, pushing my buzzer again. I gulped back the rest of my gin and went downstairs to let him in.

On seeing me, his first words were, 'Am I early?'

'Not at all,' I said, without consulting my watch. 'You're right on time.' I showed him up the stairs and into the flat, walking behind him so he wouldn't see the irrepressible spring in my step.

He was carrying his uniform again, and wearing a black sweater and jeans. We reached the sitting room and stood together on the rug. To my surprise, he gave me a small smile. He didn't seem as nervous as I'd first thought. For a second, everything seemed so simple: here he was, back at the flat. What else could matter? My policeman was here, and he was smiling.

'Right then,' he said. 'Shall we get going?' There was a new confidence, a new determination in his voice.

'I think we should.'

And he turned, walked into the spare bedroom and closed the door behind him. Trying not to dwell too much on the fact that he was undressing behind that door, I went into the kitchen to fetch him a beer. Passing the hallway mirror, I checked my appearance and couldn't stop myself giving my reflection a sly grin.

'Ready,' he called, opening the door to the 'studio'. And there he was, all dressed for me, waiting to begin.

After I'd finished drawing him, we came through to the sitting room and I gave him another drink.

The beer must have relaxed him. He unbuckled his belt, took off his jacket, slung it across my armchair, and sat himself on the chesterfield without being invited. I looked at the shape his jacket made on the back of the chair. Thought how limp it looked without his body to fill it.

'Do you like the uniform?' I asked.

'You should've seen me when I first got it. Kept pacing up and down the front room, looking at myself in the mirror.' He shook his head. 'I didn't realise, then, how heavy it would be.'

'Heavy?'

'Weighs a bloody ton. Try it.'

'It wouldn't fit me . . .'

'Go on. Give it a go.'

I picked it up. He was right: the thing was weighty. I rubbed the wool between my finger and thumb. 'It is a little coarse . . .'

His eyes glittered as they met mine. 'Like me.'

'Not at all like you.'

There was a pause. Neither one of us looked away.

I hauled the jacket on to my back, my arms floundering to find the sleeves. It was too big – the waist too low, the shoulders too wide – but still warm from his body. The smell of carbolic and pine talc was strong. The roughness of the collar prickled my neck and I shivered. I wanted to bury my nose in the sleeve, pull the fabric tightly around me and breathe in his smell. His warmth. But instead I bobbed at the knee and said, rather feebly, 'Evenin', all.'

He laughed. 'Never heard anyone say that. Not in real life.'

I took off the jacket and poured myself another gin. Then I sat next to him on the sofa, as close as I dared.

'Do I make a good subject, then?' he asked. 'Will I be a good portrait?'

I sipped my drink. Made him wait for the answer. My trochaic heart flapped in my chest.

I didn't look at him, but I felt him shift. He gave a little sigh and stretched out an arm. It went along the back of the chesterfield. Towards me.

Outside the window, the sky was black. All I could see was the glow of a few street lamps, and the watery beginnings of the room's reflection in the glass. I tried to reason with myself. Here I am, I thought, with a policeman in my flat, and I'm really going to have to touch him soon if he keeps behaving in this way, but he's a policeman, for Christ's sake, and you can't get much more risky than that, and I should remember Jackie's knowing comment, and Mrs Esme Owens, and what happened to that boy at the Napoleon . . .

I thought this. But all I felt was the warmth of his arm on the back of the chesterfield, very close now to my shoulder. The smell of ale on him, a bread-like smell. The creak of his belt as he moved his hand a little closer.

'You're going to make a wonderful portrait,' I said. 'Quite wonderful.'

And then his fingertips grazed my neck. Still I did not look at him. I let my eyes glaze over, and the reflection of the room in the window warped into a soft mass of light and dark. It all warped, the whole room, into the feeling of my policeman's fingers in my hair. He was holding the back of my neck now, cradling it, and I wanted to let my head rest there, in his large, capable hand. His touch was firm, surprisingly sure, but when I finally turned to look at him, his face was pale, his breathing quick.

'Patrick . . .' he began, his voice barely a whisper.

I flicked off the table lamp and placed a hand over his beautiful mouth. Felt the fleshiness of his upper lip as he drew breath. 'Don't say anything,' I told him.

Keeping one hand on his mouth, I pressed the other down on the top of his thigh. He closed his eyes, let out a breath.

I rubbed him through the rough wool of his police trousers until he was swallowing hard and my fingers were wet with his breath. When I felt his cock kick up towards me, I took my hand away and loosened his tie. He said nothing, kept gasping. I unbuttoned his shirt, working quickly, my heart banging out its upside-down rhythm, and he began to lick one of my fingers, lightly at first, but as I brought my mouth to his exposed neck, then to his chest, he sucked greedily at my flesh. And when I kissed the tiny hairs that crawl up to his belly button, he bit down, hard. I kept kissing. He kept biting. Then I pulled my hand from his mouth, cupped his face and kissed him, very gently, pulling back from his straining tongue. He made a little noise, a soft groan, and I reached down and took his cock in my hand, and I whispered in his ear, 'You're going to be wonderful.'

Afterwards, I lay with my head in his lap, and we were silent together. The curtains were still open and the room was dimly lit by the street lamps outside. A few cars droned past. The last of the seagulls wailed into the evening. My policeman rested his head on the back of the chesterfield, his hand in my hair. Neither of us spoke for what seemed like hours.

Eventually I lifted my head, determined to say something to him. But before I could speak, he'd stood up, buttoned his fly, reached for his coat and said, 'I'd better not come again, had I?'

It was a question. A question, not a statement.

'Of course you should.'

He said nothing. Buckled his belt, pulled on his jacket and began to walk away from me. I added, 'If you want to.'

He stopped in the doorway. 'Not that simple, is it?'

Just like Michael, every Wednesday night. Leaving. The

door slams and that's it. Let's not have this conversation now, I thought. Just stay a little longer.

I couldn't move. I sat and listened to his footsteps, and the only thing I managed to say was, 'Same time next week?'

But he'd already slammed the front door.

19th October 1957

All week, my dreams full of his groan as I kissed him. The kick of his cock beneath my flattened hand. And the sound of the front door slamming.

He's bound to be scared. He's young. Inexperienced. Although I'm aware many boys of his class are far more experienced than I was. A lad I once met at the Greyhound swore blind a friend of his father's had had him on his allotment when he was barely fifteen. And that he'd loved it. But I don't think anything like that has happened to my policeman. I think, perhaps rather romantically, that he's like I was: he's spent many years, ever since he was a very young boy, looking at men and wanting to be touched by them. He may already have begun to tell himself that he's a minority. He may even know that no woman will offer a 'cure'. I hope he knows that, although it wasn't at all obvious to me until I was almost thirty. Even when I was with Michael there was a small part of me that wondered if some female couldn't snap me out of it. But when he died I knew this to be utter folly, because there was no word for what I'd lost other than love. There. I've written it.

But I doubt another man touched my policeman before I did. I doubt he's cradled another man's head in his hand. His actions have been bold – he's surprised and delighted me in this. But does he feel as confident as he acts? How scared he really is I have no way of knowing. That laugh, those glittering eyes, are good protection, from the world and from himself.

25th October 1957

A huge scandal has just broken in the papers about Brighton CID. I believe it was even in *The Times*. The Chief Constable and a detective inspector are in the dock, charged with conspiracy. The details are shady at the moment, but no doubt they involve these men making mutually agreeable deals with various lowlifes of the type found in the Bucket of Blood. I have to say, my heart lifted when I saw the head-line in the *Argus*: CHIEF CONSTABLE AND 2 OTHERS ACCUSED – at last, our boys in blue are the ones facing social disgrace and possibly imprisonment – but it sank when I realised what this might mean for *my* policeman. Ordinary, honest members of the force will, I'm sure, have to pay for their bosses' misdemeanours. Lord knows what pressures they'll be under now.

But there's nothing I can do about all this. I just have to wait for him to come back. That's all I have to do.

4th November 1957

A glitter of frost on the pavement this morning. We're in for a cold winter.

He has stayed away for almost three weeks. And each day, a little of the memory of our evening together hardens into something lost. I can still feel his lips, but I can't quite remember the exact shape of that knobble on the bridge of his nose.

At the museum, Jackie's been eyeing me from behind her glasses, and Houghton's been droning on about the need to keep the director, the trustees and the council happy by not doing anything too outlandish. Nothing more has been said about the portrait project. But, perhaps inspired by the feeling of being able to seduce a boy in his early twenties, I've been pressing on with my reforms. All I have to do now is find a school that's willing to send its young charges through our doors and leave them under my dubious influence.

Felt I must get up to London to see Charlie this evening. It was already quite late, but I'd have a couple of hours with him before the last train back. Wanted, very badly, to tell him about my policeman. To talk. To shout his name out. In his absence, the next best thing would be to bring him to life by describing him for Charlie. Also wanted, I must admit, to boast a bit. Ever since school, it's always been Charlie telling me about the thrilling line of some boy's shoulders, the sweet way in which Bob or George or Harry looks up to him and is fascinated by his conversation, as well as providing absolute satisfaction in bed. Now I had my own tale to tell.

Charlie wasn't surprised by my visit – I never announce I'm coming – but he did keep me hanging about on the front steps for a minute. 'Listen,' he said. 'Got someone with me at the mo. Don't suppose you could come back tomorrow?'

He hasn't changed, then. I told him that I, unlike him, had to work tomorrow, so it was now or never. He opened the door, saying, 'You'd better come in and meet Jim, then.'

Charlie's recently had his Pimlico townhouse refurbished throughout – lots of mirrors and steel lamps, thin-looking furniture and modern tapestry hangings. It's clean and bright and very restful on the eye. The perfect setting, in fact, for Jim, who was sitting on Charlie's new sofa, smoking a Woodbine. Barefoot. And looking absolutely at his ease. 'Pleased to meet you,' he said, sticking out a smooth white hand, not getting to his feet.

We shook, him fixing me with eyes the colour of rust.

'Jim's working for me,' Charlie announced.

'Oh? Doing what?'

The two of them exchanged a smirk. 'Odd jobs,' said Charlie. 'So useful, having someone live-in. Drink?'

I asked for a gin and tonic, and to my surprise Jim jumped up. 'I'll have the usual, darling,' instructed Charlie, watching the boy as he made his exit. Jim was short but well-proportioned; long legs and a chunky little arse.

I looked at Charlie, who burst out laughing. 'Your face,' he chortled.

'Is he your . . . valet?'

'He's whatever I want him to be.'

'Does *he* realise that?'

'Of course he does.' Charlie sat in a chair by the fire and ran his hands through his black hair. A few flecks of grey there now, I noticed, but still thick. He was forever telling me, at school, how his hair could blunt scissors. And I could well believe it. 'It's wonderful, actually. A mutually satisfactory arrangement.'

'How long's this . . .'

'About four months now. I keep expecting to get bored. Or for him to. But it just hasn't happened.'

Jim came back in with the drinks and we spent an agreeable hour, mostly filled with Charlie telling stories about people I haven't seen for a long time or have never met. I didn't mind. Although Jim's presence inhibited me from broaching the subject of my policeman, it was wonderful to watch the two of them, so easy in one another's company. Charlie occasionally touching Jim's neck, Jim catching his wrist as he did so. Looking at them, I allowed myself a little fantasy. I could live like this with my policeman. We could spend evenings chatting to friends, sharing a drink, behaving as though we were – well, married.

All the same, I was glad when Charlie saw me to the door alone.

'Wonderful to see you,' he said. 'You look better than ever.'

I smiled.

'What's his name, then?' asked Charlie.

I told him. 'He's a policeman,' I added.

'Bloody hell,' said Charlie. 'What happened to the old cautious Hazlewood?'

'I buried him,' I said.

Charlie drew the door to behind him and we went down the steps into the street. 'Patrick,' he said, 'I don't want to come across all parental, but . . .' He stopped. Hooked me gently around the neck and drew our faces close. 'A *policeman?*' he hissed.

I laughed. 'I know. But he's not your average bobby.'

'Obviously not.'

There was a short silence. Charlie let me go. Lit us both a cigarette. We leant together on his railings, exhaling smoke into the night. Just like the bike sheds at school, I thought.

'What's he like, then?'

'Early twenties. Bright. Athletic. Blond.'

'Fuck me,' he said, grinning.

'This is it, Charlie.' I couldn't help myself. 'This is really it.'

Charlie frowned. 'Now I *am* going to be parental. Go easy. Be careful.'

A spark of anger flared in me. 'Why should I be?' I asked. 'You're not. Yours is living with you.'

Charlie flicked his cigarette into the gutter. 'Yes, but . . . that's different.'

'Different how?'

'Patrick. Jim's my *employee*. All the rules are understood, by us and by the rest of the world. He lives under my roof and I pay him for his . . . services.'

'Are you saying it's just a financial arrangement? Nothing more?'

'Of course not. But to outside eyes it could be. And this way it's clearer, isn't it? Anything else is . . . it's bloody impossible. You know that.'

After we'd said our goodbyes and he was walking back up the steps to the house, I called out, 'You wait. This time next year he'll be living with me.'

And at that moment, I really believed what I said.

12th November, 1957

Frost still on the pavements, the gas heater leaking fumes into my office, a sweater on beneath my jacket, Jackie shivering loudly at every opportunity, and he came back.

The time: seven thirty. The day: Tuesday. I was finishing a plate of goulash at the flat. And suddenly the buzzer shrieked. DUM-de went my heart, but just once. I've almost learned not to expect him to be there.

But there he was. He said nothing as I opened up. I managed to catch his eye for a second before he looked down.

'It's Tuesday, isn't it?' he said. His voice was calm, rather cool.

I showed him in. This time he carried no uniform and was wearing a long grey overcoat, which he allowed me to take from him once we were inside. The garment was large enough to make a canopy, to take shelter beneath, and I stood for a moment, holding it in my arms and watching him as he made his way to the spare bedroom without invitation from me.

In a fit of tidying, I'd removed the easel and paints, and the chair in which he'd posed was now back in its proper place, next to the bed.

He stopped in the centre of the room and swivelled round to face me. 'Aren't you going to draw me?' His normally pink cheeks were pale and his eyes were stony.

I was still holding on to the coat. 'If you like . . .' I said, looking around for somewhere to discard it. Placing it on the bed seemed a bit too forward. Like tempting fate.

'I thought that's what we were doing here. A portrait. On Tuesday evenings. A portrait of an *ordinary* person. Like me.'

I draped his overcoat across the chair. 'I can draw you, if you like . . .'

'If I like? I thought it was what you wanted.'

'Nothing's set up, but—'

'This isn't even a studio, is it?'

I ignored this. Allowed a small silence to pass. 'Why don't we discuss this in the sitting room?'

'Did you get me here under false pretences?' His voice was low, a shiver of anger running through it. 'You're one of them *importuners*, aren't you? You got me here with one thing in mind, didn't you?'

He licked his lips. Pushed back his cuffs. Took a step towards me. In that moment, he looked every inch the bully-boy policeman.

I stepped back, sat on the bed and closed my eyes. I was ready for the blow. For the big fist on my cheekbone. You've got yourself into this mess, Hazlewood, I told myself. These toughs are all the same. Just like that boy Thompson at school: fucking me by night, fighting me by day.

'Answer my question,' he demanded. 'Or don't you have an answer?'

Without opening my eyes, I replied in the softest voice I could: 'Is this how you treat your suspects?'

I don't know quite what possessed me to push him like this. Some remnant of trust in him, I suppose. Some belief that his fear would pass.

A long pause. We were still close; I could hear his breathing

174

slow. I opened my eyes. He was looming over me, but his usual flushed complexion had returned. His eyes were an intense blue.

'I can draw you,' I said, looking up at him. 'I'd like to. I want to complete the portrait. That's not a lie.'

His jaw was working slowly, as if he were keeping back some utterance.

I said his name. And when I reached out a hand and hooked it behind his thigh, he did not move away from me. 'I'm sorry if you think I got you here for one thing only. That could never be true.'

I said his name again. 'Stay the night this time,' I said.

His thigh hard against my hand.

After a moment, he let out a breath. 'You shouldn't have asked me here.'

'You wanted to come. Stay the night.'

'I don't know . . .'

'There's nothing to know. There's just these things that you and I must do.' My cheek was near his groin now.

He pulled away from my grip. 'I came here to tell you I can't come again.'

A long silence. I kept my eyes on him, but he wouldn't return my gaze.

Eventually I said, with what I hoped was a note of mirth in my voice: 'Did you have to come here to tell me that? Couldn't you have popped a note through my door?'

When he didn't respond, I couldn't help adding: 'Something along the following lines, perhaps: *Dear Patrick, It was nice knowing you, but I have to put an end to our friendship as I am a very respectable copper and also a coward—*'

He lashed out an arm. Instinctively I ducked, but no blow came. I was almost disappointed. I'm ashamed to admit that I'd wanted his hands on me, whatever it took. Instead of meeting my cheek, his fist went to his own temple and he ground his flesh with his knuckles. Then he made a strange sound – something between a gargle and a sob. His face creased into a terrible red mask, his eyes and mouth clenched.

'Don't,' I said, standing and putting a hand on his arm. 'Please don't.'

We stood together for a long time while he fought to get his breathing back under control. Finally he brought a forearm to his face and dragged it back and forth across his eyes. 'Can I have a drink?' he asked.

I fetched us some drinks and we sat together on the sofa, cradling our brandies. I kept trying to think of something to say that would reassure him, but could come up with nothing but platitudes, so kept my silence. And slowly, his face cooled, his shoulders relaxed.

I poured myself another and ventured: 'You're not a coward. It's brave of you to come here at all.'

He looked into his glass. 'How do you do it?'

'Do what?'

'Live . . . this life?'

'Oh,' I said. 'That.'

Where to begin? I had a sudden desire to stand up and stride about like a barrister, telling him a truth or two about *this life*, as he put it. Meaning my life. Meaning the lives of others. Meaning the morally dissolute. The sexually criminal. Meaning those whom society has condemned to isolation, fear and self-loathing.

But I restrained myself. I didn't want to scare the boy.

'I don't have much choice. I suppose I just jog along . . .' I began. 'Over the years, one learns . . .' I trailed off. What does one learn? To fear all strangers, and distrust even those close to you? To dissemble whenever possible? That utter loneliness is inevitable? That your lover of eight years will never stay more than one night, will become ever more distant, until you finally break into his room and find his cold, grey, vomit-encrusted body slumped across the bed?

No, not that.

Perhaps, then, that despite all this, the idea of *normality* fills you with complete dread?

'Well. One learns to live as one can.' I took a long drink of brandy and added, 'As one must.' I tried to put all images of Michael out of my head. It was the smell in there that was so awful. The sweet, rotting closeness of death by medication. Such a cliché. I thought it even then, holding his poor, beautiful body in my arms. They'd won. He'd let them win.

I'm still furious with him for that.

'Didn't you ever think of getting married?'

I almost laughed, but his face was grave. 'There was a girl once,' I said, relieved to think of something else. 'We got along well. I suppose it may have crossed my mind . . . but, no. I knew it would be impossible.'

Alice. I hadn't thought about her for the longest time. Last night I played it down to my policeman, but it all came back to me: that moment, at Oxford, when I thought perhaps marriage to Alice would be the best solution. We enjoyed one another's company. We even went to dances, although after a few weeks I sensed she wanted something to happen *after* the dance. Something I could not make happen. But she was cheerful, kind, open-minded even, and it did occur to me that with Alice as a wife I might be able to escape my minority status. I would have access to easy respectability. I'd have someone to look after me who might not make too many demands. Who might even understand if I suffered the

177

occasional lapse . . . And I was fond of her. Many marriages, I knew, were based on much less than that. Then Michael and I became lovers. Poor Alice. I think she knew what – or rather, who – was keeping me from her, but she never caused a scene. Scenes weren't Alice's style, which was one of the things I liked about her.

'I'm planning to marry,' said my policeman.

'Planning?' I took a breath. 'You're engaged, do you mean?'

'No. But I'm thinking about it.'

I put my glass down. 'You wouldn't be the first.' I tried a laugh. If I could make light of it, I thought, we could get off the subject. And the sooner we got off the subject, the sooner he might forget all this nonsense and we might get to bed. I knew what he was doing. I've experienced it a few times before. The post-consummation straight talk. *I'm not queer. You know that, don't you? I've got a wife and kids at home. This has never happened to me before.*

'Thinking about it and doing it are entirely different propositions,' I said, stretching a hand towards his knee.

But he wasn't listening. He wanted to talk.

'The other day I was called in to see the guv. And d'you know what he asked me? He said, *When are you going to make some girl a respectable policeman's wife?*'

'The impudence!'

'It's not the first time he's mentioned it . . . *Some bachelors*, he says, *some bachelors have found it hard to rise through the ranks in this division.*'

'What did you say?'

'Not much. 'Course, they're coming down hard on all of us now, what with the Chief being in the dock . . . Everyone's got to be whiter than white.'

I knew all that business wouldn't be good for us. 'You

could've told him you're far too young to be married and it's none of his beeswax.'

He laughed. 'Listen to you. *Beeswax.*'

'What's wrong with *beeswax?*'

He just shook his head. 'There's plenty married much younger than me.'

'And look at the state they're in.'

He shrugged. Then gave me a sideways glance. 'It wouldn't be so bad, would it?'

His tone was so deliberately offhand that I knew he'd someone in mind. That he was already planning it. And I guessed it was the teacher he'd mentioned, that day I showed him Icarus. Why else would he mention her at all? I'd been so utterly stupid.

And so I said, as brightly as I could, 'It's the girl you mentioned, isn't it?'

He swallowed. 'We're just friends, at the moment. Nothing serious, you know.'

He was lying.

'Well. It's as I said. I'd like to meet her.'

I have no choice, I know that. I can pretend she doesn't exist and risk losing him altogether, or I can put myself through the ordeal and keep a crumb of him.

I could even work on putting him off the woman.

So we've arranged that she will come to the museum some time soon. I deliberately avoided setting a precise date with the rather pathetic hope that he might forget the whole thing.

And he's agreed to sit and finish the portrait. I will get him on paper, whatever it takes.

24th November 1957

It's Sunday morning and I've packed a picnic for us. Listen to me. *Us.*

Yesterday I bought ox tongue from Brampton's, a couple of beers for him, a good hunk of Roquefort, a jar of olives and two iced buns. I chose everything whilst thinking of what my policeman might like to eat, but also of what I might like him to try. Dithered over whether to include napkins and a bottle of champagne. In the end decided to put both in. Why not try to impress him, after all?

All of which is utterly ludicrous, not least because it's the coldest morning of the year so far. The sun has retreated, a wet fog hangs over the beach, and I saw my breath in the lav first thing. But he's coming at twelve and I'm to drive him in the Fiat to Cuckmere Haven. Really I should take a flask of tea and a couple of warm blankets. Perhaps I'll put those in too, just in case we fail to get out of the car.

Still, the gloominess of the day bodes well for our privacy. Nothing spoils an outing more than too many suspicious glances. I hope he wears some sort of hiking gear, so as to at least look the part. Michael always refused to wear tweed of any kind and did not possess even one pair of stout walking shoes – one of the reasons we usually stayed indoors. Of course, there are places in the countryside where few people ever appear, but those that do can be a lumpen lot, glaring with weather-beaten eyes at anyone who fails to look just as they do. One learns to ignore a certain amount, but I can't bear the thought of my policeman sullied by those enraged looks.

Must go and check the Fiat's starting all right.

He arrived on time. The usual jeans, T-shirt, ankle boots. And the long grey coat over the top. 'What?' he asked as I looked him up and down. 'Nothing,' I said, smiling. 'Nothing.'

I drove recklessly. Stealing glances at him whenever I could. Throwing the car around corners. My foot on the accelerator giving me such a feeling of power that I almost started to laugh.

'You drive too fast,' he observed as we took the coast road out of town.

'Are you going to arrest me?'

He gave a short laugh. 'I didn't think you were the type, that's all.'

'Appearances,' I said, 'can be deceptive.'

I asked him to tell me all about himself. 'Start at the beginning,' I said. 'I want to know everything about you.'

He shrugged. 'Not much to tell.'

'I *know* that's not true,' I implored, throwing an adoring look his way.

He looked out of the window. Sighed. 'You know most of it already. I told you. School. Rubbish. National Service. Boring. Police force. Not so bad. And swimming . . .'

'What about your family? Your parents? Siblings?'

'What about them?'

'What are they like?'

'They're . . . you know. All right. Ordinary.'

I tried a different tack. 'What do you want out of life?'

He said nothing for a bit, then this: 'What I want, right now, is to know about you. That's what I want.'

So I did the talking. I could almost *feel* him listening, he was so eager to hear what I had to say. Of course, that's the greatest flattery: a willing ear. So I went on, and on, about life at Oxford, the years I spent trying to make a living from painting, how I got the job at the museum, my beliefs about art. I promised to take him to the opera, to a concert at the Royal Festival Hall, and to all the major galleries in London. He'd already been, he said, to the National. On a school outing. I asked him what he remembered of the place, and he mentioned Caravaggio's *Supper at Emmaus*: the clean-shaven Christ. 'I couldn't take my eyes off him,' he said. 'Jesus without a beard. It was really strange.'

'Strange as in wonderful?'

'Maybe. It didn't seem right, but it was more real than anything else in the place.'

I agreed. And we've made a plan to go together next weekend.

The fog was worse around Seaford, and by the time we reached Cuckmere Haven the road in front seemed to have disappeared completely. The Fiat was the only vehicle in the car park. I said we didn't have to walk – we could just talk. And eat. And whatever else took our fancy. But he was determined. 'We've come all this way,' he said, letting himself out of the car. It was quite a disappointment, to have him spring away from me like that, no longer held captive.

The river, with its slow meander down to the sea, was lost to us in the fog. All we could see was the grey chalk of the path, and the foot – not the tops – of the hills along one side.

Through the fog came the occasional glimpse of the dumb bulk of a sheep. Nothing more.

My policeman strode slightly ahead, hands in pockets. As we walked, we fell to a comfortable silence. It was as though we were cushioned by the quiet, forgiving fog. We saw not another soul. Heard nothing apart from our own feet on the path. I said we should head back – this was useless: we could see nothing at all of river, downs or sky. And I was hungry; I'd packed a picnic and I wanted to eat. He turned to look at me. 'We need to get a look at the sea first,' he said.

After a while I could hear the suck and rush of the Channel, even if I couldn't see the beach. My policeman's pace increased, and I followed. Once there, we stood side by side on the steep bank of pebbles, staring into the grey mist. He inhaled deeply. 'It'd be good swimming here,' he said.

'We'll come back. In the spring.'

He looked at me. That smile playing on his lips. 'Or sooner. We could come one night.'

'It'd be cold,' I said.

'It'd be secret,' he said.

I touched his shoulder. 'Let's come back when the sun's out. When it's warm. Then we'll swim together.'

'But I like it like this. Just us and the fog.'

I laughed. 'For a policeman, you're very romantic.'

'For an artist, you're very afraid,' he said.

My answer to that was to kiss him hard on the mouth.

13th December 1957

We've been meeting some lunchtimes, when he can get a long break. But he has not forgotten the schoolteacher. And yesterday, for the first time, he brought her with him.

What a great effort I made to be charming and welcoming. They are so obviously mismatched that I had to smile when I saw them together. She is almost as tall as he is, made no attempt to disguise it (wearing heels), and is not nearly as handsome as him. But I suppose I would think so.

Having said that, there was something unusual about her. Perhaps it's her red hair. So coppery that no one could fail to notice it. Or perhaps it's the way that, unlike many young women, she does not look away when you meet her eye.

Having met them at the museum, I led them both to the Clock Tower Café, which has become my policeman's and my favourite haunt for the kind of hearty, no-nonsense meals that I sometimes crave. At any rate, it's always wonderful to be in the greasy fug of the place after the dry silence of the museum, and I was determined to make no effort whatsoever to impress Miss Marion Taylor. I knew she would be expecting silver cutlery and a tablecloth, so I offered her the Clock Tower. Not the sort of place a schoolteacher likes to be seen. I can tell, just from those heels, that she's a social climber and she wants to drag my policeman up with her. She'll have his future mapped out in kitchenettes, television sets and washing machines.

But I am being unfair. I have to keep reminding myself that I should give her a chance. That my best tactic is to get her on side. If I can make her trust me, then it will be easier to keep seeing him. And why shouldn't she trust me? After all, we both have my policeman's best interests at heart. I'm sure she wants him to be happy. Just as I do.

I don't sound convincing, even to myself. The truth is, I'm a little afraid that her red hair and assured manner have turned his head. That she can offer him something I cannot. Security, for a start. Respectability (she has that in spades, although she may not be aware of it). And perhaps a promotion.

She does look to be a worthy rival. I could see her steadfastness – or was it stubbornness? – in the way she waited for my policeman to hold the door of the café open for her, and the way she watched his face carefully whenever he spoke, as if trying to fathom his real meaning. Miss Taylor is a determined young woman, I've no doubt of that. And a very serious one.

As we walked back to the museum, she held on to my policeman's arm, steering him ahead.

'Next Tuesday evening,' I said to him, 'as usual?'

She gazed at him, her large mouth fixed in a straight line, as he said, ''Course.'

I placed a hand on my policeman's shoulder. 'And I want you both to come to the opera with me in the new year. *Carmen* at Covent Garden. My treat.'

He beamed. But Miss Taylor piped up: 'We couldn't possibly. It's too much . . .'

'Of course you can. Tell her she can.'

With a nod in her direction, he said, 'It's all right, Marion. We can pay something towards it.'

'I wouldn't hear of it.' I turned my back on her and looked him in the face. 'I'll let you know the details Tuesday.'

I said my farewells and headed down Bond Street, hoping she was noting the way I swung my arms.

16th December 1957

Last night, very late, he came to the flat.

'You did like her, didn't you?'

I was groggy from sleep and had stumbled from bed in just my pyjamas, still half dreaming of him, and there he was: tense-faced, damp-haired from the night. Standing on the doorstep. Asking for my opinion.

'For God's sake come in,' I hissed. 'You'll wake the neighbours.'

I led the way upstairs and into the sitting room. Switching on a table lamp I saw the time: a quarter to two in the morning.

'Drink?' I asked, gesturing towards the cabinet. 'Or tea, perhaps?'

He was standing on my rug just as he had when he first visited – upright, nervous – and he was staring directly at me with an intensity I hadn't seen before.

I rubbed my eyes. 'What?'

'I asked you a question.'

Not this again, I thought. The suspect-interrogator routine. 'Rather late, isn't it?' I said, not caring if I sounded peevish.

He said nothing. Waited.

'Look. Why don't we have a cup of tea? I'm not quite awake.'

Without giving him time to argue, I fetched my dressing gown, then went into the kitchen to put the kettle on.

He followed me. 'You didn't like her.'

'Go and sit down, won't you? I need tea. Then we can talk.'

'Why won't you tell me?'

'I will!' I laughed and stepped towards him, but something in the way he was standing – so steady and straight, as if ready to spring – stopped me from touching him.

'I just need a moment to gather my thoughts—'

The kettle's scream interrupted us and I busied myself with measuring, pouring and stirring, aware all the while of his refusal to move.

'Let's sit.' I held out a cup.

'I don't want tea, Patrick . . .'

'I was dreaming of you,' I said. 'If you want to know. And now here you are. It's a little strange. And lovely. And it's late. Please. Let's just sit down.'

He relented, and we sat at opposite ends of the chesterfield. Seeing him so twitchy and insistent, I knew what I had to do. And so I said: 'She's a super girl. And a lucky one.'

Immediately his face brightened, his shoulders relaxed. 'Do you really think so?'

'Yes.'

'I thought perhaps you didn't, you know, take to her.'

I sighed. 'It's not up to me, is it? It's your decision . . .'

'I'd hate to think the two of you couldn't get along.'

'We got along fine, didn't we?'

'She liked *you*. She told me. She thinks you're a real gent.'

'Does she.'

'She meant it.'

Perhaps due to the late hour, or perhaps in reaction to this declaration of Miss Taylor's appreciation, I could hide my irritation no longer. 'Look,' I snapped, 'I can't stop you seeing her. I know that. But don't expect it to change things.'

'What things?'

'The way things are with us.'

We looked at each other for a long moment.

Then he smiled. 'Were you really dreaming of me?'

After I gave my seal of approval, he rewarded me richly. For the first time, he came to my bed and he stayed the whole night.

I'd almost forgotten the joy of waking up and, before you've even opened your eyes, knowing by the shape of the mattress beneath you, by the warmth of the sheets, that he's still there.

I awoke to the wonder of his shoulders. He has the most pleasing back. Strong from all that swimming, with a soft tuft of hair at the very bottom of his spine, like the beginnings of a tail. His chest and legs are covered in wiry blond fuzz. Last night I put my mouth to his stomach, took small bites at the hair there, was surprised by the toughness of it between my teeth.

I watched the movement of his shoulders as he breathed, his skin lightening as the sun came through the curtains. When I touched his neck he awoke with a start, sat up and looked about the room.

'Good morning,' I said.

'Christ,' he replied.

'Not quite,' I smiled. 'Just Patrick.'

'Christ,' he said again. 'What time is it?'

He swung his legs out of the bed, barely giving me time to appreciate the sculptural marvel that is the whole of him, naked, before stepping into his underpants and pulling on his trousers.

'After eight, I should think.'

'Christ!' he said again, louder. 'I'm supposed to start at six. Christ!'

Whilst he hopped about, looking for various items of clothing that had been abandoned in the night, I pulled on a dressing gown. It was clear that all efforts at conversation, let alone a rekindling of intimacy, were useless.

'Coffee?' I offered, as he headed for the door.

'I'll get a bollocking for this.'

I followed him into the sitting room, where he grabbed his overcoat.

'Wait.'

He stopped and looked at me, and I reached out and smoothed down a clump of his hair.

'I've got to go—'

I delayed him with a firm kiss on the mouth. Then I opened the door and checked no one was about. 'Off you go, then,' I whispered. 'Be good. And don't let anyone see you on the stairs.'

Absolutely reckless, really, to let him leave at that hour. But I was in that state again. The state where anything seems possible. When he was gone, I put *Quando me'n vo' soletta per la via* on the record-player. Turned the volume up to maximum. Waltzed around the flat, alone, until I was giddy. That's what Mother says. *I've gone all giddy*. It's a wonderful feeling.

Luckily it was a quiet morning. I managed to spend most of it locked in my office, looking out of the window, remembering my policeman's touches.

That was quite enough to fill the hours until about two o' clock, at which time I suddenly realised I had no idea when I would see him again. Perhaps, I thought, our one night together would be the last. Perhaps his rushing to work was just an excuse.

A way to escape from my flat, from me, and from what had happened, as quickly as possible. I had to see him, if only for a minute. The whole thing, already dreamlike in its improbability, would crumble if I did not. I could not allow that to happen.

So when Jackie came in to ask if I would like tea, I told her I was on my way to an urgent meeting and wouldn't be back for the rest of the day. 'Shall I tell Mr Houghton?' she asked, her mouth curling a little at one side.

'No need,' I said, pushing past her before she could ask anything else.

Outside, the afternoon was crisp and cold. The intensity of the sun convinced me I had made the right decision. The pavilion glowed a rich cream. The fountains on the Steine glittered.

Once in the fresh air, some of my urgency seemed to pass. I trotted along the seafront, welcoming the icy breeze on my face. Took in the glaring whiteness of the Regency terraces. Reflected for the umpteenth time how lucky I am to live in this town. Brighton is the very edge of England, and there's a sense here that we're almost somewhere else entirely. Somewhere far away from the hedged-in gloom of Surrey, the damp, sunken streets of Oxford. Things can happen here that would not elsewhere, even if they're only fleeting. Here, not only can I touch my policeman, he can stay with me all night, his heavy thigh clamping mine to the mattress. The thought of it was so outrageous, so ludicrous and yet so real that I let out a laugh, right there on Marine Parade. A woman passing in the other direction smiled at me in the manner of someone humouring a maniac. Still chuckling, I turned up Burlington Street and headed to Bloomsbury Place.

There was the police box, no bigger than a privy, the blue light weak in the sun. To my delight, there was no bicycle propped outside. A bicycle outside means a visit from the sergeant; he's told me that. Still, I stopped and looked up and down the street. No one to be seen. In the distance, the soft crash of the sea. The frosted windows of the box gave nothing away. But I trusted he would be in there. Waiting for me.

What an ideal location, I thought, for a tryst. Inside we'd be hidden, but we'd be in a public place. A police box offers both seclusion and excitement. Who could ask for more? Love in a police box. It could be one of those rather wonderful paperbacks that are available by mail order only.

Giddy. And anything seemed possible.

I knocked loudly at the door. DUM-de, went my heart. DUM-de. DUM-de. DUM-de.

POLICE, said the sign. IN AN EMERGENCY, CALL FROM HERE.

This did feel something like an emergency.

As soon as the door opened, I said, 'Forgive me,' and had a fancy I was like a Catholic boy begging for a confession.

There was a pause as he registered what was happening. Then, first checking the coast was clear, he grabbed my lapel and pulled me inside, slamming the door closed. 'What the hell are you playing at?' he hissed.

I brushed myself down. 'I know, I know . . .'

'Isn't it enough that I get a bollocking for being late? Do you have to make things worse?' He puffed out his cheeks, held his forehead.

I apologised, kept smiling. Giving him time to get over the shock of seeing me, I looked around the place. It was pretty gloomy in there, but there was an electric heater in the corner, and on the shelf was a sandwich box and a Thermos flask. I suddenly pictured his mother cutting him triangles of meat-paste-filled white bread and felt a new rush of love for him.

'Aren't you going to offer me a cup of tea?' I asked.

'I'm on duty.'

'Oh,' I said, 'so am I. Well, I'm supposed to be. I crept out of the office.'

'That's completely different. You can break the rules. I can't.' As he said this, he hung his head a little, like a sulky boy.

'I know,' I said. 'I'm sorry.' I reached out to touch his arm, but he moved away.

There was a pause. 'I came to give you these.' I held out a set of keys to my flat. I keep spares in the office. An impulse. An excuse. A way to win him over. 'So you can come by whenever you like. Even if I'm not there.'

He looked at the keys but made no move to take them. So I placed them on the shelf, next to his flask. 'I'll go then,' I sighed. 'I shouldn't have come. I'm sorry.' But instead of turning for the door, I caught hold of the top button of his jacket. I kept a tight grip on it, feeling its coolness between my fingertips. I didn't undo it. I just held on until it warmed in my hand.

'It's just,' I said, moving down to the next button and holding it fast, 'I can't seem to . . .'

He didn't flinch, or make a sound, so I moved down to the next button: '. . . stop thinking . . .'

Next button: '. . . about your beauty.'

His breath quickened as I worked my way down, and as I reached the final button, his hand caught my own. Gently he guided two of my fingers into his open mouth. His lips so hot on that cold day. He sucked and sucked, making me gasp. He is greedy for me, I know it. Just as greedy as I am for him.

Then he took my fingers from his lips and, pressing them against his groin, he asked, 'Can you share?'

'Share?'

'Can you share me?'

I felt him harden, and I nodded. 'If that's what it takes. Yes. I can share.'

And then I was on my knees before him.

III

Peacehaven, November 1999

Watching you look out of your window at the rain, I wonder if you remember the day Tom and I were married, and how it poured like it would never stop. Probably that day seems more real to you than this one, a Wednesday in November in Peacehaven at the end of the twentieth century, where there is no relief from the drabness of the sky or the wailing of the wind at the windows. It certainly seems more real to me.

The twenty-ninth of March 1958. My wedding day, and it rained and rained. Not just a spring shower that might have dampened frocks and freshened faces, but an absolute downpour. I woke to the sound of water hammering on our roof, clattering down the guttering. At the time it seemed like good luck, like some sort of baptism into a new life. I lay in my bed, picturing cleansing torrents, thinking of Shakespearean heroines beached on foreign shores, their past lives washed away, facing brave new worlds.

We'd had a very short engagement – less than a month. Tom seemed keen to get on with things, and so, of course, was I. Looking back, I've often wondered about his haste. At the time it was thrilling, this dizzy rush into marriage, and it was flattering, too. But now I suspect he wanted to get it over with, before he changed his mind.

Outside the church, the path was treacherous beneath my sateen shoes, and my pillbox hat and short veil gave me no protection. All the daffodil heads were bent and battered, but I walked tall down that path, taking my time, despite my father's impatience to reach the relative safety of the porch. Once there, I expected him to say something, to confess his pride or his fears, but he was silent, and when he adjusted my veil, his hand shook. I think to myself now: I should have been aware of the significance of that moment. It was the last time my father could make any claim to be the most important man in my life. And he was not a bad father. He never hit me, rarely raised his voice. When Mum wouldn't stop crying over the fact that I was going to the grammar, Dad offered me a sly wink. He'd never said I was good or bad, or anything in between. I think, more than anything, I puzzled him; but he didn't punish me for that. I should have been able to say something to my father at that moment, on the threshold of my new life with another man. But, of course, Tom was waiting for me, and I could think only of him.

As I walked up the aisle, everyone but you looked round and smiled. But that didn't matter to me. My shoes were soaked through and my stockings were splashed with mud and you were best man instead of Roy, which had caused some trouble, but none of it mattered. Even the fact that Tom wore the suit you'd bought for him (like yours, only grey rather than dark brown) instead of his uniform hardly registered with me. Because once I reached him, you passed him the ring that made me Mrs Tom Burgess.

We followed the ceremony with beer and sandwiches in the church hall, which smelled very like St Luke's – all children's plimsolls and overcooked beef. Sylvie, now actually pregnant, wore a plaid frock and sat smoking in the corner, watching Roy, who'd appeared to be drunk even before the reception started. I'd invited Julia, who I felt sure was becoming a firm friend, and she came wearing a jade-green two-piece and her wide smile. Did you talk to her, Patrick? I don't recall. I just remember her trying to start up a conversation with my brother Harry, who kept looking past her towards Sylvie's breasts. Tom's parents were there, of course; his father kept slapping everyone on the shoulder, rather too hard (I suddenly saw that this was where Tom got it from). His mother's shelf-like bosom was larger than ever and stuffed into a floral blouse. After the ceremony, she kissed me on the cheek and I smelled the slight staleness of her lipstick as she said 'Welcome to the family' and dabbed her eyes.

All I wanted was to leave that place with my new husband. What did you say in your speech? At first no one listened very hard; they were all too keen to get to the luncheon-meat sandwiches and the bottles of Harvey's. Still, you stood at the front of the hall and carried on regardless, while Tom looked around anxiously, and after a while, the sheer novelty of your fulsome, velvety voice with its Oxbridge vowels pricked people's ears. Tom frowned a little as you explained how the two of you had met; it was the first time I'd heard about the lady on the bicycle, and you enjoyed yourself telling that story, pausing for comic effect before you repeated what Tom had said about her being a batty old bird, which made my father laugh uproariously. You said something about Tom and I making the perfect civilised couple – the policeman and the teacher. No one could accuse *us* of not paying our debt to society, and the people of Brighton could rest easy in their beds knowing that Tom was pounding the streets and I was attending to their children's education. I wasn't sure how serious you were, even at the time, but I felt a little twinge of pride as you said those things. Then you raised your glass in a toast, drank your half of stout down in a few gulps, said something to Tom that I couldn't hear, patted him on the arm, firmly kissed my hand, and took your leave.

The night before the wedding, I went to Sylvie's flat. I suppose this was what people would now call my 'hen night', since Tom had gone out with some of the boys on the force.

Sylvie and Roy had finally managed to move out of Roy's mother's place in Portslade, and their flat was in a new tower block, with lifts and large windows, overlooking the municipal market. The place had been occupied for only a few months; the corridors still smacked of wet cement and new paint. But when I entered the shiny lift, the doors opened smoothly.

Sylvie had irises on the wallpaper and the curtains in the living room, I remember – the deepest blue with yellow flecks. But everything else was modern; the sofa, with its low seat and thin arms, was covered in a slippery, cold fabric that must have been mostly plastic. 'Dad felt sorry for us and shelled out,' she said, seeing me glance at the sun-shaped wooden clock above the gas fire. 'Guilty conscience.'

He'd refused to see Sylvie for months after the wedding.

'Mackeson? Sit down, then.'

She was already quite big. Little, brittle Sylvie's edges were blurring. 'Don't get yourself in the club as quick as me, will you? It's bloody awful.' She handed me a glass and lowered herself on to the sofa. 'What's really annoying,' she continued, 'is I didn't even have to lie to Roy. As soon as we were married, I got pregnant anyway. He thinks I'm six months gone, but I know this baby's going to be a late arrival.' She nudged me and giggled. 'I'm quite looking forward to it, really. My own little thing to cuddle.'

I remembered what she'd said on her wedding day about wishing she could do as she pleased, and I wondered what had happened to change her mind, but all I said was, 'You've got it nice here.'

She nodded. 'Not bad, is it? The council moved us in before it was finished – wallpaper was still damp – but it's nice to be up high. Up in the clouds, we are.'

Four storeys up was hardly in the clouds, but I smiled. 'Just where you should be, Sylvie.'

'And where you must be, what with getting married tomorrow. Even if it is to my useless brother.' She squeezed my knee and I felt myself blush with pleasure.

'You really love him, don't you?' she asked.

I nodded.

Sylvie sighed. 'He never comes to see me, you know. I know he's fallen out with Roy good and proper over this best man thing, but he could come by when Roy's not about, couldn't he?' She looked me in the face, her eyes wide and clear. 'Will you ask him to, Marion? Tell him not to be a stranger.'

I said I would. I hadn't realised Tom and Roy's rift was quite so bad.

We drank our stout and Sylvie talked about baby clothes and how she was worried about getting the nappies dry in the flat. As she fetched more drinks and continued to chatter, I let my mind wander to the next day's events, imagining myself on Tom's arm, my red hair catching the sunlight. We'd be showered in confetti as he looked at me so intently, as if seeing me for the first time. *Radiant.* That would be the word to come to his mind.

'Marion, you remember that thing I said to you, years ago, about Tom?' Sylvie was on her third stout and was sitting very close to me.

I caught my breath and placed my drink on the arm of the sofa, just to be able to look away. 'What thing?' I asked, my heart beating a little faster. I knew full well to what she was referring.

'That thing I said, about Tom not being, you know, like other men . . .'

That was not what she'd said, I thought. She had not said that. Not exactly.

'Do you remember, Marion?' Sylvie insisted.

I kept my eyes on the glass doors of her display cabinet. Inside, there was nothing but a blue jug with the words 'Greetings from Camber Sands' written on the side, and a photograph of Sylvie and Roy, unframed, on their wedding day, Sylvie's downcast eyes making her look even younger than her years.

'Not really,' I lied.

'Well. That's good. Because I want you to forget it. I mean, none of us thought he'd get married, and now here you are . . .'

There was a small silence, and then I said, having managed to calm my heart by concentrating on the photograph of Sylvie's wedding, 'Yes. Here we are.'

Sylvie seemed to exhale. 'So he must have changed, or maybe we were wrong, or something, but either way I want you to forget it, Marion. I feel awful about it.'

I looked at her. Although her face was pink and fleshy, it was still attractive, and I was back on that bench, listening to her tell me about how Roy had touched her and how I should give up all hope of ever gaining her brother's affection.

'I don't even remember what you said, Sylvie,' I stated. 'So let's just drop it, shall we?'

We sat in silence for a while. I could feel Sylvie groping around for the right thing to say. Eventually she came up with, 'Soon we'll both be married ladies, pushing our prams along the seafront.' And for some reason, this utterance seemed to increase my irritation.

I stood up. 'Actually, I plan to keep working at the school, so we'll probably put off having children for a bit.' The truth was, children hadn't featured in my daydreams about marriage to Tom at all. I hadn't even considered the prospect. I'd never imagined myself with a pram. I'd only imagined myself on his arm.

Making some excuse about having to rise early to make my preparations for the wedding, I fetched my coat. Sylvie said nothing. She walked with me into the chilly corridor and watched in silence as I waited for the lift.

When the lift doors opened, I didn't look back to say goodbye, but Sylvie called out: 'Get Tom to come here, won't you?' and, still not looking back, I grunted my assent.

'And Marion?'

I had no choice but to hold the lift and wait. 'Yes?' I asked, fixing my gaze on the button that said 'Ground'.

'Good luck.'

Our 'honeymoon' was a night at the Old Ship Hotel. We'd talked vaguely about a few days in Weymouth at some other time, but since Tom wasn't due any leave for a while, that would have to wait.

The Ship, whilst not quite the Grand, had the kind of hushed glamour that I found very impressive at the time. We both fell silent as we pushed through the revolving glass doors into the lobby. The thickly carpeted floor creaked and groaned reassuringly beneath our feet, and I repressed the urge to comment on the place even *sounding* like an old ship. Tom's father had paid for the room and for dinner as a wedding gift. It was the first time either of us had spent a night at a hotel, and I think we both experienced a slight panic at not knowing the etiquette of such places. In the films I'd seen there were bellboys who manhandled your luggage, and desk clerks who wanted to know your personal details, but all was quiet that afternoon in the Ship. I had a small case, in which I'd packed a new lace-trimmed nightgown, the palest apricot in colour, bought especially for the occasion. I'd already changed from my wedding dress into a twinset, with a short bouclé jacket, and I felt just about smart enough. My shoes were not new, and were badly scuffed around the toes, but I tried not to dwell on it. Tom had only a canvas bag with him, and I wished he'd brought a suitcase, so as to look more the part. But, I thought, that was how men did things. They travelled light. They didn't make a fuss.

'Shouldn't there be someone here?' Tom asked, peering about the place for signs of life. He approached the desk and placed both his hands on the shining surface. There was a gold-coloured bell very close to his hand, but he didn't touch it. Instead he waited, drumming his fingers on the wood and staring at the glass-panelled door behind the desk.

I made a little circuit behind him, taking in the menu board for the night (*sole au vin blanc*, lemon tart) and the list of conferences and balls for the coming week. I didn't quite dare to sit in one of the high-backed leather armchairs, in case someone should appear and ask me if I wanted a drink. Instead, I made another circuit. And still Tom waited. And still no one came.

Not wanting to keep going round in circles, I paused at the desk and brought my hand down sharply on the bell. The clear ringing sound echoed around the lobby, making Tom flinch. 'I could've done that,' he hissed.

Immediately a man with polished black hair and a starched

white jacket appeared. His eyes shifted from Tom to me and back again before he managed a smile. 'So sorry to keep you waiting, Mr and Mrs . . .'

'Burgess,' said Tom, before I could. 'Mr and Mrs Thomas Burgess.'

Tom's father's budget didn't quite stretch to a sea view. Our room was at the back of the hotel, overlooking a courtyard where the staff gathered to gossip and smoke. Once inside, Tom wouldn't sit down. Instead he stalked the place, plucking at the heavy crimson curtains that covered most of the window, stroking the liver-coloured eiderdown, exclaiming over luxuries ('They've got a mixer tap!'), just as he'd done when we were at your flat, Patrick. After a struggle with the catch and a terrible squeal of wood, he managed to get the window open, letting in the afternoon whine of the seagulls.

'Are you all right?' I asked. This wasn't what I'd meant to say. *Come away from the window and kiss me*, was what I'd wanted to say. I'd even thought, briefly, of saying nothing at all; of just beginning to undress. It was still early; not past five in the afternoon, but we were newly-weds. In a hotel. In Brighton. Where things like that happen all the time.

He gave me his lovely grin. 'Never been better.' He came over and kissed my cheek. I moved my hand up towards his hair, but he was already back at the window again, twitching the curtains and looking out. 'I was thinking,' he said, 'we should have some fun. It is our honeymoon.'

'Oh yes?'

'We could pretend we're holidaymakers,' he said, pulling on his jacket. 'There's plenty of time before dinner. Let's go on the pier.'

It was still raining. Going on to the pier, or going out at

all, was the last thing I wanted to do. I'd imagined an hour's intimacy – *canoodling*, as we called it then, and sweet talk about being newly married – followed by dinner, followed, swiftly, by bed.

It may sound to you, Patrick, as though I was interested only in one thing. You may even be surprised to think of me, in 1958, as a twenty-one-year-old girl who couldn't wait to lose her virginity. These things are commonplace now, and at a much earlier age, too; although, if truth be told, I believe I was a late starter, even for 1958. Certainly I remember feeling that I should be a little scared, at least, by the prospect of sleeping with Tom. It wasn't as though I'd any experience at all, or knew much about the act itself, save what Sylvie and I had gleaned, years ago, from the copy of *Married Love* she'd stolen from somewhere. But I'd read plenty of novels, and I fully expected a sort of romantic mist to descend as soon as Tom and I were between the sheets, followed by some mysterious, mystical state called 'ecstasy'. Pain and embarrassment didn't enter my head. I trusted that he would know what to do, and that I would be transported, body and soul.

As Tom smiled and held his hand out to me, I knew I should pretend that I was nervous, however. A good, virginal bride would be timid; she would be relieved that her husband had invited her out walking, rather than jumping straight into bed.

And so, a few minutes later, we were strolling arm in arm towards the noise and lights of the Palace Pier.

My jacket was a pretty flimsy affair, and I clung to Tom's arm as we sheltered beneath one of the hotel's umbrellas. I was glad there'd been only one available, so we had to share. We rushed across King's Road, were splashed by a passing bus, and Tom paid for us to go through the turnstiles. The wind threatened to blow our umbrella into the sea, but Tom kept a firm grip, despite the waves foaming around the pier's iron legs and throwing shingle up the beach. We battled past the sodden deckchairs, fortune-tellers and doughnut stalls, my hair coarsening in the wind, and my hand, clutching the umbrella above Tom's, going numb. Tom's face and body seemed set in a determined grimace against the weather.

'Let's go back . . .' I began, but the wind must have stolen my voice, for Tom ploughed ahead and shouted, 'Helter-skelter? House of Hades? Or ghost train?'

It was then I started to laugh. What else could I do, Patrick? Here was I, on my honeymoon, battered by a wet wind on the Palace Pier, when our warm hotel bedroom – bed still immaculately made – was only yards away, and my new husband was asking me to choose between fairground rides.

'I'm for the helter-skelter,' I said, and started running towards the blue and red striped turret. The slide – then called 'The Joy Glide' – was such a familiar sight, and yet I'd never actually been down it. Suddenly it seemed like a good idea. My feet were soaked and freezing, and moving them at least warmed them a little. (Tom has never felt the cold, did you notice that? A little later in our marriage, I wondered if all that sea swimming had developed a protective layer of seal-like fat, just beneath the surface of his skin. And whether that explained his lack of response to my touch. My tough, beautiful sea creature.)

The girl in the booth – black pigtails and pale pink lipstick – took our money and handed us a couple of mats. 'One at a time,' she ordered. 'No sharing mats.'

It was a relief to get inside the wooden tower, out of the wind. Tom followed me up the stairs. Every ten or so steps, we caught a glimpse of the grey sky outside. The further we ascended, the louder the wind howled. Halfway to the top, something made me stop and say, 'Hang her. We can share a mat. We're newly-weds.' And I threw mine down the stairs. It landed with a whump, having narrowly missed Tom's startled face. He laughed nervously. 'Will there be room?' he asked, but I ignored him and ran the rest of the way to the top without stopping. The floorboards of the narrow platform thrummed in the wind. I took in great gulps of salty air. From there, I could see the lights coming on in all the rooms of the Ship Hotel, and I thought again of our bed with its thick cover and its sheets ironed to perfect slipperiness.

'Hurry up,' I called. 'I can't get down without you.'

When he emerged, he looked very pale, and before I could think about it, I stepped forward, grasped his face between my hands and kissed his cold mouth. It was a brief kiss, but his lips didn't stiffen, and afterwards, as if catching his breath, he leant his head on my shoulder. He was shaking a little, and I breathed a sigh of relief. At last. He had responded to me.

Then he said, 'Marion. You'll think I'm a coward, but I don't like heights very much.'

I looked out over the churning sea and tried to take in this information. Tom Burgess, sea-swimmer and policeman, was afraid because he was standing at the top of a helter-skelter. Up until that moment, he'd seemed wholly capable, unflappable, even. And now here was this weakness. And here was my chance to tend to him. I held him close, smelling the newness of his suit, and was surprised by the warmth of him, even in this cold, exposed spot. I could have suggested we walk back down the steps, but I knew his pride would be wounded, and I also did not want to forfeit my chance of sharing a mat with my new husband, the two of us clinging to each other as we rushed down the slide. 'We'd better go down, then, hadn't we?' I said. 'I'll get on first, and you sit behind.'

He was holding on to the rail, his eyes fixed on my face, and I knew I had only to suggest an action for him to perform it; if I just kept talking in my best soothing-but-firm schoolteacher's voice, he would do anything I asked. Nodding dumbly, he watched as I sat on the prickly mat. 'Come on,' I instructed. 'We'll be down in no time.'

He sat behind me and wrapped his arms around my waist. I leant into him, feeling his belt buckle against the small of my back. The wind blew about us, and at least a hundred feet below, the sea foamed.

'Ready?'

His thighs were squeezing the breath out of me. I heard a grunt, took it for a 'yes', and pushed us off as strongly as I could. As soon as we moved, Tom gripped me tighter. We gathered speed around the first bend, and on the next we were going so fast that even I thought we might crash through the side and sail out over the water. Blaring music, coming from the pier's tannoy, warped and waved as we went, and the greyness of the day became a sudden blast of refreshing air, a thrilling glimpse of the waves below. For a moment, it seemed as if there were nothing between us and the deep, save for a square of raffia mat. I screamed in delight, Tom's clinging thighs forcing my squeals to a higher pitch, and it wasn't until we were nearly at the bottom that I realised it wasn't just me making a noise; Tom was wailing, too.

We overshot the end of the slide by quite some distance and crashed into the fence surrounding the mats. Our limbs were tangled in all sorts of impossible ways, but Tom was still gripping me around the waist. I began to laugh wildly, my wet cheek touching his, his breath heavy on my neck. At that moment, everything in me relaxed, and I thought – it's going to be all right. Tom needs me. We are married and it's going to be just fine.

Tom disentangled his body from mine and brushed his suit down.

'Shall we do it again?' I asked, jumping up.

He rubbed at his face. 'God, no . . .' he groaned. 'Please don't make me.'

'I'm your wife. It's our honeymoon. And I want to go again,' I said, laughing and tugging at his hand. His fingers, I noticed, were slippery with sweat.

'Can't we just go for a cup of tea?'

'Certainly not.'

Tom eyed me uncertainly, not sure if I was joking. 'Why don't you go again, and I'll watch,' he suggested, fetching the umbrella from the stand at the side of the booth.

'But it's no fun without you,' I pouted.

I was enjoying this new feeling of careless flirtation, but again Tom seemed unsure how to react.

After a pause, he said, 'As your husband, I am commanding you to come back to the hotel with me.' And he slipped an arm around my waist.

We kissed once, very softly, and without a word I let him lead me back to the Ship.

All through dinner I couldn't stop smiling and laughing at the slightest thing. Perhaps it was the relief of the wedding being over, perhaps it was the excitement of the helter-skelter, perhaps it was the anticipation of what was to come. Whatever it was, I had a breathless feeling of rushing towards something, headlong, unheeding.

Tom grinned, nodded, responded with a chuckle when I completed a long monologue about why the hotel was very like an old ship (the creaking floors, the flapping doors, the wind battering the windows, the staff looking a little seasick), but I got the impression he was simply waiting for this slightly hysterical mood to pass. I rushed on regardless, eating hardly a thing, drinking too much wine, and laughing openly at the waiter's waddling gait.

In our room, Tom switched on the bedside lamps and hung up his jacket whilst I collapsed on the bed, giggling. He'd ordered two glasses of Scotch to be brought up to us; when the boy appeared at the door with a small tray, Tom thanked him in the poshest voice I'd ever heard him use (he must have learned it from you), and I giggled all the more.

He sat on the edge of the bed, drank back his whisky, and said, 'Why are you laughing?'

'I suppose I must be happy,' I replied, gulping down a burning swig of Scotch.

'That's good,' he said. And then: 'Shall we get ready for bed? It's late.' I liked the first half of that sentence: he'd used the word *bed*; but I didn't much care for the second, with its tone of practicality, its suggestion of sleep. 'Do you want to use the bathroom?' he continued.

He was still using the quiet, drawn-out, slightly upper-class tone he'd tried out on the boy at the door. I sat fully upright, my head swimming a little. No, I wanted to say. No, I don't want to use the bathroom. I want you to undress me, here on the bed. I want you to unzip my skirt, unhook my new lacy bra, and gasp at the beauty of my naked breasts.

Of course I said nothing of the kind. Instead, I went into the bathroom, slammed the door, sat on the edge of the tub and suppressed the urge to giggle. I took several deep breaths. Was Tom undressing on the other side of the door? Should I surprise him by bursting into the room wearing only my slip?

I looked at myself in the mirror. My cheeks were blotchy and the wine had stained my lips brown. Did I look different now I was married? Would I look different in the morning?

When we'd first arrived at the hotel I'd unpacked my new nightdress and hung it on the back of the bathroom door, hoping Tom would spot it and be tantalised by the sight of its plunging neckline, the long split up one side. Leaving my skirt and twinset in a heap on the floor, I now pulled the nightdress over my head and combed my hair until it crackled. Then I brushed my teeth and opened the door.

The bedroom was dim. Tom had turned off all the lights, apart from the lamp on his side of the bed. Between the sheets and the pillow, his pyjama-jacketed shoulders lay straight and still. His eyes followed me as I approached the bed, pulled back the sheet and climbed in beside him. By this point, my heart was clattering about in my chest, and the urge to laugh had left me completely. What would I do if he merely switched off the light, said good night and turned his back to me? What, Patrick, could I possibly have done about that? As we lay there, not moving, my teeth began to chatter. I could not be the one to touch him first. We were finally married, but I had no right, I felt, to make any demands. As far as I knew, physical demands could not be made by wives. Women who pleaded for sexual contact were abhorrent, unnatural.

'You look nice,' said Tom, and I turned to smile at him, but he'd already turned off the light. My body stiffened. So that was it, then. Sleep was all that lay ahead. There was the longest silence. Then his hand brushed my cheek. 'All right?' he asked, softly, and I had no answer.

'Marion? Are you all right?' I nodded, and he must have felt the movement, because his big body shifted towards mine, and then his lips were on my mouth. Such warm lips. I wanted to lose myself then. I wanted that kiss to transport me, as the novels I'd read suggested it would. And it did, a little; I opened my mouth to let more of Tom in. Then he began to tug at my nightdress, pulling great handfuls of it up around my waist. I tried to move to make it easier for him, but it was difficult to do so when his other hand was on my hip, pinning me to the bed. My breath quickened; I stroked his face. 'Oh Tom,' I whispered, and saying it made me feel as though this was actually happening to me, here and now, in this pristine bed in the Old Ship Hotel. My new husband was making love to me. Tom planted his elbows on either side of my shoulders and heaved his whole body on to mine. I placed my hands on the small of his back and realised he'd taken off his pyjama bottoms. I let my hands stray to his buttocks, which were smoother than I could ever have imagined. He took a few lunges towards me. I knew he was nowhere near the target, but could say nothing. For one thing, I was holding my breath. For another, I didn't want to spoil things by uttering something inappropriate.

After a while, he paused, panting slightly, and said, 'Do you think you could – open your legs a bit more?'

I did as I was asked, thankful to shift down beneath him and wrap my thighs about his hips. He made no sound as he managed to enter me. What I felt was a sharp pain, but I told myself this would pass. We were there now. Ecstasy couldn't be far away.

And it was wonderful, holding on to Tom as he moved in me, feeling his sweat on my fingers, his breath hot at my neck. Just the unbelievable closeness of him had a wonder about it.

But Patrick, I knew even then – although I doubt I admitted this to myself at the time – that the delicacy with which he'd held me during our swimming lessons was absent. As he made his thrusts, I found myself picturing that scene once again, imagining how I'd gone under and Tom had found me, how he'd held me at the waist as I'd floated in the salty water, how he'd carried me back to shore.

Suddenly Tom held his breath, made one last thrust that caused me almost to moan in pain, then collapsed by my side.

I stroked his hair. When he'd got his breath back he said, very quietly, 'Was that all right?' but I couldn't reply because by then I was weeping, using my every muscle to do it silently and without moving. It was the relief of it all, and the wonder of it, and the disappointment. So I pretended not to have heard his question, and he kissed my hand, turned over and went to sleep.

I tell you all this, Patrick, so you'll know how it was between me and Tom. So you'll know there was tenderness, as well as pain. So you'll know how we failed, both of us, but also how we both tried.

We're tired today. I was up most of the night writing, and now, at eleven thirty in the morning, I've only just sat down with a coffee after bathing and dressing you, giving you breakfast and moving your body so you can look out of the window, although I know you'll be asleep again within the hour. It's stopped raining but the wind is up and I've turned the heating on, giving the house a dry, dusty smell that I find quite comforting.

I wonder how much longer we have, if I'm honest, to get through this story. And I wonder how much time I have to persuade Tom to talk to you. Last night he didn't sleep well either – I heard him get up at least three times. It won't surprise you to know we've had separate rooms for many years now. During the day he goes out, and I don't ask him where he spends his hours any more. I stopped asking at least twenty years ago, after I received the answer I'd known was coming. Tom was on his way to work, I remember, and was wearing his security guard's uniform. It was very shiny, that uniform – all silver buttons and epaulettes and a big belt buckle at the waist. A poor imitation of a policeman's uniform, but Tom looked striking in it, nevertheless. He was on night shifts at the time. On my enquiry about how he spent the day whilst I was at work, he looked me in the face and said, 'I meet strangers. Sometimes we have a drink. Sometimes we have sex. That's what I do, Marion. Please don't ask me about it again.'

On hearing that, there was a part of me that was relieved, because I knew I hadn't totally destroyed my husband.

Perhaps he still meets strangers. I don't know. I know that on most days he takes Walter for lengthy walks across the downs. I used to volunteer at the local primary on Tuesdays, helping the little ones with their reading, and Tom would stay indoors on that day. But since you came, I've told the school I'm no longer available, and so Tom goes wandering every day of the week. He is a busy man. He has always been good at being busy. He swims every morning, even now. No more than fifteen minutes, but still he drives down to Telscombe Cliffs and enters the icy water. I don't need to tell you, Patrick, that for a man of sixty-three, he is remarkably fit. He never let himself go. He keeps a close eye on his weight, hardly ever takes a drink, swims, walks the dog, and watches documentaries in the evening. Anything involving real-life crime interests him, which always surprises me, considering what happened. And he talks to no one. Least of all to me.

You see, the truth is he didn't want you to come here. It was my idea. In fact, I insisted. You'll find it hard to believe, but in over forty years of marriage, I've never insisted on anything like I insisted on this.

Every morning I hope my husband won't leave the house. But since the morning when I tried to have you sit at what Nurse Pamela calls the 'family table', Tom doesn't even break-fast with us. I used to find his absence something of a relief, after everything we'd been through, but now I want him here by my side. And I want him by your side, too. I hope that he will join us in your room, if only for a little while. I hope that he will come and at least look at you – really look at you – and see what I can see: that despite everything, you still love him. I hope this will break his silence.

Instead of four days in Weymouth, you offered us the use of your cottage on the Isle of Wight over half-term.

Although I had my misgivings, I was so desperate to escape from the separate-beds arrangement at Tom's parents' house, into which we'd moved while we were waiting for a police house, that I agreed. (There wasn't the space, Tom said, for a double bed in his room, so I'd ended up in Sylvie's old room.) Tom and I would have four nights to ourselves, and you'd join us for the final three, in order to 'show us around the place'. It would mean a whole week away, and for most of that time I'd be alone with Tom. So I agreed.

The cottage was not at all what I'd imagined. When you'd said cottage, I'd presumed you were being modest, and that what you really meant was 'small mansion', or, at the very least, 'well-appointed seaside villa'.

But no. Cottage was a more than accurate description. It was situated down a gloomy narrow lane in Bonchurch, not far from the sea, but not near enough to afford a view of the coast. The whole place was dank and close-feeling. There were two bedrooms, the double with a sloping ceiling and a sagging bed. At the front was an overgrown garden, and out the back, a privy. There was a tiny kitchen with no electricity, but the cottage did stretch to gas. Every window was small and rather grubby.

As we walked down that lane, the fruity stink of wild garlic was overwhelming. Even inside the cottage, with its mingled odours of damp rugs and gas, I could smell the stuff. I wondered how anyone could bring themselves to eat such a foul-smelling substance. To me it smacked of nothing so much as overripe sweat. I'm quite fond of garlic now, but back then, just walking along that lane with its banks of green tongues and white flowers, the heat and the smell rising, almost made me gag.

Still, it was a sunny week, and during our days alone, Tom and I indulged in all the usual holidaymaker activities. We walked along Blackgang Chine, saw a Punch and Judy show at Ventnor (Tom laughed very hard when the policeman appeared), visited the model village at Godshill. Tom bought me a coral necklace, the colour of peaches and cream. Each morning he cooked us bacon and eggs, and whilst I ate he would suggest a plan for the day, to which I always agreed. At night I was glad of the sagging bed – it rolled the two of us together, so we had to sleep very close. I spent many hours awake, enjoying the way my body would lock helplessly against his, my stomach filling the hollow of his back, my breasts squashed against his shoulders. Sometimes I blew softly on the back of his neck to wake him. We managed a repeat performance of our wedding night on the evening we arrived, and I remember there was less pain, but it was over very quickly. Still, I felt we could improve. I thought that if I could find a way to encourage Tom, to guide him without instructing him, then perhaps our bedroom activities would become more agreeable. It was early on in our marriage, after all, and hadn't Tom told me, that night at your flat, that he'd had very little experience?

And then you arrived. I almost laughed when I saw you drive up in your green Fiat sports car, from which you jumped and collected your matching luggage. You wore a light suit with a red cravat tied loosely about your neck, and you looked like the perfect English gent on his spring break. As I watched from the bedroom window, I noticed your slight frown dissolve into a smile when Tom came down the path to meet you.

In the kitchen, I unloaded the boxes of supplies you'd brought – olive oil, bottles of red wine, a bunch of fresh asparagus, purchased, you said, from a charming roadside stall en route.

'I'm so sorry about that bed,' you announced, when we'd all had a cup of tea. 'It's an awful old thing, isn't it? Like trying to sleep in a shifting sandpit.'

I reached for Tom's hand. 'We don't mind at all,' I said.

You stroked your moustache and glanced down at the table before announcing that you'd like to stretch your legs with a walk to the sea. Tom jumped up, saying he'd join you. The two of you, he informed me, would be back in time for lunch.

You must have seen my startled face, because you put a hand on Tom's shoulder and said, looking at me, 'In actual fact, I've brought a picnic with me. Let's all go down and spend the day, shall we? Shame to waste this glorious weather, don't you think, Marion?'

I was grateful to you for your graciousness.

Over the next few days, you showed us the coastal paths along the south of the island. As we walked, you made sure I was positioned between the two of you wherever the path allowed, guiding me to your side with a firm hand, never allowing me to lag behind. You seemed a bit obsessed with the stone that made up the landscape, telling us how each different type of rock, pebble and grain of sand was formed, pointing out the different sizes, shapes, colours. You referred to the landscape as *sculptural*, and talked of *nature's palette* and the texture of her *materials*.

During one particularly long walk, when my shoes had started to pinch, I commented: 'It's all an artwork to you, isn't it?'

You stopped and looked at me, your face serious. 'Of course. It's the great artwork. The one we're all trying to imitate.'

Tom looked very impressed with this answer, and to my annoyance, I could think of absolutely no reply.

Every night you cooked dinner for us, spending hours in the kitchen preparing your dishes. I still remember what we had: beef bourguignon one night, chicken chasseur the next, and on the last night, salmon in a hollandaise sauce. The idea that you could successfully prepare and eat such sauces at home, rather than in some fancy restaurant, was novel to me. Tom would sit at the kitchen table and talk to you whilst you cooked, but I generally kept out of the way, taking the opportunity to disappear with a novel. I've always found too much socialising very tiring, and although I was still at a stage where I quite enjoyed your company, I needed to escape now and then.

After we'd finished our meals, which were always delicious, we'd sit and drink wine by candlelight. Even Tom acquired a taste for your reds. You'd talk about art and literature, of course, which Tom and I both lapped up, but you also encouraged me to talk about teaching, about my family, and about my views on 'the position of women in society', as you put it. On the second evening, after the chicken chasseur and too many glasses of Beaujolais, you asked me for an opinion on working mothers. What effect did I think they had on family life? Was adolescent delinquency the fault of the working mother? I knew there'd been a big debate about this in the papers recently. One woman – a schoolteacher in fact – had been blamed for her son's death from pneumonia. It was said that if she'd been at home more she would have spotted the seriousness of the boy's illness much earlier, and his life would have been spared.

Although I'd read about the case with some interest – mainly because it involved a schoolteacher – I didn't feel quite ready to voice an opinion on the matter. All I had to go on, at the time, were my feelings. I didn't seem to have the words, back then, to talk about such things. Even so, encouraged by the wine and your intent, interested face, I admitted that I wouldn't want to give up work, even if I had children.

I saw a little smile form beneath your moustache.

Tom, who'd been busy playing with a puddle of candle wax during this conversation, looked up. 'What was that?'

'Marion was just saying she'd like to continue to work after you have children,' you informed him, watching my face as you spoke.

Tom said nothing for a moment.

'I haven't made any real decisions,' I said. 'We'd have to talk about it.'

'Why would you want to carry on working?' asked Tom, with that deliberate mildness to his voice that I would later recognise as rather dangerous. At the time, though, I did not understand this warning.

'I think Marion's quite right.' You filled Tom's wine glass to the brim. 'Why shouldn't mothers go out to work? Especially if their children are in school. It would have done my own mother the power of good to have some profession, some *purpose*.'

'But you had a nanny, didn't you? And you were away at boarding school most of the time.' Tom pushed his glass away. 'It was completely different for you.'

'Unfortunately, yes.' You grinned at me.

'No child of mine . . .' Tom began, then trailed off. 'Children need their mothers,' he began again. 'There'd be no need for you to go to work, Marion. I could provide for a family. That's the father's job.'

Back then, I was surprised by the strength of Tom's feelings on the matter. Now, looking back, I can understand them more. Tom was always close to his own mother. When she died, over ten years ago now, he took to his bed for a fortnight. Until then, he'd seen her every week without fail, usually alone. During the early days of our marriage, if I entered my mother-in-law's house I would remain largely silent, whilst Tom filled her in on his latest triumphs on the force. Sometimes, I knew, they were fabricated, but I never tackled him about it. She was immensely proud of him; the place was decorated with photographs of her son in uniform, and he returned the compliment by taking round catalogues of outsized clothes and suggesting which ones might suit her. Towards the end, he even chose and ordered the clothes for her.

'No one's debating your fitness to be a father, Tom,' you said, your voice soft and consoling. 'But what about what Marion wants?'

'Isn't all this a bit theoretical?' I asked, trying to giggle. 'We may not even be lucky enough to have children—'

'Of course we will,' Tom stated, reaching over and placing a warm hand on mine.

'That's not what we're discussing,' you said, quickly. 'We're discussing whether mothers should go out to work—'

'Which they shouldn't,' said Tom.

You laughed. 'You're very categorical about that, Tom. I didn't have you down as being so – well, *suburban* about it.'

Again you laughed, but Tom did not. 'What do you know about it?' he demanded, his voice low.

'We're just debating the issue, aren't we? Chewing the proverbial fat.'

'You don't know anything about it, though, do you?'

I stood and began to clear the plates, sensing a growing tension that I didn't quite understand. But Tom continued, his voice rising, 'You know nothing about children, or about being a parent. And you know nothing about being married.'

Even though you managed to keep smiling, a shadow passed across your face as you muttered, 'And long may that remain the case.'

I set about bringing through dessert, talking all the time about what a wonderful apple and rhubarb tart you'd made (your pastry was always better than mine – it melted on the tongue), giving the two of you time to gather yourselves. I knew Tom's moods blew over fairly quickly, and if I could just keep twittering on about custard and spoons and fruit fillings, everything would be all right.

You may have wondered, even at the time, why I did this. Why didn't I let the row build to a climax, and have us pack up and leave? Why did I sit on the fence, unable either to defend my husband or to push him to denounce you? Although I hadn't yet admitted the truth about you and Tom to myself, I still couldn't bear to see how easily you provoked his passion, how obviously he cared about what you thought of him. I didn't want to think about what that might mean.

But it was also that I agreed with what you said. I thought women who went to work could also be good mothers. I knew you were right and Tom was wrong. And this wasn't the last time I would feel this, although each time it happened, I continued to deny it.

On our last day on the island, I got my own way about a trip to Osborne House. I've never been that interested in royalty, but I've always enjoyed snooping around stately homes, and it seemed to me that a visit to the Isle of Wight wasn't complete without taking a look at Queen Victoria's holiday home. Back then, the place was open only on certain afternoons and many of the rooms were out of bounds to visitors. There was certainly no gift shop, tearoom, or even much information; the whole thing had a rather musty, forbidden flavour. It was as though you were prying on a private world, albeit one that had come to an end many years ago, and that was exactly what I liked about it.

You objected, mildly, to the idea, but after the previous night's discussion, Tom was on my side, and we ignored your smiling protestations about the terrible taste of the royals and their second-rate furnishings, and being herded around with a load of tourists (what made us so different from them, I didn't ask). Eventually you relented and drove us there.

No one's making you come, I thought. Tom and I could go alone. But you joined us in the queue for tickets and even managed, towards the end of the tour, to stop rolling your eyes at everything the guide told us.

The most striking part of the house was the Durbar Room, which seemed to have been fashioned completely from ivory and was almost blinding in its whiteness. Every surface was embellished: the ceiling deeply coffered, the walls sporting intricate ivory carvings. Even you stopped talking as we entered. The long windows looked out on a shining Solent, but inside it was pure Anglo-India. The guide told us about the Agra carpet, the chimneypiece and overmantel, shaped like a peacock, and, most wonderful of all, the miniature maharajah's palace, carved from bone. When I peered inside, I could see the maharajahs themselves, their tiny glittering shoes turned up at the ends. The guide said the room was the Queen's attempt to create a corner of India on the Isle of Wight. Although she'd never been there herself, she was entranced by Prince Albert's tales of his travels on the subcontinent, and she even employed a particular Indian boy, to whom she became very close, as a personal secretary, although he, like all servants, was instructed to look away when he spoke to his sovereign. There was a photograph of this boy in the room, wearing the turban that the Queen had apparently insisted he thread with gold, although it wasn't his custom. His eyes were large and serious-looking; his skin gleamed. I imagined him unlooping the turban to reveal the black snake of his hair, and Victoria – fifty-something, trussed up in corsets, her own hair tied so tightly it must have made her eyes ache – watching, and longing to touch it. He looked like a beautiful girl, that boy. No wonder they went in for beards and swords, I thought.

Although the room struck me as incredibly frivolous and even verging on the immoral – all those elephant tusks, just for the amusement of a queen with a liking for the exotic – I knew what you meant when you praised its audacity, its *fabulously pointless beauty*, as you put it. In fact, I was so engrossed in the place that I didn't notice you and Tom slip out of the room. When I looked up from studying yet another embroidery fashioned from a million gold threads, the two of you were nowhere to be seen.

Then I caught a flash of your red cravat, out amongst the topiary. Our guide had begun preparing the group to leave, but I hung back, close to the window. Tom, I now saw, was standing, hands in pockets, half hidden by a tall shrub. You were facing him. Neither of you were smiling, or saying a word; you were just looking, as intensely as I'd looked at the photograph of the Indian boy. Your bodies were close, your eyes locked, and as your hand fell on Tom's upper arm, I was sure I saw my husband's eyes close and his mouth fall open, just for a moment.

Last night, while you were sleeping, I stayed awake in the hope of being able to talk to Tom. This involved a disruption to our usual routine, which has been in place now ever since we both retired, and goes as follows. Every evening I prepare a rather lacklustre meal, nothing like the feasts you used to offer us: oven-ready lasagne, a chicken pie or a few sausages from the butcher in Peacehaven, who somehow manages to be both surly and obsequious. We eat at the kitchen table, perhaps engage in a little conversation about the dog or the news, after which I wash up whilst Tom takes Walter for his final walk around the block. We then watch television for an hour or so. Tom buys the *Radio Times* every week and highlights the programmes he doesn't want to miss using a yellow marker pen. We have a satellite dish, and so he has access to the History Channel and National Geographic.

While Tom watches another documentary about polar bears, how Caesar built his empire, or Al Capone, I tend to read the newspaper or complete the crossword, and it's no later than ten o'clock when I turn in, leaving him to at least another two hours' viewing.

As you'll have gathered, there is something about this routine that inhibits real conversation or deviation of any kind. There is also, I think, something about it that both Tom and I find reassuring.

Since you've been with us, I make sure you have your meal, which I feed you from a spoon to avoid upsets, before Tom and I sit down to ours. And even though you are in your bed in the room down the hall, we do not speak of your presence.

Lately, though, I've got into the habit of sitting with you whilst my husband watches television. Tom has said nothing about it, but rather than joining him in the living room, I sit at your bedside and read aloud. We are currently enjoying *Anna Karenina*. Although you still cannot speak yourself, I know you understand every word I read, Patrick, and not just because you are doubtless very familiar with the novel. I see you close your eyes and enjoy the rhythm of the sentences. Your face becomes still, your shoulders relax, and the only sound apart from my voice is the television's regular hum coming from the living room. Tolstoy's grip on the female mind is, I've always thought, remarkable. Last night I read one of my favourite sections: Dolly's reflections on the sufferings of pregnancy and childbirth, and tears came to my eyes because so often, over the years, I've longed for those sufferings, imagining that a child could have brought Tom and me closer together – despite everything, I'm convinced he wanted children; and even when I knew this could never happen, I imagined a child might bring me closer to myself.

Whilst I cried, you looked at me. Your eyes, which have a pickled look about them these days, were soft. I chose to interpret this as a look of sympathy. 'Sorry,' I said, and you made a slight movement with your head – hardly a nod, but close enough, perhaps.

When I left your room I felt curiously elated, and perhaps it was this that made me sit, fully clothed, on the edge of my bed until past one o'clock in the morning, waiting for Tom to retire.

Eventually I heard his light tread on the hallway runner, his loud yawn.

'You're late turning in.' I stood in my doorway and kept my voice low. He looked startled for a moment, then his face crumpled back into tiredness.

'Can I have a word?' I held my door open by way of invitation, feeling again like the deputy head during my last days at St Luke's, when I often had to have a 'little chat' with a new teacher about taking the responsibilities of playground duty seriously, or the dangers of becoming too close to the more needy children.

He looked at his watch. I held the door open a little wider. 'Please,' I added.

My husband didn't sit in my bedroom. Instead, he paced around as if the place were deeply unfamiliar to him (which I suppose, in some ways, it is). It reminded me of our first night together at the Ship. My bedroom is very different to that room, though: instead of curtains, I have a practical wooden-slat blind; instead of an embroidered eiderdown, I have a duvet cover that needs no ironing. These items I purchased, along with the bedroom furniture, from IKEA when we moved in. I gave the whole exercise very little thought, and IKEA helped me, as they said, to 'chuck out the chintz'. And so out went all the bits and pieces I'd inherited from Mum and Dad – not that there was much: a fringed standard lamp, a wall mirror with ornamental shelves, a scratched oak table – and in came the IKEA look. I wanted blankness, I suppose. Not so much an attempt at a new start as a refusal to engage with the process. Perhaps a longing to negate myself from the location altogether. To this end, the walls are painted a biscuity shade, and all the furniture is made of artificial wood in a colour they call 'blonde'. That word makes me smile – such an odd word to apply to a wardrobe. *Blonde.* It's so glamorous, so voluptuous. Bombshells are blonde. And sirens. And Tom, of course, although now his hair is grey; still thick, but without the shine of youth.

My one extravagance in the room is the floor-to-ceiling bookcase that I had built along one wall. I'd always admired your bookshelves at Chichester Terrace. Of course, mine are nowhere near as impressive as yours, which were fashioned from mahogany and were filled with leather-bound hardbacks and outsized art monographs. I wonder what happened to all those books. There was no sign of them in your Surrey house, where I went a month or so ago, first in a bid to find you before I knew you were in the hospital, and then to pick up some things for you to bring here. That house was a very different place to Chichester Terrace. How long must you have lived alone there, after your mother died? Over thirty years. What you did during that period I have no idea. The neighbour who told me about your stroke said you'd kept yourself to yourself but you'd always said hello and asked very attentively after his health in the street, which made me smile. That was when I knew I'd definitely found the right Patrick Hazlewood.

Tom finally came to a halt, having made a full circuit of the room, and stood in front of the blind with his arms crossed.

'It's about Patrick,' I said.

He let out a little groan. 'Marion,' he said. 'It's very late . . .'

'He asked for you. The other day. He said your name.'

Tom looked at the beige carpet. 'No. He didn't.'

'How can you know that?'

'He did not say my name.'

'I heard him, Tom. He called for you.'

Tom let out a breath, shook his head. 'He's had two major strokes, Marion. The doctor told us it's only a matter of time before there'll be another one. The man can't talk. He'll never talk again. You're imagining things.'

'There's been a real improvement,' I said, aware that I was exaggerating. After all, there's been no word from you since the day you uttered Tom's name. 'He just needs encouragement. He needs encouragement from you.'

'He's nearly eighty years old.'

'He's seventy-six.'

Tom looked me in the face then. 'We've been through all this. I don't know why you brought him here in the first place. I don't know what weird scheme you have in mind.' He gave a short laugh. 'If you want to play nursemaid, fine. But don't expect me to be part of it.'

'He has no one,' I said.

There was a long silence. Tom uncrossed his arms and drew a hand across his tired face. 'I'm going to bed now,' he said, quietly.

But I blundered on. 'He's in pain,' I said, my voice wheedling now. 'He needs you.'

Tom stopped at the door and looked back at me, his eyes glowing with anger. 'He needed me years ago, Marion,' he said. And he let himself out of the room.

Early summer 1958. It was already hot; at school, the smell of warm milk became overpowering, and the children's nap time was a lovely, drowsy affair, even for me. So when Julia proposed we take both our classes on a nature trip to Woodingdean, I jumped at the chance. The head agreed to a Friday afternoon. We were to take the bus and then walk to Castle Hill. Like most of the children, I'd never been there, and the thought of a break from the usual school routine was just as exciting to me as it was to them. We spent the whole week drawing pictures of the plants and wildlife we expected to see – hares, larks, gorse – and I got all the children to learn how to spell the words bugle, orchid and primrose. I have to admit, Patrick, that this was largely inspired by the things you'd pointed out to Tom and me, on our Isle of Wight walks.

We left school at about eleven thirty, the children clutching their packets of sandwiches, walking in a crocodile with Julia at the front and me at the back. It was a glorious day, windy but warm, and all the blowsy horse chestnuts held their candles out to us as the bus made its way over the racecourse towards Woodingdean. Milly Oliver, the quiet, rather scrawny girl with the masses of black curls from whom I'd found it hard to look away on my first day, was sick before we'd even reached the downs. Bobby Blakemore, the boy with the boot-mark hair, sat at the back of the bus and stuck out his tongue at passing cars. Alice Rumbold talked loudly all the way of the new motorbike her brother had bought, despite Julia shushing her several times. But most of the children were quiet with anticipation, looking out of the windows as we left the town behind and the hills and sea came into view.

We all got off at a stop on the outskirts of the village and Julia led the way over the downs. She was so energetic, always. At the time I found her boundless energy a little intimidating, but these days I rather long for it. She'd have you bathed in a jiffy, Patrick. On that day she wore trousers, a light pullover and sturdy shoes, but a string of bright orange beads swung from her neck and a large pair of tortoiseshell-framed sunglasses were balanced on her nose. A gaggle of children followed her, and she took every opportunity she could to touch them, I noticed. She'd pat them on the shoulder, steer them in the direction she wanted by placing a hand flat on their back, or kneel down so she was level with them, holding their elbows as she spoke. I vowed to be more like her in my approach. I rarely allowed myself to touch a child, but unlike some of the other teachers, I did not hit the children as a matter of course, and as my career progressed I felt little need of such punishments. I do remember having to give Alice Rumbold the ruler early on. She stared me in the face as I brought the wood down on her palm, her eyes steady and black; I nearly dropped my weapon, my hand was shaking so much. My own timidity, the sweatiness of my fumbling fingers and the intensity of Alice's stare actually made me hit her open hand harder than I ought, and for many weeks afterwards I regretted having done it at all.

It was a relief to drop down out of the wind and look over the deep valley. Although I'd lived in Brighton all my life, I'd never fully realised such a landscape surrounded my home town. The hills were bald of trees, but this seemed only to enhance the beauty of their curves, and their colours – everything from purplish brown to grasshopper green – sang out in the clear air. The larks were calling insistently above, just as they'd done on the Isle of Wight, and buttercups dotted the grass. We could see right down to the sea, which sent out white sparks. I stopped and stared, letting the sun warm my bare arms. I hadn't anticipated the strength of the wind up here, and had hung my cardigan on the back of my chair in the classroom, leaving only my summer blouse to protect me now.

Julia told the children they could start their lunch, and the two of us sat at the back of the group, a little apart, watching over them. Clumps of gorse, thick and prickled, surrounded us, giving off a coconutty scent that lent the whole scene something of a holiday feel.

When I'd finished my own egg and cress sandwiches, Julia offered me one of hers. 'Go on,' she said, pushing her sunglasses up into her hair. 'They're smoked salmon. A friend gets it for me on the cheap.'

I wasn't sure if I liked smoked salmon, never having tried it before, but I took a sandwich and bit into it. The flavour was intense: salty, like the sea, but with an oily mellowness. I loved it immediately.

Bobby Blakemore stood up and I commanded him to sit back down until everyone had finished their lunch. To my surprise, he obeyed instantly.

'You're getting good at this,' murmured Julia with a chuckle, and I felt myself blush with pleasure.

'So. You haven't told me about your honeymoon,' she said. 'Isle of Wight, wasn't it?'

'Yes,' I said. 'It was – well . . .' a nervous laugh escaped me. 'It was lovely.'

Julia raised her eyebrows and studied my face with such interest that I had no choice but to go on. 'We stayed in a cottage that belongs to Tom's friend Patrick. He was best man at the wedding.'

'I remember.' Julia paused to bite and chew her apple. 'That was generous of him, wasn't it?'

I looked at my nails. I hadn't told anyone that you'd joined us, not even my parents, and certainly not Sylvie.

'So you had a good time?'

There was something about the day, the warm clarity of it,

that made confession irresistible. And so I said, 'Well, yes, Tom and I had a lovely time. He came too, though.'

'Who?'

'Tom's friend. Patrick. Just for the last few days.' I took another bite of the sandwich and looked away from Julia. As soon as the words were out, I realised how dreadful they sounded. Who would endure any sort of threesome on their honeymoon? Only a damned fool.

'I see.' Julia finished her apple and threw the core into the gorse. 'Did you mind?'

I found myself unable to tell the truth. 'Not really. He's a good friend. To both of us.'

Julia nodded.

'He's an interesting man, actually,' I stumbled on. 'He's a curator at the museum. Always taking us to shows and concerts, paying for everything.'

Julia smiled. 'I liked him. He's *comme ça*, isn't he?'

I had no idea what she meant. She was looking at me rather hopefully, a little glint in her eyes, and I wanted to understand her meaning, but I could not.

Seeing my confusion, she leant towards me and said, in a voice I thought not nearly low enough, 'He's homosexual, isn't he?'

Smoked salmon turned to rancid oil in my mouth. I could hardly believe that she'd uttered the word with such careless-ness, as if she were enquiring after your star sign, or shoe size.

She must have sensed my panic, because she added, 'I mean – I thought he might be. When I met him. But maybe I'm wrong?'

I tried to swallow, but my stomach was protesting and my mouth had turned dry.

'Oh dear,' said Julia, placing a hand on my arm, just as she did when she knelt beside a child. 'I've shocked you.'

I managed to laugh. 'No, really . . .'

'I'm sorry, Marion. Perhaps I shouldn't have said that.'

Bobby Blakemore stood up once again, and I barked at him to sit down. The boy looked at me, astounded, and sank to his knees.

Julia still had a hand on my arm, and I heard her say, 'I'm such a bloody idiot – always blundering in. It's just I thought perhaps . . . well, I assumed . . .'

'It doesn't matter,' I said, standing up. 'We should get going, or the afternoon will be lost.' I clapped my hands together and ordered the children to stand.

Julia nodded, perhaps a little relieved, and took the lead, guiding the children down the hill, pointing out birds and plants as she went, naming them all. But I couldn't look at her. I couldn't look at anything save my own feet, moving heavily through the grass.

I can't say, Patrick, that I hadn't thought about it before. But up until that moment on Castle Hill, no one had spoken the word aloud to me, and I'd done my level best to press it right down in my brain and keep it in a place where it could never be fully examined. How could I begin to admit such a thing? At the time, such a thing was non-admissible. I hadn't the first idea about gay life, as I would call it now. All I knew were the headlines in the papers – the Montagu case was the most famous, but there were often smaller stories in the *Argus*, usually on page ten, sandwiched between the divorces and the traffic-law violations. 'Headmaster charged with gross indecency', or 'Businessman committed unnatural acts'. I barely looked at them. They were so regular that they seemed almost ordinary; they were something you expected to see in every newspaper, along with the weather report and the radio listings.

Looking back now, and writing this, it's obvious to me that I'd known, on some level, all along – perhaps from when Sylvie had told me that Tom wasn't *like that*, and certainly from the moment I witnessed the two of you standing together outside Osborne House. But at the time it didn't seem obvious – or, at least, *admissible* – at all, and I find it's impossible, now, to pinpoint the exact moment when I allowed the full picture to dawn on me. But the incident on Castle Hill was certainly a turning point. From then on, I could no longer avoid thinking about you, and therefore thinking about Tom, in this new way. The word had been uttered, and there was no going back.

By the time I returned home – we'd moved into a two-up, two-down terrace on Islingword Street, not a police house as we'd hoped, but one that had become available through the influence of one of Tom's colleagues on the force – I was determined to say something to my husband. Consciously, I told myself that all I was doing was giving him the chance to deny it. The matter would be cleared up quickly, and we would carry on with our lives.

I could only get as far as the words with which I'd begin: 'Julia said something awful today about Patrick.' Beyond that, I had no idea what I would say, or how far I could venture. I couldn't see past that first phrase, and I kept silently repeating it as I walked home, trying to convince myself that these were words that would actually come out of my mouth, no matter where they led.

Tom was on early shifts that week, and so was home before me. I had hoped that he wouldn't be there, giving me time to get myself settled in the house and prepare in some way for the scene that was to come. But as soon as I stepped over the threshold, I smelled soap. The house did have a bathroom upstairs and a toilet at the end of the hall, but Tom liked to strip down and wash at the kitchen sink after work. He'd fill the sink, put the kettle on, and by the time he'd scrubbed his face and neck and soaped his armpits, the water had boiled and he was ready for his cup of tea. I'd never discouraged him in this habit; in fact, I'd always enjoyed watching him wash himself in this way.

I came into the kitchen, put down my basket of books and saw his naked back. *Julia said something awful today about Patrick.* I still hadn't become used to the sight of my husband's flesh, and instead of coming straight out with it, I stopped to admire him, taking in the movement of muscled shoulder as he rubbed at his neck with a towel. The kettle was whistling, filling the small room with steam, and I took it off the ring.

Tom turned around. 'You're early today,' he said, smiling. 'How was the nature ramble?'

Despite your enthusiasm for walking, Tom was always more at home in the water, and regarded rambling as a bit of a waste of time. To him, walking wasn't quite proper exercise – not enough exertion, not enough risk. Now, of course, he spends many hours on the downs with Walter, but back then I never knew him to take a walk without having a definite destination in mind.

'Fine,' I answered, turning my back to him and busying myself with preparing the tea. *Julia said something awful today about Patrick.* The sight of him – glorious in the afternoon light coming through our small kitchen window – had scrambled my brain. It would be so much easier, I thought, to say nothing. I could just press down that word of Julia's into the place in my mind where I stored Sylvie's comments and the image of you and Tom outside Osborne House. Here was my husband, the man I'd wanted for so long, standing half-naked before me in our kitchen. I could not drag such words into our lives.

Tom patted me on the arm. 'I'll put a clean shirt on, then we'll have a cup.'

I took the tea into our front room and placed it on the table before the window, where we sat to eat our meals. We'd inherited a cloth from Tom's mother – it was mustard-coloured, made of thick velour, and I hated it. It made me think of old people's homes and funeral parlours. It was the perfect table-cloth on which to place an ugly plant, such as an aspidistra. I put my teacup down heavily, willing it to spill and stain the fabric. Then I sat and waited for Tom, looking about the room, my mind skipping from one thought to another. *Julia said something awful today about Patrick.* I had to say it. I stared at the lino, picturing the silverfish that I knew lurked beneath, metallic and wriggling. Our bedroom, which faced the street, was light and airy, with two large windows and paint instead of wallpaper, but this room was still gloomy and rather damp. I'd have to do something about it, I thought. *Julia said something awful today about Patrick.* I could buy a new lamp from one of the junk shops on Tidy Street. I could risk getting rid of this bloody tablecloth. *Julia said something awful today about Patrick.* I should have said it as soon I stepped through the door. I shouldn't have given myself time to think. *Julia said something awful today about Patrick.*

Tom came back and sat opposite me. He poured himself a cup of tea and took a long drink. Once finished, he poured another cup and drank greedily again. I watched his throat contract and his eyes close as he swallowed, and I was suddenly struck by the fact that I'd never seen Tom's face when we made love. We'd fallen into a kind of pattern by this time, and every other Saturday night things were, I told myself, a little better. I'd even begun to look, every month, for signs of pregnancy, and if my period was even a day late, I felt light-headed with excitement. But Tom always turned the light off, and his head was usually buried in my shoulder anyway, making it impossible for me to see his expression at our most intimate moments.

I held on to the anger that I felt rising in me at this injustice. Just as Tom was reaching for a biscuit, I let the words come out of my mouth.

'Julia said something about Patrick today.'

I hadn't managed to say *awful.* It was very like my first day at St Luke's, when my voice seemed completely detached from my body; there must have been a tremor in it, because Tom put down his biscuit and studied my face. I blinked back at him, trying to hold my nerve, and he asked, very evenly, 'Does she know him, then?'

He was so calm, Patrick. This wasn't the response I'd antici-pated, as far as I'd anticipated anything at all. I'd imagined, vaguely, immediate denials, or at least defensiveness, on Tom's part. Instead he took up a spoon and began stirring his tea, waiting for my reply.

'She met him. At our wedding.'

Tom nodded. 'So she doesn't know him.'

I couldn't disagree with this statement. It was as if he'd batted me, gently but firmly, to the side. Not knowing how to proceed, I stared out of the window at the street. If I looked away from my husband I might be able to keep hold of my anger. I might even be able to unleash that redhead temper. The struggle I wanted might come my way.

After a moment, Tom let his teaspoon clatter in his saucer and asked, 'So what did she say?'

Still looking out of the window, raising my voice a little, I said: 'That he was – *comme ça*.'

Tom let out a little snort of derision, a sound I'd never heard him make before. It was the sort of sound you might have made, Patrick, at some particularly imbecilic comment. But when I looked at my husband's face, I saw again the expression he'd worn at the top of the helter-skelter: his cheeks had paled, his mouth was skewed, and his wide eyes were fixed on mine. For a second, he looked so weak that I wished I'd said nothing; I wanted to reach out and take his hand and tell him it was just a silly joke, or some kind of mistake. But then he swallowed and, all at once, seemed to pull his features back into line. Standing up, he demanded, in a loud and steady tone, 'What's that supposed to mean?'

'You know,' I said.

'No. I don't.'

We held each other's gaze. I felt as though I were a suspect facing a cross-examination. I knew that Tom had been present at a few of those lately.

'Tell me, Marion. What does it mean?'

The coldness in Tom's voice made my hands shake, my jaw clench. I saw it all slipping away, everything I had: my husband, my home, my chance of a family. I knew he could take it all away from me in an instant.

'What does it mean, Marion?'

Fixing my eyes on the hateful mustard tablecloth, I managed to say, 'That he's a – a sexual invert.'

I braced myself for an explosion, for Tom to throw his cup against the wall, or upturn the table. Instead, he laughed. Not one of his big Tom-laughs. This was more a tired sound, like someone letting out long-pent-up bitterness. 'That's ridiculous,' he said. 'Completely ridiculous.'

I didn't look up.

'She doesn't even know him. How could she say something like that?'

I had no answer.

'If you want sexual inverts, as you call them, I'll show you some, Marion. They're brought into the station every week. They wear stuff – rouge and that – on their faces. And jewellery. It's pathetic. And they have this walk. You can tell one a mile off. Vice squad haul the same ones in over and over. The new chief wants us to clean the streets of their type. He's always on about it. Vice catch them in the gents at Plummer Rodis, did you know that?'

'All right,' I said. 'I get the picture . . .'

But Tom was in full flow now, and he warmed to his subject. 'Patrick isn't one of them, is he? A mincer with a limp wrist. That's not him, is it?' He laughed again, softer this time. 'He's got a respectable job. Do you think he'd be where he is now if he was – what you said? And he's been bloody good to us. Look how he helped with the wedding.'

It was true that you'd paid for Tom's suit.

'I think you need to put this friend of yours straight. She could cause a lot of trouble, saying things like that.'

Not wanting to hear another word of his smooth policeman's voice, I stood to clear away the crockery. But when I carried the tray into the kitchen, Tom was right behind me.

'Marion,' he insisted, 'you do know how ridiculous what she said is, don't you?'

I ignored him, putting the cups in the sink, reaching for the bacon from the fridge.

'Marion? I want you to promise me you'll put her straight.'

At that moment I was very close to throwing something. To slamming the fridge door and yelling at him to stop. To informing him that I could turn a blind eye, but I would not, under any circumstances, be patronised.

Then Tom put his hands on my shoulders and squeezed. At his touch, I let out a breath. He kissed the back of my head.

'Do you promise?' His voice was gentle, and he turned me towards him and touched my cheek. All the fight left me, and I felt only exhaustion. I could see it in his face, too: a weariness around the eyes.

I nodded my agreement. And although he smiled and said, 'Are we having chips? Chips are my favourite. Especially yours,' I knew we'd say nothing more to each other all evening. I did not anticipate, however, the fierceness with which Tom would make love to me that night. I still remember it. It was the only time he undressed me. He pulled my skirt to the floor with one hand and pushed me on to the bed. There was some new intent in his body. It felt, Patrick, as though he meant it. It made me forget Julia's words, if only for that night, and afterwards I slept deeply on Tom's chest, dreaming of nothing.

Weeks went by. In July, Tom announced that he'd arranged to spend every other Saturday afternoon as well as every Tuesday evening with you, as you were still finishing his portrait. I didn't protest. Some Thursdays you came to our house, always bringing wine and talking jovially about the latest plays and films. One evening, over my rather tough steak pie, you said you'd finally persuaded your boss to agree to a series of art-appreciation afternoons for children at the museum, and would my class like to be the first to benefit? I said yes. Mostly it was to please Tom, to convince him that

I'd forgotten Julia's utterance, but it was also, I think, to give myself the opportunity to see you alone. I knew I couldn't possibly discuss matters with you, but, without Tom there, I could perhaps weigh you up for myself.

The afternoon of the visit was sunny, and on the bus into town I regretted agreeing to your plan. It was nearing the end of term; the children were tired and fractious in the heat, and I was nervous about displaying my teaching skills in front of you, worrying that Bobby Blakemore or Alice Rumbold would defy me in your presence, or Milly Oliver would take it upon herself to disappear, prompting a search of the entire museum.

But once I stepped inside, out of the glare of the street, it was something of a relief to be in that dim, cool place, the hush of it quietening the children's row. It felt very different this time: not as forbidding or hidden as it had once been, perhaps because I was now determined to assert my right to be there. The beautiful mosaic floor swirled before me, and everywhere I looked there were scalloped edges and wooden embellishments – around the windows, framing the doors – in the shape of little turrets, echoing the pavilion outside.

The children also stopped and stared, but we didn't have long to take it all in, because, to my surprise, you appeared almost immediately to greet us. It was as if you'd been watching from an upstairs window, waiting for our arrival. You came towards me, smiling, holding out both hands, saying how pleased and honoured you were to have us. You were wearing a light suit and you smelled, as always, expensive; when your hands clasped mine, your fingers were cool and dry. You appeared absolutely at home here, completely in control of your environment. Your footsteps, I noted, were even louder than mine on the tiles, and you didn't hesitate to raise your voice and clap your hands loudly as you guided the children along the hallway, saying you had something magical to show them. It was, of course, the money cat, which you demonstrated using a shiny penny. The children pushed and shoved to get to the front, to see for themselves the cat's belly lighting up, and you used several of your coins, making sure each child had witnessed the marvel. Milly Oliver, however, backed away from its devilish-looking eyes, and I thought her the most sensible girl of all.

As the afternoon went on, I saw that you were genuinely excited about having the children here, and they warmed to you in response. You glowed, in fact, as you led them around your selected exhibits, which included a wooden mask from the Ivory Coast, decorated with bird bones and animal teeth, and a black velvet Victorian bustled dress – which caused all the girls to press their noses to the glass for a closer look.

After the tour, you took us to a small room with large arched windows where tables and chairs, along with aprons, pots of paint, jars of glue and boxes full of treasure – drinking straws, feathers, shells, paper stars coloured gold – had been laid out. You asked the children to make their own masks, using the cardboard templates provided, and together we supervised them as they stuck and painted all sorts of things both on their masks and all over themselves. Occasionally I heard you laughing loudly, and would look up to see you trying a mask on yourself, or giving instructions as to how to make one more frightening, or, as I heard you say, 'a touch more showbiz'. I had to hide a smile as Alice Rumbold stared at you in disbelief when you told her that her creation was 'truly exquisite'. She'd probably never heard the word before, and if she had, I'm certain it wouldn't have been applied to anything she'd made. You patted her on the head, stroked your moustache and beamed, and she looked over at me, still uncertain as to how to interpret your reaction. Alice went on to display quite a talent for art. It was something I'd completely failed to pick up on, but you saw it clearly. I remembered what Tom had told me about you, early on: *He doesn't make assumptions just because of how you look.* At that moment I knew it to be true, and felt a little ashamed of myself.

As I was about to leave, you touched my elbow and said, 'Thank you, Marion, for a lovely afternoon.'

We were standing in the shady hallway, the children all gathered around me, each one gripping their mask and looking towards the glass doors, eager to go home. It was already late; I'd been having such a good time that I'd forgotten to keep an eye on my watch.

It had been a lovely afternoon. I couldn't deny that.

And then you said, 'It's terribly good of you to let Tom come to Venice. I know he appreciates it.'

As you uttered these words, you did not look away from me. There was no hint of shame, or of malice, in your tone. You were just plainly stating the facts. Your eyes were serious, but your smile broadened. 'He has mentioned it?'

'Miss. Milly's crying.'

I heard Caroline Mears's voice, but could not quite understand what she was saying. I was still trying to comprehend your words. *Good of you. Tom. Venice.*

'I think she's wet herself, miss.'

I looked over at Milly, who, ringed by about five others, was sitting on the mosaic floor, sobbing. Her black curls hung in untidy strings about her face, there was a tiny white feather stuck to her cheek, and she'd thrown her mask to the side. I was used to the vinegary odour of children's urine. At school, the problem was easily dealt with – if the child was too ashamed to draw attention to their own wetness, and they hadn't badly soaked the floor or the seat, I would generally turn a blind eye. If they complained, or if the stench was unbearable, I'd send them off to Matron, who had an efficient but kindly line in warnings about the dangers of not using the lavatory during break times, together with a huge pile of clean, if old, underpants.

But there was no Matron here, and the reek now was unmistakable, as was the yellowish puddle surrounding Milly.

'Oh dear,' you said. 'Can I assist in any way?'

I looked at you. 'Yes,' I responded, loudly enough for all the children to hear. 'You could take this girl down to the toilets, wipe her sodden behind and conjure a clean pair of underpants out of thin air. That would be a good start.'

Your moustache twitched. 'I'm not sure I'm quite up to that . . .'

'No? In that case, we'll be off.' I pulled Milly up by the arm. 'It's all right,' I said, stepping over the slippery mosaic. 'Mr Hazlewood will see to the mess. You can stop crying now. Children, say thank you to Mr Hazlewood.'

There was a weak chorus of thank-yous, at which you beamed. 'And *thank you*, children—'

I cut you off. 'Lead the way, Caroline. It's past home time.'

As I guided the children through the doors, I didn't look back, even though I knew you were still standing to one side of Milly's slick of urine, one immaculate hand held out, ready to meet mine.

Arriving home and finding Tom not there, I threw a tea plate across the kitchen. I took particular delight in selecting one that his mother had given us on our wedding day, thin china decorated with blood-red dots. The ecstatic sound of it smashing and the force with which I found I could hurl it against the back door were so pleasurable that I immediately threw another, and then another, watching the last plate narrowly miss the window, causing not two explosions, as I'd hoped, but just one. The disappointment of this calmed me a little, and my breathing steadied. I was, I realised, sweating heavily, the back of my blouse damp and the waistband of my skirt rubbing against my skin. I kicked my shoes off, unbuttoned my blouse and marched about the house, throwing open every window, welcoming the early-evening breeze on my skin, as if I could let my rage out this way. In the bedroom, I rooted around in Tom's half of the wardrobe, ripping his shirts, trousers and jackets from their hangers, searching for something that could make me even angrier than I already was. I even shook his shoes out and unfurled the balls of his socks. But there was nothing there, save for a few old receipts and cinema tickets, only one of which was for a film we hadn't seen together. I slipped this into my pocket in case I should need it later, in case I didn't manage to find any better evidence, and moved on to Tom's bedside cabinet, where I found a John Galsworthy novel, half read, an old watch strap, a pair of sunglasses, a clipping from the *Argus* about the sea-swimming club, and a photograph of Tom outside the Town Hall after he'd been sworn in to the force, flanked by his mother in a floral frock and his father who, for once, was not scowling.

I don't know what I was hoping to find. Or praying I would not find. A copy of *Physique Pictorial*? A love letter from you? Both ideas were ludicrous; Tom would never have taken such risks. But out it all came, and looking at Tom's things around me on the rug, I saw that they didn't amount to very much. Nevertheless, I carried on, digging about in the debris under the bed, sweeping aside odd socks and an unopened box of handkerchiefs, my blouse sticking to me, my hands grey with dust, finding nothing that could further fuel my rage.

Then there was the sound of Tom's key in the front door. I stopped searching but continued to kneel by the bed, unable to move, as I listened to him calling my name. I heard his footsteps pause by the kitchen doorway, pictured his astonishment at seeing the tea plates in bits on the floor. His voice became urgent: 'Marion? Marion?'

I looked around at the destruction I'd caused. Shirts, trousers, socks, books, photographs, all thrown about the room. Windows flung wide open. Our wardrobe emptied. The contents of Tom's bedside cabinet scattered across the floor.

He was still calling for me, but he was taking the stairs slowly now, as if a little afraid of what he might find.

'Marion?' he called. 'What's going on?'

I didn't answer him. I waited, my mind utterly blank. I couldn't think of any excuse for what I'd done, and at the sound of Tom's uncertain voice all my anger seemed to shrivel into a tight ball.

When he came into the room, I heard his gasp. I remained on the floor, staring at the rug, holding my unbuttoned blouse tightly closed. I must have looked a sorry sight, because his voice softened and he said, 'Bloody hell. Are you all right?'

It crossed my mind to lie. I could say we'd been broken into. That I'd been threatened by some hooligan who went about the place smashing up our plates and throwing Tom's things around the bedroom.

'Marion? What's happened?'

He knelt beside me, and his eyes were so gentle that I could not formulate any words at all. Instead I began to cry. It was such a relief, Patrick, to take this woman's way out. Tom helped me up on to the bed and I sat, sputtering out loud sobs, opening my mouth wide, not bothering to cover my face. Tom put his arm around me and I allowed myself the luxury of resting my wet cheek on his chest. That was all I wanted at that moment. The oblivion of tears cried into my husband's shirt. He said nothing; just rested his chin on the top of my head and slowly rubbed my shoulder.

After I'd calmed myself a little, he tried again. 'What's going on, then?' he said, his voice kindly but rather stern.

'You're going to Venice with Patrick.' I spoke into his chest, keeping my head down, aware that I sounded like a petulant child. Like Milly Oliver, sitting in a puddle of her own urine. 'Why didn't you tell me?'

His hand stilled on my shoulder and there was a long pause. I swallowed, waiting – half hoping – for his anger to hit me like a blast of heat.

'Is that what all this is about?' He was using his policeman's voice again. I recognised it from our last discussion about you. He'd repressed the lilt, the hint of a laugh that was usually behind all his utterances. He has this talent, doesn't he, Patrick? The gift of being able to remove oneself utterly from one's words. The gift of being physically in a place, talking, responding, whilst not actually – not emotionally – being there at all. At the time I thought it was part of a policeman's training, and for a while I told myself that Tom needed to do this, that he couldn't help it. Removing himself was his way of coping with his work, and it had leaked into his life. But now I wonder whether it wasn't always a part of him.

I straightened up. 'Why didn't you tell me?'

'Marion. You have to stop this.'

'Why didn't you tell me?'

'It's destructive. Very destructive.' He was staring ahead now, speaking in a calm monotone. 'Do I have to tell you everything immediately? Is that what you expect?'

'No, but – we're married . . .' I mumbled.

'What about freedom, Marion? What about that? I thought we had, you know, an *understanding*. I thought we had a – well, a modern marriage. You've got the freedom to work, haven't you? I should have the freedom to see whoever I like. I thought we were different from our parents.' He stood up. 'I was going to tell you tonight. Patrick only asked me yesterday. He has to go to Venice for his work. Some conference or other. Just a few days. And he'd like some company.' As he spoke, he began picking his clothes up from the floor and folding them into piles on the bed. 'I can't see the problem. A few days away with a friend, that's all it is. I didn't think you'd deny me the chance to see a bit of the world. I really didn't.' He scooped the contents of his bedside drawer from the rug and put them back in their proper place. 'There's no need for all this – I don't know what to call it. Hysterical behaviour. Jealousy. Is that what it is? Is that what you'd call it?'

Whilst he waited for my answer, he continued to tidy the room, shutting the windows, hanging his jackets and trousers in the wardrobe, avoiding my gaze.

Listening to his perfectly even tone, watching him neatly tidy away the evidence of my anger, I'd started to shake. His coolness terrified me, and with every item he lifted from the floor, my own sense of shame at having torn through the house like a woman demented increased. A woman demented was not what I was. I was a schoolteacher, married to a policeman. I was not an hysteric.

I managed to say, 'You know what it is, Tom – it's what Julia said . . .'

Tom brushed down the arms of his best jacket, the one you bought him to wear on our wedding day. Gripping the cuff, he said, 'I thought we'd settled that.'

'We have – we did—'

'So why bring it up again?' He turned to face me at last, and whilst his voice remained perfectly even, his cheeks flamed with outrage. 'I'm beginning to wonder, Marion, whether you've got a dirty mind.'

He snapped the wardrobe doors closed, pushed the bedside cabinet drawer to, straightened the rug. Then he strode to the door and paused. 'Let's agree,' he said, 'to say no more about it. I'm going downstairs. I want you to clean yourself up. We'll have dinner and we'll forget this. All right?'

I could say nothing. Nothing at all.

By now you'll have gathered that for months I'd tried my hardest to remain blind to what was between you and Tom. But after Julia's naming of his disposition, my husband's relationship with you began to come into sharp, terrifying focus. *Comme ça*: the words themselves were dreadful – they conjured an offhand knowingness that utterly excluded me. And I was so stunned by the truth that I could do nothing but stumble through the days as normally as possible, trying not to look too closely at the vision of the two of you that was always there, no matter how much I wished I could turn my eyes away.

I was, I decided, lacking in precisely the way Miss Monkton at the grammar had pinpointed all those years ago. She was right. *Enormous dedication and considerable backbone* were things I did not have. Not when it came to my marriage. And so I took the coward's way out. Although I could no longer deny the truth about Tom, I chose silence rather than further confrontation.

It was Julia who tried to rescue me.

One afternoon during the last week of term, after all the children had gone home, I was in the classroom, washing up paint pots and hanging wet artworks on a string I'd rigged across the window especially for this purpose. This gave me the kind of satisfaction I imagine my mother experienced on wash days, seeing the line of clean white nappies blowing in the sunshine. A task well done. Children well cared for. And the evidence pegged out for all to see.

Without a word, Julia strolled in and sat on a desk, which immediately looked ridiculously small with her long limbs on it – she was almost as tall as me. Putting a hand to her forehead, as if attempting to stem the pain of a headache, she began: 'Is everything all right?'

There was never much preamble with Julia. No skirting around the issue. I should have thanked her for it. But instead I said, rather surprised, 'Everything's fine.'

She smiled, tapping herself lightly on the forehead now. 'Because I had this silly idea that you were avoiding me.' Her bright blue eyes were on mine. 'We've hardly spoken since we took the children to Castle Hill, have we? I hope you've forgiven my clumsiness . . .?'

Pegging up another painting so I didn't have to look at her questioning face, I said, 'Of course I have.'

After a pause, Julia jumped up and stood behind me. 'These are nice.' She touched a corner of one of the paintings and peered at it closely. 'The head mentioned that your museum visit was a great success. I'm thinking of taking my lot next term.'

When the head had asked me about the visit, it had crossed my mind to tell him that you were nothing but an incompetent toff with plenty of artistic pretensions but no real idea of how to handle a roomful of children. However, I'd been unable to lie, Patrick, despite what had happened at the end of that day. And so I'd given him a positive if brief report of your activities and shown him some of the children's creative efforts. He'd admired Alice's mask in particular. Needless to say, I'd mentioned Milly's puddle to no one. But I was reluctant, now, to give you any more credit. 'It was fine,' I said. 'Nothing extraordinary.'

'Shall we go for a drink?' Julia asked. 'You look like you deserve one. Come on. Let's get out of this place.' She was grinning, gesturing towards the door. 'I don't know about you, but I'm very ready for a drop of the hard stuff.'

We sat in the snug of the Queen's Park Tavern. Julia's glass of port and lemon looked somehow wrong in her hand. I'd thought she would have a half of stout, or something in a shot glass, but she declared herself a slave to the sweet drink, and had bought me one too, promising that I would love it if only I gave it a try.

There was something wonderfully illicit about being in the dark, slightly dingy pub, with its heavy green curtains and almost black wood panelling, on such a bright afternoon. We'd chosen a gloomy booth in the almost-empty snug, and there were no other women in the place. Several of the middle-aged men who lined the bar stared at the two of us as we ordered our drinks, but I found I didn't care. Julia lit my cigarette, then her own, and we both blew out and giggled. It was like being a schoolgirl again, in Sylvie's bedroom, except I would never have smoked back then.

'It was fun,' she said, 'on Castle Hill. Good to get out of the classroom.'

I agreed and drank several gulps of port and lemon, getting over the sickly sweetness of it and enjoying the weak feeling it carried to my knees, the warmth it created in my throat.

'I try to take them as often as I can,' Julia continued. 'We have this wonderful landscape all around us, and most of them haven't seen anything beyond Preston Park.'

I knew I could trust her with a confession. 'Neither had I.'

She merely raised her eyebrows. 'I *thought* perhaps you hadn't. If you don't mind my saying so.'

I shook my head. 'I don't know why not, really . . .'

'Your husband isn't the outdoors type?'

I laughed. 'As a matter of fact, Tom's in the sea-swimming club. He goes in every morning. Unless he's on early shifts. Then it's after work.'

'He sounds very disciplined.'

'Oh, he is.'

She gave me a sidelong glance. 'You don't join him?'

I thought of Tom holding me in the waves and carrying me back to shore. I thought of how light I felt in his arms. Then I thought of myself with all his possessions scattered around me on the bedroom floor, my blouse open, my hands grubbied. Taking another drink, I said, 'I'm not a strong swimmer.'

'You can't be any worse than me. All I can do is doggy paddle.' Putting down her glass, Julia lifted both hands in the air, let her wrists go limp and paddled furiously at nothing, pulling her mouth into a woeful grimace. 'If I had bigger ears and a tail, someone might throw me a stick. Want another?'

I looked at the yellowed clock over the bar. Half past five. Tom would be home by now, wondering where I was. Let him wait, I decided. 'Yes,' I said. 'Why not?'

At the bar, Julia stood with one foot on the brass rail that ran along the bottom, waiting to be served. A man with very few teeth stared at her, and she nodded at him, causing him to look away. Then she looked at me and grinned, and I was struck by how strong she appeared, standing at that bar as if ready for anything, or anyone. Her flat black hair, her red lipstick made her stand out wherever she went, but here she was like a beacon. Her voice, when she ordered, was clear and loud enough for everyone in the snug to hear, but she did not lower it. I wondered what she really thought of this place that was so obviously not her natural environment. Julia didn't belong in beer-stained pubs, I thought; at least, this was not the sort of world into which she'd been born. I imagined her growing up riding a horse at weekends, attending guide camps, holidaying with her family in the western isles of Scotland. But the funny thing was, the difference in our backgrounds didn't bother me at all. I found that her apparent independence, the way she was not afraid to look or sound different, was something I wanted for myself.

Placing our drinks on the table, she asked me cheerfully, 'So. Marion. What are your politics?'

I almost spat a mouthful of port and lemon into her lap.

'Sorry,' she said. 'Is that an inappropriate question? Perhaps I should have waited until we'd had a few more drinks.' She was smiling at me, but I got the feeling I was being tested in some way, and it was a test I badly wanted to pass. I remembered our conversation around the dinner table on the Isle of Wight, Patrick, and after knocking back half my drink, I stated: 'Well. I think mothers should be able to go to work, for a start. I'm all for equality. Between the sexes, I mean.'

Julia nodded and murmured her agreement, but was obviously waiting for further revelations.

'And I think this H-bomb testing business is awful. Terrifying. I'm considering joining that campaign against it.' This was not entirely true. At least, it didn't become true until the moment I said it.

Julia lit another cigarette. 'I went on the march at Easter. They have regular meetings about it in town, too. You should come along. We need all the help we can get to spread the word. A disaster's waiting to happen, and most people are more concerned about what the bloody royals are wearing.'

She looked away from me, towards the bar, blowing smoke upwards.

'When's the next one?' I asked.

'Saturday.'

I said nothing for a moment. Tom had promised to take me out on Saturday afternoon, even though it was your turn to see him. It was his suggestion; a way, I knew, of making amends for going to Venice with you. Your trip had been fixed for mid-August, and Tom had said he'd spend every Saturday with me until then.

'Of course,' said Julia, 'they won't let you in without a Fair Isle sweater and a pipe.'

'Then I'll have to do my best to get hold of those things,' I said. We smiled at each other and raised our glasses.

'To resistance,' said Julia.

When Tom asked me where I'd been that evening, I told him the truth – it had been a hard day and Julia and I had discussed it over a drink. He seemed almost relieved to hear this, despite what Julia had said about you. 'I'm glad you're seeing friends,' he said. 'Going out. You should see more of Sylvie, too.'

I said nothing to Tom about my plans for Saturday. I knew he wouldn't approve of me going to a political meeting. It wasn't the sort of thing policemen's wives were supposed to do. When I'd described to him my horror at the head's recent announcement that all staff would be expected to teach a session on how to survive a nuclear attack, his response had been, 'Why shouldn't they be prepared?' And he'd moved from the bread and butter to the cake I'd placed on the table in an effort to prove myself a good and loyal wife.

You can see, Patrick, that I was very confused about everything at this time. The only thing of which I felt sure was that I wanted to be more like Julia. At school, we ate lunch together and she told me about the march she'd been on. There was colour in her cheeks as she described the way that all kinds of people – Christians, beatniks, students, school-teachers, factory workers, anarchists – had come together to make their voices heard. On that cold spring day they'd joined ranks and walked from London to the nuclear research centre at Aldermaston. She mentioned a friend, Rita, who'd marched with her. They'd walked all the way, despite the dismal weather and the fact that, towards the end, they'd wished they were in the pub instead. She laughed and said, 'Some of them can be a bit – you know – po-faced. But it's a wonderful thing. When you're marching, you feel like you're doing something. You're all in it together.'

It sounded magical to me. It sounded like another world entirely. One I couldn't wait to enter.

Saturday came and I insisted that Tom go to see you after all, saying that he shouldn't let you down, and he could make it up to me next weekend. He looked confused, but he went anyway. At the door, he kissed my cheek. 'Thanks, Marion,' he said, 'for being so good about everything.' He was watching my face, obviously still unsure whether to take advantage of my apparent generosity or not. I waved him off with a smile.

After he'd gone, I went upstairs and tried to work out what might be a suitable outfit to wear to a meeting of the local Campaign for Nuclear Disarmament group. It was a warm

July day, but my best summer frock – light tangerine in colour with a cream geometric print – would have been, I knew, deeply inappropriate. Nothing in my wardrobe seemed serious enough for the occasion. I'd seen pictures in the paper of the Aldermaston march, and knew that Julia was only half joking when she'd mentioned the need for a Fair Isle sweater and a pipe. Spectacles, a long scarf and a duffel coat seemed to be the uniform of those marchers, male and female alike. I looked through the pastel colours and flower prints of my wardrobe and felt disgusted with myself. Why didn't I have a pair of trousers, at least? In the end I decided upon one of the outfits I regularly wore to school: a plain navy skirt and a light pink blouse. Taking up my cream cardigan with the big blue buttons, I set off to meet Julia.

When I arrived at the Friends' Meeting House, I knew I needn't have worried about blending in. Julia obviously had no such concerns: her jade green dress and orange beads were easily spotted in the crowd. I write 'crowd', but there can't have been more than thirty people in the Meeting House lecture room. The room was white-walled with high windows at one end, and sunlight filled the place with warmth. At the back of the hall there was a trestle table with cups and an urn of tea set out on a paper tablecloth. At the front of the room was a large banner with the words CND BRIGHTON appliquéd on. As I arrived, a man with a short beard and a very crisp white shirt, the sleeves of which were neatly rolled to his elbows, was standing up to speak. Julia spotted me and gestured that I should sit on the bench next to her. I crept over to her as quietly as I could. She grinned, patted my arm, then turned a serious face towards the front.

The room didn't look like a religious place, but a sense of quiet awe was present on that Saturday afternoon. The speaker had no platform on which to stand, let alone a pulpit from which to preach, but he was dramatically back-lit by the sunshine pouring through the windows, and everyone fell silent even before he began his speech.

'Friends. Thank you all for coming today. I'm especially pleased to see some new faces . . .' He turned his gaze to me, and I found myself smiling back. 'As you know, we're here to unite in the struggle for peace . . .'

As he spoke, I noticed how gentle yet firm his voice was, and how he managed to appear both casual and urgent. It was something to do with the way he leant back very slightly as he spoke, smiled around the room and let his words do the talking, without the dramatic gestures or the shouting that I'd expected. Instead, he was quietly confident, as were, it seemed to me, most of the people in the room. What he said was so evidently sensible that I found it hard to understand why anyone should disagree. Of course survival should come before democracy or even freedom. Of course it was pointless to argue about politics in the face of the destruction a nuclear attack would bring. Of course the H-bomb tests, which could cause cancer, should be stopped immediately. He explained how Britain could lead the world by its example. 'After all, where we go, others follow,' he declared, and everyone clapped. 'We are supported by many great and good men and women. Benjamin Britten, E.M. Forster and Barbara Hepworth are just a few of the names I'm proud to say have added their voices to our campaign. But this movement cannot afford to be complacent. We rely on the grass-roots support of men and women like you. So please, take as many leaflets as you can and disseminate them as widely as you can. Leave them in public house, classroom and church. Without you, nothing can be done. With you, much is possible. Change is possible, and it will come. We will ban the bomb!' As he spoke, there were vigorous nods of approval, and murmurs of assent, but only one woman shouted out, and she did so at odd moments. I saw a pained look pass across the speaker's face as she bellowed 'Hear, hear!' at the words 'Collect your leaflets from Pamela, who's stationed at the tea table . . .' Pamela gave a little wave, then patted her tight curls. 'After you've had tea, of course,' she added, and everyone laughed.

I thought, for a moment, how pleased you would be that I was part of something that involved such an esteemed group of writers and artists. You'd introduced Tom and me to the work of the people the speaker had mentioned, and you would be proud, I knew, to see me sitting there and listening to this speech. You'd be proud that I'd taken, in my own small way, a stand for what I believed in. You might even help me, I thought, to convince Tom that he should be proud too.

But I knew that such exchanges and understandings between the two of us were impossible. I would never tell you about this day. It would be my secret. You and Tom had your secrets, and now I had mine. It was a small, rather harmless secret, but it was my own.

After we'd collected our leaflets, Julia suggested a stroll along the seafront. As we got closer to the sea, we were harangued by salesmen hollering their wares to the crowds of day-trippers: big-banger sandwiches, fresh-shelled oysters, cockles, winkles, dirty postcards, ice cream, sun hats, sticks of rock, toilet-roll holders with naughty inscriptions. Reaching the prom, we leant on the railing and watched the scene on the beach below. The high sun felt like a slap in the face, I remember, after the gentle light of the Meeting House. Behind windbreaks, families were busy consuming sandwiches and cream cakes; children cried to go in the sea, and then cried to come out again; young men in coloured shirts sat in groups, drinking bottles of beer, and young women dressed in black tried to read novels in the glare of the sun; little girls shrieked at the water's edge, their skirts tucked into their knickers; ladies wearing head-scarves, sitting silently in deckchairs, lined the pavement, surveying the whole thing.

It was a very different picture to the one that had greeted me the morning I'd first met Tom for our swimming lessons. Now there was endless noise: the clatter of coins from the amusement arcade, gun blasts from the shooting gallery, laughter and music from Chatfield's bar, screams from the helter-skelter. The image of Tom's face at the top of the stairs, pale and childlike, came to me again. That had been the only time, I realised, he'd shown me any real weakness. I looked at Julia, who was shading her eyes against the sun, smiling down at the chaos of the beach, and I had a sudden urge to tell her everything. My husband is afraid of heights. And he's also sexually abnormal. I thought I might be able to say these things to her and she wouldn't be shocked or disgusted; I might even be able to say such things without fear of ending our friendship.

'Let's paddle,' said Julia, lifting her bagful of leaflets back on to her shoulder. 'My feet are so hot I think they might burst.'

Letting the bright light blur my vision a little, I followed her on to the pebbles. We stumbled together to the water's edge, grabbing at each other's elbows for ballast. Julia unstrapped her sandals and I looked out at the hard glitter of the waves.

I wanted, I realised, to wade deep into the water, to go under and let the sea hold me again, let it wash away all the noise of the beach, let its coldness numb my scorching skin and slow my thoughts to a stop. I kicked off my shoes and, without thinking about it, reached under my skirt to unhook my stockings. Julia was already paddling, and she looked back at me and gave a hoot. 'You hussy! What if one of the school-children should see you?'

But I ignored her. I focused on the sea's glint, and the cacophony of the beach receded as I walked into the water. I didn't stumble on the stones or hesitate as I had with Tom. I just walked right in, hardly feeling the shock of the sea's cold touch, the hem of my skirt soaking up the water until I was up to my waist in it. Still I went further, keeping my eyes on the horizon.

'Marion?' Julia's voice sounded very far away. As I went deeper, I thought about how the sea could knock me one way or the other, or take me fully under. The current was playing around my legs, making me rock back and forth. But it didn't seem like a threat this time. It seemed like a game. Letting my body go limp, I swayed with the waves. Tom's body had been so springy on that day, I remembered. He'd moved with the sea. Perhaps I could do the same.

Lifting my feet off the bottom, I thought: he taught me to swim, but what use has it been? It would have been better never to have gone in the water at all.

I heard Julia's voice again. 'Marion! What are you doing? Marion! Come back!'

My feet found the bottom and I saw her standing in the shallows, one hand on her forehead. 'Come back,' she called, laughing nervously. 'You're scaring me.' She held out a hand. I walked towards it, my wet skirt sticking to my thighs, water dripping from my fingers as they met hers. Once she had my hand in her grip, she pulled me towards her with some force, wrapping her hot arms around me. I smelled the sweet tea on her breath as she said, 'If you want to swim, you'll need a costume. You'll have the lifeguard out otherwise.'

I tried to smile but could not. Panting and shivering at the same time, I let my head rest on her shoulder. 'It's all right,' said Julia. 'I've got you.'

You sent a postcard from Venice. The picture on the front was not one of the classic views of St Mark's Square or the Rialto Bridge. There wasn't a canal or a gondolier in sight. Instead, you sent me a reproduction of a scene from Carpaccio's *Legend of St Ursula* cycle: *The Arrival of the English Ambassadors*. The card showed two young men in tomato-coloured tights and fur-collared jackets leaning on a railing, their extravagant hair curling on to their shoulders. One of them held a peregrine falcon on his arm. It struck me that the pair were both onlookers and poseurs, watching and undoubtedly aware of being watched. On the back you wrote, 'This painter gave his name to the slices of cold beef they eat here. Raw, thrillingly red; thin as skin. Venice is too beautiful to describe. Patrick.' Below, Tom had written, 'Journey long but OK. A great place. Missing you. Tom.' You had done such a good job of saying everything, and Tom had said absolutely nothing. I almost laughed at the contrast.

It arrived days after you returned, and I burned it immediately.

The two of you left on a Friday morning in mid-August. Tom had borrowed one of your suitcases, which he'd been packing all week, taking items out, putting them back in. He packed his wedding suit, although he must have done this secretly, at the last minute, because I didn't notice it was gone from our wardrobe until he'd left and I touched the empty wooden hanger on which it had hung since March. He'd also borrowed a guidebook to Italy from the library. I told him this would be pointless, as you'd been there many times before and you would, I knew, act as Tom's guidebook. Hadn't you already told us both, many times, about the wonders of the vaporetti and the must-sees in the Galleria Accademia?

However, I did look through the section on Venice in that book. Tom had told me that he didn't know where you were staying, or what you would do when you got there. That, of course, was up to you. He smiled and said, 'I expect I'll just wander around on my own a bit. Patrick will have to work.' But I knew you would never let this happen. Skimming through the guidebook, I guessed you would make it your business to show Tom the major sights on the first day, perhaps queuing to go up the Campanile for the views, which the book said were worth the wait; you'd have coffee in Florian's, and you'd know – without consulting the book – not to order cappuccino after eleven in the morning; you'd take a photograph of Tom on the Rialto Bridge; you might even end your day with a gondola ride, the two of you floating side by side along what the book called the 'glorious waterways of the city'. 'No trip,' the guide went on, 'is complete without a gondola ride, especially for honeymooning couples.'

I've since been to Venice myself. I went this September, in fact, whilst on an organised opera trip to Verona with a coachload of strangers, who were mostly my age, and mostly travelling alone, like me. For many years now, Tom and I have taken holidays apart, and I'm always careful to laugh off enquiries about my husband's whereabouts whilst travelling. Oh, I say, he detests opera. Or gardens. Or historic houses. Whichever it happens to be at the time.

I've never mentioned to Tom that the Verona visit included a day trip to Venice. *Venice* is one of the many words we do not utter to one another since you took him there. I'd imagined it many times before, but nothing could have prepared me for the *detail* of the place, the way that everything is beautiful, even the drainpipes and the back alleys and the water buses. Everything. Wandering around the city, alone, my head was filled with images of the two of you. I saw you arriving at Santa Lucia station, stepping from the train into the sunlight like film stars. I saw you slipping across bridges together, your reflections shimmering queasily in the water below. I saw the way you'd stand close to one another at the quay, waiting for the vaporetto. In every *calle* and *sotoportego* I imagined the pair of you, backs turned to me, heads inclined towards one another. You would have looked at Tom with a new intensity in this strange and magnificent city, loving the way his blond hair and large limbs made him stand out from the dark, nimble Venetian crowd. At one moment, I found myself wanting to cry as I sat on the cool steps of the Santa Maria della Salute, watching a couple of real young men read a guidebook together, each tenderly holding the edge of a page, sharing the information. I wondered, for the hundredth time, where you were and what had happened to you. I even sought out the Carpaccios in the Accademia and stared for a long time at the two men in the English Ambassadors painting. I could almost hear your voice as you told Tom all about it; I could picture the serious look on his face as he drank it down. As I walked around, footsore and sweating, I wondered what, exactly, I was doing. Here I was, a lone woman in her early sixties, trying to retrace the steps of her husband and his male lover in an unknown city. Was it some kind of pilgrimage? Or perhaps a purgative act, a way of seeing off the ghosts of 1958 for ever?

It turned out to be neither of those things. It was, instead, a catalyst. Long overdue, perhaps too late, but a catalyst nonetheless. Soon after, I took the action I'd been meaning to for years: I sought you out. I brought you back.

On the Saturday the two of you were gone, I spent most of the day between the sheets after a sleepless night, phrases and images from the guidebook running through my head. *The tranquillity of a city built entirely on water has to be experienced to be believed.* In my fitful sleep, I dreamed I was on a gondola, going far out to sea whilst the two of you waved to me from the shore. There was no way of reaching you, because in the dream I was back where I started: I couldn't swim, and was afraid to go in the water.

At about six o'clock, I forced myself to rise and dress. I tried not to look at the empty space in the wardrobe where Tom's suit had been, or the spot by the door where his shoes usually were. By some enormous effort of willpower – or perhaps it was merely fatigue – I thought only of the port and lemon that awaited me. The sickly first mouthful, the burning after-taste. I'd arranged to meet Julia for a drink in the Queen's Park Tavern, and had invited Sylvie to join us. She'd looked excited when I asked her; this would be the first time she'd left her baby girl, Kathleen, who was only a few weeks old, alone with her mother-in-law for the evening. Kathleen had Roy's black hair and slightly bulging eyes, and when I'd visited it had struck me that Sylvie was already disappointed in her daughter. She had a way of talking about the baby as if she were a fully formed personality, capable of consciously defying her mother's intentions. 'Oh,' Sylvie had said, when I'd held Kathleen and the girl started to cry, 'she's a little attention-seeker.' From the start, it was a battle of wills between Sylvie and her daughter.

I arrived at the pub deliberately early in order to have a drink before facing Sylvie's questions about Tom's whereabouts, even though it meant I had to sit alone, enduring the stares of the regulars. Choosing the booth where Julia and I had sat together that evening after school, I slotted myself into a corner. Once I'd taken my first sip, I allowed myself to think again of the two of you, who, I imagined, would be eating spaghetti on some sun-drenched terrace. I'd let Tom go, I told myself. I'd let him. And now I'd have to live with it.

Sylvie came in. She'd had her hair set, I could see, especially for the occasion – not a strand was out of place – and she was wearing a lot of make-up: bright blue metallic streaks across her eyelids, a pearly peach colour on her lips. I guessed this was an attempt to hide her tiredness. She was sporting a white belted mac, despite the warmth of the evening, and a tight sweater. Watching her walking over, I was newly aware of how different she was from Julia, and I experienced a small stab of anxiety that the two of them would not get on at all.

'What are you drinking?' asked Sylvie, eyeing my glass with suspicion. She laughed when I told her. 'I think my Aunt Gert's very partial to a port and lemon. But what the hell? I'll try one.'

She sat opposite me and clinked her glass against mine. 'Here's to . . . escape.'

'Escape,' I agreed. 'How's Kathleen?'

'Getting all the attention she wants from Roy's mother. Who is actually quite keen on me since the baby was born. The only thing I could've done better is to have had a boy. But since Kath looks so much like Roy, it's not much of a problem.' She lifted her glass again. 'And to the girls, eh?'

'To the girls.'

We both drank. Then Sylvie said, 'This Julia. What's she

like? Only I'm not used to meeting teachers. Except for you, that is.'

'You'll be fine, Sylvie,' I said, ignoring her question and finishing off my drink. 'Want another?'

'I've hardly finished this one. Gruesome it is, too. I'll have a stout next.'

As I stood up to go to the bar, Sylvie grabbed my wrist. 'You all right? I heard Tom's gone away with that – with Patrick.'

I stared at her.

'Dad mentioned it.'

'What of it?'

'I'm only asking. Seems a bit rich, that's all. Leaving you on your own, I mean.'

'Can't a bloke go away with a friend for a few days?'

'I didn't say anything, did I? It's just you look – out of sorts.'

At that moment, Julia arrived. I let out a long breath as I saw her striding towards us, swinging her arms lightly, grinning. She touched me on the arm and held a hand out to Sylvie. 'You must be Sylvie,' she said. 'Lovely to meet you.'

Sylvie looked at Julia's hand for a second before taking it limply. 'All right?' she said.

Julia turned to me. 'Shall we get the drinks in, then?'

'I'll have half a stout,' said Sylvie. 'This stuff's horrible.'

When we were all sitting with our drinks, Julia asked Sylvie about Kathleen, and Sylvie seemed to enjoy telling her what a pain in the backside her daughter was. 'Mind you,' she added when she'd finished, 'she's nothing compared to my husband . . .' and off she went again, listing Roy's shortcomings, the details of which she'd rehearsed with me many times over. He was lazy. He drank too much. He didn't help with the baby. He refused to push himself forward at work. He knew nothing about anything except cars. He was too attached to his mother. As was always the case when Sylvie attacked Roy, though, she said these things with so much animation, and such a big smile on her face, that I knew she loved him for these very faults.

Julia listened to all this, nodding occasionally in encouragement. When Sylvie had finished, Julia asked, in a voice I guessed wasn't nearly as innocent as she made it sound, 'So why did you marry him, Sylvie?'

Sylvie stared at Julia, her face blank. Then she finished her drink, tugged at a lock of hair that curled up on her neck and said, in a low voice, 'Do you want to know the truth?'

Julia said that she did, and we both leant forward as Sylvie beckoned us closer with one finger. 'He's very, very considerate,' she said, 'in the bedroom department.'

At first Julia looked a bit flummoxed, but when I began to giggle and Sylvie covered her mouth to stifle her mirth, Julia laughed so loudly that several people in the pub turned to look at us.

'He's irresistible, isn't he, Marion?' said Sylvie, gazing rather sadly into her glass. 'You know how it is. Once they've got hold of you, there's no going back.'

Julia sat up straight. 'You don't think? Even if you realise it's no good?'

'I'm telling you. There's no going back,' Sylvie said, looking directly at me.

Not long before closing time, Roy appeared in the doorway of the snug. I noticed him before Sylvie did, and saw his face cloud over as he took in the scene: three tipsy women in a booth, sniggering, empty glasses piled up around them.

'Looks like a proper party over here,' he said, letting his hand fall on Sylvie's shoulder.

Sylvie gave a start.

'Sylvie. Marion.' Roy nodded to me. 'And who's this?' He was looking at Julia with curiosity. When she held a hand out to him, I noticed it was slightly unsteady. Her voice was absolutely even, though, as she said, 'Julia Harcourt. Pleased to meet you. And you are . . .?'

'Sylvie's husband.'

'Oh!' said Julia in mock surprise. 'She's been telling us all about you.'

Roy ignored this comment and turned to Sylvie. 'Come on. I'm walking you home.'

'Don't you want a drink?' asked Sylvie, her words slightly slurred. 'You usually do.'

'How are you, Roy?' I asked, attempting to make light of the situation.

'Sensational, thanks, Marion,' said Roy, still looking at his wife.

'And Kathleen?'

'She's a little treasure. Isn't she, Sylvie?'

Sylvie took a long drink and said, 'It's not even bloody closing time.'

Roy spread his hands wide in an apparently helpless gesture. 'But here I am anyway. Come on, get your coat on. Your daughter's waiting for you.'

Now Sylvie's face turned bright pink.

'Why don't you have a drink with us, Roy?' I tried again. 'We'll all go after this one.'

273

'I'll get them in,' said Julia, standing up. 'What are you having, Roy?'

Roy made a sideways move, blocking Julia's way. 'That's all right, love. Thanks anyway.'

Julia and Roy looked at each other. She looked so much taller than him that I had to suppress a giggle. Just you try getting in her way, I thought. I'd like to see that.

Sylvie slammed down her glass. 'Sorry, girls,' she mumbled, and began putting on her coat. It took her a few attempts to find the sleeve, and no one helped her. When she looked at me, her eyes were so bleary that I wondered if she was about to cry.

As Roy took hold of his wife's arm, he turned to me and said, 'I hear your Tom's in Venice. Must be nice, having a friend like that. Someone to take you places.'

Sylvie gave Roy a shove on the shoulder. 'Come on,' she said. 'If we're going, let's move it.' From the door, she offered Julia and me a resigned wave.

After they'd gone, Julia looked into her glass and gave a rueful laugh. 'He's a bit . . . heavy-handed, isn't he?'

'He knows nothing about her,' I said, surprised at the venom in my own voice. I was suddenly outraged by Roy's behaviour. I wanted to run after the pair of them and yell at him: *She trapped you! She wasn't even pregnant when you married her! How can you have been so stupid?*

But Julia put a hand on my elbow and said, 'I don't know. They seem pretty well matched. And he is *irresistible*, after all.'

I tried to laugh, but found I was close to tears and couldn't raise a smile. Julia must have seen my distress, because she said, 'Come for a drink at my place? We can walk through the park.'

Outside, the night was warm and quiet. My legs seemed to carry me down the hill with very little effort after all that port, and as we walked through the elaborate portico, Julia slipped her bare arm through mine. The seagulls cried occasionally from the rooftops as we wandered along the dark pathways of Queen's Park. I could smell the impossible sweetness of honeysuckle and orange blossom, mixed together with stale food and beer from the park's bins. We walked in silence across the parched summer grass, stopping at the rose garden. The low glow of one of the park's few lamps lit the flowers the deepest crimson, and it struck me that the colour was like someone's insides. Like my own insides, perhaps. Mysterious and changing. Julia brought a bloom to her face and inhaled; I watched the petals touch her pale skin, her lips almost meeting the flower.

'Julia,' I said, stepping close to her. 'I don't know what to do about Tom.'

We looked at each other. Julia shook her head and gave a small laugh. 'He doesn't know you, either, does he?' she said, quietly.

'What you said,' I began, 'about Patrick . . .' But I could get no further, and a small silence grew.

'We don't have to talk about this if you don't want to, Marion.'

'What you said,' I tried again, closing my eyes and taking a deep breath. 'It's true, and I think it's true about Tom, too.'

'You don't have to tell me,' she said.

'They're in Venice. Together.'

'You said.' Julia sighed. 'Men have such freedom. Even married ones.'

I stared at the ground.

'Let's sit down,' she said, and she led me towards a patch of black lawn, beneath a willow tree. I wasn't crying, Patrick. I felt curiously light. The fact that I'd spoken had lightened me. And now I'd started, now I'd begun to let the words go, I couldn't stop. We sat on the grass and I told her everything – how I'd met Tom, how he'd taught me to swim, the proposal in your flat, the way I'd seen the pair of you look at one another on the Isle of Wight. Sylvie's warnings. It all came out. Halfway through my story, Julia lay back and stretched her arms above her head, and I did the same, but still I didn't stop. My words spilled into the darkness. It was so good to speak, to let it all float upwards into the tree's branches. I didn't look at Julia once as I spoke, knowing that to do so would cause me to falter, or to lie. Instead I looked at the flickers of moonlight between the leaves. And I kept on talking until it was all said.

When I'd finished, Julia was quiet for a long time. I could feel her shoulder against mine, and I turned to look at her, hoping for a response. Without returning my gaze, she placed a hand on mine and said, 'Poor Marion.'

I thought of how strongly she'd held me on the beach, and wished she'd do it again. But she only repeated, 'Poor Marion.'

Then she sat up, looked me straight in the eye and said, 'He won't change, you know.'

I stared at her, open-mouthed.

'I'm sorry to tell you that, but it's really the kindest thing I can do.' Her voice was hard and clear.

Propping myself up on my elbows, I began to protest, but Julia interrupted me. 'Listen to me, Marion. I know he's deceived you and it's painful, but he won't change.'

I couldn't believe she was being so matter-of-fact about it. I'd told her things I'd hardly dared admit to myself, let alone anyone else, and instead of offering comfort, it seemed she was turning against me.

'I know it's difficult. But it will be better for both of you if you can accept that.' She looked off into the darkness.

'But it's his fault!' I said, close to tears now.

Julia gave a soft laugh. 'Perhaps he shouldn't have married you . . .'

'No,' I said. 'Of course he should. I'm glad he married me. It's what he wanted. What we both wanted. And he could change,' I spluttered, 'couldn't he? With me by his side. He could get – help, couldn't he? And I can help him . . .'

Julia stood up, and I noticed for the first time that her hands were trembling. In a very quiet voice, she said, 'Please don't say those things, Marion. They're just not true.'

I stood to face her. 'What do you know about it?'

She looked to the ground. But my temper had flared, and I raised my voice. 'He's *my* husband! I'm his wife. I know what's true and what isn't.'

'Maybe you do, but—'

'All this . . . lying. It's not right, what he's doing. He's the one in the wrong.'

Julia took a deep breath. 'If that's the case,' she said, 'then I'm wrong, too.'

'You?' I asked. 'What do you mean?'

She said nothing.

'Julia?'

She sighed heavily. 'Good grief. Didn't you know?'

I couldn't speak. I had no idea, at that moment, what I was feeling.

'Really, Marion. You have to open your eyes. You're too bright not to. It's such a waste.'

And she walked away from me, her arms held tightly at her sides, her head bowed.

Julia. I've written to her many times over the years, in the hope that she will forgive me. I've kept her up to date with all my activities – at least the ones of which I knew she would approve. Becoming deputy head at St Luke's. Starting the school CND group. I've shared my thoughts on the women's movement (whilst I never went on a march or burned my bra, I did take an evening course at Sussex University in feminism and literature, and found it fascinating). I have never mentioned, in these letters, Tom or you. But I think she knows what happened. I think she knows what I did. Why else would her replies be so perfunctory, even now? With each letter I hope for personal revelations, or a flash of the humour I so loved in her. But all I get are updates on her latest walks, her house and garden renovations, and sympathetic but formal declarations of how much she also misses teaching.

Sometimes I think that if I'd been braver, Julia would still be a close friend, and she would be here to help me manage your care properly. As it is, it's impossible for me to lift you on and off the commode, even though you must weigh less than I do now. Your arms are thin as a young girl's, your legs all bone. And so I take no chances. Every morning I rise at five thirty to change your waterproof pants and incontinence pad, which you wear at all hours. Nurse Pamela says we should restrict these awful garments to night-time wear, but she doesn't realise how little Tom is prepared to help, and I have no intention of mentioning this to her, knowing it will mean she'll question the suitability of our home as a base for your care. Although I'm not strong enough to lift you, I do feel, Patrick, capable in other ways. I know I am up to this task. My own body, whilst potentially on the verge of decrepitude, actually works fairly well, considering I have never done a scrap of deliberate exercise in my life. The classroom kept me fairly active, I suppose. Lately I've noticed aches and stiffness in odd places – my knuckles, my groin, the backs of my ankles. But this is most likely through looking after you. The changing of sheets every day, the turning of your body to wash you, the reaching to pull on your clean sets of pyjamas or to bring food to your mouth. All these things have taken their toll.

At the table by the window, on Tom's mother's terrible cloth, at four thirty on a Sunday morning, the seagulls protesting outside my window, smelling the dried sweat and alcohol on my own skin, my throat dry and aching, the house silent with Tom's absence, Julia's words in my head, I wrote a letter, sealed it in a plain envelope, scribbled the address on the front, affixed a stamp, and, before I could change my mind, walked to the postbox at the corner of the street and let it fall into the slot. There was a cleanness to that fall; I heard the letter find its place on top of the other post with a soft slap. I did not think about the consequences of what I had written. Over the years I've told myself that all I meant to do was give you a fright. I imagined you perhaps receiving a warning from your boss; being banned from seeing the children; losing your job at the very worst. But I knew, of course, about the sex cases in the papers. And I knew that the local police were doing all they could to restore their tarnished reputation after the corruption scandal earlier in the year.

But I felt very, very tired, and could think of nothing except the hot tea I would drink upon arriving home, and the soft bed I would curl myself into until Tom came back.

This, Patrick, is what I wrote.

Mr Houghton
Head Keeper of Western Art
Brighton Museum and Art Gallery
Church Street
Brighton

Dear Mr Houghton,

I am writing to draw your attention to a matter of some urgency.

As I understand that Mr Patrick Hazlewood, Keeper of Western Art in your museum, is currently holding art-appreciation afternoons for schoolchildren on your premises, I believe it is in your best interests to know that Mr Hazlewood is a sexual invert who is guilty of acts of gross indecency with other men.

I'm sure you'll share my concern at this news, and do your utmost to preserve both the safety of the children and the museum's good reputation.

Yours faithfully,
A Friend

IV

HMP Wormwood Scrubs, February 1959

My fingers so frozen, I can hold this pen for only seconds at a time. A word, another word, then another and another. And then I must sit on my hands to coax the blood back. The ink itself may soon freeze. If it froze, would the nib burst? Would even my pen be disfigured by this place?

But I am setting down words on a page. Which is something. In here, it is close to being everything.

Where to begin? With the policeman's knock on my door at one in the morning? The night in the cells at Brighton police station? Mrs Marion Burgess in court, describing me as a 'very imaginative' man? The slamming of the van door after being led from the dock? The slamming of every door since?

Begin with Bert. Bert, who has given me this gift of writing.

Anything you want hidden, Bert says, I can hide. Screws won't have a clue.

How does he know what I want? And yet he does. Bert knows everything. His petrol-blue eyes may well have the ability to see through walls. He is the most feared and powerful prisoner in D Hall, and he is, he's announced, my friend.

This is because Bert likes to listen to an 'educated fucker' like me talk.

As soon as I was allowed out on association, Bert made himself known to me. I was collecting the pitiful scraps they call lunch (cabbage boiled until translucent, globs of unrecognisable meat) when someone in the queue felt the need to urge me forward with the words, 'Get a move on, queer.' Not the most original of insults, and I was ready to keep my head down and do exactly as asked. This strategy had got me through the last three months without too much aggravation. Then Bert appeared by my side.

'Listen, fucker. This man's a friend of mine. And friends of mine ain't queer. Got it?'

His voice low. His cheek pale.

For the first time, I looked straight ahead as I walked to a table. I followed Bert, who somehow communicated that this was his wish without uttering a word or even making a gesture. Once we were seated with our trays, he nodded in my direction. 'Heard about your case,' he said. 'Diabolical liberty. They done you, just like they done me.'

I didn't contradict him. It's possible that because I don't flounce about wearing 'powder' (flour from the kitchen) and 'nail varnish' (paint lifted from the art class), Bert believes I am a normal. Many of the minorities in here are very, very blatant. I suppose they think they might as well pass the time as well as possible. The grey woollen capes we've been issued for the winter months – which fasten at the neck and fall full to the waist – do make a quite theatrical effect when swept over one shoulder in the yard. So why not make the most of them? I'm a little tempted myself. God knows they're quite the best item in the prison wardrobe. But old habits, as they say, die hard. And so Bert, if no one else, has been fooled. And no man contradicts Bert.

I'd known about him before he introduced himself. He's a tobacco baron. Every Friday he collects his profits from the men for the 'snout' that he's let out to them at a huge rate of interest. He's nothing to look at. Short, ginger-haired, stout about the middle. Tattoos up both forearms, but he's told me these were a youthful mistake, one he now regrets. 'Got them up Piccadilly,' he said, 'after me first proper tickle. Got a grand that time. Thought I was the king or summat.'

But Bert has natural leadership. It's in his soft, low voice. His all-seeing face. The way he stands as if he's grown out of the ground. As confident in his right to exist as any tree. And it's in the way he befriends people who need him, like me, and then makes the most of them. So. Bert has agreed to hide this exercise book. He's told me himself that he can't read. And why would he lie about a thing like that?

All I need do in return, he says, is talk. Like an educated fucker should.

I've been thinking a lot about razor blades. And fingerless gloves. I find these two items can occupy my mind quite fully.

Fingerless gloves because my hands are cracked and red around the joints due to the extreme cold. I daydream of the pair I had whilst at Oxford. Dark green, boiled wool. At the time I believed they gave my hands a rather workmanlike appearance. Now I know what a luxury those gloves were.

And razor blades. The ones they issue here each morning are too blunt to cut a decent shave. At first this nearly drove me to distraction. The itchiness of stubble was intolerable to me, and I spent much of the day scratching, or wanting to scratch, my face. I yearned for my own razor. Kept picturing how I'd simply walked into Selfridges and purchased it without thinking twice.

It's easy to become very focused, I've found, on such small things. Especially when every day is the same, bar a few differences in the food offered (on Friday we have stale fish in thick batter, on Saturdays a dab of jam with our teatime bread) or the routines adhered to (church on Sunday, bath on Thursday). To think of larger things is madness. A bar of reconstituted soap. A clean chamber pot. A sharper razor blade than yesterday. These things come to mean a lot. They keep one just about sane. They are something to think about that is not Tom. Because to think about my policeman would be hell. I do everything I can to avoid such thoughts.

Razor blades. Chamber pots. Dabs of jam. Soap.

And for fantasy: fingerless gloves.

I've never been so aware of the dimensions of any room before this cell. Twelve foot long, nine foot wide, ten foot high. I've paced it out. Walls painted dull cream halfway up, then white-washed. Floor of scrubbed bare planks. No radiator. Canvas bed with two scratchy grey blankets. And in the corner, a small table, at which I write this. The table is covered in characters carved into its poor surface. Many are statements of time: 'Max. 9 months. 02.03.48'. Some are pathetic jibes at the screws: 'Hillsman sucks cock'. The one I'm most interested in, and sometimes spend many minutes just rubbing my thumb over, is the word 'JOY'. A longed-for woman's name, I suppose. But it's such an unlikely word to find on a table in here that occasionally it's tempting to read it as a small message of hope.

There's one window, high up and made of thirty-two (I've counted them) dirty panes of glass. Every morning I wake long before the bolts on the door are unlocked, and I stare at the dim outlines of these squares of glass, trying to convince myself that today the sun might make it through and cast a jewel of light on to the floor of the cell. But this has yet to happen. And perhaps it's better like this.

No way to tell exactly what time it is, but soon the lights will go out. And then the shouting will begin. *My God. My God.* Every night the man shouts, over and over. *My God. My God. My GOD!* As if he believes he really can summon God to this place, if only he can shout loud enough. At first I expected another prisoner to shout back, order him to shut his mouth. That was before I understood that once lights are out, no other prisoner will ask you to deny your pain. Instead we listen in silence, or call back our own grief. It's left to the screws to bang on his door and threaten him with solitary.

The knock at the door. A quarter past one in the morning. A loud knock. The sort of knock that won't stop until answered. That may not stop, even then. A knock designed to let all your neighbours know that someone has come for you in the dead of night and will not leave until they have you.

Knock. Knock. Knock.

I must have slept through the downstairs buzzer, because someone was right outside the door to my flat. I knew it couldn't be Tom. He had his own key. But I had no idea it would be another policeman.

His hand still in the air when I opened up. His face comically small and red beneath his helmet. I looked behind him for Tom, thinking – in my sleep-drugged state – perhaps this was some kind of joke. And there were three more of them. Two in uniform, like the one doing the knocking. One plain clothes, hanging back, peering down the stairs. I looked again. But Tom's face was nowhere.

'Patrick Francis Hazlewood?'

I nodded.

'I have a warrant here for your arrest on suspicion of committing acts of gross indecency with Laurence Cedric Coleman.'

'Who?'

The red-faced one sneered. 'That's what they all say.'

'Is this some kind of joke?'

'They all say that, too.'

'How did you get up here?'

He laughed. 'You have very obliging neighbours, Mr Hazlewood.'

As he was reciting the usual lines – *anything you say may be taken down and used as evidence, etc. etc.* – I could think nothing. I stared at the deep dimple in his chin and tried to understand what could possibly be happening. Then his hand was on my shoulder, and the feel of that policeman's glove made the reality of what was going on begin to seep into my brain. My first thought was: it's actually Tom. They know about me and Tom. Something – some police code – is stopping them from saying his name, but they know. Why else would they be here?

They didn't handcuff me. I went quietly, thinking that the less fuss I made, the less awful it might be for him. The red-faced man, whose name I later learned was Slater, said something about a search warrant; I saw no such document, but as Slater led me away, the two other uniformed men swooped into my flat. No. Swooped is too dramatic. They slipped in, grinning. My journal was open, I knew, on the desk in my bedroom. It wouldn't take them long to find it.

Slater seemed rather bored by the whole business. As we rode through town in the Black Maria, he started chatting to his plain-clothed colleague about another case in which he'd had to 'cosh' the criminal. His victim had cried, 'just like my mum when I told her I was becoming a copper'. The two of them sniggered like schoolboys.

Once in the interview room, it became clear who Laurence Coleman was. An unflattering photograph of the boy was slapped on the table. Did I know this young man? Had I, as he'd said in his statement, 'tapped him up for a beefer' outside the Black Lion conveniences? Had I committed acts of gross indecency in said public conveniences with this man?

I almost laughed with relief. This was not about Tom, but the dark-haired youth at the Argyle.

No, I replied. I had not.

Slater gave a smile. 'It will be better for you,' he said, 'if you tell the truth and plead guilty.'

What I remember now is the number of tea stains on the chipped table, and the way Slater gripped the edge of his chair as he leaned forward. 'A guilty plea,' he said, 'often saves a lot of trouble. Trouble for you. And trouble for your *associates*.' The redness in his cheeks had drained and the creases around his mouth showed clear in the blast of the overhead light. 'Family and friends are often hurt in these cases.' He shook his head. 'And it's all so easily avoided. Breaks my heart.'

A cold rush of panic spread through my chest. Perhaps this was really about Tom after all, and this was Slater's way of saving a friend and colleague.

I looked him in the eye. 'I understand,' I said. 'And now I come to think of it, I did meet that young man, and we fucked right there in the lav and we both loved it.'

A short smile crossed Slater's face. 'That'll make the jury's job very easy,' he said.

At nine this morning, a warder – Burkitt – arrived in my cell. Burkitt has a reputation for being something of a sadist, but

I'd yet to see any evidence of this. He's a slim, tall man with large brown eyes and a closely cropped beard, and would be handsome were it not for his non-existent chin. He said nothing for a few moments. Just stood there in front of me and slowly unwrapped a mint humbug.

Then: 'Hazlewood. Get a move on. Visit to the trick cyclist.'

'Trick cyclist?' I still don't understand all the prison language. Some of it is impressively imaginative, if gruesome. 'Dry bath' for strip search seems particularly appropriate to me.

Burkitt popped the humbug in his mouth, gave a little push on my shoulder and did not see fit to enlighten me. As we walked, he kept very close behind, saying, 'You queers have it cushy in here, don't you? Plenty of business.' His mouth was so close to my ear that I could smell the sweet mint of his breath. So, I thought, this is where his reputation comes from: he knows how prison tobacco leaves our mouths with the taste and texture of a rough hound's backside, and so he tortures us with his minty freshness.

We walked out of D Hall, along a long corridor, through several locked doors, out into the yard, through a locked gate and into a miraculous place: the hospital wing. I'd heard rumours of the existence of this clean, new building, and know men who've tried everything – including burning their own arms with slugs of hot oil in the kitchen – to win a short stay there.

As soon as we stepped inside the white walls, the smell of new plaster hit me. After the prison stench of boiled cabbage and the stale sweat of hundreds of terrified, unwashed men, this new smell brought tears to my eyes. It was a smell almost like bread. I wondered, briefly, what a recently plastered wall would taste like, if licked. Everything was brighter, too. Large windows ran the length of the corridor, washing the whole place with light.

Burkitt jabbed a finger between my shoulder blades. 'Up.'

At the top of the staircase was a door with the words DR R.A. RUSSELL attached in modern silver script. Burkitt unwrapped another humbug and began to suck, staring at me all the time. Then he knocked on the door.

'Come in.'

A fire roared in the grate. Beneath my feet was a new carpet. Although it was a thin, synthetic monstrosity – multicoloured cubes on a royal-blue background – the feel of it beneath my boots was wonderful. Standing there, I felt suddenly lifted from the floor.

A man rose from behind a desk. 'Patrick Hazlewood?'

'Yes.'

'I'm Dr Russell.'

He couldn't have been more than twenty-eight. Dimples on his ample cheeks. Wearing a boxy blazer, unbuttoned. Around his cushiony middle a very new-looking belt bit into his flesh. He didn't look at all threatening, but I still had no idea what kind of treatment I'd been sent for.

'Thank you, Burkitt,' he said, beaming at the scowling screw.

'Right outside,' said Burkitt, slamming the door.

Russell looked at me. 'Sit down.'

It was unexpected, this order. Seduced, I suppose, by the carpet, the fire and Russell's schoolboy cheeks, I'd almost been anticipating the word *please.*

He settled himself into his leather office chair and picked up a fountain pen. Despite the comforts of the room, my chair was the familiar wooden type. He must have seen me looking at it in disappointment, because he said, 'I'm working on that. Ridiculous to expect a person to talk freely whilst perched on a school chair. No one tells teacher their secrets, eh?'

Of course, I thought. He's the psychiatrist. I relaxed a little. I've never believed they could offer any type of 'cure', but I've always been curious about what it would be like to visit one.

'So. We start by you telling me how you are at the moment.'

I said nothing. I was lost in the print of Matisse's *La Danse* that hung above his desk: the first piece of art I'd seen for three months. Its bright colours seemed almost obscene in their beauty.

Russell followed my gaze. 'Lovely, isn't it?' he asked.

I couldn't speak for a full minute. He waited, turning his pen over and over. Then I blurted: 'Did you get it to torture your patients into a confession?'

He flicked an imaginary piece of lint from his knee. 'I'm not here for confessions. There's a priest who will gladly hear them every Sunday. Do you believe?'

'Not in any god who condemns so many.'

'So many of – your kind?'

'Of all kinds.'

There was silence for a while.

'I'm interested in why you find torture in that picture.'

'I would have thought that was rather obvious.'

Russell raised his eyebrows. Waited.

'It's a reminder of beauty. Of what's outside these walls.'

He nodded. 'You're right. But some can find beauty wherever they are.'

'There's not much in this place.'

Another long pause. He tapped his pen three times on his notepad and smiled, very suddenly. 'Do you want to be cured?' he asked.

I almost snorted. Checked myself when I felt the intensity of Russell's serious gaze.

It was an easy question to answer. Did I want to spend more time up here in this light, warm room, chatting with Russell by the fire? Or did I want to be sent back to my cell?

'Yes,' I said. 'Oh yes.'

We are to meet once a week.

I say I do everything possible to avoid thinking about Tom, but, of course, Tom is mostly what I think about. And it is hell. Not least because the more I think about him, the more I cannot remember the reasons why we could not be together. The more I think about him, the less I remember anything that was wrong, or difficult. All I remember is his sweetness. And that is the hardest thing to bear. Yet my mind keeps returning to it. Keeps returning to Venice. Most especially to the water taxi we took in the dead of night, over the lagoon to the city. We climbed into the shining wooden cabin, sat together at the back of the boat, and our captain closed the hatch to give us privacy. Then we sped across the waves, so fast we couldn't stop laughing at the sheer daring of that little boat on the black water. Zoom, we went. Zoom. Our thighs touching. Our bodies forced back by the speed of the thing. And then the boat suddenly slowed, and the beauty of Venice unrolled itself outside the tiny windows. Tom gasped, and I smiled at his wonder. But to me the wonder was the touch of his hand on mine in that cabin which was ours alone for the time it took to reach our hotel.

Like most who experience these things, throughout the arrest and trial, and the first few days in here, I truly thought someone would appear to announce that there'd been a terrible mistake and ask that I accept the apologies of everyone involved. And all the doors that had slammed shut would open again and I would walk through them, out into the clean air, away from the strange piece of theatre my life had become.

But thirteen weeks in, I've grown as used to the routine as most of the others. And I perform it with the same dead-eyed, accepting stare. 6.30 a.m. Buzzer signals it's time to get up. 7 a.m. Slop out, being careful to carry one's metal chamber pot with the utmost nonchalance. Fetch cold water and shave with allocated blunt blade. I'm now, since being on association, allowed to 'dine out' with the other men, rather than eating all meals alone in my cell. But it's the same dishwater tea, stale bread, smear of marge and – almost tasty – bowl of porridge. Perhaps porridge is so vile there's not much one can do to make it worse. Then it's to work in the library. My position there has enabled me to gain access to exercise books and pens, but as a description of the place, the word 'library' is something of a joke – the books are all filthy (in strictly a literal sense) and obsolete. It's impossible for a prisoner to obtain anything he really wants to read, save for the few paperback Westerns available on each of the corridors. The library is dingy, but at least it's slightly warmer than the rest of the prison. One of the radiators actually works. The warder in charge – O'Brien – must be nearing retirement, and spends most of the day sitting in the corner barking for silence and refusing requests. However, he is rather deaf, so the noise must reach a certain volume before he barks. This makes it possible for the men to speak to one another quite freely, so long as they keep their voices fairly low.

Much of the work involves dealing with new deliveries from public libraries. We always get the absolute dregs. In yesterday's shipment, for example: a guide to the maintenance of Norton motorcycles from the 1930s, a history of the village of Ripe, a book on the coinage of the Middle East, another on the dress of the people of Latvia, and – the only slightly interesting volume among the whole lot – a biography of William of Orange, written in 1905.

With me in the library is Davies, a large, quiet man with grey eyes, who is apparently in for causing his wife grievous bodily harm. Impossible to imagine anyone less likely to commit such a crime. But one learns not to question a man too closely on his conviction. Also with me is Mowatt, a young fair-haired lad festooned with freckles. A habit of licking his lips as he works. Mowatt was a Borstal boy, like so many of them here. Talks a lot about his next 'twenty-two-carat doddle', which I now understand to mean his next fantastically large-scale yet utterly risk-free robbery. He walks as though his feet are too long, picking them up and placing them down so carefully you want to offer him an arm.

Yesterday Mowatt said nothing at all as we sorted through our shipment of books. At first I was glad to be spared the usual fantasies of how, on his release, he'd *hook up with this gorgeous bird* who's waiting for him and make use of the *ton* he's *got stashed for a new life in Spain*. But later I noticed that his hands trembled more than usual on the book spines, and he walked as if his feet were not only too long but also incredibly heavy. At last Davies shed light on it. 'Family visit,' he whispered. 'Tomorrow. He's saved enough for a bit of hair oil but he's obsessed with the state of his boots. I told him. He can't borrow mine. I'd never get them back.'

And so this morning, whilst we were sitting together at the library table, I slipped off my boots, which I'd left unlaced, and kicked them in Mowatt's direction. No response. So I shoved an out-of-date theology textbook towards him, deliberately nudging him in the ribs with one corner. 'Oi!' he began, making O'Brien look up. But I put my hand on his, very gently, to silence him, and the deaf old screw chose to ignore us.

Mowatt looked down at my fingers, lost for words for a minute. I gestured beneath the table, seeking his boot with my foot. After a second, he understood what was going on. He looked at me with such warmth in his eyes that I almost laughed. I almost opened my mouth and roared with laughter in that stinking, cold room, amongst those useless, forgotten books.

Another visit to Russell's warm sanctuary.

'Why don't we start with you telling me about your childhood?'

'I didn't think psychiatrists really said that.'

'Begin wherever you like.'

My first instinct was to make something up. *At the age of nine I was taken brutally over the nursery rocking horse by my Russian uncle, and ever since I've been drawn to other men, Doctor.* Or: *My mother dressed me in flowered smocks and rouged my cheeks when I was five, and ever since I've longed to attract a strong man to my bed, Doctor.* But instead I told him a kind of truth: that mine was a happy childhood. No brothers or sisters to knock me off my perch. Many idyllic hours spent playing in the garden (with a sailor doll named Hops, but *outside* nonetheless). My father largely absent, like many fathers, but not overly mysterious or abusive, despite his later dalliances. Mother and I always got along well. Whenever I was home from school, we enjoyed our times together, going up to town to the theatre, museums and cafés . . . I ran away with myself rather, telling him about the time in Fortnum's when a stranger at the next table had tried to buy Mother a glass of champagne. She'd smiled and very firmly turned him down. I'd been so disappointed. The man had a blue silk cravat, wonderfully waved blond hair and had worn a sapphire ring on his index finger. He'd looked to me as though he knew all the secrets of the world. As we left the place, Mother had commented hotly on his impertinence, but that afternoon her whole being had been lit up in a way I'd never seen before. She'd moved in an easier way, laughed at my silly jokes and bought all sorts of things that hadn't been on our list: a new scarf for her, a leather-bound notebook for me. I still think of that man sometimes, remembering the way he'd sipped his coffee and shrugged at Mother's rejection. I'd wanted him to weep or become angry, but he'd merely put down his cup, bowed his head and said, 'What a shame.'

'That's our time almost up,' said Russell.

I waited for his comments about how I had projected myself into my mother's situation and this was really most unhealthy and it was no *wonder* I was in prison for gross indecency. But none came.

'Before you leave,' he said, 'I want you to know that you could change. But the question is: do you really want to?'

'I told you last week. I want to be cured.'

'I'm not sure I believe you.'

I said nothing.

He let out a long breath. 'Look. I'll be honest with you. Therapy can help some individuals to overcome certain . . . proclivities, but it's very hard work, and it takes a lot of time.'

'How much time?'

'Years, probably.'

'I only have six months left.'

He gave a rueful laugh. 'Personally,' he said, leaning forward and lowering his voice, 'I think the law is an ass. What two adults get up to in private is their business.' He was looking at me very seriously, dimpled cheeks aglow. 'So what I'm saying is, if *you* want to change, then therapy could help you. But if you don't . . .' he held his palms upward and smiled, 'then it's really not worth the effort.'

I held out a hand, which he took, and thanked him for his honesty.

'No more fireside chats, then,' I said.

'No more fireside chats.'

'That's a great shame.'

Burkitt took me back to my cell.

I'm trying to keep the image of *La Danse* in my head.

I don't suppose a man of Russell's integrity will last long here.

In Venice we'd spend the morning in bed, have a long lunch on the hotel terrace, then walk through the city. Delicious freedom. No one glanced our way, even when I took Tom's arm and guided him through the throngs of tourists on the Rialto Bridge. One afternoon we stepped out of the summer fug and into the sweet coolness of the church of Santa Maria dei Miracoli. What I've always loved about the little place is its paleness. With its pastel grey, pink and white marble walls and floor, the Miracoli could be made of sugar. We sat together in a front pew. Utterly alone. And we kissed. There in the presence of all the saints and angels, we kissed. I looked at the altar with its image of the miraculous Virgin – reputed to have brought a drowned man back to life – and I said, 'We should live here.' After just two days of the possibilities of Venice, I said, 'We should live here.' And Tom's answer was, 'We should fly to the moon.' But he was smiling.

*

Every fortnight I am allowed to receive and reply to one letter. So far, most of these have been from Mother. They're typed, so I know she dictates them to Nina. She says nothing of her health, merely rattles on about the weather, the neighbours, what Nina has cooked for supper. But this morning there was one from Mrs Marion Burgess. A short, formal letter requesting permission to visit. At first I was determined to refuse. Why would I want to see her, of all people? But I soon changed my mind. The woman is my only link to Tom, whose absolute silence I hardly dare consider. I've heard not one word from him since my arrest. At first I almost hoped he would appear in the Scrubs, to serve his sentence, just so I could see him again.

If she comes, perhaps he will come too. Or perhaps she will carry some message from him.

The courtroom was small and stuffy, with none of the embellishments I'd expected. More like a school hall than a chamber of the law. Proceedings began with the public gallery being warned that the trial would contain material of a nature offensive to ladies, who might wish to leave. Every single one of them made an immediate bolt for the exit. Only one looked slightly rueful. The rest blushed to their hairlines.

As the counsel for the prosecution, Jones – Labrador eyes, but the voice of a bichon frise bitch – presented the case against me, Coleman stood shaking in the witness box, never once meeting my eye. In his blue flannel suit he looked older than when we last met. When he was cross-examined it became clear – to me, at least – that he'd made his claim to get himself out of trouble; he admitted to being involved in a petty piece of thievery. But even this realisation did not wake me from my daze. Everyone in the courtroom seemed to be going through the motions, the police yawning occasionally, the judge looking on impervious, and I was no different. I stood in my box, all the time aware of a uniformed man sitting behind me, biting his nails absent-mindedly. I found myself listening to the sound of the saliva in his mouth, rather than the court proceedings, as he nibbled away. I kept telling myself: in a few moments I'll receive my sentence. My future will be decided. But somehow I could not comprehend what was happening to me.

Then everything changed. My barrister, the amiable but ineffectual Mr Thompson, began his presentation of the defence. And he called Marion Burgess.

I was prepared for this. Thompson had asked me who I'd recommend as a character witness. My list did not include anyone who was both female and married, as he'd soon pointed out. 'Don't you know any really dull ladies?' he'd asked. 'Librarians? Matrons? Schoolteachers?'

Marion was my only choice. And I calculated that, even if she did know the truth about my relationship with Tom (he'd always reassured me that she did not, although in my estimation she seemed too sharp to miss it for long), she would not risk denouncing me because of the damage it would cause her husband and, by extension, herself.

She was wearing a pale-green dress, too loose for her. She'd lost weight since I last saw her, and this accentuated her height. Her red hair was set into an absolutely unmovable shape. She stood very straight and clutched a pair of white gloves as she spoke. I could hardly hear her voice as she stated the usual formalities – her oath, her name, her occupation. Then she was asked in what capacity she knew the accused.

'Mr Hazlewood was kind enough to take my pupils for an art-appreciation afternoon at the museum,' she stated. And suddenly her voice was not her own. Long ago I'd guessed her teaching had chipped the edges from her Brighton accent – which is not nearly as pronounced as Tom's – but in that witness box she sounded as though she'd been to Roedean.

She confirmed that I had performed my duties thoroughly, she would not hesitate to call on me again, and I was absolutely not the sort of man one might ordinarily find committing acts of gross indecency in a public convenience. Then the counsel for the prosecution stood and asked Mrs Burgess if she knew the accused in anything other than a professional capacity.

A flicker of concern passed across her freckled face. She said nothing. I willed her to look at me. If she would only look at me, I might have a chance of staring her into silence.

'Is it not the case,' continued Jones, 'that the accused is a close friend of your husband, Constable Thomas Burgess?'

The sound of his name made me gasp. But I kept my eyes on Marion.

'Yes.'

'Speak up so the court can hear you.'

'Yes. He is.'

'How would you describe their relationship?'

'It's as you said. They're good friends.'

'So you know Mr Hazlewood personally, then?'

'Yes.'

'And you still say he is not the sort of man who would commit the crime of which he is accused?'

'Of course he's not.' She was looking at Jones's shoulder as she answered him.

'And you completely trusted this man with your pupils?'

'Completely.'

'Mrs Burgess, I would like to read an extract from Patrick Hazlewood's diary to you.'

Thompson objected, but was overruled.

'Some of it is rather purple, I'm afraid. It's dated October 1957.' Jones spent a long time fixing his glasses to his nose, then cleared his throat and began, one hand waving airily about as he read. '*And then: the unmistakable line of his shoulders. My policeman was standing, head on one side, looking at a rather mediocre Sisley . . . Magnificently alive, breathing, and actually here, in the museum. I'd pictured him so many times over the past days that I rubbed my eyes, as disbelieving girls do in films.*' A short pause. 'Mrs Burgess, who is "my policeman"?'

Marion pulled herself up taller, stuck out her chin. 'I have no idea.'

She sounded quite convincing. More convincing than I would have done, under the circumstances.

'Perhaps another extract will help you to remember. This time dated December 1957.' Another clearing-of-throat-placing-of-glasses-on-nose performance. Then: '*We've been meeting some lunchtimes, when he can get a long break. But he has not forgotten the schoolteacher. And yesterday, for the first time, he brought her with him . . . They are so obviously mismatched that I had to smile when I saw them together.*'

I winced.

'*She is almost as tall as he is, made no attempt to disguise it (wearing heels), and is not nearly as handsome as him. But I suppose I would think so.*'

A long pause from Jones.

'Mrs Burgess, who is "the schoolteacher"?'

She made no reply. She was still standing very tall and straight, looking at his shoulder. Cheeks red. Blinking a great deal.

Jones addressed the jury. 'This journal contains many more intimate details of Patrick Hazlewood's relationship with "his" policeman, a relationship that can only be described as deeply perverse. But I'll spare the court any further account of such depravity.' He turned back to Marion. 'Who do you think the accused is writing about, Mrs Burgess?'

'I don't know.' Bite of the lip. 'Perhaps it's some fantasy of his.'

'There's an awful lot of detail for a fantasy.'

'Mr Hazlewood is a very imaginative man.'

'Why, I wonder, would he imagine his male lover to be engaged to a schoolteacher?'

No response.

'Mrs Burgess, I don't want to embarrass you, but I must put it to you that Patrick Hazlewood was having an indecent relationship with your husband.'

Her eyes dropped and her voice became very faint. 'No,' she said.

'Do you deny that the accused is a homosexual?'

'I – don't know.'

She was still standing tall. But I could see her gloves trembling. I thought of how she'd walked down North Street with Tom on the day we'd first met. Her pride and assurance emanating with every step she took. And I wanted to give those qualities back to her. Her husband she could never have, and I was glad of it. But I'd no desire to see her like this.

Jones the bichon bitch would not give up, however. 'I have to ask you again, Mrs Burgess. Is Patrick Hazlewood the kind of man who would commit acts of gross indecency?'

Silence.

'Please answer the question, Mrs Burgess,' the judge interrupted.

There was a very long pause before she looked straight at me and said, 'No.'

'No further questions,' said Jones.

But Marion was still talking. 'He was very good with the children. He was wonderful with them, in fact.'

I nodded at her. She gave a small nod back.

It was a swift, unsentimental and wholly civilised exchange.

After that, all I could think was: what will happen to Tom? What will they do to him now? And how can he ever forgive my stupidity?

But my policeman was not mentioned again, despite his name being on the tip of my tongue during the rest of the trial, and ever since.

On our last day in Venice, we went to the tiny island of Torcello to see the mosaics. Tom was quiet on the boat, but I imagined he was lost, like me, in the sight of the city disappearing behind us. One is never sure, in Venice, what is reality and what reflection, and when seen from the back of a vaporetto, the whole place looks like a mirage, floating in an impossible mist. The silence of Torcello was a shock after the continuous clanging of bells, coffee cups and tour guides that is San Marco. Neither of us spoke as we entered the basilica. Had I overdone it on the culture front? I wondered. Would Tom rather have spent the afternoon drinking Bellinis in Harry's Bar? We looked at the glittering reds and golds of the Last Judgement. Those doomed to hell were pushed down by devil's spears. Some were consumed by flames, some by wild beasts. The most unlucky did the job themselves, eating their own hands, finger by finger.

Tom stood there for a long time, looking at the awful corner into which the sinners had been shoved. Still he said not one word. I felt myself begin to panic at the thought of going back to England. At the thought of being apart. At the thought of sharing him. I found myself clasping his arm, searching his face, saying his name. 'We can't go back,' I said.

He patted my hand. Smiled a rather cool, amused smile. 'Patrick,' he said. 'You're being ridiculous.'

'Don't make me go back.'

He sighed. 'We have to go back.'

'Why?'

He looked to the ceiling. 'You know why.'

'Tell me. I seem to have forgotten. Other people do this. Other people live in Europe, together. They leave, they have happy lives . . .'

'You have a good job in England. So do I. I can't speak Italian. We both have friends, family . . . We can't live here.'

He sounded so calm, so conclusive. My comfort, still, is that he did not mention her. Not once did he say, *Because I'm a married man.*

A letter from Mother.

> *My dear Tricky,*
>   *I have come to a decision. When you are released, I want you to come and live here with me. It will be like old times. Only better, because your father won't be here. You can have EVERY freedom you desire. I ask only for your company at mealtimes, and for a glass or two after that. As for what the neighbours think – hang them, I say.*
>   *Forgive the ramblings of an old lady.*
>   *Your ever-loving*
>   *Mother*

> *PS I hope you know I would visit were it not for doctor's orders. But it is NOTHING for you to worry about.*

The terrifying thing is, at the moment this seems like a very good offer.

Marion came to visit today.

I'd spent all night wondering whether to stand her up. Let her come and wait, gloves trembling, perfectly set hair beginning to dampen with sweat. Let her wait with the painted wives of con men, the screaming children of cosh boys, the disappointed mothers of the sexually perverse. And let her be the one who has to turn and leave, her presence rejected.

But in the morning, I knew I would do nothing of the sort.

Burkitt took me to the visiting room at three. I'd made no effort to look decent. In fact, I shaved particularly badly that morning and was glad of my cuts and grazes. Some rather pathetic wish to shock her, I suppose. Perhaps I even wanted to gain her sympathy.

As soon as I saw her – she was alone, face lined with fear – disappointment flooded me. *Where is he?* I wanted to scream. *Why isn't he here, instead of you? Where's my darling?*

'Hello, Patrick,' she said.

'Marion.'

I sat on the metal chair opposite her. The visiting room – small, fairly bright, but just as cold as the rest of this place – smelled of Harpic and stale milk. There were four other visits going on, Burkitt watching over each. Marion stared at me very intently, her eyes unblinking, and I realised she was trying to focus exclusively on the spectacle of Patrick Hazlewood, prisoner, rather than watching the scene unfolding next to us, where man and wife were desperately grappling at each other's knees beneath the table. In a strange attempt to afford us privacy, a radio tuned to some inane quiz show on the Light Programme played at mid-volume. *Fingers on buzzers, please . . . Here's your starter question . . .*

Marion removed her gloves and placed them on the table. Her fingernails were painted a lurid orange, which surprised me. And now that I really looked at her, I could tell she was wearing much more make-up than was usual, too. Her eyelids were covered with some shiny substance. Her lips were a plasticky-looking shade of pink. Unlike me, she'd obviously made quite an effort. But the overall effect wasn't much superior to that which the Scrubs queens manage. And all they have is flour paste and poster paint.

She folded the sleeves of her cardigan back and patted her collar down. Her face was pale and composed but a red rash spattered her throat. 'It's good to see you,' she said.

Just from the way she'd arranged her features – in a look of distant, respectful sympathy – I knew she'd no message from Tom. The woman had nothing for me at all. Rather, I realised, it was she who wanted something from me.

'I don't know how to begin,' she said.

I offered no assistance.

'I can't tell you how awful I feel about what's happened.' She swallowed. 'It was a complete miscarriage of justice. Coleman should be in here, not you.'

I nodded.

'It's a scandal, Patrick.'

'I know that,' I burst out. 'I've already received a letter from the museum, relieving me of my duties. And one from my landlord, letting me know my flat has been rented to a very nice family from Shoreham. Only my mother swears she's not ashamed of me. Isn't that funny?'

'I didn't mean . . . I meant it's a scandal that you should be in here . . .'

'But I am a homosexual, Marion.'

She stared at the table.

'And I wanted to have sex with Coleman. He looked rather pathetic in the courtroom, but I can assure you on the night we met he was anything but. Even if we never actually managed to perform the act itself, the intention was there. That's enough, in the eyes of the law, to condemn a man. I was *importuning*.' She was still looking at the table, but I was in full flow. 'It's grossly unfair, but that's how it is. I believe there are committees, petitions, lobbyists and the like who are trying to get the law changed. But in the British mind, intimacy between two men is right up there with GBH, armed robbery and serious fraud.'

Marion rearranged her gloves. Looked around the room. Then said, 'Are they treating you all right?'

'It's a bit like public school. And a lot like the army. Why did you come?'

She looked startled. 'I – don't know.'

There was a long pause. Eventually she tried: 'How's the food?'

'Marion. For God's sake tell me about Tom. How is he?'

'He's – all right.'

I waited. Imagined grabbing her shoulders and shaking the words out of her.

'He's left the force.'

'Why?'

She looked at me as if I should know the answer without her having to spell it out.

'I hope there wasn't too much trouble,' I mumbled.

'He refused to discuss it. He just said he left before he was pushed.'

I nodded. 'What will he do now?'

'Security guard. At Allan West's. It's not as much money,

but *I'm* still working . . .' She broke off. Studied her orange nails. 'He doesn't know I'm here,' she said.

'Oh?'

A brittle laugh, a lift of the chin, a flash of that metallic eye shadow. 'About time I had my own secrets, isn't it?'

I said nothing.

She waved a hand in the air as if wiping away what she'd said. Apologised. 'I didn't come here to – go over what's past.'

'Past?'

'Between you and Tom.'

'One more minute,' barked Burkitt.

Marion picked up her gloves and started fiddling with her handbag, gabbling something about coming again next month.

'Don't,' I said, grabbing her wrist. 'Ask Tom to come instead.'

She looked at my fingers on her skin. 'You're hurting me.'

Burkitt stepped forward. 'No physical contact, Hazlewood.'

I removed my hand and she stood, dusting off her skirt.

'I have to see him, Marion,' I said. 'Please ask him.'

She looked down at me, and I was surprised to see she was blinking back tears. 'I'll ask. But he won't come,' she said. 'You must see that he can't. I'm sorry.'

Bert says: Talk, then.

We're in the Old Rec after supper. Some men are managing to play a limp game of table tennis, despite the freezing conditions. Others, like me and Bert, are leaning on the wall furthest from the stinking lavatory, talking. Most are hunched over with cold, clutching their capes around themselves or blowing futilely on chilblained fingers. Davies told me recently that the best way to deal with chilblains is to wrap them in a piss-soaked rag. I've yet to try this myself. The Light Programme blares from the set in the corner. Usually these sessions where

I entertain Bert with my wit, erudition and knowledge are the highlight of my day. But today I don't feel like telling him about the plot of *Othello*, the Battle of Hastings (about which I know very little but have, on previous occasions, managed almost to re-enact for Bert, such was my enthusiasm), the works of Rembrandt or even Italian cuisine (Bert loves to hear about my trips to Firenze, and almost drooled when I described to him the joys of tagliatelle with hare sauce). I don't feel like saying anything at all. Because all I can think about is Tom. Tom, who will not be coming to visit.

'Talk, then,' Bert says. 'What are you waiting for?'

There's an edge to his voice. It's a reminder of who this man is: the tobacco baron. The unofficial leader of D Hall. This man always gets what he wants. He knows nothing else.

'Have you heard of Thomas Burgess?' I ask. 'The policeman from Brighton?'

'Nah. Why would I?'

'His is a very interesting story.'

'I know enough about the filth already. What about a bit more on Shakespeare? The tragedies. I love tragedies.'

'Oh, this is a tragedy. One of the best.'

He looks dubious but says, 'Go on, then. Surprise me.'

I draw a deep breath. 'Thomas – Tom to his friends – was a policeman with a problem.'

'You don't say.'

'He wasn't a bad policeman. He turned up on time, did his job to the best of his abilities, tried to be fair.'

'Don't sound like any copper I know.'

'That's because he wasn't like any other copper. He was interested in the arts, in books and music. He wasn't an intellectual – his education meant he couldn't be that – but he was intelligent.'

'Like me.'

I ignore this. 'And he was very handsome. He looked like one of the Greek statues in the British Museum. He loved to swim in the sea. His body was strong and lithe. His hair was golden and curled.'

'Sounds like a bloody queer.'

A few other men have gathered around to listen. 'That's what he was,' I say, keeping my voice even. 'That was Tom's problem.'

Bert shakes his head. 'Fucking filth. I don't think I want to hear no more, Hazlewood.'

'It was his problem, but it was also his joy,' I continue. 'Because he met a man, an older man, whom he liked very much. This older man took Tom to the theatre, to art galleries and the opera, and opened up an entirely new world to him.'

The muscles in Bert's face have stopped moving. His eyes flicker.

'Tom liked to listen to this man talk, just as you like to listen to me. He took a wife, but that meant nothing. He continued to see the older man as much as he could. Because Tom and the older man loved each other very much.'

Bert comes up close to me. 'Why don't we change the fucking subject, mate.'

But I don't stop talking. I can't stop. 'They loved each other. But the man was sent to prison on a trumped-up charge because he'd been careless. Tom's pride and his fear stopped him from ever seeing the man again. Despite this, the man went on loving him. He will always love him.'

All the time I talk, more men gather round, summoned by Bert's silent rage. And I know they'll have made sure the screw is looking the other way whilst Bert punches me quietly in the stomach until I fall to the floor. I'm talking all the time,

311

even as the punches take the air from my body. He'll always love him, I say. Over and over. Then Bert's kicking me in the chest and someone else is kicking me in the back and I cover my face with my fists but it does no good because the blows keep coming. And still I'm getting the words out. He'll always love him. And I remember the time Tom came to the flat and was so angry with me for lying to him about the portrait and I imagine it's him kicking me again and again and again and I keep whispering his name until I no longer feel anything at all.

V

Peacehaven, December 1999

Dr Wells, our GP, came today. He's a youngish man – not past forty – with one of those funny little beards that cover only the chin. He has a swift but careful manner, moving about the room almost silently, which I find slightly unnerving. I'm sure his quietness upsets you, too. When he's examining you he doesn't do any of the hearty yelling that most of them go in for ('AND HOW ARE WE TODAY?' – as if being ill immediately renders you stone deaf), which is something of a relief, but this *creeping* about is almost worse.

'We need to have a quick discussion, Marion,' he said, after we'd left you to sleep. I have never suggested he use my first name, but I let it pass. We sat at opposite ends of the sofa and he refused my offer of tea, obviously wanting to get on with it.

He launched straight into his speech. 'I'm afraid Patrick's health is deteriorating. There's been no real improvement in muscle coordination, speech or appetite for the past few weeks, as far as I can see. And he seems considerably worse today. I think he may have suffered a third stroke, in fact.'

Knowing exactly where this 'quick discussion' was heading, I leapt to your defence. 'He did speak. He said my husband's name. Quite clearly.'

'You said. That was some time ago, wasn't it?'

'A few weeks . . .'

'Has this happened again?'

I couldn't lie, Patrick, although I wanted to. 'No.'

'I see. Anything else?'

I really tried to think of some other evidence of the improvement I'm sure you're going to make. But we both know that, up to this point, you've shown very little sign of getting better. And so silence was my only answer.

Dr Wells touched his beard. 'How are you and your husband coping? The carer's role is a challenging one.'

Have you noticed how everything these days is *challenging*? What happened to difficult and downright bloody awful? 'We're coping fine,' I said, before he could start talking about social workers and support networks. 'Very well, in fact.'

'Tom's not here at the moment?'

'I've sent him to the shops.' The truth was he'd left early with the dog and I had absolutely no idea where he might be. 'For some milk.'

'I'd like to talk to him next time.'

'Of course, Doctor.'

'Good.' He paused. 'If there's no improvement in the next few days, I really think we should consider a nursing home.'

I'd known this was coming, and I had my response ready. Nodding gravely, I stated, in a firm but friendly voice, 'Dr Wells. Tom and I want to look after him here. Patrick's very comfortable, even if he isn't making the progress you'd – we'd all – like. And you said yourself that he stands a much better chance of recovery amongst friends.'

The doctor drummed his fingers on his corduroyed knee. 'Yes. That is true. But I don't know how much longer we can talk about recovery in any meaningful way.'

'Are you saying he definitely won't recover?' I knew he wouldn't give a straight answer to that one.

'No one can say that. But if he doesn't, things may

become – unmanageable fairly soon.' He started to speak rapidly. 'For example, what if Patrick can no longer tolerate liquidised foods? He may need nose-feeding. That's not something I recommend carers do at home. It's tricky and can be distressing.'

'Every day is tricky and distressing, Doctor.'

He gave a quick smile. 'The deterioration in stroke patients can be quite sudden, and we want to be prepared. That's all I'm saying.'

'We'll manage. I don't want him amongst strangers.'

'You could spend every day at the home, if you like. It would be much easier on you. And on your husband.'

Ah, I thought. So that's it. He feels sorry for the displaced husband. He thinks my looking after you is at Tom's expense. He's concerned that I'm risking the stability of my marriage over an infatuation with you. I almost burst out laughing.

'Talk about it with Tom,' he said, rising from the sofa and reaching for his briefcase. 'I'll be back next week.'

We finished *Anna Karenina* last night. I've been staying up late to complete it, even though you're often asleep before I stop reading. I'm sure you slept during the final chapters, and to be honest, I rather gabbled my way through them. Once she's thrown herself under the train, I lose interest. And my mind was fixed on what I would read next. Because what Dr Wells said has made me sure that it's time you heard what I've written. Just in case they take you away from me. And a thought has just struck me: perhaps my story will prompt some response from you. Perhaps it will trigger the movement or gesture Dr Wells is so keen to see.

After sending my letter to Mr Houghton, I slept very deeply for many hours. And when I woke, there Tom stood, his nose a little sunburned, a puzzled look on his face as he scrutinised me.

'Nice welcoming party,' he said. 'What's going on?'

I blinked, unsure if I was quite awake.

'Doesn't a man even get a cup of tea when he comes back from his travels?'

No, I wasn't dreaming: that was definitely my husband, in the flesh. It took me a moment to dredge up the energy to speak. 'How – how long have I been asleep?'

'*I* don't know. Ever since I left, by the look of it.'

'What time is it?'

'About two. Why are you in bed?'

I sat up quickly, my mind rushing over the past few days' events. I glanced down at myself and saw I was fully clothed, right down to my shoes, which were still dusty from the park. I covered my mouth, feeling suddenly queasy.

Tom sat on the edge of the mattress. 'You all right?'

He was wearing a white shirt, open at the neck. The collar was very stiff and bright, and the sleeves had sharp creases running down their length. He saw me looking and smirked. 'Hotel laundry service. Fantastic.'

I nodded and said nothing. But I knew that shirt was brand new, and a gift from you.

'So. What's going on here?' he asked.

I shook my head. 'Nothing. I can't believe I've slept this long. I had a drink with Sylvie and we got home late, so I just collapsed on the bed . . .'

But he'd already lost interest. Patting my hand, he said, 'I'll make us some tea, eh?'

I've never asked him anything about his time in Venice with you. And he's never volunteered any information about it. I've imagined it many times, of course. But all I really know of that weekend is that Tom experienced the luxury of a hand-made Italian shirt.

A few days later, I took a great deal of pleasure in washing and ironing that shirt in my usual haphazard way, neglecting to starch the collar and deliberately pressing the sleeves so the creases fell in broken lines.

At first, I waited for the storm to break over my head. Every day I imagined Tom coming home and telling me you'd lost your job. I imagined myself giving a shocked response, asking why and receiving no valid explanation. I then imagined myself becoming angry with Tom for this lack of explanation, and pictured him finally breaking down and apologising to me, maybe even confessing a little of his weaknesses whilst I remained the strong, forgiving wife. *We'll get through this together, darling*, I would say, cradling him in my arms. *I'll help you to overcome these unnatural longings*. I enjoyed that little fantasy.

But nothing happened for weeks, and I began to relax, thinking that Mr Houghton had chosen to ignore my message, or perhaps had never even received it due to some postal error. You continued to visit us every Thursday and remained your usual ebullient, entertaining, infuriating self. Tom continued to hang on your every breath. And I continued to watch the two of you, sometimes wondering when on earth my letter would take its desired effect, sometimes regretting ever having set pen to paper.

With Tom working all hours, Julia and I avoiding each other, and Sylvie busy with the baby, the rest of August was, I remember, long and rather tedious. I looked forward to getting back to my desk and to seeing the children again, now that

I knew my way around a classroom. But most of all I looked forward to seeing Julia. Although I dreaded breaking the ice, I missed our conversations and I missed her. I told myself that we could pick up our friendship again. She'd been angry and I'd been upset, but we'd get over it. As for what she'd implied about her personal affairs – well, I suppose I hoped she'd just drop the subject and we could carry on as before.

I know, Patrick. I know how stupid I was.

It rained heavily on the first day of term. The usual accompanying Brighton wind was absent, but my umbrella still did little to protect me: by the time I'd reached the school gates, my shoes were sodden and a dark patch of wetness had spread across the front of my skirt.

I squelched along the corridor and opened the door to my classroom. Julia was sitting on my desk, her legs crossed. I wasn't surprised; it was just like her to plunge straight in, and I'd been half expecting to have to face her in this way. I stopped in the doorway, water dripping from the tip of my umbrella.

'Shut the door,' she said, jumping to her feet.

I did as commanded, taking my time so as to get my breath back. Still facing the door, I removed my jacket and propped my umbrella against the wall.

'Marion.' She was standing very close behind me. I swallowed and turned to face her.

'Julia.'

She smiled. 'The very same.' Unlike me, Julia was completely dry. Her voice was grave but her face was composed in a friendly grin.

'It's good to see you . . .' I began.

'I've got a new job,' she said, quickly. 'At a school in Norwood. I want to be closer to London. I'll be moving up

320

there, in fact.' She took a breath. 'I wanted you to be the first to know. I've been planning it for a while.'

I looked down at my waterlogged shoes. My toes were starting to go numb.

'I should apologise,' I began, 'for what I said . . .'

'Yes.'

'I'm sorry.'

She nodded. 'Let's not say any more about it.'

There was a long pause during which we stared at one another. Julia's face was pale, and her mouth was set in a determined line. I was the first to drop my eyes. For a terrible moment I thought I might cry.

Julia sighed. 'Look at you. You're soaked. Have you got anything to put on?'

I said I hadn't. She clicked her tongue and caught my arm. 'Come with me.'

In the corner cupboard of Julia's classroom, two tweed skirts and a couple of cardigans hung on the back of the door. 'I keep them,' she said, 'for emergencies. Here.' She unhooked the larger skirt and pushed it into my chest. 'This one should fit. It's a bit monstrous, but beggars can't be choosers. Take it.'

It was not monstrous at all. The fabric was finely woven, the colour a rich purple. It looked a little strange with my flowered blouse, but it fitted perfectly, skimming my thighs and kicking out just on the knee. I kept it on all day, even after my own skirt had dried out. I wore it home and hung it in the wardrobe next to Tom's wedding suit. Julia never asked me to return it, and I still have it, folded carefully in my bottom drawer.

The next night I was late home, having spent a few extra hours preparing for the following day's class. I slung my basket into the corner of the kitchen, tied on an apron and rushed about peeling potatoes and flouring pieces of cod for Tom's dinner. When I had the chips cut and resting in water, I looked at my watch. Half past seven. He'd be home by eight, so I had half an hour to tidy myself up, straighten my hair and sit down with a book.

Soon, however, I found myself pretending to read, because my eyes kept straying towards the clock on the mantelpiece. Quarter past eight. Half past. Twenty to nine. I put the book down and went to the window, opening it and leaning out to look up and down the street. When I couldn't see any sign of Tom, I instructed myself not to be silly. Being a copper wasn't a job with regular hours. He'd told me that often enough. Once he'd been over six hours late. He'd come in with a bruise on his cheek and a cut above his eye. 'Fight at the Bucket of Blood,' he'd announced rather proudly. 'We had to raid the place and things got nasty.' I have to admit I enjoyed bathing his wounds, fetching a bowl of warm water, adding a drop of Dettol, soaking a ball of cotton wool in the liquid and gently applying it to his skin like a good nursemaid. Tom had sat quite happily and let me fuss over him, and when I'd kissed the bruise on his cheek and told him not to get himself into such situations again, he'd laughed and said this was the least of it.

Tonight would be something similar, I told myself. Nothing he couldn't cope with, nothing to worry about. I might even be able to nurse him again when he did come home. And so I put the fish back in the fridge, fried myself a few chips, ate alone and went up to bed.

I must have been very tired because, when I woke, it was getting light and Tom was not in our bed. I jumped up and hurried downstairs, calling his name. He'd have come in late and fallen asleep in the armchair. That had happened before, I reminded myself. But not only was there no Tom in the living room, there were no shoes by the door, and no jacket on the peg. I rushed back upstairs and pulled on the dress I'd flung to the floor the night before. As I left the house, my plan was to go to the police station. But as I hurried down Southover Street, realising I should have worn a jacket – it wasn't past six and was still chilly – I changed my mind. I could hear Tom's voice – *What did you do that for? Do you want them to call me henpecked?* – and decided to try his mother. I'd come out, though, with just my keys in my hand and no money for the bus. It would be at least a half-hour walk from here. I began to run and, as I reached the bottom of the street, I found myself turning instead towards the seafront. Although my mind was slow, my body seemed to know what to do. You see, I knew where he was. I'd known all along. He'd stayed the night – all night – with you. He hadn't even bothered to think up some excuse. Tom was at your flat.

I rushed along Marine Parade, sometimes running, sometimes slowing down to a jog as a stitch grew in my side. My rage was thrillingly complete. If Tom had been before me at that moment, I have no doubt I would have struck him repeatedly and called him every name I knew. As I ran, I imagined myself doing just this. I was almost excited by it. I couldn't wait to get to the two of you and unleash my wrath. It wasn't just anger at you and Tom. I'd lost Julia, too. She'd told me her secret and now she couldn't trust me, and she was right not to. I'd failed as a friend, I could see that even then. And I'd failed as a wife. I couldn't make my husband desire me in the right way.

About halfway there, it struck me that I could say I was leaving Tom. I had a job, after all. I could afford a little flat of my own. There were no children to think of, and the way things were going, there never would be. I would refuse to live a life of misery. I would simply walk out. That would teach him. No one to cook and clean. No one to iron his blasted shirts. The thought of the shirt you'd bought for him made me break into a sprint. In my haste, I almost knocked down an old man, I slapped into his arm so hard. He shouted out in pain, but I didn't stop or even look back. I had to reach your flat, find the two of you together and make my announcement. Enough was enough.

I rang your buzzer, leaning my forehead against the door and trying to catch my breath. No reply. I pressed again, letting it ring longer this time. Still nothing. Of course. The two of you would be in bed. You might well know it was me. You would be hiding. Hiding and laughing. Keeping a finger on the bell for at least a minute, I thumped at the big brass doorknocker with the other hand. Nothing. I began to press the bell and then let go, ringing out an impatient tune. BUZZ. BUZZ. BUZZ. BU-BU-BUZZ. BU-BU-BUZZZZZ.

Nothing.

I would start shouting soon.

Then the door opened. A middle-aged man in a yellow paisley-print dressing gown stood before me. He wore a pair of gold-rimmed spectacles and looked very tired. 'For pity's sake,' he said, 'you'll wake the whole building. He's not in, my dear woman. Please stop ringing that infernal buzzer.'

He made to close the door, but I held it open, trapping it with my foot. 'Who are you?' I asked.

He looked me up and down. I must, I suddenly realised, look a fright: pale and sweaty, hair not brushed, wearing a creased dress.

'Graham Vaughan. Top-floor flat. Very awake. And rather annoyed.'

'Are you sure he's not in?'

He folded his arms and said, very calmly, 'Of course I'm sure, my dear. The police took him away last night.' He lowered his voice. 'We all knew he was queer – so many of them are around here – but one can't help but feel sorry. Sometimes this country is too brutal.'

You and I are really very alike, aren't we? I knew it that time on the Isle of Wight, when you challenged Tom's views on child-rearing. All these years I've known it, but I've never really felt it until now, until writing this and realising that neither of us got what we wanted. Such a small thing, really – who does? And yet our ridiculous, blind, naive, brave, romantic longing for it is perhaps what binds us together, for I don't believe either of us has ever truly accepted our defeat. What is it they're always saying now, on TV? *You have to move on.* Well. Neither one of us managed that.

Each day I look for a sign and am disappointed. The doctor is right: you are worse. I suspected another stroke long before he said it. Your fingers, capable of holding a spoon a few weeks ago, now drop everything. I hold a cup of liquidised pasta to your lips and most comes dribbling out in a gloopy stream. I've bought some of those adult-sized bibs and we're using those quite successfully, but I keep thinking about the nose-feeding Dr Wells mentioned. It sounds like some Victorian torture for wayward women. I can't let that happen to you, Patrick.

You sleep most of the afternoons, and in the mornings I arrange your body in an armchair, propped on both sides with pillows to stop you from sliding too far in one direction, and we watch television together. Most of the programmes are about buying and selling things: houses, antiques, food, clothing, holidays. I could play Radio 3, which you'd prefer, but I feel at least the TV brings some life into the room. And sometimes I hope your exasperation will spur you into speech and movement. Perhaps tomorrow you will hold up your hands and command me to TURN OFF THIS UTTER CLAPTRAP.

If only you would.

I know you can hear me, though. Because when I say the word *Tom*, your eyes brighten, even now.

After finding no one at your flat, I went to see Sylvie.

'What's up with you?' she asked, letting me in. I was still in my crumpled dress, my hair unbrushed. A hot smell of unwashed nappies came up to greet me.

'Where's the baby?'

'She's asleep. At last. Up at four, down by seven. What sort of madness is that, eh?' Sylvie stretched her arms upwards and yawned. Then she looked me in the face and said, 'Blimey. You need a cup of tea.'

The offer of tea and Sylvie's sympathetic face were so wonderful that I had to clamp a hand over my mouth to stop myself crying. Sylvie put an arm round me. 'Come on,' she said, 'let's have a sit-down, shall we? I don't need any more wailing this morning.'

She brought two cups through and we sat on her plastic sofa. 'God, this thing's terrible,' she said. 'Like sitting on a park bench.' She took two noisy slurps of tea. 'I drink tea all day now,' she said. 'Just like my bloody mother.'

She seemed to be babbling in order to give me time to compose myself, but I couldn't wait any longer. I had to unburden myself. 'You remember Patrick, Tom's—'

''Course I remember.'

'He's been arrested.'

Sylvie's eyebrows shot up to her hairline. 'What?'

'He's been arrested. For – indecency.'

There was a small silence before Sylvie asked, in a hushed voice, 'With *men*?'

I nodded.

'The dirty . . . When?'

'Last night.'

'Christ almighty.' She put her cup down. 'Poor bugger.' She smiled, then put a hand over her mouth. 'Sorry.'

'The thing is,' I said, ignoring her, 'the thing is, I think it might be because of me. I think it's all my fault.' I was breathing very fast, and had trouble getting the words out evenly.

Sylvie stared at me. 'What are you talking about, Marion?'

'I wrote an anonymous letter. To his boss. Telling him about Patrick being – you know.'

There was a pause, before Sylvie said, '*Oh.*'

I covered my face with my hands and gave a loud sob. Sylvie put an arm round me and kissed my hair. I could smell tea on her breath. 'Calm down,' she said. 'It'll be all right. It must have been something else, mustn't it? They don't arrest people just because of a letter, do they?'

'Don't they?'

'Silly,' she said. ''Course not. They'd have to catch him *doing* something, wouldn't they? In the act, you know.' She patted me on the knee. 'I'd have done the same, in your situation,' she said.

I looked at her. 'What do you—'

'Oh, Marion. Tom's my brother. I've always known, haven't I? Although I hoped he'd changed, of course. I don't know why you . . . Well. Let's not talk about that now. Drink your tea,' she said. 'Before it gets cold.'

I did as she instructed. It tasted sour and heavy.

'Does Tom know?' she asked. 'About the letter?'

'Of course not.'

Sylvie nodded. 'Don't go telling him, neither. It won't do any good.'

'But—'

'Marion. It's like I said. They don't arrest people over a letter. I know you're a schoolteacher and everything, but you don't have that much power, do you?' She nudged me and smiled. 'It's for the best, isn't it? You and Tom can have a new start with him out of the picture.'

Just then, Kathleen let out a sudden shout of displeasure that made us both jump. Sylvie pulled a face. 'Little madam. Don't know where she gets it from.' She squeezed my shoulder. 'Don't you worry,' she said. 'You kept my little secret. Now I'll keep yours.'

I left Sylvie to see to her daughter and went to school. I didn't care about my crumpled dress or messy hair. I would have to do. It was still early, so I sat at my desk, staring at the print of *The Annunciation* with its unsuspecting Mary that hung above the door. I have never been religious, but at that moment I wished I could pray, or even pretend to pray, for forgiveness. But I could not. I could only weep. And in the silence of the eight a.m. classroom, I laid my head on the desk, banged a fist on the register and let my tears flow.

When I'd managed to stop crying, I went about readying myself for the day. I patted down my hair as best I could and put the cardigan I kept hanging on the back of my chair over my dress. The children would arrive soon, and I could be Mrs Burgess for them, at least. They would ask me questions to which I would mostly know the answers. They would be grateful when rewarded, fearful when scolded. They would – for the most part – react in ways I could predict, and I could help them with small things that would, perhaps, eventually make big differences in their lives. That was some comfort, and I was to hold on to it for many, many years.

That evening, Tom was waiting for me at the table by our front window. I glimpsed his stricken face through the glass and almost carried on walking, right past our door and to the end of the street. But I knew he'd seen me, and so I had no choice but to enter our house and face him.

When I came in the door, he stood up, nearly knocking over his chair. His shirt was creased and his hands shook as he attempted to smooth down his hair. 'Patrick's been arrested,' he blurted, before I'd taken two steps into the room. I nodded briefly and went into the kitchen to wash my hands.

Tom followed me. 'Didn't you hear me? Patrick's been—'

'I know,' I said, shaking water from my fingers. 'After you didn't come home last night, I went to his flat to look for you. Patrick's neighbour took some pleasure in informing me of the situation.'

Tom blinked. 'What did he say?'

'That the police arrived late last night and took him away.' I reached past Tom for a tea towel on which to dry my hands. 'And that everyone in the terrace knew he was – an invert.' I didn't look at Tom as I spoke. I concentrated on drying each finger very thoroughly. The tea towel I used was thin and frayed, with a faded picture of the Brighton Pavilion on it. I remember thinking that I should replace it soon; I even told myself that it was no wonder Tom was not the husband I expected if this was the sort of housewife I'd become. One with threadbare, stained tea towels.

Whilst I was standing in the kitchen, thinking all this, Tom had gone into the living room and was smashing up the furniture. I went to the doorway and watched as he threw a wooden chair repeatedly to the floor until its back was broken and its legs shattered. Then he picked up another and gave it the same treatment. I hoped he'd start on the table, perhaps ripping up that terrible cloth of his mother's. But once two chairs were destroyed, he sat heavily on a third and put his head in his hands. I stood in the doorway and watched my husband. His shoulders moved in great heaves, and he let out a series of strange, animal-like groans. When he eventually lifted his face, I saw the same expression I'd witnessed on the helter-skelter after we were married. He was chalk-pale and his mouth had a strange, undefined look about it. He was utterly terrified.

'I was there when they brought him in,' he said, staring at me, his eyes wide. 'I saw him, Marion. Slater had him by the wrist. I saw him and I got out of there, quick as I could. I couldn't let him see me.'

And it suddenly hit me: in attempting to destroy you, Patrick, I'd risked destroying Tom. When I'd written my letter to Mr Houghton, I hadn't given a single thought to what the consequences could be for my husband. But now I had no choice but to face them. I'd betrayed you, but I'd also betrayed Tom. I'd done this to him.

Tom had his head in his hands again. 'What am I going to do?'

What answer could I give him, Patrick? What could I say? At that moment I made a decision. I would be the woman

I'd thought I was on top of the helter-skelter. The one who knew Tom's weakness and could save him.

I knelt beside my husband. 'Listen to me, Tom,' I said. 'It will be all right. We can put all this behind us. We can start our marriage again.'

'Jesus!' he shouted. 'This isn't about *our marriage*! Patrick will go to prison, and I'm bloody ruined! They'll find out about – everything – and that will be it.'

I took a breath. 'No,' I said, surprised by the evenness and authority of my own voice. 'No one knows. You can resign. You can work somewhere else. I'll support us for as long as you need . . .'

'What are you talking about?' asked Tom, looking at me, utterly bewildered.

'We'll be fine. It'll be a new start.' I placed my hands on either side of his face. 'Patrick will never tell them about you. And I will never leave you.'

He began to cry, his tears wetting my fingers.

He wept a great deal over the following weeks. We would go to bed and I'd be woken in the night by the sound of his dry sobs. He would whimper, too, in his sleep, so that sometimes I wouldn't know if he were awake or dreaming as he cried. I would draw him to me and he would come freely, resting his head on my chest as I held him until he was still and quiet. 'Shush,' I whispered. 'Shush.' And in the morning we would carry on as usual, neither of us mentioning the crying, what had been said that day when he smashed up the chairs, or your name.

Before your case went to court, Tom did as I'd suggested. He resigned from the force. During your trial, to my absolute horror, passages from your journal, detailing your relationship with Tom, whom you referred to as 'my policeman', were read aloud. Those passages have been with me ever since, like a low but constant ringing in my ears. I have never been able to shake myself free of your words. *They are so obviously mismatched that I had to smile when I saw them together.* I've always remembered that particular sentence. Your casual tone is what hurts the most. That, and the fact that you were right.

But by the time of the trial, Tom was close to the end of his notice and, despite your incriminating journal, somehow escaped any investigation. He told me very little about it, but I suspect the force was glad to let him go quietly. I'm sure the authorities wanted to avoid any further scandals, after all that fuss in the papers about corruption in the highest ranks. Another officer in the dock would have been a disaster.

About a month later he got a new job, as a factory security guard. He worked night shifts, which suited us both. We could barely look at one another and I could think of nothing to say to him. I visited you in prison once, mostly out of remorse for what I'd done, but I'd be lying if I said there wasn't a part of me that wanted to witness just how much misery you were experiencing. I didn't tell Tom about the visit and I never suggested he do the same. I knew the mention of your name would be enough to make him walk out the door and never return. It was as though everything could continue only in conditions of complete silence. If I were to touch this wound, to probe its boundaries, it would never heal. And so I carried on, going to work, preparing meals, sleeping on the edge of the bed, away from Tom's body. In some ways it was just as it had been before I'd married Tom. My access to him was so restricted that I began to cling to clues of his presence. When I washed his shirts, I'd press them to my face just to smell his skin. I'd spend hours arranging his shoes neatly under the bed, ordering his ties in the wardrobe, pairing his socks in his drawer. He'd gone, you see, from the house, and all that was left were these traces of him.

This evening I told a lie. It was late, and Tom was in the kitchen, making himself something to eat. He'd been out all day, as usual. I stood in the doorway, watching him slice cheese and tomatoes and arrange them on bread. Standing there, I remembered how, when we were first married, he would sometimes surprise me by making lunch at the weekend. I recalled a soft omelette with cheese melting inside, and, once, French toast with streaky bacon and maple syrup. I'd never tasted maple syrup before, and he'd told me, very proudly, that you had given him a bottle of the stuff, as a gift.

He peered beneath the grill, watching his cheese bubble in the heat.

'Dr Wells came today,' I announced, sitting at the table. He gave no response, but I was determined to do this. So I waited for him. I did not want to lie to my husband's back. I wanted to lie to his face.

When he'd put his meal on a plate and collected a knife and fork, I asked him to sit with me. He'd got through most of his food before he wiped his mouth and looked up.

'He said Patrick doesn't have long to live,' I said, keeping my voice steady.

Tom continued to eat until he'd cleaned the plate. Then he leant back in his chair and replied, 'Well. We've known that all along, haven't we? It's time for a nursing home, then.'

'It's too late for that. He's got a week.'

Tom's eyes met mine.

'At the most,' I added.

We held one another's gaze.

'A week?'

'Maybe less.' After giving this information a moment to sink in, I continued, 'Dr Wells says it's vital that we keep talking to him. It's really all we can do now. But I can't do it all by myself. So I was thinking maybe you could.'

'Could what?'

'Talk to him.'

There was a silence. Tom pushed his plate away, crossed his arms and said, very quietly, 'I wouldn't know what to say.'

I had my answer ready. 'Read, then. You could read to him. He won't respond, but he can hear you.'

Tom was watching me carefully.

'I've written something,' I said, as casually as I could. 'Something that you could read aloud to him.'

He almost smiled in his surprise. 'You've *written* something?'

'Yes. Something I want you both to hear.'

'What's all this about, Marion?'

I took a deep breath. 'It's about you. And me. And Patrick.'

Tom groaned.

'I've written about – what happened. And I want you both to hear it.'

'Christ,' he said, shaking his head. 'What for?' He was staring at me as if I'd gone utterly mad. 'What on earth for, Marion?'

I couldn't answer him.

He stood up and turned to leave. 'I'm going to bed. It's late.'

Springing from my chair, I grabbed his arm and made him face me. 'I'll tell you what for. Because I want

336

something said. Because I can't live with this silence any more.'

There was a pause. Tom looked down at my hand on his arm. 'Let go of me.'

I did as he asked.

Then he fixed me with a stare. 'You can't live with the silence. I see. *You* can't live with the silence.'

'No. I can't, not any more.'

'You can't live with the silence, so you make *me* break it. You subject me and that sick old man in there to your rantings, is that it?'

'Rantings?'

'I see what this is all about. I see why you dragged the poor bastard here in the first place. So that you could give him a bloody telling-off, just like at school. You've written it all down, have you? A catalogue of wrongs. A bad school report. Is that it, Marion?'

'It's not like that . . .'

'This is your revenge, isn't it? That's what this is.' He took hold of my shoulders and shook me, hard. 'Don't you think he's been punished enough? Don't you think we've both been punished enough?'

'It's not—'

'What about *my* silence, Marion? Did you ever think about that? You have no idea . . .' His voice cracked. He loosened his grip on me and turned his face away. 'For God's sake. I lost him once already.'

We stood together, both breathing heavily. After a while, I managed to say, 'It's not revenge. It's a confession.'

Tom held up a hand, as if to say, *No more, please*.

But I had to see this through. 'It's my confession. It's not about anyone's wrongs but my own.'

He looked at me.

'You said he needed you years ago, and that's true. But he needs you now, too. Please. Read it to him, Tom.'

He closed his eyes. 'I'll think about it,' he said.

I let out a breath. 'Thank you.'

After heavy rain, this morning was coldly bright. I woke feeling oddly refreshed; I'd got to bed late but had slept deeply, exhausted by the day's events. I had the usual lower backache, but I went about my morning duties with what you might call *considerable brio*, greeting you cheerfully, changing your bedclothes, bathing your body and feeding you liquidised Weetabix through a straw. I chatted all the while, telling you it wouldn't be long now before Tom was coming to sit with you, and your eyes watched me with a hopeful light.

As I was leaving your room, I heard the kettle boiling. Funny, I thought. Tom had left the house at six for his regular swim, and I didn't usually see him again until the evening. But when I went into the kitchen there he was, holding a cup of tea out for me. In silence, we sat down for breakfast with Walter at our feet. Tom looked over the *Argus* and I gazed out of the window, watching last night's rain dripping from the conifers outside. It was the first time we'd had breakfast together since that morning you spilled your cereal.

When we'd finished eating, I fetched my – what shall I call it? – my manuscript. I'd kept it in the kitchen drawer all along, half hoping that Tom would stumble across what I'd written. I placed it on the table, and I left the room.

Since then, I've been in my bedroom, packing a case. I've picked out only a few essential items: nightdress, change of clothes, washbag, novel. I don't expect Tom will mind sending the rest on. Mostly I've been sitting on my plain IKEA duvet and listening to the low hum of Tom's voice as he reads my words to you. It's a strange, frightening, wonderful sound, this murmur of my own thoughts on Tom's tongue. Perhaps this is what I've wanted all along. Perhaps this is enough.

At four this afternoon I cracked open your door and looked in on the two of you. Tom was sitting very close to your bed. At this hour you are usually asleep, but this afternoon, although your body wasn't coping very well with the pillows Tom had arranged for you – you were wilting to one side – your eyes were open and fixed on Tom. His head (still beautiful!) was bent over my pages and he stumbled briefly on a sentence but continued to read. The day had darkened, and I slipped into the room to turn on a corner lamp so the two of you could see one another clearly. Neither of you looked my way, and I left you alone together, closing the door softly behind me.

You've never liked it here and neither have I. I won't be sorry to say goodbye to Peacehaven and to the bungalow. I'm not sure where I will go, but Norwood seems a good place to start. Julia still lives there and I would like to tell her this story, too. And then I would like to listen to what she has to say, because I have had enough of my own words. What I'd really like now is to hear another story.

I won't look in on you again. I'll leave this page on the kitchen table in the hope that Tom will read it to you. I hope he will take your hand as he does so. I cannot ask for your forgiveness, Patrick, but I hope I can ask for your ear, and I know you'll have been a good listener.

Acknowledgements

Many sources were helpful to me in writing this novel, but I am particularly indebted to *Daring Hearts: Lesbian and Gay Lives in 50s and 60s Brighton* (Brighton Ourstory Project); Peter Wildeblood's searing memoir, *Against the Law,* and – not in the same class of brilliance but still illuminating – *The Verdict of You All* by Rupert Croft-Cooke. Thanks, too, to Debbie Hickmott at Screen Archive South East, Philip Meeson at the Brighton Old Police Cells Museum, and to my parents and Ruth Carter for sharing their memories of the period with me. I'm also grateful to Hugh Dunkerley, Naomi Foyle, Kai Merriott, Lorna Thorpe and David Swann for their comments on early drafts, to David Riding for his commitment to the book, and to Poppy Hampson for her editorial excellence. And thank you, Hugh, for all the other things.

penguin.co.uk/vintage